The Jamais Vu Papers

The Jamais Vu Papers

—or—

Misadventures in
the Worlds of Science,
Myth, and Magic

Wim Coleman and Pat Perrin

HARMONY BOOKS / NEW YORK

The Jamais Vu Papers is a work of fiction. Certain actual people agreed to appear as themselves in the fictional events of this story and they are specifically identified on pages 326–327. We have also made use of several historical or mythological figures. With those exceptions, any resemblance to actual or fictional persons or events is entirely coincidental.

Grateful acknowledgment is made to the following for permission to reprint artwork and previously published material:
"Aesthetic Consciousness Survey," and the drawing, "The Regeneration of Pavlov's Dog," by William T. Squires, Department of Art, The University of Georgia, reprinted by permission of the author.
"Black Hole Theory" and "Kritic's Korner," graphics by Tom Hammond, Department of Art, The University of Georgia, reprinted by permission of the artist. His work is represented by Art South, Washington, D.C.; Galerie Petit, Amsterdam, Netherlands; The Print Consortium, St. Joseph Missouri; and the Chicago Center for the Print.
"The Book of Sand," from Jorge Luis Borges: *Labyrinths*. Copyright © 1962, 1964 by New Directions Publishing Corporation. Summarized by permission of New Directions Publishing Corporation. U.S. and Canadian Rights.
"Cardiff Giant," sculpture by Henry Salle and Fred Mohrman, reprinted by permission of New York State Historical Association, Cooperstown, New York.
"Media Neutral" appeared, in an earlier version, in *Speculations: The Reality Club 1* (Prentice-Hall, 1990), John Brockman, editor.
"One Thing" and "Tristan und Isolde," paintings by Nancy Witt, Ashland, Virginia, reprinted by permission of the artist.
"Pan Returns to a New Tune," sculpture by Margaret Ford, reprinted by permission of the artist. Her work is exhibited at the Susan Cummins Gallery in Mill Valley, California and is available in southern California through Wita Gardiner Associates, La Mesa, California.
"Smoke Gets In Your Eyes," music by Jerome Kern and lyrics by Otto Harbach. Copyright © 1933 PolyGram International Publishing, Inc. (3500 West Olive Avenue, Suite 200, Burbank, California 91505). Copyright Renewed. International Copyright Secured. All Rights Reserved. Used By Permission.
"Snailboy" ceramic sculpture by Sergio Bustamente, reprinted by permission of the artist. His work is represented internationally by numerous galleries. Locations of some of the Sergio Bustamente Galleries are: 89 So. St., Pier 17 Pavillion, New York; Water Tower Place, Chicago; 2435 Kaanapali Parkway, Lahaina, Maui; Mani Bldg., Roppongi 5-16-22 Roppongi, Minato-Ku, Tokyo; Campos Eliseos 204, Colonia Polanco, Mexico City; 134 Adelaide St. E, Toronto; 1130 Mainland St., Vancouver; Paseo de la Florida 35, Madrid; Fasanen Strasse 73, 1000 Berlin 15.

Design by Pat Perrin
Page layout and typesetting was done with the help of Macintosh computers and PageMaker software. Computer illustrations for the comic book newsletter, pages 123–128, by Wim Coleman. Illustrations for Llixgrijb chapters and other miscellaneous graphics by Pat Perrin.

Published by Harmony Books, member of the Crown Publishing Group.
HARMONY and colophon are trademarks of Crown Publishers, Inc.
Manufactured in the United States of America

Coleman, Wim.
The jamais vu papers: or misadventures in the worlds of science,
myth, and magic/Wim Coleman and Pat Perrin.—1st ed.
        p.·   cm.
I. Perrin, Pat. II. Title.
PS3553.047448J36 1991
813'.54—dc20   90-5304
ISBN: 0-517-57513-2   CI

10 9 8 7 6 5 4 3 2 1

First Edition

to Sylvia, for help and friendship

CONTENTS

*Did you ever get
the strangest feeling
you've never
been here before?*

The joy of lucidity
at first seems like poison
but is in the end like ambrosia
from the calm of self-understanding.

The Bhagavad-Gita
Barbara Stoler Miller, trans.

———

Of all the several ways of
beginning a book which are now in
practice throughout the known
world, I am confident my own way
of doing it is the best————I'm
sure it is the most religious————
for I begin with writing the first
sentence————and trusting to
Almighty God for the second.

Laurence Sterne
Tristram Shandy

The Jamais Vu Papers

Volume One
Number One
December

In all my years as a psychotherapist, I have never encountered anything like the "Hilary Case." So I am turning to you, esteemed colleagues, for advice.

"Hilary" is, of course, a pseudonym. Aside from the imperative of patient confidentiality, I must also consider my client's celebrity. Hilary is an extremely well-known figure in the entertainment world. So I dare not even reveal whether my patient is a man or a woman.

Hilary suffers from what I can only describe as an extremely intransigent form of boredom. This talented, wealthy, and universally beloved human being simply has nothing whatever to live for.

You will ask, why this fuss over a simple case of upper-class jadedness? You will say that it is hardly a pathological condition.

Until now, I would have agreed with you. As a Beverly Hills psychiatrist, I am familiar with cases of ennui. But the vast majority are easily treated with talk therapy, any of the latest electronic gadgets, or mild antidepressants.

But Hilary's case, I can assure you, is quite perilous. This most envied of people is unenviably close to suicide.

The technique of homeopathic trauma

I cannot even trace Hilary's condition to some childhood trauma. My patient's life has been blessed with good fortune from the beginning.

Perhaps, suggested certain colleagues, this was the very problem. They proposed that, in a hypnotic trance, I take my patient back to some delightful childhood memory and plant a minute quantity of awful recollection there.

I have rejected this "homeopathic trauma" approach. Philosophically, it seems to imply that human happiness depends upon a germ of misery.

The state of JAMAIS VU

Although all my attempts at treatment have failed, it is my well-informed hunch that the key to this case resides in a too-little-studied mental phenomenon known in the textbooks as *jamais vu*.

How do you treat a patient who has everything?

CONTENTS

In this brief newsletter, I have set forth the questions that concern me. Unfortunately, I know too little to proceed with further treatment. The situation is at a standstill. Hence this appeal to other professionals in my own field—as well as to brilliant minds in all disciplines—to help me unravel a tragic mystery.

There is no need to rush to your psychiatric desk dictionaries. I'm sure that the literal meaning of *jamais vu* is apparent enough. It is the opposite of *déjà vu*.

Now *déjà vu*, as I'm sure you are aware, literally means "already seen." It is typically a fleeting but eerie sense of familiarity and return—an unsettling feeling of having "been here before."

But *jamais vu* is quite the opposite. It is a state of *"never*-having-seen," a numinous moment of strangeness, wonder, and perhaps even fear. But it is just as likely to be joyous and creative. During such an episode, one would feel a stranger to one's surroundings—indeed, to this planet and to this life.

Surely, the inducement of such a state would be the perfect treatment for a pervasive and debilitating sense of the ordinary.

But how am I to bring it about? Talk therapy has proven useless so far. And any drugs which might evoke a state of *jamais vu* have, alas, been declared Schedule I by the FDA. I am at a loss.

My query, ladies and gentlemen, is fourfold:

1) How often do you experience the state of *déjà vu*? Have you ever treated a patient with a persistent *déjà-vu*-like condition?

2) What treatment did you employ, and with what degree of success? Please give me your sources for specific electronic equipment and/or medications.

3) Have you experienced spontaneous or deliberately induced states of *jamais vu*? Please also inquire among your friends and associates.

4) If so, how have you induced them? In whom?

I am sending this newsletter not only to psychiatric professionals, but to brilliant minds in other disciplines as well. Perhaps it will open up a floodgate of research into this hitherto neglected state called *jamais vu* and serve as a valuable forum for ideas. Colleagues, I do believe that we might be onto something important!

A *matter of consequence to millions*

I cannot overemphasize the urgency of this plea for assistance. Try as I might to consider all my patients equally, it is hard not to place this one in a unique light.

Doubtless, you have already guessed my patient's identity, and fully appreciate the public magnitude of this case. Should I lose Hilary, the loss would be crushing to millions.

Boredom: *a zeitgeist malaise*

At the start of the 1990s, boredom is an almost universal malaise. It is a pathology of the American *zeitgeist*, if you will.

Scrutinize your own lives closely. Do you see nothing of my patient in yourselves? Unique though the Hilary case might seem, we may well live in a veritable wilderness of untreated Hilarys.

By exploring the use of *jamais vu* as the antidote to ennui, we are likely to create the therapeutic state-of-the-art for the 1900s. We will gain the lasting gratitude of a generation. Great honors, awards, and accolades await us all.

Expecting your responses hourly,

I am,

Hector Glasco, M.D.

■Eternity Has
Gone into Reruns

For the longest time Hilary maintained a trancelike silence. Then she spoke.

"Dr. Glasco, would you do something for me?" she queried. "Imagine that you're sitting in a movie theater."

Then she was quiet again.

Hector Glasco was taken aback. He wasn't used to patients giving *him* instructions, particularly ones which sounded suspiciously like the beginnings of guided imagery. He didn't much like this reversal of roles. But he closed his eyes, anyway.

"Is the theater dark? Or am I watching a movie?" he asked.

"You're watching a movie," said Hilary.

More silence followed. Hector's imagination was a befuddled blank. His eyes popped open. "What kind of a movie?" he asked.

"I don't care. It doesn't matter. A screwball comedy or a love story or a suspense thriller or a horror flick. Anyway, you've come wanting to be delighted, *to be surprised*. Now don't we all hunger for surprise? And what's a movie without surprise?"

Hector closed his eyes again. And a movie started playing in his mind with startling clarity. It didn't surprise him that it was a movie with Hilary in it. Even though it was her first session and she had shown up without so much as an appointment, he immediately knew who she really was. He had seen her on-screen in real-life theaters. Still, she chose to call herself Hilary. She would admit to no other name and Hector respected her wish.

But this movie in his mind wasn't one he'd ever seen. The scene which unfolded was standard-issue romantic comedy. Hilary played a fire-and-ice society girl, quarreling with an uncouth but dashing furniture salesman over the price of a rather Byzantine-looking dining room table. Although Hector couldn't make out the words, they came fast and furious in a steady stream of witty banter. It was one of those moments which might easily turn into a love scene—but might just as easily not. Hector was impressed by the sudden lucidity of his imagination.

"Are you watching it?" asked Hilary.

"Yes," said Hector, thoroughly hypnotized.

"Good. Now. Imagine there's somebody sitting next to you. He's seen the movie before. He talks a lot. He annoys you."

And sure enough, the obnoxious entity appeared on Hector's right. He was short, squat, and smelly, chattering and munching obscenely on wads of popcorn.

"I seen this before," said the entity. *"I seen it dozens of times. You'll love this part. Oh, you're really gonna love this."*

Hector tried to ignore him and watch the screen. The furniture salesman had just said something a little too injurious. The society girl turned away defenseless, trying to hide her tears. Apologetically and gently, the salesman touched her on the shoulder. She turned toward him, suddenly vulnerable.

"What's happening in the movie?" asked Hilary.

"It's hard to tell just yet. A man and a woman have been quarreling, but they seem to be making up."

"Well let's just say that our should-be lovers are lingering, their lips oh-so-close together, *possibly* ready for a kiss. But you can see doubt in their eyes, can't you? They fear something. Perhaps it's a suspected husband or wife. Perhaps it's disease, betrayal, or the pods from outer space. So who can guess what the distance between those lips might mean? A tender collision, or a bittersweet retreat? Passion fulfilled, or passion put on hold?"

And the scene continued vividly, right down to the glistening in the heroine's eye, the hero's breathlessness, the swelling love theme. And at that very moment, the entity next to him barked out:

"Yup! They're gonna kiss now!"

And in less than a tick of a stopwatch came the burst of delicious osculation—but the moment was utterly ruined! The film got stuck. A flaming, bubbling hole burned into it and the screen erupted into blazing whiteness. Hector could even smell the toasted celluloid.

"He told you, didn't he?" queried Hilary.

The projector shut down. The theater was dark. Hector nodded idiotically, his eyes still closed. His face flushed and anger burned. Anger, he noted, at *Hilary*. It was she who had set the scene, had ruined everything.

"And that's the way it's going to be for the rest of the movie," said Hilary, "once they splice up the film, anyway. As every moment of the movie unfolds, he'll tell you what's going to happen next. He'll tell you everything *the split second before it happens*."

Hector's eyes snapped open. Hilary was staring at him intently, smiling. He noticed again the peculiar correctness of her face. It was sculpted perfectly. Her nose and cheekbones seemed to follow some ancient aesthetic principle—the Golden Section, perhaps. Her lips were thin and precise and seemed incapable of any truly inelegant expression. And she wore no makeup. Why should she?

Her skin was immaculate, each uniformly perfect pore in its own aesthetically regimented position. Surely there was something unnatural about so much poise.

"And that's my life, Dr. Glasco. I go around with a voice inside me, giving my life away by increments, squandering my spontaneity piecemeal."

Hector scratched his head. He sat in his office chair opposite hers, notebook in hand. To make matters worse, he couldn't take his eyes off her. He tried not to stare, but he'd never seen anyone inhabit a chair in quite the way this Hilary did. She didn't really *sit* there. She was languidly *draped* there, hanging against the upholstered leather in exquisitely arranged folds. Hector felt a certain professional embarrassment as his mouth began to water. He didn't like it. And despite his obvious attraction, he didn't like *her*.

Of course, he felt a certain clinical fascination. "Forgive me, but I'm not sure I understand. Are you telling me you experience, uh, audio hallucinations?"

"It's not *really* a voice, it's—" Hilary sighed wearily. "Let me put it another way. How often do you experience *déjà vu?*"

"Oh, not very often," said Hector. "Maybe two or three times a year."

"And how does it feel?"

"Well, a little alarming. Not exactly frightening, but discomforting. Sort of like getting hit on the funny bone. Fleeting and disagreeable."

"Yes," said Hilary. "When I was a child, I suppose I experienced *déjà vu* about as often as you do now. The first few times it happened, I ran frightened and crying to my mother, begging her to explain. When I was a teenager it started happening two or three times a month. Then it got more and more frequent. The episodes went from a few seconds to two or three minutes, then a quarter of an hour, then longer and longer and longer. I learned to ignore it. I learned to go on with life as if it weren't happening. And now, at last, my life has become one long, continuous episode of *déjà vu*. Can you imagine what that's like?"

Hector tried to imagine. He couldn't. He knew that Hilary knew he couldn't. She emitted a sad, peculiar giggle.

"So tell me, Dr. Glasco," she said. "Have you seen any good movies lately?"

Hilary came to three sessions every week. Hector insisted quite strenuously that Miss Bellows, his receptionist, control her flurry of excitement every time the star crossed their threshold. He vowed to let no one else know about his newest and most famous patient.

Hector was puzzled that his odd resentment of Hilary persisted. It seemed completely unfounded. In fact, Hilary was the first patient in the history of his practice who had ever carried out his every instruction. He persuaded her to give up an exceedingly dangerous regimen of skydiving, rock climbing, and hang gliding—activities calculated to put her life at risk in the vain hope that she might shock herself into a sense of surprise and wonder. He suggested she pursue less self-destructive activities: that she visit zoos, gardens, and amusement parks; that she roam blindfolded through familiar places; that she walk barefoot through early morning grass; that she meditate, burn incense, and explore new culinary sensations; and that she routinely introduce herself to total strangers on the street. But her perpetual sense of *déjà vu* and her terrible despair remained. It really began to grate on his nerves.

One afternoon he sat in his chair opposite Hilary as usual. The session had begun quite typically, in complete silence. He was startled to notice his own foot swinging impatiently and exerted considerable self-control to sit quietly and offer an encouraging smile.

Hector attempted not to stare at Hilary, trying instead to focus his gaze on the rug spread out between them. It was a very old-looking thing, almost worn through in some places, with ancient letters or hieroglyphs embroidered around the edges. He supposed that it was dull green, although his color-blind eyes were easily fooled. He couldn't even remember where he'd purchased it.

His mind was riddled with annoyances. He'd never had such thoughts in all his years as a therapist. But Hilary evoked something obsessive in him. These extended intervals of silence provoked him further.

He found the woman increasingly disturbing. Her resolute sadness seemed untouchable. And he found his occasional flights of erotic fantasy unbearable. Was it her star status that stirred his body, even when he mentally rejected her?

Today he even found himself rationalizing the possibility of making a pass at her. Yes, it might even be therapeutic! Surely the last thing Hilary expected was a rude sexual advance from her staid and conservative psychotherapist. The shock of it might free her from her spell.

His truant imagination created a scene in his mind:

Hilary is in the midst of a particularly heart-baring revelation. I walk over to her. I kneel before her chair, touch her hair, take both of her hands in mine. Ah, such presumption! But she is far too troubled, distracted, and vulnerable to push me away. She needs my comfort terribly. She looks into my eyes . . .

. . . and she yawns.

Hector sighed. Of course, that rude inner voice of hers would snidely announce his approach. Try as he might to imbue his passion with spontaneity, to Hilary the whole thing would be just another weary incident devoid of wonder. Even if he proved the most dazzling lover in her life, it might turn out to be the fatal incident which bored her past all endurance, broke her spirit with the absolute mediocrity of it all. It was the ultimate male sexual nightmare. Hector felt a grumpy relief in the squelching of his guilty dream.

It was now twenty minutes into the session. Right on schedule, Hilary broke the long silence, this time by popping her bubble gum. This was a brand new habit. Hector made a note of it. He thought for a moment of asking her why she had suddenly taken up so coarse a practice. But he knew the reason. It was in the very hope that it would make her ungraceful, awkward, imperfect. He decided not to tell her that it wasn't working.

"I understand now," said Hilary. "I know how I got like this. I know what's the matter."

"You do?" asked Hector, quickening slightly.

"It's eternity," said Hilary.

Hector squirmed in his seat a little. This didn't bode well for the remaining thirty minutes of the session.

"Yes," said Hector. "Eternity. What about it?"

"It's over," said Hilary. And a sigh came from deep inside of her—a sigh of extraordinary finality. "Eternity is over." And she paused to blow a bubble—a slow, enormous one which climactically burst and spread all over her lips and chin. She picked the sticky blue substance off her face and shoved it back into her mouth, chewing noisily. The entire action seemed graceful and perfect. Hector shivered a little. He feigned a chuckle, trying to stifle a vague feeling of alarm.

"Surely," he said, "the end of eternity would be more, well, *dramatic*."

"You just haven't noticed," said Hilary with resignation. "Nobody else has noticed. I'm not so lucky. I'm the only one who's noticed that eternity is over." She craned forward in her chair and peered closely at Hector. "Do you know what eternity *means?*"

Hector shook his head stupidly.

"Eternity is the amount of time it takes *for everything to happen,* for all possibilities to occur. It's the amount of time it takes for starfish to compose waltzes, for ice to burn like kerosene, for peace to prevail on earth, and for cows to jump over the moon. It's the amount of time it takes for pigs to sing Puccini, for popes to shit in the woods, and for bears to turn Catholic. It's the amount of time it takes for elephants to forget, for cheese to elope, and for dice to sneeze. It's the amount of time it takes for sextillions of big bangs and big crunches to happen—and infinitudes of big plunks and big wiggles and big belches and big splashes and big whimpers. It's the amount of time it takes for time itself to begin and end, again and again and again. It's the amount of time it takes for asteroids to weep for lost youth and for lovers to stay faithful forever. And all of it has happened. Everything. The universe has run out of things to do. So it has to start all over again. Do you know what Nietzsche called it?"

Hector drummed his fingers frantically on his notebook, trying to concentrate on the rug. He was getting nowhere at all with this case. It was bad enough that she had turned suddenly delusive, thinking herself the sole mortal to recognize the end of absolutely everything. But now she had to drag Nietzsche into it.

It was a bad sign when patients brought up German philosophers. That always meant they had reached the very brink. And Hector knew nothing about

Nietzsche except that he had gone crazy from syphilis. That pretty well invalidated him as a psychiatric role model. But he couldn't very well tell Hilary not to discuss him.

"Perhaps," he finally said, "you should tell *me* what Nietzsche called it."

Perhaps you should tell me was the handiest phrase in his arsenal, so beautifully ambiguous, possibly a confession of ignorance, and yet just as possibly a Socratic tactic. It said exactly what Hector wanted it to say: that he might know what Nietzsche said, and he might not—and that it didn't matter in either case.

"*Eternal recurrence*," said Hilary. "That's what Nietzsche called it. There are just so many possibilities in the universe. Everything that takes place eventually has to recur exactly the same way over and over." Hilary emitted a low, grim chuckle. "Eternity has gone into reruns! And I've seen all the shows before. I know them all by heart. I remember every last second of eternity, and I have to sit through the whole damn thing again."

She popped her gum desperately.

T...   ...is Vu Papers

**Volume One
Number Two
January**

Dear Colleagues —
Much has happened,
but no time to comment.
A query — Does the
attached have any sig-
nificance to you?
I need to know quite
urgently! — H.D., M.D.

se *Question:* yes this says a great deal for you
...tivity and also *Question:* your chances for succ
Question: treatment so just relax and tell me a
..u experiencing any *Question:* any auditory ef

nd I so seldom seeing seen ces any mayb
d as **oft and scoffed** k if anything vi
and skein and sherbert shapes of rotund
n: correspo **raspberry to be** nding to
__ f color or of depth has any well *Questio*
...ion of y **just see!** our sense of time set in and do
you see me do *Question:* do you see this hand in front of you how
many fingers am I holding in **Wage wonder, small sage self!**
fro **Brush with blunder barely -- burst** nt of you *Questio*
n: this won't last long I promise **open whirls of open sail:**
high, high feverish and air-nautical! don't be frightened j
usttry to tell me are *Question:* you no longer in this office wher
e are you ho **All fallen before me, dropped and drape-like**
flat as a world I knew and morning-mocked merry w wou
ld you de **knew to hang hopeful over long livid life!** scr
ibe the place you're *Question:* in try to remember that you are my
patient and I am y **Thrilled fingers poked and poked** our t
herapist and all will be quite alri **throughout and three**
to make the stars the stars. ght and normal *Question:* soon
te **Light shone punctured through the perforated outward**
ll me of any **and the finger-painted universe before me:**
light of desire physical *Question:* well any side effects any
any headach **light from home.** iness any clenching of the j
aw any dehydration but m **This was my world.** ore to the *Ques*
tion: point are you privy to or witness to **This was yours.**
sense of *Question:* surprise or *Question:* jamais vu or *Question:*
Sky stars these were: fear *Question:* since that is what *Ques*
tion: we' **but I never meant to stop** re trying to get at a
fter all if you *Que* **with blue-black rendered regions:**
stion: don't feel like **no!** answering my question directly j
But meant to fill the birches ust go with whatever flow of
thought *Questio* **and the intimate walnuts** *n:* comes to you
but do tell me *Question:* I would ver **and the tortoise-earth**
y much app **and the coughing rivulets** reciate knowing *Ques*
and the boulders great-lunged and shouting *tion:* if you f
eel any alteration any diminishme **with star-holes punctured**
nt of the M's effect **everywhere!** because to be perfectly *Ques*
tion: honest the duration of the drug in my *Question:* opinion sh

INSTITUTE OF NEUROREALITY
New Prague, Minnesota 10001

Dr. Savonarola, is, alas, nowhere to be found. Thus, my 2nd query: Does anybody know the antidote to M?

H. D., M. D.

Dear Dr. Glasco:

After studying your inquiry with extrem[e] ... have something unique to offer each other a[nd] ... with the elusive nature of the mind. I have ... which I am convinced will completely revolu[tionize] ... pharmacology, neuroscience, psychology, psyc[h] ... metaphysics -- well, I cannot do justice to ... paradigm from within our current understanding of mind and reality.

I have determined that the brain possesses <u>receptors for paradox</u>. Correspondingly, I have hypothesized the existence of a neurotransmitter which I call the "oxymorphin" -- a natural narcotic, if you will, which induces a state of perceptual freshness, paradoxical comprehension, or what you rightly term <u>jamais vu</u>. This letter is no place for me to document the experiments leading to this conclusion. But I hope I can give you a sense of the implications of my work.

The oxymorphin is almost wholly dormant in modern man, except when it is occasionally sparked by direct encounter with a common metaphor. These experiences are exceedingly brief in our age. This is because we have developed an involuntary tendency to explain metaphors away the instant we experience them. Indeed, critics, theorists, and professors of literature and the arts may share an insidious role in the degeneration of human perception.

But I may very well have discovered a way to reverse this unfortunate trend in our culture. After some intriguing experiments with the poetry of Gerard Manley Hopkins, I am convinced that I can translate metaphors into chemical terms. In other words, I can take a potent literary metaphor and make a drug out of it. An experience with a chemical metaphor will be more intense and more prolonged than an experience with a written one. The culturally-instilled impulse to "explain" the experience will simply vanish.

I have not had the opportunity to test this drug, which I have nicknamed "M", on human subjects. Would you care to study M's effect on Hilary? It might be an epoch-making enterprise.

Enclosed, please find a capsule of this substance. I eagerly await the results of your experiment.

In shared scientific destiny, I am,

Yours truly,

Imogene Savonarola

Imogene Savonarola, M.D., Ph.D.

☐Natural Cataclysms

Hector sat in his Beverly Hills apartment. It was night and raining, one of those rare Southern California winter thunderstorms. Hailstones were probably falling in the valley. Well, it would clear up the air.

He fingered the gelatin capsule which had arrived that morning by Federal Express and studied it carefully. It really didn't look like much, just crushed herbs. He sniffed it. It had a slight minty smell. A drug called M, Imogene Savonarola had written. The chemical equivalent of a metaphor. Yes, just what he'd asked for in his newsletter: a drug designed to create a state of *jamais vu*— the opposite of *déjà vu*. She said she'd derived it from a verse of a poem by—who was it? He couldn't remember. Some poet he'd never heard of.

Metaphor. The word dredged up disagreeable classroom memories. In his mind, an eighth-grade teacher scrawled two sentences on the blackboard: *My love is* like *a red, red rose*, and then, *My love is a red, red rose*. She waved a pointer at the two phrases and chattered shrilly about similes and metaphors. Hector didn't give much of a damn about the difference, then or now. And now he was supposed to believe he was holding a tiny metaphor in his hand.

He perused Savonarola's letter yet another time, looking again for some note of instruction, some indication of what the capsule really contained. Was it a mild mood elevator, some gentle amphetamine? Or was it something much more dangerous? Might it be one of those notorious designer drugs? Then again, perhaps it was merely a placebo, spiked with vitamin niacin to give it a certain physiological kick, a slight but rapid flushing of the cheeks, just enough to convince Hilary she had really taken a drug and provoke a positive reaction— or any reaction.

Hector frowned at that last consideration. If that was the idea, he had a right to know it—unless, of course, this was some sort of a double-blind experiment. In that case, both he and Hilary were experimental subjects. The thought made him queasy. But he reminded himself of Savonarola's many distinguished accomplishments. He knew her reputation well. Who didn't? Aside from her Ph.D. in biochemistry, she was widely known to hold degrees in medicine and several of the humanities, and had published scholarly papers in an eclectic variety of fields, including the occult sciences. Whatever the result, surely he could depend upon the judgment of so authoritative a personage.

And it was, after all, a heady thought to collaborate with such a celebrated thinker. Might this be the breakthrough that earned her the Nobel Prize the world had so long anticipated for her? And might he share an equal portion of her glory? Hector pictured himself in front of a wildly applauding audience, side by side with the renowned Dr. Savonarola—her face rather a blank, of course, as Hector had no idea what she looked like. Together, they were accepting the most exalted citation known to humankind.

"And yet," Hector wondered aloud, "suppose something goes wrong?"

But there was no point in debating the issue. His decision was already made. He would give the mysterious substance to Hilary. He closed his eyes and conjured up a picture of his patient. He tried, briefly, to re-attach the image with her real name.

Interesting, he thought. *I can't. She's really Hilary now. She's just plain Hilary.*

He went to the window, gazing over the metropolis. Great clouds rolled over the skyscrapers of Century City. Their underbellies absorbed weird colors from the Christmas lights, signs, and buildings below. The city turned them into garish billboards. Rain was their retaliation.

Then came a flash of lightning at least ten seconds long, spreading its fingers in all directions, reaching between skyscrapers, making every square inch of the streets below suddenly vivid, striking some unseen target. Hector waited for the thunderclap, counting the seconds, *One, two, three, four, five, six, seven, eight . . .*

The thunder never came.

But that was impossible. A flash like that should have produced a roar to shake him off his feet. What happened to the thunder? It seemed to have been abducted, stolen, swallowed up by the sheer greed and insatiability of the city.

That's L.A. for you, thought Hector. *It even cheats you out of natural cataclysms.*

At the very beginning of their next session, Hector handed the capsule to Hilary with a glass of water. He took a little satisfaction in the knowledge that, for once, he wasn't going to have to endure twenty minutes of silence. But he was nervous. Very nervous.

"Swallow it," he said, without preamble.

"What is it?" asked Hilary, mildly interested.

"Why don't we let that be our little surprise?"

Hilary showed just a trace of amusement. "Surprise is a little tough to come by, Dr. Glasco. Why don't you want to tell me what it is?"

Hector considered for a moment. Yes, a dose of honesty was in order. It might very well be a valuable part of the procedure.

"I don't know what it is," he said. "But I want you to take it anyway. Does that frighten you?"

Hilary laughed. "Why, Dr. Glasco, the very idea. If I could get frightened, you'd have to stop getting those fat, juicy checks I keep giving you. Where did you get it?"

"Someone sent it to me. A colleague. Someone I respect. Someone much wiser than I am. I think it might help you."

"Didn't this person tell you anything at all?"

"Yes, she said a few things in a letter, but. . ." Hector was surprised at what he said next. "I don't think they were true. I think they were all lies."

"And yet you trust this person?"

Hector was silent for a long moment. All he could muster was a mute shrug.

"Well," said Hilary, "that's good enough for me."

And she dispatched the capsule and the glass of water in the blink of an eye.

"That was fun, Dr. Glasco," she said. "That was the first genuinely stupid thing you've allowed me to do in a long time."

Hector stared at her. He didn't know what to say. What had he expected, anyway? Did he expect her to refuse? Now he almost wished she had. He wondered if he had made the worst mistake of his life.

"I know what's going on here, you know," said Hilary impishly. "That capsule was full of tobacco or tea leaves or some such thing. Really powerful stuff, huh, Dr. Glasco? And there was no trusted colleague. You just made that part up. It's a scam. A hoax. A placebo, right? You're trying to mess my mind back to normal."

With a rush of discouragement, Hector knew the capsule was worthless, that nothing was going to happen. He went wild with resentment. He snapped.

"I'll have no more of your glib goddamned mockery!" he barked. "Do you hear me?"

Hilary stared at him. Her expression changed profoundly.

Hector wanted to shut up, but couldn't. "I'll have you know," he shouted, "I've got patients who really hurt, who've been insulted and raped and abused and downright *shafted*, who've suffered the wounds and humiliations and injustices of the *world!* Do you get what I'm saying? I've got work to do! I don't *need* your hundred dollars an hour! I don't *need* your infernal non-suffering, your interminable numbness! And damn it, woman, I don't need *you!*"

But something had happened to Hilary. She was weeping. The most enormous teardrops he had ever seen were cascading down her face in gigantic beads. Hector was thunderstruck. *Did I cause this?* he wondered. He had never seen such voluptuous tears. And her face wasn't grotesquely distorted or disfigured. Rather, it was transfigured. It glowed like a saint's.

"Who are you?" she asked, wonder-stricken. "Where am I?"

Hector craned forward in his chair. "I'm Hector Glasco. You're in my office."

"I know that," she sobbed. "But you're not answering my question. Who are you? Where am I? And—who am I?"

15

"You're—you're Hilary," said Hector. He thought to himself, *That's not even true.* And yet, strangely, it was the only true thing he could say.

"Hilary," she said with a radiant smile. "Hilary."

"It's taken effect then?"

"I have no words," said Hilary, quickened with rapture. "I have no words. I have no words. I have no words."

"Well," stammered Hector stupidly. "I hadn't expected such a quick response."

"I have no words. I have no words. I have no words."

Hector tried to talk above his rising panic. "Yes, this says a great deal for your receptivity, and also your chances for successful treatment."

"I have no words. I have no words."

"So just relax and tell me, are you experiencing any auditory effects?"

"I have no words."

"Any voices?"

"I have no words."

"Maybe I should ask if anything visual, anything—"

"It's starting!" cried Hilary suddenly, almost exploding with wonder. "It's just beginning!"

"What is?" asked Hector.

She clapped her hands, which produced a deep, booming peal of thunder, at least ten sonorous seconds long. It seemed to come from inside of both of them. It resonated everywhere. It rumbled through the building and shook the furniture. Vases and statuettes on the bookshelves teetered and threatened to topple. Framed certificates and expensive paintings tried to leap off the walls.

Hector looked out the window. There wasn't a cloud in the sky. He looked back at Hilary.

"Something you misplaced, I believe," she said, laughing. "I thought I'd give it back. You see, I really do have no words. Only—gifts! Events! Actions! Stories! Many beautiful things lost and found! Because all things lost and found are the same!"

He had to struggle to even look at Hilary. She was blindingly radiant. Her face was riddled with color, as if illuminated by a hundred prisms. Her pupils dilated. They glowed like a cat's in the dark. They got brighter. They seemed to explode like novas. Hector could see whole universes inside those eyes.

He backed away from her. She rose from her chair. She danced, twirling slowly and majestically, accompanied by unheard but strangely resonant music. She moved as if she were walking a tightrope, hovering at an incredible height over some profound abyss. She poked her finger all about her, as if perforating the air itself.

"*Stars!*" she said, giggling. "*Stars! Stars! Stars!*"

The rug seemed to undulate beneath her feet. Even to Hector's color-blind

eyes, it had turned a wild and vivid green. The mysterious letters and hieroglyphs came crazily alive, dancing like naiads around Hilary. Abruptly, she sat
down on the rug and smiled up at him.

His astonishment was interrupted by his receptionist's frantic scream on the
intercom:

"Dr. Glasco, I . . . You'd . . . Please come!"

Hector tore out of his office and found poor Miss Bellows transfixed, staring
at the computer screen. It was a blaze of psychedelic color. Images exploded off
it, almost holographically. It popped with *I Ching* hexagrams, runes, signs of the
zodiac, alchemical symbols. And it sang a wordless song which nonetheless
related untold myths and legends—the very unheard melody that Hilary
danced to.

Hector's attention was distracted by the roar of the computer printer.
Unbidden, it spewed out reams of words. Hector tore off a sheet and tried
frantically to make some sense of it. It seemed mostly gibberish, but a weird and
cryptic message coiled snakelike down through the middle of it. Hector read the
first few words:

> You child
> and I so seldom seeing seen
> oft and scoffed
> right reckoned sky and skein and sherbert shapes of rotund
> raspberry to be
> to be
> just see!

Hector didn't stop to consider its meaning. He sensed calamity, and dashed
back into his office.

But he was too late. Hilary was gone. The office was eerily quiet, with just a
remnant of a breeze whistling through. A window was open. Hector walked
over to it and looked out. Beverly Hills spread out before him in its abnormal
serenity, twenty-seven stories below.

Imagine. . .

. . . if you will, a realm in which there is no height, width, depth, or time—a realm with fifteen dimensions, but none you've ever heard of. Imagine an entity who lives in this realm—an entity named Llixgrijb.

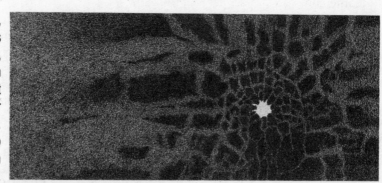

Imagine that poor Llixgrijb is trapped by some sort of extra-dimensional cave-in—completely immobilized and separated from its fellows. There's no escape. But here's the real problem—Llixgrijb cannot die.

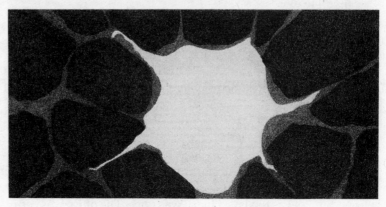

It's consciousness will continue, all alone and completely paralyzed for eternity—or whatever the equivalent of eternity is in such a realm.

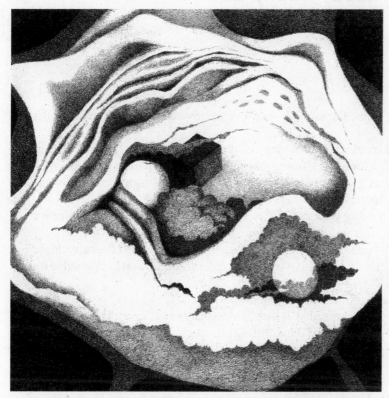

How would you deal with this situation? Think about it. You've got an imagination, haven't you? That's right, you're catching on. *Imagination*.
That's the key.
You'd create something to entertain yourself.
You'd create worlds in your mind, worlds within yourself.
You'd create universes with exotic dimensions no one ever dreamed of before.
You'd become strange creatures and share the company of other such creatures.
You'd try to make these realms and beings so real that you could completely forget the horror and boredom of your actual situation . . .

and that's exactly what Llixgrijb has been doing!
But—what *is* a world? . . .

19

Lies, Lies, Lies

After eleven rings, the familiar reedy voice answered: "Institute of Neuro-reality."

"Yes, could I speak to Dr. Savonarola? This is Hector Glasco again. I've been trying to reach her for a week now." The letter from Savonarola was still on his desk. He had read it so many times, looking back upon his original hope with loathing, trying to understand his error.

"Was she expecting your call?" The whiny, adolescent-sounding voice immediately grated again.

"Look, we've been through all this before. I'm calling about the capsule she sent along to me, the chemical metaphor. I'm calling about what happened to my patient. Is she in?"

"I don't believe so."

"Can you give me a number where I can reach her? It's terribly urgent."

"Let me see." Hector heard the shuffling of papers. "No, I'm afraid not," came the sluggish reply. "Dr. Savonarola is in a Tibetan monastery right at the moment."

"Has she taken a vow of silence or something?"

"It's not unlikely," droned the voice self-righteously. He could imagine her at her desk, wearing a fake leopard-skin miniskirt, a purple lamé blouse and giant-rimmed glasses with multicolored plastic inset jewels.

"When do you expect to hear from her?"

"That's hard to say."

"Please, please, just tell her I called. Tell her to get in touch with me."

"I will do that, Dr. Belasco."

"It's Glasco! G-L-A-S-C-O!" He hung up angrily. Then a vague suspicion crossed his mind. He had called the Institute of Neuroreality once daily, and each day the secretary had told him that Savonarola was someplace entirely different. Now what could that mean? Hector grabbed the phone and dialed again.

"Institute of Neuroreality," came the secretary's voice.

Hector affected a British accent. "Hello, this is Tobias Benz, the theoretical physicist."

"Oh, yes, Dr. Benz," said the secretary, with sudden amiability. "How are you?"

"Well, I'm calling from a restaurant in Vancouver. Frankly, I was expecting Imogene for lunch, and she's dreadfully late."

"Oh, dear. I'm afraid it slipped her mind. If memory serves—" and again came the shuffling of paper. Probably her nose was buried in a copy of *People* magazine. "Yes, Dr. Savonarola is speaking in Moscow. It's some sort of *glasnost*-related thing. Can I reschedule?"

"No, thank you. I'll reach her later."

Hector hung up. He stared at the phone dumbfounded. Then he dialed again. The secretary answered in her accustomed way. She relentlessly stalked Hector's imagination, the very image of clerical intractability. He felt sure that she was painting her nails some unfathomable hue, or writing her boyfriend's name all over the company stationery with a scented pink ballpoint, dotting the i's with little hearts. Hector affected a woman's voice.

"Hello," he said. "This is Shirley Cohen, with *I Ching Monthly.*"

"Oh, yes, Ms. Cohen. How can I help you?"

"I was scheduled to do a phone interview with Dr. Savonarola right about now."

"Oh, I'm terribly sorry, you *were* on the schedule, but she seems to have forgotten."

"Well, is she in?"

"No, I don't think so. Let me see." And again, the papers rattled briefly but noisily. "She's in Australia, communing with the aborigines. I could have her paged, but I doubt she'll be able to get back to you."

Hector dropped his vocal disguise and yelled furiously. "Listen to me, you mendacious little bimbo! I want to know where Imogene Savonarola really is, and I want to know right now!"

"Is this Dr. Glasseye again?"

"Glas*co*, damn it!"

"Well, if you must know, Dr. Savonarola is at the North Magnetic Pole, experiencing certain unique ionic resonances. But it's very hush-hush, so I would appreciate if you didn't call all the newspapers or—"

But Hector slammed the phone down before she could finish. He held his throbbing head between his hands.

"Infernal *lies!*" he cried aloud. "What on earth have I gotten myself into?" His head raced with disturbing possibilities. Maybe the secretary really didn't know Savonarola's whereabouts. Maybe Savonarola had taken M herself, and was now wandering abroad in the world, spouting mad prophecies or some such thing. Maybe the eminent biochemist was in the same fix as Hilary.

Savonarola's fateful letter stared up at him. "Would you care to study M's effect on Hilary?" she had written. "It might be an epoch-making enterprise."

"Epoch-making enterprise, indeed!" growled Hector. "You created your monster, then vanished before you had to deal with the consequences!"

But then Hector wondered, who had *really* created the monster? He blushed with shame at the Faustian impulse which had led him into this mess. He paced his office. Then, palms pressed flat on the sill, he leaned forward and gazed out his office window. Twenty-seven stories down. How the hell had Hilary gotten out of the building? No answer came. He resumed pacing. Now everything in the office reminded him of Hilary. The homelike ambiance of end tables with magazines, coffee table for servings of fruit juices, herbal teas, and sometimes coffee, framed watercolors and luxurious green plants, the two spacious armchairs . . .

The empty space on the floor caught his eye again, that slightly pale rectangle which marked where the green rug had been.

Yes, there was the enigma of the rug—the rug which had disappeared with Hilary. But how? Had she rolled it up and tucked it under her arm and jumped out the window? *No*, he thought fleetingly, *whatever* really *happened was much stranger*. Hector's flesh tingled slightly. He didn't want to think about that.

The worst of it was the guilt. *If only I hadn't lost my temper!* But was that really the cause? He doubted it.

In the days following Hilary's disappearance, Hector took to the streets. He frantically searched for his lost patient, stalking the halls of both elegant and run-down hospitals, fruitlessly roaming the plazas of Century City. He ignored all preparations for the Christmas season, pushing his way through interminable crowds of people and automobiles each time he got a new idea about where to look.

Then, of course, there were the personal ads. Hector placed them in everything from the *Times* to the sleaziest of tabloids. But they stirred up no clues except a handful of crank responses.

He never went to the police, of course. How could he explain his own role in it all? "You see, officer, I gave her this drug . . ." No, the whole idea was completely out of the question. Besides, Hilary's absence was already a public concern. The papers buzzed with rumors about the disappearance of a certain beloved movie star. Friends and family denied everything, but Hector was quite sure a team of detectives were already investigating the matter.

And yet, for the time being, nobody had connected Hector with her disappearance. And Miss Bellows, as amazed as Hector by Hilary's high-altitude vanishing act, steadfastly promised to keep quiet.

But Hector knew it was only a matter of time. One day soon, some shrewd and dogged detective would come knocking at his door. The terrible truth would be revealed. Then Hector would be accused, found guilty of the crassest negligence and irresponsibility, and stripped of all his credentials. The very thought made him flush and break out into a sweat.

His only recourse was to find Hilary before anyone else did.

And he had to find an antidote to that infernal drug!

The holidays came and went with no word from Hilary. One morning early in January, Hector staggered into his office, looking and feeling even more haggard than usual. He muttered something to Miss Bellows, which she took to be his usual request for a cup of coffee. She presented him with a steaming mug. Hector growled his thanks and lurched into his enclave.

He sat at his desk, immobile and hopeless, for several long minutes. Then he reached across his desk for a book he had checked out of the library the day before. He opened it at random, silently reading the first line which caught his eye.

> But ah, but O thou terrible, why wouldst thou rude on me
> Thy wring-world right foot rock? lay a lionlimb against me?

Could those be the words he was looking for? He closed the book and opened it again. This time he read aloud, to see if it would help to hear the words.

> "No wonder of it: sheer plod makes plough down sillion
> Shine, and blue-bleak embers, ah my dear,
> Fall, gall themselves, and gash gold-vermilion."

The language staggered Hector into increasing wakefulness. It seemed to make no logical sense, but it exhilarated him despite the fact. He read aloud still another time, trying to put a little feeling into it.

> "My cries heave, herds-long; huddle in a main, a chief
> Woe, world-sorrow; on an age-old anvil wince and sing—
> Then lull, then leave off."

Hector was interrupted by a loud guffaw. He whirled around to face a jolly gentleman standing in his office doorway.

"Dr. Glasco, I presume," said the rather portly man. "Can it be that we share a passion for Gerard Manley Hopkins?"

"Somewhere in here . . . ," Hector waved the book at the intruder, "is a clue to the condition of one of my patients. Somewhere in this book, there's an extremely dangerous metaphor—a burst of figurative language that . . ."

Hector collapsed into a chair. "That I'd be the last man on earth to find." Then he straightened up and glared at his visitor. "Who the hell are you?"

"Max Henderson." The intruder stepped forward and extended a hand. "We had an appointment."

Hector bounded up out of the chair and shook hands. "Of course, of course, I apologize. But my receptionist . . . ?"

"Seems to be away from her desk at the moment," Max answered. Hector sighed. The once-steadfast Miss Bellows was becoming less and less reliable. Hector suspected his own recent dispiritedness might be the cause.

Max settled comfortably into a chair and started unwrapping a peppermint from the dish on the coffee table. "You know, I'm only here because my wife insisted. She's being pretty silly about this whole thing. But she's sold on you as a shr— I do beg your pardon."

"Shrink is quite acceptable."

"Anyway, I'm just trying to keep things peaceable."

Hector sat down again in the chair on the other side of the table. He strained to clear his mind, to focus on the case at hand. "Yes," he said, thinking hard. Hector looked around nervously for his clipboard and the file for this new case. It was all the way over on his desk, and he did hate to be obtrusive about reading notes. It often made clients uneasy. He should have reviewed the records before Max Henderson arrived. He vaguely recalled that Max was an English professor at one of the local universities. He had no idea which.

"Let's see," said Hector. "After you phoned to make an appointment, your wife came in. I talked with her."

"Did you?" returned Max, raising his eyebrows in mild amazement. "Not an easy thing to accomplish. So. What did she say about me?" He munched on the candy.

"She said . . ." Hector couldn't carry it off. He stood up casually and edged over to his desk. He peeked into the file. "She said that you aren't there for her," he reported triumphantly.

"*I'm not there for her,*" said Max, mulling the phrase thoughtfully. "*I'm not there for her. I'm not there for her.* Hmmm." He pursed his lips and raised his fingers to his chin, lost in thought.

"What do you have to say to that?" queried Hector, sitting down once again, this time with the clipboard and file on his lap.

"Well, what did she mean by *there*, Dr. Glasco? Did she mean our kitchen, our bedroom, the basement, the garden, where she works? *Where*, exactly, is *there*? I take it she didn't mean your office, otherwise she would have said *here*, not *there*."

Hector was more than a little nonplussed. "I believe," he explained, "that she simply meant that you weren't really *present*. You know, with her."

Max laughed. "Well, that's so obvious it's trivial, isn't it? I mean, at that very moment, I was probably in some infernal faculty meeting or giving a lecture or hiding in the library or catching a beer at the local bar or some such thing. I certainly wasn't *with* her."

Hector was a little alarmed by Max's obtuseness. Was this the sort of man we entrusted with the instruction of our young adults? "No, Max," he said urgently, "I'm afraid you're missing the point. She was speaking *figuratively.*"

"Yes, yes, yes, I understand that. I'm not stupid. But those *words* are so revealing—or unrevealing. She says them to me time and time again, day in and day out, over and over and over, *ad infinitum.* 'You're not *here* for me,' she says. Now, she doesn't say that I'm not *there* in these instances, mind you, but that I'm *not here,* since she's not describing some hypothetical or figurative *elsewhere,* but a literal *here* and *now.* 'You're not here for me. You're not here for me.'

"'And what does that mean?' I always ask her. 'If I'm *not here* for you, then surely you're sitting in the room alone. And if you're sitting in the room alone, you must be talking to yourself. And if you're talking to yourself, then speaking from your own perspective, the *"you"* that's not here for *"me"* must be *"myself."* Or, speaking from my perspective, the *"I"* that's not here for *"you"* must be *"yourself."* But since I'm not here for you, I'm not even present in the room, so my perspective doesn't exist. In fact, I'm not even present to the degree that I *can not* be present. Which brings the whole question back to you alone. *Ipso facto:* You, yourself, are really the absent party.'"

Hector stammered confusedly. "How does she respond when you, er, put it that way?"

"Well, how should I know? As a non-present observer, I haven't the faintest idea. In fact, at those moments, I'm not even saying the words I'm saying, so she must be saying them herself. So I guess you'd better ask her. Except you can't, because she's not here."

Max folded his hands over his knee and smiled wistfully. "It's sad, really. She misses herself so badly, and believes that she's me."

Hector knew, without a moment's reflection, that this was the most ridiculous blather he'd ever heard. It was time to put a stop to it.

"I've got news for you, Max," he said commandingly. "That poor woman means exactly what she says: *You're not there for her!*"

"And I've got news for *you,* Dr. Glasco: *Nobody's there!*"

Forgetting his professional demeanor, Hector pulled his hair with frustration. "What the hell kind of gibberish is this?" he barked.

"Deconstructionist criticism," said Max proudly. "My specialty." He said it exactly as if he were a chef speaking of a particularly tasty recipe. He popped another peppermint into his mouth. Hector found the whole thing unbelievably annoying.

But then he thought back to his perplexity at reading Hopkins's poetry. And here was an academic, just when one was needed. Glasco wondered, *Is this the guy who can help me find the Hopkins metaphor? Could he help me rationally explain it to Hilary—provided, of course, I can* find *Hilary?*

"Excuse me for asking," he said shyly, "but what do you do with, er, *literary metaphors* when you run into them?"

"A metaphor," said Max fondly, "is a lamp which guides us down dark corridors to the heart of the mystery—only to extinguish itself at the crucial moment! It is the perfect joke of language! And when the joke's on us, we have no choice but to laugh."

"But could you . . . *rationally explain* a metaphor?"

Max smiled benignly. "And take away its sublime comedy? Oh, no, Dr. Glasco. Besides, I'm afraid rationality's no longer a tenable concept in a culture so fraught with binary oppositions. It's a lie from start to finish. But what isn't?"

Hector threw his arms up in exasperation. "But aren't there any good old-fashioned *critics* left? Doesn't anybody just *interpret* literature anymore?"

"Only a handful of academic bores and dunderheads," said Max.

Hector quickened at these words. Of course! It wasn't enough to find an annoying academic. He had to find one who was boring as well. It would require a *superior level of mediocrity* to solve the Hopkins riddle—the dreariest academic he could find! He poised his pen over a blank sheet of paper.

He leaned forward and stared at Max challengingly.

"Name one," he said.

The Jamais Vu Papers

Volume One
Number Three
February

My Dear Colleagues:

I must reluctantly report that the treatment prescribed by Dr. Savonarola—the drug called M—was not entirely successful.

Since my collaborator is not available for consultation (being out of the country on important scientific matters) I once again beg your assistance.

What was the metaphor?

I admit that my primary failure in this matter was this: I never learned from the renowned biochemist *what metaphor was used* in creating the drug M. From her letter, I could only assume it was derived from a poem by Gerard Manley Hopkins.

If I had known what the metaphor was, I could have counteracted its somewhat undesirable side effects by literally explaining it to Hilary. The wondrous moment of *jamais vu* would have been reduced to the prosaic normalcy of a college literature course, and I could then have proceeded with more conventional treatments.

Recourse to academia

I needed academic assistance to divest the metaphor of its magic. After some enquiries, I enlisted the aid of a midwestern academic renowned for his stodgy and lackluster approach.

This was none other than Dr. Joseph Xavier Brillig, Chairman of English at James Fenimore Cooper Junior College in Sequester, Missouri. As you can see from his letter (included here), his opinion are somewhat at odds with mine.

A strange manifesto

Alas, Professor Brillig's input thus far has been thoroughly plodding and unimaginative. He did, however, turn up an interesting document which you will find reproduced on page 2.

Who are these so-called "Brothers and Sisters of Thaumaturgy"? Is there anything in their arcane literature to shed any light on the Hilary Case? And is it true that Imogene Savonarola is of their number?

As always, I anxiously await any information you may have to offer.

H. Glasco

Complete text of a letter from a Dr. J.X. Brillig

Dear Dr. Glasco,

I assure you, I will lend every assistance to this "Hilary problem." Of course, try as you might, you cannot hope to conceal your patient's true identity. But I, too, will go along with your androgynous pseudonym.

I do believe you have been seriously bamboozled about the role of the alleged wonderdrug M in Hilary's disappearance. I have some trouble swallowing (forgive the pun) this little "metaphor in a capsule."

Don't you see, Glasco? The very *idea* of a chemical metaphor is nothing but a figurative lie—and hence a *metaphor*. There's not a shred of truth to it.

And I seriously question the complicity of so authoritative a thinker as Imogene Savonarola in this preposterous "M" business.

In fact, I very much doubt that you corresponded with the *real* Dr. Savonarola at all. Surely someone used her name and letterhead to convince you of this M hoax and put you in an uncharacteristic (I sincerely hope!) state of gullibility.

This plot probably made it easy for some nefarious group to kidnap Hilary right under your nose.

Well. Now we get to the puzzling role of Gerard Manley Hopkins in this caper. Why did our kidnappers bring an inscrutable nineteenth-century poet into their scheme?

As a man of literary insight, I believe I might be able to help with this question. But I warn you, it won't be easy. Poets are, by definition, unprincipled liars. And that metaphor-mongering, syntax-smothering rascal Gerard Manley Hopkins may be the most deceitful of them all. If there is a clue to your case concealed in his poetry, it will be devilishly hard to find.

An obscure society

At the end of your phone call, you also inquired about a group called the "Thaumaturgists." I did a little research on that pack of mystical nitwits.

The Ancient Order of the Brothers and Sisters of Thaumaturgy claims to date back to ancient Egypt, and to have come into existence to counteract such "disagreeable" innovations in human consciousness as empiricism and cause-and-effect reasoning. Members believe in the literal reality of metaphors and fiction. As

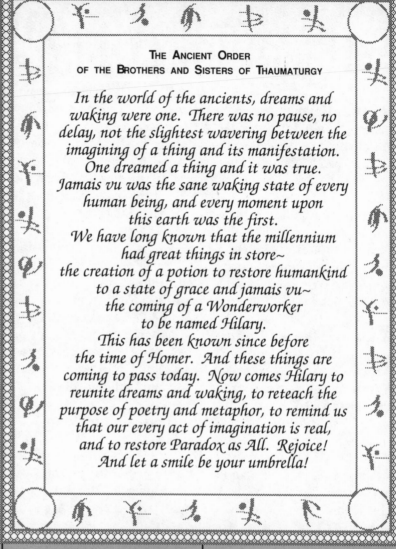

**THE ANCIENT ORDER
OF THE BROTHERS AND SISTERS OF THAUMATURGY**

*In the world of the ancients, dreams and
waking were one. There was no pause, no
delay, not the slightest wavering between the
imagining of a thing and its manifestation.
One dreamed a thing and it was true.
Jamais vu was the sane waking state of every
human being, and every moment upon
this earth was the first.
We have long known that the millennium
had great things in store~
the creation of a potion to restore humankind
to a state of grace and jamais vu~
the coming of a Wonderworker
to be named Hilary.
This has been known since before
the time of Homer. And these things are
coming to pass today. Now comes Hilary to
reunite dreams and waking, to reteach the
purpose of poetry and metaphor, to remind us
that our every act of imagination is real,
and to restore Paradox as All. Rejoice!
And let a smile be your umbrella!*

if I didn't contend with enough literal-mindedness in my literature classes!

They claim such unlikely past brothers and sisters as Socrates, Sir Isaac Newton, Thomas Carlyle, Gertrude Stein, Virginia Woolf, Bernard Shaw, and Charles Edward Ives. Living members are rumored to include author Tom Robbins and your supposed collaborator, Imogene Savonarola. And as you may gather from the enclosed credo, the Order may have adopted your patient as a sort of messiah.

They are also said to be devising a new list of Seven Deadly Sins for the postmodern age. Call me old-fashioned, but I found the old list more than adequate.

Sincerely yours,
Joseph Xavier Brillig, PhD

*Take note, then, that a being
endowed with any poetic sense is
sensitive to the supernatural.*

It is around us; it is in us.

*Have you come across your
image already present in an old
mirror?*

*That some people never perceive
the encompassing supernatural
proves nothing. Let us say that
they are impervious to everything,
to poetry, to music, to light, to love,
to the cries of the world, to the
chorus of the dead, to the
phosphorescence of the living, to
metamorphosis, to anamorphosis
. . . I don't say that everything
breathes the supernatural; but
could you dissociate it from art
without great damage?*

Michel de Ghelderode
The Ostend Interviews

The Dreaded Explicator

The minute Max left his office, Hector rushed to his phone and dialed the number Max had given him—the English department at James Fenimore Cooper College in Sequester, Missouri. After a few rings came the most pompous and overbearing voice he'd ever heard.

"Joseph Xavier Brillig here."

"Professor Brillig, my name is Hector Glasco. I'm a psychiatrist in Beverly Hills. A certain Max Henderson suggested I call you. He said you might be able to help me with a difficult psychiatric case."

"Max Henderson!" cried Brillig gleefully. "That disgrace to academia! We go way back, Max and I. Dozens of conferences over the years. Tell me, why on earth did he give you my name? And what sort of postmodern claptrap is that hack mixed up in these days?"

Hector thought it best to ignore the query. "Could I ask you a couple of questions?"

"Certainly."

"Have you ever taught a course in Gerard Manley Hopkins?"

"Well, the powers that be try to discourage me. But yes, on occasion."

"What was the most recent enrollment?"

"Two," said Brillig, with perverse but unmistakable glee. "And one of them dropped out in less than a week. Old J. M. H. got cancelled that term, I'm afraid. I'm not the most popular professor at Fenimore Cooper. I know that. I'm proud of it. Oh, lots of folks today think that literature courses should be entertaining. I don't subscribe to that damn fool notion. If students want to have fun, they should go to an amusement park. In my classes, we get down to serious business."

Hector was breathless. He sensed he had a real dud on his hands. He could barely contain his excitement as he asked the crucial question:

"What's your perspective on metaphors?"

"Metaphors!" Brillig chortled. "Dr. Glasco, let me tell you a little story."

Hector immediately felt a yawn welling up. He was pleased. After only a few words of conversation, he already found this character unspeakably dull.

Brillig's capacity to produce boredom was swift and uncanny.

"When I was a boy," continued Brillig sententiously, "a teacher tried to explain the difference between metaphors and similes. She wrote two sentences on the blackboard: *My love is like a red, red rose*, and then, *My love is a red, red rose*."

Well, well, well, mused Hector boredly. *Did we have the same English teacher? No, of course not. They all use that example.* Hector's eyes watered from the inexplicable tedium of the conversation.

"And I immediately knew the awful truth," continued Brillig. "A metaphor was nothing more than a bold-faced, shameless lie. What kind of botanical pervert could honestly say that his love *is* a red, red rose? Why, the guile of it! And here I was, with all my Boy Scout ideals, being told that this duplicitous and brazen practice was the very heart and soul of poetry! So much the worse for poetry!"

Hector yawned and couldn't stop. He began to ache all over. He became alarmed by the dangerous surge of ennui. Was he growing physically ill with sheer disinterest? Could this prove fatal? Desperate to stay awake, he got up from his desk and paced back and forth, striding across the patch of floor where the rug had been. He slapped himself, trying to get the blood flowing in his head. Brillig continued relentlessly.

"It was then, my good Dr. Glasco, that the die was cast. Possessed of a resolute impatience with such chicanery, I decided that I would have none of it. From that day forward, I was fated to be a critic, an enemy of literary subterfuge."

Hector became dizzy. He swayed on his feet. The room started to darken. This was worse than any lecture he'd endured in college—but he wasn't sure why.

"Yes," continued Brillig, "I became that most dreaded and most feared of all breeds of academics: an *explicator*, always looking for just one true meaning lurking in any heap of falsehoods parading in the insidious guise of poetry! I devoted my talents and my very life to . . ."

Those were the last words Hector heard before the room went completely black. He collapsed in a senseless heap on the floor.

Blackness surrounded Hector. *Oh no!* he thought with embarrassment, *I fell asleep during Brillig's phone call—and now it's night! Why the devil didn't Miss Bellows wake me up? Didn't I have any more appointments? My God, it's dark! How did it get so dark?* Even his windows seemed to be shuttered over, blocking out the lights of the city.

Hector groped around, trying to get to his feet. Nothing familiar met his searching fingers. There were no solid objects within his reach. He could touch this darkness somehow—it was a kind of surface, a strangely dimensional thing. But it seemed to occupy the air, too.

He was breathing it! Hector gasped, feeling the whoop of his childhood asthma about to erupt. Automatically he calmed his panic, letting the sweat turn cold on his face. As his breathing gradually returned to normal, Hector realized that he could see . . . something. The floor he was sitting on was illuminated by a faint flicker, as if a candle burned nearby. He looked around but could find no source of light.

When he peered closely at the floor, figures slowly took shape before his eyes, characters and hieroglyphs sewn into a badly worn fabric. Hector was sitting on his missing rug! It had been returned to him somehow! And now he heard voices through the darkness, voices on the other side of the darkness.

Then came a flash of light, and another, and another. They became successively brighter until Hector was almost blinded. Each flash looked like a star exploding. They were so close by that he might touch them if he were only quick enough. He tried to, but his hand movements were slow and suspended, as if he were underwater. The stars blazed briefly and wildly, like Hilary's eyes when she'd taken that damnable drug.

That's what the voices were chanting! "Hilary! Hilary! Hilary! Hilary!"

Hector tried to peer into the bursts of light, which now seemed like sudden gashes in the darkness—openings which just as suddenly repaired themselves. In each moment that they appeared, he caught glimpses of eyes, faces, and wildly colored masks and costumes. Yes, there was a multitude nearby, celebrating, performing some wild ritual. They almost seemed to occupy the same space as he did. At the same time, he was irrevocably separated from them by this intangible sheet of darkness.

The voices grew steadily louder: "Hilary! Hilary! Hilary! *Hilary!*"

Hector heard his own voice cry out, for no reason he could imagine, "No comment!"

"*Hilary! Hilary! Hilary!*" continued the voices.

"No comment!" cried Hector, baffled by his own words. "No comment! No comment! No comment!"

As the voices reached a shattering crescendo, Hector covered his ears and shouted at the very top of his lungs, "There is such a thing as patient confidentiality!"

Then came a silence. *I guess that got through to them,* he thought smugly, still not understanding what he'd said, or why. But he knew the celebrants were still there somewhere.

The flashes had died down to tiny, self-detonating pinpoints. A figure dimly appeared in front of him, illuminated only by that dim, candlelike flicker. It spoke with a voice which spanned several pitches, rich and resonant, at once harmonious and dissonant, neither man's nor woman's. "In the world of the ancients, dreams and waking were one. There was no pause, no delay, not the slightest wavering between the imagining of a thing and its manifestation. You ask how the great Pyramids were built? Thaumaturgists know the one true answer: They were dreamed. And they are always dreamed."

The surrounding throng joined in accompaniment, in a whisper at first. "One dreamed a thing and it was true." Then the voices swelled in a slow, steady crescendo, humming, chanting, singing some wordless, age-old song. The figure intoned with a tragic solemnity which verged on mockery and laughter: "*Jamais vu* was the sane waking state of every human being, and every moment upon this earth was the first."

Hector was a few inches away from the figure, which nevertheless seemed as indistinct as before. The surrounding chorus reached an ear-shattering pitch. The figure extended a chalice toward him. Hector took it in his hands. It changed in shape and texture as he held it, feeling rough and jewel-encrusted one second and smooth and metallic the next.

Then the palpable darkness dispersed somewhat. The figure before him became considerably clearer. It was a robed and hooded personage. Its face was shrouded with blackness.

Hector shuddered, and turned and looked from side to side. He was surrounded by an ocean of masks, some plain and pale, others wildly sculpted and painted. Their eyeholes were all black. But Hector could sense the presence of hundreds of staring eyes. He could feel their presence in the pit of his stomach.

Hector looked forward. The robed figure bent over him. Its eyes seemed to glow a little.

"What are you hiding from the Thaumaturgists?" the voice demanded.

Hector cowered. He stammered incoherently. He had no idea how to respond. Without thinking further, he lifted the chalice to his lips and drank from the sour and pungent liquid within . . .

"And so, Glasco, in answer to your question . . ."

Hector opened his eyes and found himself lying on the bare patch on his office floor, staring at the phone receiver which lay right in front of him. Brillig's voice was still chattering away.

Light surrounded Hector. *Oh no!* he thought with embarrassment, *I fell asleep during Brillig's phone call—and I dreamed something, too. What was it?* He shook his head. *What was it?*

But Hector had no knack at all for remembering dreams. And his mouth was filled with the unmistakable taste of tequila—a substance he hadn't imbibed since his college days. His memories of tequila were not agreeable.

A word lingered on his tongue along with the aftertaste. It repeated itself in an obsessive but barely audible whisper. What was it? He could barely make it out.

Oh, yes . . .

Thaumaturgists.

Groggily, Hector grabbed the receiver. How much of Brillig's performance had he missed? The professor seemed to be wrapping things up.

". . . metaphors are rather like ghosts and ESP and telekinesis, all that foolishness. There's not a metaphor in the world that can't be *rationally explained.*"

Hector rubbed his head. A hangover seemed to be setting in. But weary and disoriented as he was, he knew he'd found the perfect pedant.

"I think you can help me, Professor Brillig," he said finally. "Here's my problem . . ."

The Jamais Vu Papers

**Volume One
Number Four
March**

My Dear Colleagues,

I must, at last, come forward with the unfortunate truth. My patient, Hilary, disappeared immediately after taking the drug M, and has not been seen since.

Forgive my prior lack of forthrightness in this matter. I won't pretend that professional embarrassment didn't play its role in my reticence.

This being said, any clues to my patient's whereabouts are urgently needed. And I yet know of no antidote to M.

Further perplexities

Among the responses to my publication, I have received a weirdly assorted collection of objects, news clippings, photographs, books, etc. These materials apparently have produced the state of *jamais vu* in some of my readers.

They include 168 copies of the novels of Tom Robbins. These were unaccompanied by explanation or return addresses. I delved into the author's work with a mixture of delight and perplexity. Finding no immediate clues to the Hilary Case therein, I wrote to Robbins himself for information.

He was quick to respond to my query. "Simply send me seven questions," he wrote cheerily, "and I will return eight answers."

Following are the fruits of our correspondence.

H. Glasco

Tom Robbins replies

Q #1: Mr. Robbins, do you have any idea why, in response to the first few issues of the jamais vu papers, *I am receiving dozens of copies of your books?*

A #1: Probably a Communist plot intended to unravel your moral fabric.

Q #2: It is rumored that you belong to the Ancient Order of Brothers and Sisters of Thaumaturgy. Do you wish to deny or confirm this?

A #2: In recent years, my name has been mentioned in connection with several organizations, including the Union of Mad Scientists, the College of 'Pataphysics, and Friends of the Missing Link. It is my practice neither to confirm nor deny these associations, although it's public knowledge that I once belonged to the Columbia Record Club. (I was forced to resign because it was too disciplined.) As for my alleged membership in the Ancient Order of Brothers and Sisters of Thaumaturgy, I shall have no further comment except to say that I'm well acquainted with the history of that order, and thus can flatly assure you that never at any time did it harbor Virginia Woolf under its luminescent wings. In fact, the only official body to which that little hysteric ever belonged was Bedwetters Anonymous, where she lost her good standing due to a resumption of habits.

While we are on the subject of group activity, I should mention that on more than one occasion I have been petitioned to join a certain well-known authors' organization. Why have I declined? Well, to paraphrase J. Gustafson, "Better one writer in love with language than a thousand in love with each other."

Q #3: Your writings suggest that a richer time is behind us; for example, gods die because people stop believing in them. Do you think a wondrous state of jamais vu *might once have been everybody's normal waking condition? What might such a world have been like?*

A #3: Human experience is, indeed, thinning out, but in the way that rubber thins out before it reaches the limits of its elasticity, where either it rips in half or else snaps back into a fair approximation of its original shape.

I like to think that the latter is our fate, and that an epoch is coming when we (in great variety) will once again live outside of time and history—but not outside of the pizza delivery zone.

Q #4: As a master of figurative language, what do you think are the transformative and evolutionary properties of metaphors?

A #4: When we say that "Johnny runs fast," what have we said that anyone except Johnny's mother is apt to recall? When we say that "Johnny runs like a deer," we have provided a memorable totemic image to which our notion of Johnny's speed might be conveniently stapled.

Should we say, however, that "Johnny *is* a deer," we

have eternalized Johnny, fitting him out forever with antlers and hooves from the unyielding deep forest of primal unconsciousness.

Q #5: What will happen if chemical metaphors hit the streets?

A #5: My suspicion is that chemical metaphors may not belong on the streets. In ancient Greece, the fungoid metaphors dispensed at Eleusis were restricted to those who were deemed spiritually and intellectually evolved enough to benefit from them. Public discussion of the M(ysteries) by initiates was forbidden under penalty of death.

That's probably a sound idea. The problem is, who decides who is or who isn't qualified for the experience? Certainly, it's a bit elitist, but as Hermann Hesse pointed out, "The M(agic) Theatre is not for everyone."

Q #6: I'm hardly a literary critic, but I find your writing a delightfully paradoxical mixture of elegiac lamentation and irreverent celebration. How do you pull this off?

A #6: About twenty years ago in Morocco, a Ukrainian neurosurgeon turned Sufi master inserted a device into my right ear. The

Ukrainian word for the device means "right brain stretcher." In Arabic, the word for it translates as "Q-tip." In any case, to the extent that I live up to your kind praise, I am indebted to that marvelous device.

Q #7: The Brothers and Sisters of Thaumaturgy are said to be very interested in determining the "Seven Deadly Sins" for our age. Could you suggest a list? What sin might you strike from the old list, and why?

A #7: Religion
       Politics
       Advertising
       Real Estate
          Development
       Gentrification
       Nationalism
       Disco Dancing

Of the old Seven Deadly Sins, Lust was definitely the pick of the litter. Come to think of it, Smut Sniffing (the misguided activities of porn hounds) ought to be included on any list of deadly sins.

Q #8:_____?

A #8: Men and women need to be told that their lives are not nearly as limited as they think they are, that we are on this planet to enlarge our souls and light up our brains, and that a good cigar is a smoke.

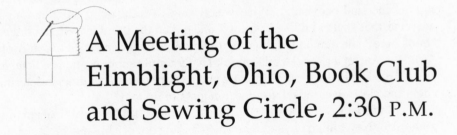

A Meeting of the Elmblight, Ohio, Book Club and Sewing Circle, 2:30 P.M.

"This is such a fine way to spend an afternoon," said Myrtle Roebuck, contentedly sewing another image of a ritual mask into a quilting square. The Tlinglit shaman's design would look admirable opposite the double-faced Ekoi, she decided. They were both so fundamentally naturalistic. "It's really essential to my peace of mind to take time out every single week for our book discussion club."

"And I do so enjoy our tea and biscuits," injected Lida June Laramie. Lida June was a minimalist. Meticulously, she appliquéd white squares onto her granddaughter's white sundress.

"But the sewing is the best part," said Myrtle. "And weaving and knitting and whatever you like. It's so holistic."

"After all, the vigorous stimulation of both hemispheres of the brain is the secret of maintaining vigor in other parts of the body as well," said Ethel Wainwright, waving her knitting needles so erratically that she was in danger of dropping several stitches. Ethel was knitting a poncho to wear on cooler days when she rode her moped to the grocery.

"We needn't go into personal details," Lida June hastened to say.

"Some people would just like us to think they had personal details to go into," grumbled Addie Gaines, stitching yellow yarn—apparently at random—into an already chaotic composition on white burlap.

"Well, there is Myrtle and her brigadier general," interjected Ethel. "Tell us, Myrtle, are you going to run away to Texas and marry that retired test pilot?"

"Jack's only semiretired," explained Myrtle. "And he still manages to set his share of altitude records."

"Robbing the cradle, I call it," muttered Lida June.

"Now, Addie," said Myrtle. "He *is* sixty-three."

"Just my point," said Lida June.

"Well, I don't know what to decide," sighed Myrtle. "Jack's so conservative, such an old cold warrior. And he's so philosophically unadventurous, still living in the Newtonian/Cartesian paradigm. Besides, I'm not sure I'm ready to settle down. And I'd miss you all so much."

There came a little chorus of affirmation. But then Lida June ducked her chin, snapped her needle even more precisely in and out along the edge of the white square, and said peevishly, "What was wrong with the good old Newtonian universe, that's what I'd like to know." She pulled the thimble from her finger. "Look here," she demanded, holding the thimble over her lap. She let it drop. "You see, you let it go and it falls down. That's simple enough, and predictable, too. It's too late in life to start thinking of curvatures in space/time, indeterminacy, and electron clouds. I, for one, am just not up to it."

Then, with a severe look at Myrtle, she added: "I'll bet your spaceman is grateful for Newtonian physics when he's coming out of a lunar orbit. Ask him. He'll tell you."

"Jack's not a spaceman," said Myrtle, a little hurt. "And he's never been to the moon."

"Are you so sure?" grumbled Lida June. "I'll bet you don't know *where* he's been."

"Lida June, stop it right this instant," snapped Addie. "And kindly join the rest of us in the twentieth century."

Lida June drew a deep sigh, but said nothing. There was a short silence.

Phoebe McNair paused from her multicolored tapestry of Quetzalcoatl, the Feathered Serpent. The small frame-loom weaving dangled a dozen tiny shuttles. "I think I'll just put my pan of brownies in the oven," she said. "This won't take a minute."

"Look here, ladies," said Lida June, "let's get back to the subject. What's the name of that book we're reading now?"

"Oh, this is it!" Ethel Wainwright waved a book that she picked up from the table beside her. Phoebe returned from the kitchen, dug around in her handbag and produced another. The other ladies all reached under chairs and into sewing baskets and came up with more copies of *The Jamais Vu Papers*.

"It seems to me this Hector Glasco has so far made a mess of things," said Phoebe. She started up her weaving again. "Losing a patient is quite careless, I should think."

"Well, I don't much like the beginning at all," said Myrtle. "It makes me sad. And uncomfortable, too. Like I was too involved in it somehow."

"Really, Myrtle," cautioned Lida June, without interrupting her neat chain stitch. "When will you learn to maintain a healthy aesthetic distance?"

"Aesthetic distance is the author's job, not mine. What's Keats's term for it?"

"Negative capability," said Ethel.

"Yes, negative capability," continued Myrtle. "This book is running way short on negative capability."

Ethel opened up her copy of *The Jamais Vu Papers* and was about to start reading where they had left off the week before. But Addie's stitchery caught her eye, and not for the first time. Addie had a stash of hundreds of scraps of fabric and yarn in an enormous cardboard box sitting next to her. Without even looking, she would dip her hand into the box, pull out a piece of fabric followed by a short length of yarn, and stitch away. The trouble was, the pieces were so bizarrely different, and Addie didn't seem to care how they went together.

There was a bright, solid vermilion sewed to the background with orange cotton yarn. The next was blue with yellow polka dots, stitched all over with lavender silk thread. The next was plaid. And the one after that was paisley. Bright red wool stitches wandered between them. The burlap was becoming an outrageous jumble to the eye.

"Addie, do forgive me for speaking up," said Ethel, "but that . . . uh . . . work of yours does alarm me so. Whatever will you use it for?"

"I haven't the slightest idea," Addie replied, stitching complacently.

Ethel persisted, "Isn't there any rhyme or reason to it?"

"Nope," said Addie without elaboration.

"But why not? You used to come up with such lovely patterns."

"I'm through with patterns," said Addie, with a certain world-weariness. "I'm through *making* patterns. The only thing you can really depend on in this universe is chaos itself. The only real pattern is one of recurrent randomness."

"Oh, Addie," said Lida June. "Don't start on chaos and randomness again. Give me a chance to get used to quantum mechanics."

"I'm through pretending that order prevails, that's all," said Addie defensively. "The rest of you can go around with blinders, just like that damned weatherman on channel four."

"You mean the one who's only on TV because he looks studly beyond belief?" queried Phoebe.

"The very one," said Addie. "Why, just yesterday I heard that gigolo predict that we're in for snow—in exactly two weeks!" She chuckled contemptuously.

"Laugh if you like," said Ethel, "but I'm getting this poncho ready just in case."

"Experts can tell you," pronounced Addie, "that weather forecasts aren't worth much beyond two or three days. And beyond six or seven weeks—forget it! Remember the butterfly in Peking." And she nodded with finality, volunteering no further comment. The ensuing silence was a bit unsettling.

"Addie, may I remind you," said Lida June, "that the rest of us have never *been* to Peking, so we don't know what butterfly you're talking about."

"I am referring," said Addie, "to the butterfly which beats its wings in Peking and, a month or so later, changes the weather *here*."

"Oh yes," sighed Lida June with resignation. "*That* butterfly. It was only a figure of speech, Addie." *

---

* "What on earth are they going on about?" whispered Phoebe to Ethel, so that Addie and Lida June wouldn't hear.

But Addie wouldn't listen. "'*Sensitive dependence upon initial conditions*,'" she continued. "That's what scientific-types call it. Just tell me how you can count on anything in a world chock full of 'initial conditions'! You can't, that's all!"

"Not that I buy all this talk about chaos and randomness for a blessed second," rejoined Lida June, "but if you choose to swallow it hook, line, and sinker, why get all upset about it? After all, chaos is *supposed* to generate complexity, setting creative processes in motion. Is that so bad?"

"Who said I'm upset about it?" snapped Addie, returning abruptly to her stitching. "I'm just saying, somebody should tell that pretty weatherboy about the butterfly in Peking."

"Honestly, Addie," said Myrtle, who had been listening raptly. "What got you to carrying on so about the weather?"

"Surely it had something to do with this new book we're reading," said Ethel, hoping to change the subject.

"Must have," remarked Addie with frustration, scratching her head with her thimble. "Seems to have completely escaped my mind."

"I'll just start reading where we left off," said Ethel. "I'm sure it'll come back to us. . ."

"Oh, it's that book Addie and Lida June read last year: *Chaos*, by James Gleick."

"Yes, I remember," said Phoebe. "They sure had some lively conversations about that one."

"Too lively, for my taste," said Ethel. "And Addie's never been quite the same since. Still, I've been reading it myself, and it's not half bad." And she surreptitiously reached into her purse, produced a copy, and read in a whisper to Phoebe:

> "In a way, art is a theory about the way the world looks to human beings. It's abundantly obvious that one doesn't know the world around us in detail. What artists have accomplished is realizing that there's only a small amount of stuff that's important, and then seeing what it was."

Ethel returned the book to her purse while Addie and Lida June quibbled on about randomness and the butterfly in Peking.

"I like that, don't you?" said Ethel to Phoebe.

Phoebe nodded in assent.

The Jamais Vu Papers

**Volume One
Number Five
April**

I confessed. I asked for your help.
I reached down into the darkest region of my heart
and revealed all.
I unflinchingly recounted how I foolishly jeopardized the health,
sanity, and perhaps the very soul of a patient. This took greater
reserves of courage than I thought I even possessed.
I sent *The Jamais Vu Papers* to every thinking person I could
reach—whether in medicine, the sciences, education, or the arts.
I hoped for assistance. It seems, instead, that the entire
intellectual community thought I was joking.
My Dear Colleagues, I'm not joking.
To make matters worse, I have continued to receive in the mail a
dreadful clutter of random objects, news clippings, books,
manifestos of improbable societies,
and pre-paid orders for vast quantities of M.
Now I am anxious to learn if my readers can derive any clues
from these items, some of which are included on page 2.
But, to be blunt and truthful,
I despair of meaningful responses from any of you.
Despite my disappointment,
I will continue this newsletter.
I have directed my secretary and my printer to present
the continuing facts of Hilary's case in a dignified
and straightforward manner.
Can this issue help me convince you of my sincerity?
You hold the answer in front of you.

MAGIC: Physicist's Flying Carpet Lifts Off

STANFORD — In 1964, Stanford physicist William Little wrote that someday it would be possible to produce plastic materials that had no electrical resistance at relatively high temperatures, room-temperature superconductors.

He predicted flying carpets, superconducting skis, trains that levitated over the track and glided smoothly at 300 miles an hour, and electrical trasmission lines with no resistance.

His theory was quickly ridiculed by his colleagues around the world as flying in the face of the "correct" theory. The *New Scientist* in Lon-

"People think that scientists are open to new ideas and that's not really true. We ar_ When something ne_ you are comfortab_ ings and it's very _ change."

"I find it very, _ a little bewilde_ people who we_ cs of this, whe_ xperimental di_ n another look_ out a smile, '_ g there's absc_ you can't get_ room temper_ for 23 years th_ cientifically (_ were openly h_

tle predicted _ were plac_ ductir_

Stanford received _ calls from scientists wondering _ it employed such a screwball, _ says.

Little's predictions appear r_ to come true.

He actually uses a small ver_ of his flying carpet in his ph_ class. He has won a teaching a_ for his inventive teaching _ niques.

THE LEGEND OF PRINCE AHMED AL KAMEL

«O King» replied Ahmed, «I care not for silver or gold or precious stones. One relic hast thou in thy treasure, handed down from the Moslems who once owned Toledo— a box of sandalwood containing a silken carpet. Give me that box and I am content».

All present were surprised at the moderation of the Arab, and still more when the box of sandalwood was brought and the carpet drawn forth. It was of fine green silk, covered with Hebrew and Chaldaic characters. The court physicians looked at each other and shrugged their shoulders and smiled at the simplicity of this new practitioner who could be content with so paltry a fee.

«This carpet», said the prince, «once covered the throne of Solomon the Wise; it is worthy of being placed beneath the feet of beauty».

So saying, he spread it on the terrace beneath an ottoman that had been brought forth for the princess, then seating himself at her feet.

«Who», said he, «shall counteract what is written in the book of fate? Behold the prediction of the astrologers verified. Know, O King, that your daughter and I have long loved each other in secret. Behold in me the Pilgrim of Love!»

These words were scarcely from his lips when the carpet rose in the air, bearing off the prince and princess. _ king and physicians gazed after it with open mouths _ eyes, until it became a little speck on the _ _ _ _ _ _ disappeared in the blue

*THE SIGHTS AND SOUNDS OF THE _ CREATE A CARNIVAL ATMOSPHERE IN WON_*

Hector! Greeting! How Life being since Firstness! Beyond Is Worlds! Is Time! Is Ordinary! Ride Rug Upon Roads of Air to Venice! Here Worldsprite take Idea Bird, Away take Feather, Unto give Paper Strings Sticks and send on Nojourney. Womonworldsprite see Hand, say use only seem tobe to Work Feel Other- such, but truly is to Read-Speak! Worldsprites of Wood String Brass latch-sing to Fleshthings! Worldsprites sprout Wheels, Ride Every-Where and No-! How Everstrange Alway Ordinary. Wish We Here!

D. Finking
c/o jamais vuing
5607 N.Figueroa St.
Los Angeles CA 90042
(Approx 11 kilometers
below stratosphere, U.S.A)

▪Smoke Gets In Your Eyes

Two months had passed since the puzzling phone call. And now, Joseph Xavier Brillig had just noticed the February issue of that Glasco fellow's newsletter, *The Jamais Vu Papers,* in the pile of unread literary journals and advertisements for educational materials. He skimmed it irritably.

". . . prosaic normalcy of a college literature course."

". . . academic assistance to divest the metaphor of its magic."

". . . his opinions are somewhat at odds with mine."

There was something wrong with it. Skimming it quickly at first, he couldn't decide just what. But as he read it more closely, it dawned on him.

I've been made the butt of a heartless joke!

Every word of the confounded thing seemed calculated to make him look ridiculous for getting mixed up in such a transparently bogus yarn, with its celebrity patient and its chemical metaphors and . . .

And, yes, its *midwestern academic renowned for his stodgy and lackluster approach.*

Brillig threw the newsletter on the floor and stomped off to the kitchen. He seethed with fury as he shoved a Lean Cuisine Salisbury steak into the preheated oven. *Who does that Hector Glasco think I am, anyway?* But then came another flash of realization.

There was no Hector Glasco. He was made up just like the rest of it, performed over the telephone by some third-rate actor reading from a fourth-rate script.

"Lies!" exclaimed Brillig. "Nothing but lies!"

He longed to get his fingers around the perpetrator's throat. And he knew exactly who it was. It was that California flake Max Henderson, his nemesis at so many conferences. He should have known he was in for trouble the minute Henderson's name was mentioned on the phone.

And so he'd walked right into the trap. His letter, *his signed letter,* was reprinted in that blasted epistle, proclaiming him the chump of the year. And Henderson had probably acquired a second class mail permit to send copies of *The Jamais Vu Papers* to every professor in every English department across the country.

He'd never be able to attend a conference again. He was a laughing stock—
or in his students' parlance, *dead meat.*

Brillig dropped into his living room chair and moaned aloud. He felt like
weeping. But he wouldn't let himself weep. "Touch me with noble anger," he
whispered, "And let not women's weapons, water drops, /Stain my man's
cheeks."

Still, even without tears, the anger subsided and he was seized by an awful
sadness. *Why?* he wondered. *Why is it always me?*

He had long tried to believe that he was hardened to it all, even though
hardly a day went by when he didn't turn around in a classroom or a hallway
and catch insolent students imitating him, laughing at him, sharing a joke at his
expense. His colleagues were no better. His comments at committee meetings
were greeted by barely concealed snickers. He got anonymous memos weekly,
some of them false alarms about faculty cutbacks, others cruel parodies of
whatever he had published recently.

In Brillig's existence, every day was April Fool's Day. And he was the fool.

And the worst of it was being alone, not having someone to come home to,
someone warm and companionable, someone who was unconditionally *there.*

His eyes darted about nervously. He felt strangely on the verge of suffoca-
tion, as if his little house had become a coffin.

This existence of mine—can it really be a life? he wondered. *Or is it just some cruel
hoax masquerading as a life?*

He found himself staring at the top of the buffet, at that empty, dusty place
where his and Marie's wedding pictures used to be. He had removed them
when she left him five years ago. But still he stared in spite of himself, as if they
were still there.

"You've got no magic," she had said, turning toward him one last time as she
walked down the sidewalk toward the car. "You never had any. I thought I
could give it to you, but I couldn't."

He hadn't known what to say then. The shock of her departure had left him
speechless. Now he thought to himself, *No magic, eh? A good thing, too! Isn't it the
mark of a truly civilized man to know there's no such thing as magic?*

A song wafted its way into Brillig's mind.

> They asked me how I knew
> my true love was true . . .

Why did he find himself thinking of that old song? Of course. It was *their*
song in better days, during the sweet sojourn of courtship, during their
wedding reception and that splendid honeymoon in Colorado. The song hadn't
come to mind for a very long time, perhaps twenty years.

> I, of course, replied
> something here inside
> cannot be denied . . .

Brillig shut his ears, but that didn't help. And he wanted not to look at that empty place on the buffet, but couldn't avert his eyes. Marie stood there in her white dress, he in his tuxedo holding a cake knife—vivid phantoms of memory, and so extremely young. A vast, white wedding cake spread out before them. *Like our lives*, he remembered thinking. *Like our lives.*

> They said someday you'll find
> All who love are blind . . .

Blind indeed. Who would have thought, after twenty-five uneventful years, two children, all those mortgage payments . . . ?

> When your heart's on fire
> you must realize
> smoke gets in your eyes.

"No!" cried Brillig in protest. "More lies, more lies! A heart's a pump, not a thing of passion, love, romance. It's an instrument that keeps this desolate machine alive, not some magical thing that burns. And smoke is not the source of grief, sorrow, betrayal, broken promises.

"*Other people* are . . ."

He closed his eyes. A tear welled up. Brillig wiped it away brusquely, unceremoniously. Where had it come from? Did it arise out of painful reminiscence?

Or was it caused by that distinct burning odor?

Brillig rushed to the kitchen and rescued his TV dinner. Unable to find a pot holder, he used a dish towel to take hold of the plastic tray and carry the inauspicious meal to the living room. He set the smoldering dish on the coffee table and sat down on the couch. He grabbed the TV remote switch and clicked it on. "Anything," he muttered. "Anything to dispel these morbid thoughts."

The news was on. A female newscaster, pert, smartly dressed, a little too perfect, stood in the hallway of an office building. She was jostled by dozens of other reporters, many of them wielding flash cameras.

". . . and so I'm coming to you live," she said, "to report the latest word on the vanished celebrity."

Oh, no, thought Brillig. *Not another feature about what's-her-name, the missing movie star, the one I almost got conned into thinking was that bogus psychiatrist's patient.*

The media was positively obsessed by her disappearance. Brillig was sick of the whole pathetic business taking time away from the real issues of the day. He lifted the remote switch to change the channel.

But the camera zoomed in on an office door upon which was printed:

HECTOR GLASCO, M.D.
CLINICAL PSYCHOTHERAPIST

Slowly, Brillig set the remote switch down. The woman turned and spoke confidentially to the viewers, "Now we bring you an exclusive first report."

But the background noise increased, and she shouted above the commotion of her fellow reporters:

"Rumors surfaced early this morning that she was undergoing psychiatric treatment before her disappearance. But who is this Hector Glasco? Is he just some obscure and unsought-after shrink who barely ekes out the rent on this less-than-glamorous suite here in Beverly Hills? Or is he, as some think they have reason to believe, some sinister cult guru preying on the sufferings of celebrities, an unregenerate quack whose methods are a scandal to the psychiatric community? We're awaiting his comment."

And sure enough, the office door opened to reveal a tall, gangly, awkward man, taken completely aback by the crush of reporters. They surged forward, pushing him back into the office, battering him with a barrage of questions. Only semi-meaningful fragments could be heard: ". . . really her shrink? . . . responsible for her disappearance? . . . charge per hour? . . . referred to by whom? . . . sexual manipulation of clientele? . . . other movie stars? . . . would you care to explain? . . ."

Flashbulbs exploded wildly. Hector Glasco covered his eyes. He cried out aimlessly, helplessly, "No comment! No comment! No comment!"

The woman managed to articulate the only completely audible question: "What about the rumors of electric shock treatments, or even a lobotomy?"

Hector Glasco backed farther into his office. Flashbulbs continued to blaze.

"There is such a thing as patient confidentiality!" he cried.

And then, in the midst of the surrounding chaos, Brillig watched the strangest expression cross Glasco's face, as if he fleetingly remembered something, as if he was experiencing a particularly vivid moment of *déjà vu*. For a moment he seemed completely unaware of his journalistic assailants and was in a different world, in the middle of a dream.

Then the psychiatrist got pushed even farther back into the office by the crazy bombardment of flashing lights and strident voices. He made a mad dash for the first door he could find, the women's washroom. He rushed inside. The reporters tried to follow him, but the door was locked.

The woman stepped away from her colleagues, who pounded on the door and shook the doorknob.

"You can be sure," said the woman, "that I'll be keeping watch over this Beverly Hills washroom. And now, back to you, Ron."

Brillig rubbed his eyes with disbelief as the anchorman came on the screen. The man he had just seen was certainly not Max Henderson. *So there is a Hector Glasco!* he thought. *And it wasn't some practical joke! He's real after all! And he does need my help!*

"There's a last-minute development in the case of America's missing sweet-heart," said the anchorman. "Just a few moments ago, this station received a videotape from a group which calls itself 'The Ancient Order of the Brothers and Sisters of Thaumaturgy.' They claim to know something of her where-abouts. Let's take a look."

"Those blasted Thaumaturgists!" growled Brillig. "I thought I'd heard the last of them after I did that research for. . . Hector Glasco! Yes!"

The tape was of very poor quality. The picture kept threatening to vanish in a veritable blizzard of television snow. All that Brillig could see was a face in extreme shadow. The features were completely invisible.

"Greetings," said a voice. "I am the Grand Matron of The Ancient Order of Brothers and Sisters of Thaumaturgy."

Despite her pretentious and overly solemn delivery, the woman's voice was nasal, awkward, unprepossessing.

"We want you to know that your beloved friend is safe and well. More than that: she is transformed, transfigured. So think no longer of her by her old name. Now she is *Hilary!*"

The woman leaned toward the camera. There was the glint of reddish hair in the dim light. She continued. "Too long has humankind suffered in this prison of time and space and causality! The world seems empty and absurd; we are told this is what it means to understand reality. The creations of our minds are in exile; they long for amnesty.

"We no longer understand the meanings of our most precious words. A 'myth' is now a lie; once it was the most profound truth—a truth at once ever-changing and ever-still. We no longer believe it is possible to 'see heaven in a wild flower.' We no longer believe in 'fiends angelical, dove-feathered ravens, or wolvish-ravening lambs.' We no longer believe the yellow smoke really 'licked its tongue into the corners of the evening.' And how can you drink to anyone 'only with thine eyes?'

"We are told these are all lies—good lies, useful lies, lies that explain, *white* lies, but lies nonetheless."

A knot of irritation formed in Brillig's throat. He didn't like the sound of this at all.

Now the voice rose with clumsy eloquence. "We are told that the purpose of poetry and metaphor is not to give birth to the new and vital, but to explain the old and tired. We are told the world existed long before our dream of the world, so the world must be very old indeed. This decrepit world isn't good for much, except to be explained."

The woman peered closely into the camera. Brillig thought he could see her eyes glowing. "And who stole the sheen of newness from the world? Scholars, rational thinkers, *critics*—mental and emotional automatons, bereft of intuition and spontaneity—bereft of *magic*."

Brillig grabbed his TV dinner with the sudden urge to throw it at the television. But his scorched hands retreated hastily.

"But now comes Hilary, greatest of all Thaumaturgists, to reunite dreams and waking, to remind us that our every act of imagination is real, and to restore Paradox as All.

"Rejoice!" she concluded, waving jauntily. "And let a smile be your umbrella!"

The image dissolved into snowy whiteness. The anchorman reappeared.

"Who are these Thaumaturgists?" he enquired, putting on his very best investigative manner. "A gang of terrorists, or a satanic cult? Kidnappers, or perpetrators of a tasteless hoax? You can count on us to follow this story through to the bitter end."

Brillig snapped the TV off. He had forgotten his sadness. He was fuming, absolutely livid with rage.

"The gall!" he cried. "The infernal, unequivocal gall! Just where the hell does this woman get off, anyway? Just who do these Thaumaturgists think they are?"

Brillig rose from the couch and paced the room angrily.

"'Mental and emotional automatons,' indeed! 'Bereft of intuition and spontaneity,' my foot! Just who does she think she's talking to?"

Seized by an impulse, Brillig rushed to the bookshelf and grabbed the first volume which came within his reach. It was *Tales of the Alhambra* by Washington Irving—a charming little tome which he had not taken off the shelf in years. He opened it utterly at random, grabbed one of the pages firmly, and ripped it out.

"There!" he shouted, waving the page at the blank TV screen. "How's *that* for spontaneity, you mystical flake?"

Hector awoke to find himself sitting uncomfortably against a washroom stall. He sighed as he tried to get his aching limbs moving. His legs were numb and tingling from having been awkwardly crossed for hours. *How did* this *happen?* he wondered. He did hope he wasn't going to make a habit of falling asleep in unseemly places. Maybe he was getting narcoleptic. The absence of urinals told him this was a women's rest room. He blushed at the thought and struggled to remember, *What was I doing here in the first place?*

As he rose stiffly to his feet, he asked himself, *Did I dream this time? Yes, I seem to recall some horrible nightmare.* Hector took fleeting pride in being able to remember this dream—and pretty vividly, too. *I was surrounded by reporters with flashbulbs and television cameras, shouting questions at me, pushing me. I wound up having to hide in the . . .*

Then he looked at his surroundings. "Oh, no," he muttered. "Oh, no. Oh, no."

He crept toward the door and tried the handle. It was locked—from the inside, fortunately. It all came back to him. He had been holed up here for hours, hiding from the reporters who had seemed determined to keep an eternal vigil.

Yes, they'd finally caught up with him. He'd known all along it was inevitable. And now the worst had happened—but maybe not. Maybe the worst was yet to come.

Anyway, things seemed quiet on the other side of the door. The reporters were no longer exchanging monotonous banter, bragging about past exploits, planning elaborate orders for pizza and donuts, occasionally pounding on the door and barking questions at him. They'd given up and left—thank God.

As he reached for the lock, Hector was jolted by a sharp rapping on the door.

"No comment!" he cried reflexively.

"Dr. Glasco, it's me, Miss Bellows. Please open the door."

Hector did so. As imposing as ever, Miss Bellows stood in the doorway, smiling from ear to ear.

"How long was I in there?" asked Hector.

"All night, I guess," said Miss Bellows. "I gave up and went home at six last evening."

"What the hell are you smiling about?"

"Oh, Dr. Glasco, forgive me, but I've never worked for anyone who was on *television* before!"

In the days that followed, life lost its canniness.

Or so it seemed to Hector Glasco. True, the tabloid reporters and TV crews quickly gave up their assaults on his office. At first, they followed him like faithful puppies everywhere he went—as long as he kept exclaiming "No comment!" and running like the devil. A true reporter enjoys nothing more than a man proclaiming his own reticence, a man resolutely in flight from the camera.

But then Hector changed tactics. He told them the truth as he knew it. He read his entire first two newsletters aloud. He explained that he had given their beloved missing celebrity the chemical equivalent of a metaphor out of Gerard Manley Hopkins. He discussed various clinical statistics on the experiences of *déjà vu* and *jamais vu*. He read a detailed letter from the head of a research project. He showed them slides and flip charts.

"But what the hell is a chemical metaphor?" asked reporter after reporter indignantly. "Wasn't there any *sex* involved?"

No, it wasn't what the press wanted. Maybe it was true and maybe it wasn't, but you couldn't make it into a good story. Hector Glasco made bad copy, pure and simple. And he was immensely relieved.

Still, life just wasn't canny anymore.

Mail still poured in. Hector didn't know if it was in response to his plea for help in his newsletter or to his brief exposure in the media. But it came in fifty-pound bags every day. People sent anything they had at hand: seashells, old flashlight batteries, spatulas, lampshades, hats of all kinds, fossils, shoestrings, pressed flowers, diaper pins, high school graduation gowns, Garfield dolls with suction cups on their paws, monkey wrenches, teddy bears, rosaries, incense burners, broken light bulbs, pipe joints, empty whiskey bottles, cloves of garlic—to name but a few.

The randomness of such mute objects was troubling enough. But the printed, written, and recorded material really unnerved him. This unwieldy hodge-podge included bumper stickers, Spike Jones records, antique editions of Victorian pornography, antique postcards from Niagara Falls, recent newspaper articles, old copies of *Mad* magazine, Scandinavian recipes, baseball cards, tarot decks, reel-to-reel recordings of baby talk, a heavily spliced sixteen-millimeter print of *Plan Nine from Outer Space*, cheap cassette recordings of the last Beethoven quartets, astrological charts, exotic postage stamps, drivers education manuals, and countless books of all kinds.

He found himself hopelessly, obsessively sorting through this enigmatic mess for something remotely meaningful—a clue, perhaps, to Hilary's where-abouts. Nobody sent him anything straightforward or comprehensible. If they included letters at all, they made such claims as, "This object evoked the state you talked about," and, "If this doesn't stir up a bit of *jamais vu*, nothing will." Perhaps it was true for the people who had sent the objects. But none of them had any such effect on Hector.

Max Henderson kept his appointments weekly, but more often than not he and Hector simply retired to a Hollywood bar. Together they drank a thick, dark brand of English beer which Hector found laboriously difficult to get down. And Hector did most of the talking, about his own problems.

Whenever he appeared at Hector's office before these barroom sessions, Max chuckled delightedly at the proliferation of objects piled everywhere.

"I do envy you, Hector," he said one day as they were leaving the office together. "So many toys to play with!"

"Toys, hell!" exclaimed Hector. "There's got to be meaning here somewhere! There's got to be some kind of connection!"

"Oh, I do hope not!" said Max. "That would be most boring! Do take my advice and stop looking for meaning and connection. Start looking for absurdity. Start looking for disconnection. You shouldn't have much trouble with this kind of raw material. Remember the words of Laurence Sterne: 'Mysteries which must explain themselves are not worth the loss of time which a conjecture about them takes up.'"

But of course, Hector found that an utterly unacceptable philosophy. He became more irrational and obsessed. He didn't much like it. *I'm getting worse than my patients,* he thought. It was ironic. Surely, after being so thoroughly trained to help other people with their problems, he could do something meaningful about his own. He was, after all, an expert.

Then came the amusing idea of seeking therapy from himself. Hector decided to give himself the full treatment. He plopped himself in the patient's chair, recounted the whole history of his problems, and then asked pitifully, "What do you think I should do, Dr. Glasco?"

He trotted back to his own chair, sat, and pressed his fingers together pensively. "First of all, Hector, consider your environment. You're not likely to make progress in a mess like this."

Then he dashed back to the patient's chair. "Don't I know it, Doctor. But what choice have I got? I've got to figure out what all this means!"

Then, playing the psychiatrist, he paced the office thoughtfully, ruminatively. "I wouldn't be too sure, Hector. Stop to consider: What does this conglomeration mean to you?"

"Perhaps," said Hector the patient, sensing an impending breakthrough, "it's some sort of symbol."

"Of what, do you suppose?" asked Dr. Glasco.

Hector shrugged. "Of all the troubles in the world, I guess. Of all the unfairness and confusion and injustice I'm powerless to do anything about."

Dr. Glasco nodded. "I see. So you've created your own little world away from the world, your own little Quixotic battlefield—"

"—where I can never win!" said Hector, completing Dr. Glasco's thought. "So Max was halfway right after all! There's no point in seeking order in this mess."

"You could spend the rest of your life finding disorder," said Dr. Glasco.

"But I don't want to do that," said Hector.

"Very well then. What do you think you should do?" asked Dr. Glasco.

"I suppose it's time to fight my losing battles in the world of people again," said Hector.

"It sounds like a fine idea. Might I make a suggestion?"

"Certainly."

"What most occupied your thoughts before this 'Hilary' thing took over your life?"

"Why, I was writing a paper of some sort. I was quite caught up in it at the time, but now I can't seem to remember what it was about."

"You might want to dig it out of your files and dust it off. It might just be the tonic you need."

"Yes, I'll do that."

"Very good, Hector," concluded Dr. Glasco. "I believe we've made excellent progress today."

A few minutes later, Hector was shoving his entire junk collection into plastic garbage bags. *Excellent progress is right!* thought Hector. *If only all my patients were so responsive!*

Pretty soon all the stuff was bagged up. Hector dragged it out into the hallway for the janitor to take away. As he strode back into his office, wiping his hands with satisfaction, he noticed Miss Bellows's relieved expression. *Poor woman,* thought Hector. *She's really seen me at my worst lately.*

He went back into his office and scrambled through his files. After a few moments of searching and shuffling, he found the paper he had abandoned the day Hilary had first come to his office:

Synchrophobia:
toward an etiology of coincidence
by Hector Glasco, M.D.

ABSTRACT:

The purpose of this paper is to discuss a hitherto unrecognized syndrome I call synchrophobia—the irrational fear of co-incidence, brought on by those ostensibly accidental concurrences of everyday life which Jung and Kammerer termed synchronicities. Such a fear can become obsessive—even delusive. Sufferers often develop the misguided notion that they are living in a clumsily crafted and exceedingly contrived work of fiction, written by some unusually incompetent author.

This bizarre condition may seem so anomalous as to be hardly worth discussing. To the contrary, based on observations made in my own clinic and on consultations with other therapists, I strongly suspect that this condition is reaching epidemic proportions in our culture—perhaps even rivaling depression as the so-called common cold of mental health. And yet it has gone ignored in the psychiatric literature. Why?

The text stopped there. The rest of the file consisted of notes and ideas.

Oh, it's a dandy opening! thought Hector. *Funny, I barely remember working on this at all.*

He set the brief manuscript aside and put his feet up on his desk. At last! Something new to think about, something original and yet respectable—and most importantly, something *solvable.* Yes, things were looking much, much better.

He surveyed his surroundings. The office was suddenly spacious and comfortable. He sure could breathe more easily with all that clutter gone. He looked again at the bare spot on the floor where his rug had been. After

52

worrying and fretting over its whereabouts during the last few weeks, he now found himself relieved not to have it there. It was always something of an eyesore. Now he could thank whatever agency had spirited it away.

He closed his eyes, and a most enjoyable image came to him. It was his rug flying through the air, carrying all the weight and baggage of this damned Hilary case far, far away from him. Hector smiled.

Then came a knock at his door. Miss Bellows came in.

"A Federal Express letter from Professor Brillig," she said, all efficient and happy, obviously delighted by Hector's welcome change of disposition. Then, with a wave, she left.

As Hector opened the package, he thought, *Better call Brillig and tell him not to waste his time on this stuff. The last thing I need is for him to suddenly turn helpful!*

But Hector shuddered as the envelope came open. Attached to Brillig's letter was a yellowed, torn-out page from a book. In its upper right-hand corner was a woodcut of a young man and woman—*flying on a magic carpet!* The following words caught his eye:

> . . . the carpet rose in the air, bearing off the prince and princess.
> The king and physicians gazed after it with open mouths and
> straining eyes. . .

Hector slowly lowered the nightmare to his desk. Then something else caught his attention. Leaning against his desk lamp was a postcard with one corner torn away. Hector could swear it hadn't been there a moment before. He was certain he had cleared his office of every speck of debris. The handwriting was a childish scrawl, but Hector knew that it had to have been written by Hilary. His eyes were riveted to one particular line:

Rode Rug Upon Roads of Air to Venice!

Breath failed him. "A flying carpet!" he gasped aloud. "Is that how she got out of here?" Then, realizing the very absurdity of the idea, he cried, "Who's *writing* this story, anyway?"

He rushed out of the office and into the hallway. He grabbed as many of the plastic bags as he could and lugged them back into the lobby. As he lurched toward his office door, he caught Miss Bellows' look of irritation and disapproval out of the corner of his eye.

But there was nothing to be done.

"No time to write a paper on synchrophobia," he muttered under his breath. "I'm my own classic case."

I have been studying how I may compare
This prison where I live unto the world:
And for because the world is populous
And here is not a creature but myself,
I cannot do it; yet I'll hammer it out.
My brain I'll prove the female to my soul,
My soul the father; and these two beget
A generation of still-breeding thoughts,
And these same thoughts people this little
world,
In humours like the people of this world,
For no thought is contented.

Shakespeare
Richard II

What is a Universe?

. . . Slowly, Llixgrijb thought about it.

It thought of a concept called place, and set about creating one . . . then another . . . then connecting them together. It found that very entertaining for a while.

Llixgrijb created a universe in which everything was connected to everything else in exactly five different ways—and another in which nothing was connected to anything else at all.

Then Llixgrijb had an idea called time. It created three worlds in which absolutely everything had already happened and four in which everything was permanently just getting ready to happen.

Then it created parallel worlds which did the sidestep shuffle—moving always from one present moment to another with no common past or future.

Llixgrijb thought of a concept called light, and thereby discovered dark. It created one world made up of only shadows, with no objects.

It conceived of largeness and smallness, and spent a few eons going to exremes in both directions.

But none of these beautiful new universes lasted. Something was wrong—something was imperfect.

Imperfection!
That was a new concept!

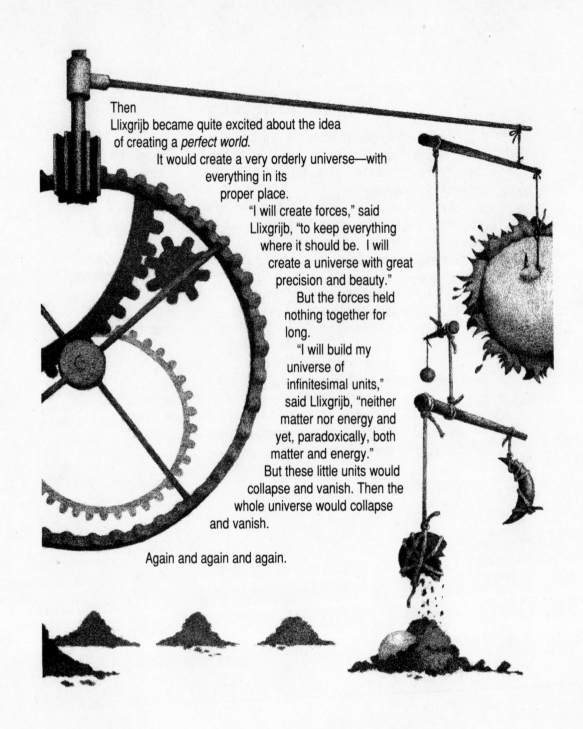

Then
Llixgrijb became quite excited about the idea
of creating a *perfect world*.
It would create a very orderly universe—with
everything in its
proper place.
"I will create forces," said
Llixgrijb, "to keep everything
where it should be. I will
create a universe with great
precision and beauty."
But the forces held
nothing together for
long.
"I will build my
universe of
infinitesimal units,"
said Llixgrijb, "neither
matter nor energy and
yet, paradoxically, both
matter and energy."
But these little units would
collapse and vanish. Then the
whole universe would collapse
and vanish.

Again and again and again.

Then Llixgrijb had a new idea . . .

The Jamais Vu Papers

**Volume One
Number Six
May**

[23] Ibid., 25:2-5

[24] Ibid., 24:13-14

[25] Licorice Root.

[26] His "many strange women." (1 Kings, 11:1)

[27] I.e., solve et coagula (see n. 13).

[28] Solomon here bemoans the advance of scientific and empirical thought. Solomon's surveyors and navigators had taken quantitative measurements and determined that the world was not round, as had always been said in legend. It was, in all scientific certainty, flat. This staggered the prevailing cosmology.

Solomon here expresses his sadness at this discovery. How many more of our splendid multiplicity of mythical truths, he asks, will fall to humankind's idolatry of fact and senseless craving for absolutes? (See n. 48)

[29] Bayberry.

[30] I.e., freemasons, who are still said to meet secretly in Solomon's mines.

[31] Black holes.

[32] The earliest historical reference to Hilary.

[33] I dare not explicate this overtly arcane passage. To quote another noted Thaumaturgist, "Who hath ears to hear, let him hear."

[34] Sun spots.

[35] The renowned "magic carpet" of Solomon — useless to him, now that men have lost their "gods." (See n. 48) But he prophesies that Hilary will restore its use.

[36] Again, we must harken back to the death of Girolamo Savonarola. When he had been long since strangled and was burning on the gibbet, it is said that the ropes which bound his wrists burned quite through. One hand raised itself up with two fingers pointed at the crowd of onlookers. Assuming this to be a sign of benediction from beyond the threshold of death, the crowd went quite insane. Screaming, "Miraculo! Miraculo!" again and again and again, they ran about the

square trampling one another.

Such a delusive schism between coincidence and mysticism marks everyday life in the Waking World. Hence, the all-too-urgent need of the Elixir.

[37] Solomon speaks here _____ _____ frustration at civilization "changi__ _____ ____ ____. What does he mean by this? Preced___ _____ _____ ____ human beings had little or _____ _____ _____ _____ed under the halluci___ _____ _____ _____ ____ibited the right side _____ _____ _____ ____ coming of ego-c_____ _____ _____ _____ of the gods _____ _____ _____ ____ __ and the Bre__ _____ _____ _____ ___ n moving __ _____ _____ _____ ____ a ration__ _____ _____ _____ _____ of histo__ _____ _____ _____ ____ d fuse ____ _____ _____ _____ restor____

[38] Ibi__

[39] Ore__

[40] Holo__

[41] A re__ _____ _____ _____ _____ tern cuisine.

[42] A simil__ _____ _____ _____ _____ath of my namesake __ _____ _____ _____ ___ was overrun by a _____ _____ _____ ___llars with strange physic__ _____ _____ _____eir heads and a circle which__ _____ _____ _____atures had never been recorded b__ _____ ___ been seen since. Apparently unable to breed, ____ ____ out.

Did this come about as a result of an extraordinary level of morphic resonance arising from the departure of such an exalted spirit? We in the Sleeping World are all too numb to such occurrences. Those in the Waking World are not.

[43] Quasars.

[44] An unrequited yearning for an end to ambiguity.

[45] Cf. Harpo Marx's response (worthy of the most adept Thaumaturgist) to the vagrant who "could really use a cup of coffee."

Cf. also: 1 Kings 3:16-28.

"ONE THING"
painting by
Nancy Camden Witt

Reality Lag

Hector Glasco stared at the frantic parade of intrepid heroes, impossibly beautiful women, senseless killings, flights of grossly imbecilic behavior, and random sexual collisions. He felt trapped. He could neither escape nor take part in the gratuitous sex and violence. The images before him leered and gestured in a hushed frenzy.

One particularly glamorous woman ran a manicured hand enticingly across mountainous, swarthy regions of male sinew. She wrapped perfectly formed limbs around waist and neck, brushed long golden hair across a craggy, stubbled chin. Her fresh, moist lips were parted slightly. . .

What stupid, infantile dreams, thought Hector, slightly embarrassed at his inability to turn away. He adjusted his position carefully. He pulled his right elbow out from under the heavy arm that overlapped his space. He shifted uncomfortably, trying to gain a little room without disturbing the other body on his left. His legs were bent uncomfortably by the bulk that pushed against his feet. Every nerve, muscle, and bone in his body was tired and bored.

Once again, Hector pushed the button requesting service. That made at least twelve times now. Although he wore the headsets brought by the flight attendant, there was no sound—just the dutiful background drone of the 747 engines to accompany the pictures on the movie screen. Perhaps the whole world has gone mute, he thought. But the woman at his left was snoring loudly. And several scattered passengers uttered deathlike chuckles at an unheard joke.

It was eight exhausting hours into the flight, and his reservation had been too hastily made for comfortable seating. The plane was probably over the Atlantic. *It's Purgatory,* he grumbled in his mind. *An endless, wretched Purgatory.*

Once again, he looked at the battered postcard he held clutched in his hand. "Rode Rug Upon Roads of Air to Venice!" he read for the hundredth time.

"Right, Hilary," he whispered between clenched teeth. "A rug must be nice. A flying carpet, no less. I could really do with one of those, Hilary. Think you could supply me with one? One that erases time zones, maybe? One that exceeds the speed of nausea?"

Jet lag. That was the nemesis he loathed most. Every passing minute meant

59

increasing desynchronization. Some of his globe-roving patients suffered from illness, depression, and even mild schizophrenia from their constant forays. After all he'd been through during the last few weeks, to finally go completely mad from simple trans-Atlantic travel . . .

That would be the final irony.

"I'll just think of this as a well-deserved vacation," Hector decided.

Well, why not? For years he had harbored a desire to visit Venezia, that magical city of canals, lovers huddled in gondolas, and handsome, pole-bearing gondoliers singing Puccini and Verdi—that timeless little world where the Renaissance never died.

But now, as love scenes and hair-raising escapes, high-speed car chases and great explosions transpired in mute absurdity, Hector could only mutter, "Some vacation."

He craned his head upward, struggling to taste the insignificant stream of fresh air which trickled through the nozzle above him. Only staleness met his nostrils. He wearily shoved the postcard into his jacket pocket and swallowed the residue of his third glass of scotch.

At last, a flight attendant peered down at him with a grotesquely professional smile. Her mouth was filled with teeth which looked like they'd never been used. She tilted her head to one side in a puppetlike gesture of concerned inquiry and said, "Are your headphones not working, sir?"

"To hell with the headphones," growled Hector. "Get me another scotch."

◼Carne Vale

La Serenissima, they called it—the most illustrious, the most sublime.

But did Venice look that way? Not quite.

It was growing dark as the airport boat skirted the island cemetery of San Michele, rounded the eastern end of the city, and moored at last near the mouth of the Grand Canal. From the boat, Venice hardly looked magical at all. In fact, it looked strangely sad and empty. Now, in the off-season, the city was not enlivened by tourists. But where was the regular population? Where were the lights? The lagoon city seemed lonely and unwelcoming—rather like a gray bullfrog brooding over a swampy pond. It was surrounded by stale mist. Dark water sucked at its edges and a dank breeze blew across the dock.

Hector disembarked with a dozen somber tourists. He was in a dazed state, unable to decide what to do next. There were gondolas and motorboats waiting to take travelers to their hotels, but he had no reservations. Nearby were several cafés, although only one was open. Perhaps he could walk to a pensione.

He clutched his small bag in one hand and resolutely crossed the piazza, but soon found himself in an intricate maze of tiny streets. There were no automobiles, nor could a car have traversed these claustrophobic lanes. Empty clotheslines were draped overhead. Hector continued to feel that eerie sense of loneliness about the city, as if there was nobody home. In fact, the only pensione that he saw was closed and dark. It was a shuttered city.

Most streets were barely lit, and some not at all. There was a stomach-sinking dampness everywhere, and a discomforting sense that, with his every single step, Venice sank just a little deeper into the surrounding water, like some sort of stop-action Atlantis.

Hector came to a little arched bridge. On the other side, a pale face lingered in the mist—a woman's face, long and elegant. As he peered into the darkness, he detected golden tresses surrounding the visage, and a black, velvet gown clinging to a tall, regal figure. The woman's body almost dissolved into the surrounding blackness.

Could it be Hilary? Hector's thoughts lapsed into slow motion as he stepped forward, hypnotized. *Not Hilary . . . but someone . . . familiar.*

She gazed straight at him, momentarily still, then nodded to him invitingly. Then she began to dance to the unrhythmical lapping of the water. Hector cautiously began to cross the tiny bridge. He wanted to call out to her, but found that he couldn't make a sound. As he approached, her face altered weirdly. It became paler, chalky white, barely human. Full, crimson lips smiled at him mockingly. An orange-and-black butterfly bloomed huge and flowerlike over her right eye.

And her eyes were completely black.

Hector shuddered, but kept walking. Now he could see that the woman had companions. Faces peered out of the darkness behind her. One was painted gold like a statue of Buddha, with a great jewel in the center of its forehead. Another was black on one side and white on the other, with a string of brightly painted tears trickling down the white cheek. Another was encrusted with rows of pearls. Another was painted with dozens of tiny faces. And yet another was the face of a devil, deep red with a hooked nose and an arched, furrowed brow. Their eyes, too, were all black. They seemed to move closer and closer.

Hector was within reach of the apparition now. She stared at him with those cold, empty eyes. He wanted more than ever to speak, but his mind was completely empty. He reached out and touched her face.

Then he plucked it down from the air like a piece of ripe fruit. He held it in his hand.

It was a mask made of papier mâché, painted and glazed to look like fine china. It had been dangling by a string from a clothesline. It was wet from the mist. As he held the mask, the butterfly melted beneath his fingers.

And her companions? he wondered. *Masks just like this one, of course.*

He peered again into the passageway. There were still more faces in the darkness now, staring at him, completely motionless. His lips shaped the silent question, *Are you masks, too?*

But no sound came out.

Chills seized him. He turned and ran. He didn't know where to go, or how he'd gotten here. He only wanted to find his way back to the lighted piazza, to the one open café, and to the water taxis which might deliver him to a world he could understand.

To his own amazement, he quickly emerged again into the light. Had he been only half a block away, or lost in some momentary nightmare? He went straight to the water taxis and chose a motorboat. This was no time for a leisurely gondola tour along the Grand Canal. He could barely keep his eyes open.

"Take me anywhere," he said to the driver. "Anywhere with a clean bed."

"What are you hiding from the Thaumaturgists?" a voice demanded.

Hector cowered before the robed figure. Its eyes were glowing. It was all so familiar. He sensed—or perhaps vaguely remembered—that he was surrounded by a throng of masked faces. But he didn't dare look. He was holding a chalice in his hands. He lifted it to his lips and drank. He almost choked on the intoxicating power of the liquid.

When he lowered the chalice, the figure was gone. Now he found himself standing knee-deep in stagnant water which seemed to rise very slowly about him. The fog was even thicker than before, and he couldn't make out where he was. He was surrounded by partially submerged artworks—marble sculptures, great canvases, a ruined column here and there, swaying back and forth, almost toppling, all slowly being swallowed up by the water. Slime clung to his pants legs. He heard voices close by—the strange, mournful cries of disembodied souls. *Ridiculous*, he thought confusedly. *They really should clean this sort of thing up.*

Then, from out of the mist came that elegant, pale face again. But was it a mask this time? Hector lifted his hand and discovered that he was holding the mask he had encountered—how long ago was it now? A few minutes, or a few centuries? Its glaze was losing its sheen from the misty dampness; its lips were bleeding red paint.

He looked again at the face before him. Though it was partially obscured, this face was certainly a fleshly one, not papier mâché, not porcelain, not china. As he moved closer, the most exquisitely lovely female form he had ever seen emerged from the mist—rounded and voluptuous, but delicate in movement. She laughed and played in the water—a strange contrast to the wounded voices in the surrounding fog.

Then the last trace of fog swept away from her face. She turned toward Hector and he was stunned by her beauty. Her golden hair was swept up in a delightfully careless bundle atop her head. She had the most alert, most electric eyes he had ever seen—not wild and altered like Hilary's when she'd taken that drug, but deeply sane and full of wisdom.

"Hello, Hector Glasco," she said, "I'm happy to meet you at last." And her smile weakened him. Perhaps, he considered, she wouldn't astound him so if she weren't posed against such dank surroundings.

But as her eyes met his, her expression darkened a little. She listened to the cries around them. "Sad, isn't it?" the vision said. "They came to this place hundreds of years ago because they feared something on the land. And now they must rush to the land again, for fear of the sea. But this is hardly the sort of place where I'd hope we'd meet."

And at that very moment, they were both in an Edenic garden, separated by a lovely stream filled with swans. They were standing at each end of an arched footbridge. It might even have been the same bridge he had crossed earlier in darkness and uncertainty. But now, the apparition on the other side was vastly warmer, more inviting. She wore a gorgeous silk robe, printed and dyed with wonderful leaves and flowers.

"You know who I am, don't you?" she asked.

"Yes," Hector said, much to his own astonishment.

"And who am I?"

"You're Imogene Savonarola."

The apparition laughed. "Good!" she said. "That's very good!"

Hector's mind was in a flurry of confusion. What could be going on? Was this a dream, or—?

Then Hector realized that was exactly what it was: a *dream*. He waited, fearfully, for the dream to dissolve, but everything stayed in its place. He was delighted.

"I'm dreaming," he explained amiably to the sumptuous phantasm.

"That's nice," came the sweet-voiced reply.

"Well, you see," he continued, "the problem is this: I can't know if you're really you. I mean, are you dreaming me, too, or am I just making this up on my own?"

"You mean you don't know?" she asked, with just a trace of melancholy. "Perhaps a mere touch will tell you. Why don't you come over to this bank to join me?"

Hector hesitated for a moment. There were no lurking masks in the background, just luscious expanses of garden. Still, he experienced a certain trepidation, an unsettling sense of danger—and also the sinking feeling that they were not alone. He sensed the presence of a multitude nearby.

"Why don't you come over *here?*" he replied.

And, inexplicably, she was in his arms. The bridge, the stream, the very space which had separated them had suddenly vanished. She ran her fingers through his hair. Had he chosen this, or she? Whose dream was this? And why was it more real than anything he had ever experienced while awake?

"I've been trying so hard to reach you," said Hector. "I have so much to ask you."

"I know."

"But does this mean you are here, in Venice?"

"Don't worry. You'll learn everything—*all in good time*. But now, you must answer one very important question for me . . ."

Suddenly, a rhythmic, percussive sound shattered the serenity of the scene. Hector shot up from his bed. Someone was knocking on the door—not hard, but insistently. It took Hector an interminable split second to realize he was awake.

An urgent voice whispered loudly from the other side of the door: "Glasco! Hector Glasco! Wake up! Wake up at once!"

Hector heard his own voice hazily reply, "Wait just a minute, damn it." Then he collapsed back into the bed and longed for more sleep, to go back to his beautiful dream-vision. If he lost her now, would he ever find her again?

"Glasco!" the voice persisted. "Can you hear me? You've got to wake up!"

Hector sat up in bed. He was wearing all his clothes. He could barely remember checking into the pensione, much less going to sleep. He must have collapsed onto the bed the moment he arrived. He looked at his wristwatch. Ten-thirty A.M., it said. But Hector couldn't recall if he'd reset it to Italian time. He peered closely at the watch and noticed something which vaguely bothered him. The watch said it was Sunday. Now why was that so odd?

Hector suddenly remembered why. He had arrived on Wednesday.

"Good God!" he cried aloud. "Have I been asleep for three days?"

Hector plopped down into a chair. The knocking and whispering continued. He tried to remember. He didn't feel hungry, and when he thought hard, he had vague memories of lunches and dinners in the hotel dining room. Yes, there was even a tray here in the room with the remains of a meal. So, he had obviously been up and about. But why was it all so hard to remember? His dreams had seemed more real.

"Amnesia!" he groaned. "What'll it be next?"

The knocking got louder. "Glasco! Are you all right? Is somebody with you?"

"I'm coming," grumbled Hector, and he slouched toward the door and opened it. A short and rather homely, large-nosed gentleman wearing horn-rimmed glasses and a food-stained wool jacket stood outside the door. He extended his hand with nervous formality.

"Upton Orndorf, *Magister Templi* of the Ancient Order of Brothers and Sisters of Thaumaturgy. Hector Glasco, I presume."

Hector nodded dumbly.

"Thaumaturgists?" he mumbled. Then he backed away, "I'm not hiding anything!" he said reflexively.

"Ah, but perhaps you should be," said Orndorf.

"If you're one of that bunch of weirdos . . ." Hector began.

But Orndorf brushed aside his protest. "First of all, sir," he said, "I must ask if you've been dreaming."

"Yes," said Hector. "And most pleasantly—until you came along."

"And did you meet anyone in your dreams who asked you any questions?"

"Now look here," protested Hector, "I believe my dreams are a private matter."

"Dreams are *never* a private matter," Orndorf replied.

Hector tried to shut the door, but it collided with Orndorf's wing tip shoe.

"Please," Orndorf protested. "It's extremely important."

Too tired to argue, Hector scratched his head and remembered Imogene's last words: *"You must answer one very important question for me . . ."*

"Somebody started to ask me something," said Hector. "Then you interrupted."

Orndorf looked alarmed. "Then they'll be looking for you! We must both keep wide awake and out of their hands! Come with me at once!"

Orndorf grabbed Hector by the arm and started to lead him out of the pensione.

"Wait . . . wait just a minute!" stammered Hector, resisting. "Why all this . . . *theatricality?*"

"Forgive me," whispered Orndorf intensely, glancing furtively up and down the hallway. "But this is a matter of international, historical, and evolutionary importance. A feeling of high drama is necessary."

Then Orndorf ushered Hector out of the pensione. "I know the finest little trattoria," he said. "Follow me."

Orndorf obviously enjoyed playing the secret agent. At every corner, he looked to see if the coast was clear. And he had a knack for perceiving invisible pursuers. As they wound their way through the Venice streets, they had to double back or change directions more than once because of some imperceptible assailant. As he scurried along he muttered audibly to himself, but Hector couldn't catch any of the words.

He wondered if he would ever see Venice by daylight. His watch still insisted that it was morning, but a heavy dusk had fallen, and with it the pervasive Venetian mist. And he seriously wondered if this Orndorf character really knew his way around. Time and time again they went up the wrong lane and had to turn back. They indiscriminately crossed one bridge after another until it was impossible to determine which of Venice's hundred or so islands they were on. Some of the streets were untraversable, knee-deep with water. Frail planks served as temporary footbridges here and there.

"Doesn't anybody live in this desolate city?" enquired Hector.

"Haven't you heard?" replied Orndorf. "Venice is sinking into the sea. I'm sure the inhabitants of Atlantis or Lemuria would have moved away if they'd had this kind of advance warning."

"Slow down a little," Hector grumbled, panting for breath, but Orndorf wasn't winded in the least and their meanderings continued at a brisk pace. Despite his chronic furtiveness, Orndorf seemed to exult in the confusion of it all.

"Ah, the lanes of Venezia!" he rhapsodized as they found themselves up yet another blind alley. "How like the mazes of Escher or Borges. And yet, unlike those passageways, here we have no dreary paradoxes, no tired illogic, no bland incongruity. You never turn a corner and find yourself walking upside-down. You never walk to the end of a straight and narrow street and wind up in the same place where you started. And you never pass yourself by on your way. Perspective tells the truth here." Orndorf hit the side of a building with his fist. "You see, it's solid. All paths lead exactly where they seem to. Ah, the thrilling clarity of it all! The exhilarating logic! Don't you find it simply wondrous?"

None of this seemed exhilarating or wondrous to Hector, so he said nothing.

"No, I don't suppose you do," said Orndorf. "How sad. But we must hurry. Wakefulness! Wakefulness is of the essence!"

"But what's this all about?" said Hector, trying to catch his breath.

"Be patient," said Orndorf. *"All in good time."*

Why am I following this absurd character? wondered Hector fleetingly. But he knew the reason. It was in the frail hope that Orndorf was leading him to Hilary. *Or the even more bizarre hope that he's leading me to . . .* But Hector shook off the thought. No, that had only been a dream.

They came upon yet another flooded street, and this time a half a dozen papier mâché masks drifted in the water, pale white. They looked like drowned swimmers, improbably floating on their backs. Hector believed he recognized certain of their ghastly number. He grabbed Orndorf by the arm.

"Those masks!" he cried. "Where do they come from? What do they mean?"

"Carnival masks," explained Orndorf. "The Venice Carnival just ended—a supreme celebration of the waking state! The streets go wild with Harlequins, Pantalones, and Columbines; with monarchs, knights, and pages of pentacles, wands, cups, and swords; with devils and angels, tricksters and saints. These masks are cheap; you can buy fine ones of china almost anywhere in town. But why such alarm, Dr. Glasco?"

Hector preferred not to relate his encounter with the apparitions. Besides, he was no longer sure whether it had taken place while he was dreaming or awake.

Before they continued to wend their way, the *Magister Templi* actually stopped and leaned against a railing for a moment. Apparently his energy was not inexhaustible after all. Still, he chattered on.

"The Carnival! A last binge of wakefulness before that desultory dream called Lent. *Carne vale,* that's where the word comes from. 'Farewell to meat.' A poignant phrase, to my reckoning, but a prosaic one to yours. Perhaps if you think of it as meaning 'farewell to wonder, farewell to magic,' you might get some idea of what it means to me."

As they crossed an open courtyard, Orndorf's eyes drooped visibly. When they entered another street, he began to lean against the walls for support. But despite his increasing tiredness, he forged on bravely.

From not far away came the lullabylike song of a gondolier. It seemed to float ubiquitously upon the air wherever they wandered. But they never saw the singer or his craft. Hector wondered if the crooner was serenading the only pair of lovers in the city, or if he was singing himself sadly to sleep.

At last, they arrived at a dismal little trattoria. Orndorf was indeed exhausted. His head nodded. With a last remaining burst of energy, he swung the door open and staggered forward. He almost collapsed in a weary heap on the floor, but successfully made his way to the nearest table.

"But we must hurry, Dr. Glasco," he cried wearily. "I cannot stay awake much longer."

It was a grimy little place, with a dozen or so cats stalking the tabletops. Hector and Orndorf plopped themselves down at the nearest table. Hector had little appetite, so he just ordered a cup of espresso. Besides, the Italian menu was too much of a puzzle for him. He was already confused enough.

Bleary and exhausted as he was, Orndorf spoke to the waiter with hoarse urgency in fluent Italian. Although Hector had no idea what he was ordering, the list sounded absolutely endless.

Soon, a number of dishes began to arrive. At first, Orndorf barely had the energy to lift his fork. But, slowly at first, he dispatched the dishes one by one. First came various plates of seafood. Although Hector could identify the oysters and clams, other dishes were quite exotic and unrecognizable; still others were apparently raw. These were followed by artichoke hearts and a host of other fresh vegetables. The rich smell of garlic did not resuscitate Hector's appetite. To the contrary, it made him slightly ill. A rather dissolute-looking black-and-white cat jumped up on the table and poked its nose in Hector's espresso.

Orndorf's eating accelerated rapidly. He consumed the food with preternatural zeal. The color returned to his cheeks. His eyes brightened. He grew more wakeful and alert with every bite.

"And now," said Hector, "perhaps you can tell me why you dragged me here."

"Soon," said Orndorf, his mouth stuffed with broccoli. "All in good time. First, we both have to be fully awake. Drink your strong coffee. And I must advise you to eat up, my friend."

Orndorf's spirits, in such a decline but a few moments before, had now become quite exuberant. The table was cleared and a tiny bowl of sorbetto was brought forth. Hector believed that Orndorf had eaten enough to satiate the most gluttonous of desires. But then came pasta with rice, beans, peas, celery. These were accompanied by bottles of wine, which Orndorf guzzled with ardor.

All this in the quest for wakefulness? wondered Hector. *Surely, the digestion of so much food and drink would leave any ordinary mortal completely exhausted—to say nothing of violently ill!* He was nonplussed. If, indeed, Orndorf had sought him out on a "matter of international, historical, and evolutionary importance," why couldn't he think about anything except food?

The table was cleared again, and another dish of sorbetto came and went. Then came fish. Orndorf's teeth turned completely black as he bolted down an inky serving of squid. *Carne vale, indeed,* mused Hector.

Afterward came a decadent procession of desserts. By now, all the waiters in the restaurant had come to Orndorf's ministration. They brought strudel, fresh fruit, ice cream, and several luxurious hunks of chocolate sponge cake all-too-liberally soaked in rich liqueur. Orndorf gulped down one cappuccino after another.

At last, the pace of Orndorf's gastronomy began to slow. His eyes were brighter than ever. He was now in a state of high excitement. Between resonant belches, uttered with litanylike reverence, he even began to articulate a few coherent syllables.

"So," he said, "have you found your missing patient?"

"Sadly, no," said Hector. "But then, I've been rather out of it since I got here."

"So. No Hilary," said Orndorf, wiping his chin. "I believe you, my friend. I knew she'd never come. It's all just a lot of dreaming, superstitious rot. But unfortunately, *she's* not likely to believe you."

"She?" said Hector. "Who do you mean by she?"

"You know who *she* is as well as I do. I am no more ignorant of your sleeping itinerary than I am of your waking one. And, frankly, I have little time for feigned ignorance. Once she finds out about the document I am about to put in your possession, don't even think of sleeping, friend. She'll pursue you through your dreams like the Furies."

And from his jacket, Orndorf produced a burlap bag, tied shut with a leather drawstring. He handed it to Hector.

"I advise you to summon up all your waking powers and study this document with extreme care. It may be that you won't fully understand what they are trying to do, but, believe me, it would be an abomination."

"Whatever are you talking about?" Hector demanded. "And who the hell are *they*?"

"They want it joined, don't you see? *Merged into sameness.* No more of this lovely solidity, no more of this sensuous and delicious physicality."

Orndorf began to look impatient as Hector just sat and stared blankly at him. Finally the *Magister Templi* shoved the envelope toward the therapist. "The book will explain what they're about—you'll see—read her very own notes, read her preface, her *plan!*"

Hector took the hefty bag and held it in his hands. It was fat and formidable. But when he opened it, he found that it only contained two battered typewritten pages. He glanced over them hastily.

"Ibid . . . Ibid . . ."

Hector peered more closely at the pages.

"Footnotes!" he exclaimed. "This is nothing but a bunch of footnotes!"

Then he looked up, expecting some sort of explanation.

Upton Orndorf was gone. The remaining dishes had been emptied and wiped clean. And Orndorf had left Hector with the bill for his epic feast.

Llixgrijb's Masterpiece

. . . Meanwhile, outside of time and space, Llixgrijb started working on its greatest achievement: a universe with height, width, depth, and time . . . a universe with the illusion of chronological history. And it created imaginary entities for its entertainment . . . imaginary entities like *yourself,* patient reader! And it observed this delightful illusion with wonder.

But Llixgrijb was afraid.

"Suppose my creatures discover that they are only phantoms," wondered Llixgrijb. "Suppose they become aware of *me,* their creator. Suppose they learn that *I* am the only reality. A phantom aware of its own nonexistence—is a *nothing,* that's all! These lovely creatures of mine will simply collapse into the recesses of my imagination, just like all the failed universes which preceded them."

Llixgrijb could not allow that to happen.

So Llixgrijb devised its masterstroke . . . IGNORANCE!

Yes, Llixgrijb determined that Ignorance must be the glue which held its cosmos together, the fire which gave its creatures life. And the sure way to keep Ignorance alive was to send knowledge forever chasing its own tail . . .

"*Rationality,* the seeming means of escaping Ignorance, will actually lead my creatures deeper into confusion," decreed Llixgrijb. "It will take them further away from me, further away from the truth about themselves!"

But to introduce *Rationality* into its cosmos, Llixgrijb also had to allow its opposite: *Intuition.* Llixgrijb shuddered at what might happen if all its creatures simply stopped reasoning and paused to sense its presence. Rationality was Life, the ultimate illusion. Intuition was Death, the ultimate reality . . .

Desperate to preserve Ignorance against the forces of Intuition, Llixgrijb created Institutions of Higher Education.

"There!" said Llixgrijb with a note of fleeting satisfaction. "That ought to do it!"

But even so, Llixgrijb was discontented . . .

70

*And she, with a sad smile—which
was already a smile of surrender to
the impossible, the unreachable—
said: "Yet you won't remember
anything during the day." And she
put her hands back over the lamp,
her features darkened by a bitter
cloud. "You're the only man who
doesn't remember anything of what
he's dreamed after he wakes up."*

Gabriel García Márquez
"Eyes of a Blue Dog"
Collected Stories
Gregory Rabassa, trans.

———

*What I know, then, is that having
dreamed is only a part of
something different, a kind of
superimposition, a different zone,
even though the expression might
not be right, but I also have to
superimpose or violate words if I
want to get close, if I hope to be
there sometime.*

Julio Cortázar
"There, But Where, How"
*A Change of Light and Other
Stories*

Dream Berlitz

Reality jarred.

It was like a splice passing jerkily through a movie projector. For a second, it seemed as though consciousness itself would grind to a halt.

But then . . . an Edenic garden filled with flowers and swans . . . a beautiful woman clasped in his arms, bedecked in a gorgeous silk robe, printed and dyed with wonderful leaves and flowers . . . staring smilingly into his eyes . . .

Hector vaguely realized that she had just started to ask him a question. He mumbled, "I'm sorry, I must have been dreaming for a moment."

The woman threw back her head and laughed. Then she cooed sweetly, "Your lovely patient, how did she respond to that substance I sent along to you?"

Hector just stood there, gaping in confusion. Then he began to remember. *Yes*, he realized. *Now I know. This is a dream. And this is Imogene Savonarola—or at least I think she is.*

There was yet another splice. Hector staggered with disorientation again, but this time kept his wits about him. Imogene became annoyed.

"Hector, you're not staying with me at all," the woman said with exasperation. "All of these interruptions are ridiculous—these silly delays while you run about hither and thither."

She paced up and down before him. Gone was the flowered robe; now she was attired in a blue suit with severe padded shoulders. A pencil and a notepad appeared in her hand.

"Please pay attention!" she commanded. "I need your help. Don't you understand?"

He didn't understand. Her curtness irritated him. The fleeting romantic mood had evaporated. He said nothing.

"Hilary," she snapped. "What happened to Hilary?"

"I didn't have much of a chance to find out," he finally replied. "She disappeared so quickly. And I haven't been able to find her."

Imogene's eyes grew black and fierce, and her face turned chalky white. A great monarch butterfly took shape across one eye. The world around them got darker. Demons peered out of the surrounding blackness. Gently, she stroked Hector's face with her fingertips. Her nails had become razor sharp. Hector's skin crawled. Just the slightest pressure, and . . .

"I'm disappointed in you, Hector," she said. "The Waking-Born so seldom lie in dreams."

Hector shuddered. "I assure you I'm not lying," he said.

Swiftly the butterfly expanded, filling all his vision, and then she took the shape of a gigantic and ghastly white bird. She flew all around Hector, screeching and diving, flapping her wings angrily. Hector was buffeted by wild winds.

Imogene grabbed the back of Hector's jacket in her claws and carried him off into a flaming red sky filled with green, rectangular clouds. Beneath his panic, Hector was amazed. *But my dreams are always in black and white!* he marveled. But suddenly, with a final screech, she released him.

Then came that splicelike jarring again. Once again, he could barely remember the previous few moments. Hector shook his head vigorously to clear the confusion. That was when he saw that there was nothing immediately beneath him. He was falling!

And with an awful splash, Hector plunged into cold water. He choked on the taste of salt. He held what remained of his breath until he floated to the surface, then gasped desperately, trying to fill his lungs with air.

He could perceive that he was adrift upon some vast and rocky sea. His short-term memory slightly scrambled, he was not quite sure why he was anxiously searching the sky for a glimpse of wings.

Hector trembled as a shadowy form glided by in the water, and a huge fish tail lifted into the air. He was terrified, but then a mermaid's gorgeous torso broke the surface. The lovely specter looked at him, giggled, and swam on her way. Bobbing helplessly in the water, Hector gazed after her.

Then he realized, *Dreaming, yes, I must be only dreaming.*

There came yet another jolt in the fabric of reality, like a mild earthquake in the ocean. Hector was still in the water. In the distance, he saw a ferryboat chugging through the waves. For a moment, it seemed familiar, almost as though he knew where it was going. He swam in the direction of the ferry, but it kept moving away from him. Soon it was gone.

Hector was left alone in the thick gray sea. It heaved with a slow rolling motion and he treaded water with leaden arms and legs. He tried to assess his situation. If this was some sort of a recurring, continuous nightmare, then what of his waking reality? Perhaps wakefulness took place during those awful, jarring moments. Alas, he could remember none of it.

But perhaps, he considered with dread, *wakefulness is just some vain fantasy of mine. Perhaps there is nothing else but this recurring dream. Perhaps I've never been awake! Or perhaps this is the only waking that there is!*

Terror struck at him at the thought. He thrashed in the water. Soon he heard the roar of an engine. A purple Maserati, churning across the surface of the water, skidded to a halt beside him. The passenger door swung open. A dashing, dark-haired gentleman wearing a black bow tie and a white dinner jacket was sitting in the driver's seat. Somehow, Hector knew that it was Upton Orndorf.

"Glasco, old sport," said Orndorf. "Better jump in, and quickly."

"I'm afraid that might prove a little difficult," said Hector, pluckily flailing about in the heavy water.

"What's the problem?"

"I don't seem to be very good at this—lucidity business."

"Well, I don't have time to give you lessons. Jump in."

"But how?" asked Hector, nearly sinking.

Orndorf revved the engine impatiently. "Don't be such a neophyte, Glasco," he barked. "It's a dream. You can do anything you damn well want to."

Hector was surprised to feel a perverse trace of disappointment. "But . . . but if anybody can do anything," he stammered, "then how does anybody. . . I mean, how can . . . ?"

"Why do you think dreams are so bloody boring?" snapped Orndorf.

And in a blink of an eye, Hector was bone dry, sitting next to Orndorf in his fancy car, sipping a martini.

"That's better," Orndorf commented. Hector sank comfortably into the plush bucket seat. The engine roared as the Maserati accelerated, faster and faster and faster. The waves of the endless sea blurred into a smooth, solid sheet of grayish azure. Suddenly, there was no sound at all, except for the ticking of Hector's watch. The car hurtled on.

Twilight came on in a matter of seconds. Then an extraordinary structure rose up over the horizon. It was a gigantic wheel constructed out of girders, trimmed with tiny colored lights which shone gaudily against the steel gray twilight. It carried what looked like tiny railroad cars. It was colossal, perhaps many miles high, and rotated very slowly. Despite the unearthly silence of the car, Hector almost fancied he could hear calliope music and the pounding of engines turning the wheel.

"It's a Ferris wheel!" he exclaimed, turning toward Orndorf.

"Damn!" cried Orndorf. "That's her! She's on to us!"

And Orndorf spun the steering wheel. The Maserati whirled 180 degrees and tore off in the opposite direction. Despite this maneuver, the Ferris wheel still loomed in front of them. Orndorf uttered a stream of curses. But then, like a sun that couldn't quite manage to rise, the wheel slipped back below the edge of the sea.

Orndorf breathed a sigh of relief. "Safe—for now!" he said. "But she'll corner us before too long. We can't know where—or how. It's a good thing I came along when I did. Now didn't I warn you not to go to sleep? This realm is no safe place for you as long as you've got that manuscript—and as long as she thinks you know where Hilary is. And now, we've both got to wake up, and fast!"

"Relax" said Hector smugly. "There's little chance of the old girl catching up with us in this betsy, is there?"

"Don't be a fool. She'll be on us like a hawk at any second."

"But this is a dream," whined Hector. "My dream. I thought you said I could do anything I wanted to."

"Yes, but so can she."

"But how can she do something I don't want her to?"

"Surely you don't think the Sleeping World is your own private beach. It's consensual, just like any other reality."

"But all this is just a figment of my imagination. You're just a figment of my imagination."

"That's right. And you're just a figment of mine, and she's just a figment of of ours, and we're just figments of hers. And as a matter of fact, you're just a figment of your own imagination. Now kindly stop being so damned sophomoric and wake the hell up!"

A fragment of waking memory emerged in Hector's mind. "Do you have any idea how much cash I had to fork over to pay for that feast of yours?" he griped.

Orndorf's apology was brusque and embarrassed.

"I'm sorry," he said. "I fell asleep."

"You fell asleep?" exclaimed Hector. "You fell asleep right at the table?"

"That's right. I have trouble waking these days. Call it the insomnia of the Sleeping-Born. I'm sorry."

"Oh, I get it," said Hector sarcastically. "You fell asleep and magically dematerialized from the face of the planet!"

"Don't you understand a goddamn thing?" shouted Orndorf. "My body's here! I was born here, I live here!"

Hector's brain fumbled to make sense of it. "Are . . . are you telling me that you live in dreams?"

Orndorf glared crankily at the sea in front of them, saying nothing.

"And are you telling me," jabbered Hector, "that your waking is my sleeping, and my waking is your—?"

But it was too late for explanations. The water in front of them bubbled and boiled. The facade of a gigantic Mycenaean temple rose up in front of them. It sent water cascading in all directions. The sea rolled back around the edges of a tiny island.

The Maserati engine screamed, decelerating rapidly. Spinning wildly, the car squealed to a stop.

"You've got no time to lose," yelled Orndorf. "Wake up, now!"

But Hector had no idea how to do that. He threw the car door open, jumped out, and made a run for it across the waves. Orndorf followed in pursuit.

They fled away from the island. Nevertheless, Hector and Orndorf immediately found themselves running into the marbled courtyard of the temple. They slid to a halt. The Maserati rocked in the waves behind them.

Before them, majestic cedar doors swung solemnly open to reveal Imogene sitting on a golden tripod. She wore a gleaming chiton and her hair was garlanded with laurel. She looked, for all the world, like some resplendent oracle of old.

Orndorf laughed contemptuously.

"Really, Savonarola," he said. "The *deus ex machina* went out of style twenty-five hundred years ago. I preferred the Ferris wheel."

"So whoever called me a slavish follower of fashion?" retorted Imogene. "And now, Orndorf, if you'll excuse us, I've got things to discuss with Hector."

"I'm not leaving him at your mercy," snapped Orndorf. "He's barely achieved a level of low lucidity. He doesn't know how to handle himself here."

Imogene was about to protest. But she and Orndorf were immediately distracted by a water-skier, an elderly man wearing Bermuda shorts and out-sized sunglasses. He yelled and waved cheerfully as he circled the island. He wasn't being towed or propelled by anything visible, but his single ski whisked along in the water with exhilarating speed.

"What's Bruno doing here?" Imogene demanded, glaring at Orndorf.

"Why ask me?" replied Orndorf irritably. "He's sleeping off another drunk, I'm sure." The skier continued to circle them, going by on one foot, then on one hand, grinning their way all the time.

"He's an exhibitionist," Imogene said indignantly.

"No, he's just a very good lucid dreamer." Orndorf sounded wistful. "I wish I could do as well over there."

"I don't trust him."

"You don't trust anybody."

"He's never been of any help to us at all."

Orndorf laughed contemptuously. "He's a lazy bastard who wants nothing but a good time. You couldn't possibly understand that, could you?"

At that moment, the skier let out a bloodcurdling war cry. He burst out of the water with a wild rush and skidded across the surface of the island. Prankishly, he skied in tight circles around Imogene, splashing water all over her. Imogene spun around confusedly and dizzily. She screeched and clutched to her chest some bulky object that she had hidden under her robe.

Then the skier careened back into the sea. He continued circling the island impishly. Hector sensed that the mad fellow was looking straight at him. The skier cupped his hand over his mouth and yelled, "Lucidity isn't only for dreaming, my friend!" Laughing loudly, he roared off and vanished into the waves.

The Book of Solomon

Hector sensed some dire import in the skier's message. "What did he mean?" he asked Imogene. "What was he trying to tell me?" he asked Orndorf.

They both ignored him.

"He tried to take it!" cried Imogene.

"Take what?" grumbled Orndorf.

"You're in on this together!" shouted Imogene, waving an accusing finger.

"In on what? What? What?" Orndorf roared back at her.

"The two of you! Trying to steal my life's work! A conspiracy!"

"If you mean your manuscript, that's safely in the realm of the Waking-Born."

Imogene just looked a little puzzled.

"And Bruno had nothing to do with it!" Orndorf said smugly. "It was me! Me alone! And all I wanted was some answers! Oh, and I got them, all right! I know what you and your cronies are up to!"

"My manuscript?" she asked.

"I'm sure you've noticed that it's missing by now."

Imogene reached into the folds of her chiton and produced an enormous, leather-bound, pearl-studded volume with marbled panels. The title, *The Elixir of Solomon,* was embroidered across the cover in ornate, gilt-edged letters.

"Do you mean this manuscript?" she asked Orndorf.

Orndorf's eyes glazed with incomprehension. "No. I took it. I know I took it. I took it and I—"

"Tell me, Upton," said Imogene sneeringly. "Did you really think you could transmit objects from one realm to another? A novice like you? Really? What made you think you could do what all those great Thaumaturgists of the past—all those venerable masters and magicians—could not?"

Orndorf turned and marched defiantly toward his car. "Maybe I couldn't steal your book. Maybe it just snapped back here somehow. But I read it. And I know your plan."

Imogene stalked after him. "Oh, so you think you know something, do you?" she demanded challengingly.

Orndorf simply snarled and climbed into the Maserati. "I know all I need to know," he said, revving up the engine. "I'll be back. And I'll stop you. I'll put an end to your infernal scheme—and I don't care about any half-baked prophecies!"

Orndorf roared off. As the Maserati peeled away without Hector, a yawning, whirling maelstrom growled and churned in the sea before it. Naiads danced around the rim of the foaming contagion, singing forlorn and tragic warnings to all wayward travelers. But with enraged perversity, Orndorf roared the Maserati's engines and drove the vehicle in a wild, careening, inverse orbit down into the raging vortex. The car vanished, the maelstrom gradually ceased its mad whirling, and the sea was calm again.

Hector stood staring after him, feeling perplexed and abandonded.

"What do you know? What did Orndorf tell you?" Imogene demanded.

"He said a lot of things I could barely make sense of. He said he was Dreaming-Born. He said I was Waking-Born. But which are you?"

"You're not in a position to ask me questions," she retorted. And Imogene was all mask now, that grim white one with the orange-and-black butterfly over one eye. The hideous visage filled his entire field of vision. Hector tried to turn away, only to find himself facing the terrible vision again.

In the face of imminent danger, Hector found his memory of certain waking events cleared up remarkably.

"I know something else, though," he said, attempting a bluff. "I know what's in the book. I read part of it, too."

"You couldn't have," said Imogene.

"I did. Orndorf brought it to me. And I was definitely awake at the time."

"Impossible!"

"I read something about Solomon finding that the world was flat, and about Fra Girolamo Savonarola burning. I read the part about Harpo Marx and the vagrant and the cup of coffee."

A startled silence ensued. The mask shriveled. Imogene was herself again. Oh, her garlands had wilted slightly and her chiton had lost some of its gleam, but she still looked quite formidable—and angry and dangerous as well.

She withdrew the book from the folds of her dress and thumbed through it frantically, glancing immediately toward the end. At last, she found the missing pages.

"Pages 7,900 and 7,901," she gasped. "Footnotes."

"Yes, yes! Footnotes! Exactly!"

"And where are the pages now?" But before Hector could even offer a mute shrug, she said, "Never mind. I know. They're on your Waking Self."

Then, rather timidly, Hector enquired, "By the way, what did Harpo say to the vagrant?"

"Harpo never said anything," said Imogene sadly. "Harpo doesn't talk."

"I see," said Hector, a little embarrassed at the irrelevance of this query. But all his other questions seemed too enormous to even ask.

The garden courtyard was shriveling into a dead ruin all around them. Imogene still looked youthful, but at the same time terribly sad and ancient. Now there were great circles under her eyes from exhaustion and long weeping. And the temple, so grand just a moment before, was melting slowly into a puddle. Imogene sat sadly down on a chipped marble bench.

"So he did it," she murmured tiredly. "Orndorf really did it, or at least part of it. He's more capable than I thought."

"What is this book?" Hector ventured another question. "Did you write it?"

"No, no, it has been verbally channeled at various times during human history," Imogene said. "I was the first to write it down. And I edited it."

"But why is it so important?"

"It contains a prophecy," she said. "And a secret Elixir . . . but even Solomon never discovered the seventh ingredient." Imogene gave a long, tired sigh. "Perhaps none of it is true."

Hector sat down beside her. "Can you please explain what's happening to me?" he pleaded. "Can you tell me how all this can possibly be a dream?"

"It hardly matters," she said wearily. "One realm fades into the other now, and neither gives me any comfort. Neither seems complete. What a dreadful bore, isn't it, Hector? An awful farce, a ghastly charade. So sad, so sad." Imogene looked up at him with melancholy eyes. "But tell me, your patient, where is she really?"

"Gone," said Hector sympathetically. "I have no idea where."

Imogene hung her head in despair. All threat had vanished. Gone was the wild virago who had pursued Hector so far. What he saw now was a confused and disappointed girl.

Hector felt pity for her. He reached over and touched her gently on the shoulder. Her body trembled slightly. She seemed on the verge of giving herself up to the comfort of his arms.

"Imogene," he said tenderly.

But instead of surrendering to him, Imogene briskly rose from the bench. She snapped her fingers. Hector was abruptly blinded by a terrible, bright light. There was a loud hum in the air, as if of a powerful electrical current. Hector covered his eyes and squinted. Slowly and painfully, he adjusted to the light. He could see that he was surrounded by an ocean of masks, some plain and pale, others wildly sculpted and painted—and all eerily familiar. Their eyeholes were all black.

I thought we were alone! thought Hector.

Imogene walked toward the monolithic wall of masks and spoke to them.

"Well, Brothers and Sisters," she said to them. "You heard it yourself. He doesn't know where Hilary is."

"Lying!" whispered the multitude of masks in unison.

"He's not lying and you know it," returned Imogene. "Why would he lie? We've terrified him into submission. No, good friends. I have failed you all. Our messiah has fled. The prophecy is null and void. What's more, we have a formidable enemy."

"Orndorf!" whispered the masks.

"Yes. Orndorf."

"But what of Solomon?"

"I shall go and tell him of my failure."

"But what of Fra Girolamo?"

"I shall have to tell him too."

Hector felt a rush of indignation. He strode toward Imogene angrily.

"You didn't tell me I was in the middle of some sort of public inquisition," he complained.

"It was none of your business."

Hector ruthlessly seized Imogene by the arm. "I believe what happens in my own dreams is very much my business," he said angrily.

"You're hurting me," said Imogene.

"How can I hurt you?" growled Hector. "You're not even real. You're just a figment of my dreams."

He gripped her and pulled her roughly against him. He kissed her—rudely, coarsely, thoughtlessly. He was surprised at the vivid feeling of her body against his, so real, so palpable, even in a dream. She struggled and managed to turn her face away from him.

The masks were now murmuring discontentedly. Hector could feel their eyes gazing at both of them. The air was riddled with their disapproval. He took Imogene's chin in his hand and turned her face toward him again. He could see a whole range of feelings in her eyes. He saw her humiliation at her confessed failure. He saw rage and humiliation at the present scene. But he saw something else as well.

"You want me," he said. "You desire me."

Imogene looked straight at him. Her eyes flared. For a moment, he expected her to hotly deny his words. Instead, she broke away from his grip. She walked rapidly from him. The ocean of masks parted before her. She headed straight toward a balcony which loomed over a bottomless cliff.

Sensing what was about to happen, Hector rushed toward her. He seized her by the wrist just as she threw herself over the railing. He, too, sailed over into the abyss.

Hand in hand, they tumbled into pure blackness. They fell as though down an endless well, through a hole in the earth—or in the universe itself.

And as they fell, Hector wrapped his arms around her. Imogene gasped and returned his embrace. Locked together, they fell and fell on through the darkness.

A gigantic clock face appeared at the bottom of the well. It was round and perfect, a pool of translucent white. The clock had gnarled hands and was marked by severe Roman numerals. Its ticking echoed around them like the rolling of timpani. The image seemed to waver and ripple as they tumbled helplessly toward it. Was the clock face really there, and what would happen when their bodies struck it?

The hour hand pointed directly at the twelve. The minute hand was a fraction of an inch from meeting it. An inane question took shape in Hector's mind. In a flash, it became an obsession:

Is it noon or midnight?

Time itself slowed achingly as they neared the clock face. The last split second was interminable.

They were six feet away . . .

. . . a foot . . .

. . . an eternal fraction of an inch . . .

. . . and the chimes began. Hector shot up in bed.

He stared out of an open window, gazing down the Victoria Embankment at the great clock tower a mile or so away. Its chimes resounded, resonant and mellow and unthreatening. Then Big Ben tolled twelve times. A couple of barges passed one another listlessly on the Thames. Black taxicabs scurried to and fro over the broad thoroughfare. A flock of pigeons filled the bright blue sky.

It was noon in London.

A Question of Elmblight

London! What on earth am I doing here?

Hector looked around the hotel room. It was vast and much too elegantly decorated, with antique furniture and rococo flourishes all about.

Good God! I hope I knew what I was doing when I checked into this *place. How much is it costing me?*

But his feeling of alarm quickly faded into drowsiness. All he wanted was to go back to sleep

What was that dream? A flash of a memory was so vivid that it actually woke him up more. Just moments ago he had been locked in some beautiful woman's arms. He remembered falling and falling. Now he was here in dreary old London, alone and filled with longing.

Oh, how I would like to get back into that *dream!*

He lay in bed for a moment, staring at the decor. Then he closed his eyes. He tried hard to go back to sleep, but couldn't. Big Ben had stopped tolling. But it would soon toll again.

Damn that clock. Wish I could turn it off. Ought to be a law against that sort of thing.

He turned in his bed and observed a stack of postcards on the end table. He picked them up and thumbed through them. One was a photograph of the great column marking the end of the Via Appia, the greatest of all roads which led to ancient Rome. It was addressed to Max Henderson, and was scrawled with Hector's own handwriting. But the words were not familiar:

> Dear Max,
>
> Greetings from Brindisi, Italy, the end of the road from Rome—and the end of the road from anywhere! No need to come to Italy and deconstruct *this* town. Somebody beat you to it. Am awaiting a ferry to Piraeus, Greece, which I may prove too lazy to board. Am sleeping a great deal!
>
> With fond wishes for your complete rehabilitation,
>
> H. Glasco

And beneath that postcard was another one with a photograph of a ruined Greek amphitheater. It, too, was addressed to Max:

> Dear Max,
> Came to Greece after all. This is some sort of old-style theater, I'm told—the Theater of Dionysis. You'd know more about that sort of thing than I do. Those big stone chairs in the middle were reserved for the fellows who judged the plays. I had a good snooze in one of them. I'll bet those judges used to catch a few winks during performances, too. Sleep hearty!
> Yours in lethargy,
> H. Glasco

Following this was a postcard with a statue of a mermaid on it. This one was addressed to his own office in Los Angeles:

> Dear Miss Bellows:
> Yes, I understand your concern, but this trip is all for the best. I'm sorry about the patients' irritation at my absence, but obviously I needed the R & R. Tell them to put their psychoses on hold. I wish I could tell you all about "wonderful, wonderful Copenhagen," but frankly, this lovely mermaid was the only thing I saw. Slept the rest of my stay away.
> Warm wishes,
> Dr. Glasco

There were other postcards from all over Europe—the Prado Museum in Madrid, the Coliseum in Rome, the Eiffel Tower in Paris, and a dozen or so other sights. They were all addressed to Hector's Los Angeles acquaintances. And they all spoke, almost boastfully, of his unquenchable sleepiness. Why hadn't he mailed any of the brief epistles? Hector could only think of one plausible answer:

Too lazy, I guess.

But he had no answer to some other crucial questions:

Why can't I remember writing them? And why can't I remember being in any of these places?

Hector puzzled over the evidence in front of him. It seemed that he had been traveling a great deal—but doing considerably more sleeping than sight-seeing.

But how long have I been traveling?

He fumbled around the room vainly looking for his wristwatch. Instead, he came across an envelope addressed to him, which he had never opened. When he tore it open he found a copy of his own newsletter, dated May. *Volume One, Number Six. But I've only published five issues.*

How long ago had he received it? He unfolded the newsletter. Its contents were strange.

Footnotes! What the hell—?

But then he remembered his meeting with the ravenous Upton Orndorf in Venice.

Oh, those footnotes. I guess I must have sent them along to Miss Bellows and told her to put them in the newsletter. I suppose she chose the embellishment. I should have added some sort of explanation. My readers will be most confused. Well, no more than I am, I suppose.

Glancing at the notes, his eyes lighted on the following:

"Cf. Harpo Marx's response (worthy of the most adept Thaumaturgist) to the vagrant who 'could really use a cup of coffee.'"

Hector scratched his head and tried to remember the handful of Marx Brothers movies he'd seen.

How did *Harpo respond to the vagrant?*

Then in a frantic burst of *déjà vu,* he wondered, *And who did I —very recently— ask that same question?*

But the puzzle was too great for his sleepy mind. He dragged himself wearily to the bathroom and washed the sleep out of his eyes, taking note of the name on the towels: "Queen's Guard Hotel."

Well, as long as I can't get back to sleep, I might as well take a bit of a walk.

He struggled into some clothes and ventured downstairs to the lobby. He stopped at the desk.

"Any messages for me?" he asked the clerk.

"Ah, Dr. Glasco. Let me see."

So he knows my name, mused Hector as the clerk glanced through the mail slots. *How long have I been here, anyway?*

"There's nothing at the moment," said the clerk. "But the mail is due shortly. Might want to check back then."

"Very well," said Hector. He walked out of the hotel and stood facing the stately Thames. Several floating pubs and restaurants were moored to the embankment. County Hall stared across the river at him, squat, stolid, and riddled with British self-importance.

And how many noontimes has this sight met my all-too-sleepful eyes?

He began to walk south along the broad thoroughfare.

Let's see where my footsteps take me. How well do I know my way around?

And sure enough, he instinctively turned right on Horse Guards Avenue, then right again on Whitehall Road, and headed straight for a pub called the Clarence. It was gaslit on the inside, with sawdust on the floors and great oak-beamed ceilings. Except for its clientele, the Clarence appeared much as it must have looked two hundred years before. The barmaid knew him by name and promptly brought him his "usual"—a pint of beer and a shepherd's pie.

Hector glared at the beer. He remembered his dislike of the sour, strong imported brew Max had ordered for him at that Hollywood bar. Then, to his own surprise, Hector picked up the glass and dispatched the contents with familiarity and gusto. The barmaid quickly brought him another. It didn't exactly waken him. It had, in fact, quite the opposite effect.

And that's as it should be. Just the right level of alcoholic sleepiness is exactly what I'm looking for. Soon, very soon, I'll be ripe for a good, long nap—and another meeting with that woman of my dreams.

After another pint, Hector's eyelids got heavy. He wended his way back to the hotel.

I do feel sleepy. Yes, I believe I'll head back to my room and go directly to sleep.

As he passed by the hotel desk, the clerk flagged him down.

"Dr. Glasco," he said, "a letter for you."

Hector glanced at the envelope on his way to the elevator. The letter came from—but was he reading the address correctly?—a place called Elmblight, Ohio. It failed to inspire his curiosity.

Maybe I'll open it later in the day—after I've had a nice nap.

Once in his room, he promptly climbed back into bed. He closed his eyes and tried to conjure up that dream again.

What was her name? Oh, yes! I had this silly idea that it was Imogene Savonarola. Well, that won't do. I'll give her a different name when I get back into the dream.

He painstakingly recollected radiant eyes, a voluptuous figure. Yes, it was all coming back to him—the smooth touch of her hair and gown beneath his fingers, and an exquisite sense of falling, falling, falling . . .

The phone rang. Hector winced. He tried to will the ringing away. It continued. He answered the phone. The voice on the other end was all too familiar.

"Blast you, Glasco. Don't you ever do anything but sleep?"

"Orndorf," said Hector, unable and unwilling to suppress a yawn, "you've got a hell of a nerve."

"Don't think I don't know what you've been up to. You've been sleeping endlessly, all over Europe. And whenever you're not sleepy, you travel for no other reason than to wear yourself out and get sleepy again. Don't you see the fix you're in? Can't you see how she's manipulating you?"

"*She?* Who do you mean by *she?*"

"You know perfectly well who I mean! Imogene Savonarola!"

"How do *you* know what goes on in my dreams?"

"Glasco, I'm telling you, she's got you completely in her power. You've got to wake up."

"I don't have any idea what you're talking about," said Hector.

"I'm coming to London to talk sense to you. You stay right where you are."

"I'll do as I damn well please," said Hector. And he hung up.

He rolled over in the bed and the phone began to ring again. "That fool Orndorf," he groaned. "He behaves as though dreams were real. Would that they were!"

He tried to lull himself to sleep by counting the rings. It was no good. The phone rang persistently. Perhaps it would never stop.

If I knew where that idiot was, I'd have him arrested. Well, I guess now's as good a time as any to read my mail.

He opened the envelope as the phone kept ringing. It read as follows:

> Dear Dr. Glasco,
>
> I'm enjoying your adventures very much, and so are all the members of my book club and sewing circle.
>
> Perhaps it's not my place to say this, but there are *other* Venices where you might wish to look for Hilary. There is one in Florida (too full of retired Republicans for my taste) and, of course, one in your own backyard—Venice Beach, California. I remember it well from my Bohemian days. Sadly, those days of cheap rents are gone.
>
> Best of luck to you in your quest,
> Myrtle Roebuck
>
> P.S. I believe that Harpo pulled a steaming hot cup of coffee out of his overcoat. The exact movie escapes me.

Hector's mind exploded with questions.

Who the hell is Myrtle Roebuck? And how did she know where to write me? And what prompted her to answer a question I had asked myself only an hour or so ago?

But one question loomed over all the rest:

Can it be that I went to the wrong Venice?

The only answer was the interminable ringing of the telephone. Despite the noise, Hector collapsed in the bed and fell into an exasperated slumber.

But this time he did not dream at all.

 **3:15 P.M.**

. . . Ethel looked up in surprise. "Why Myrtle, how clever!" she exclaimed.

Myrtle said nothing.

"That was *your note* poor Hector received, wasn't it?" asked Addie Gaines. "Myrtle Roebuck, it says right here on page eighty-seven."

"Yes, it was," Myrtle said with great dignity, fighting back a grin. "Just a little experiment of mine. I wanted to check out that negative capability thing. I wanted to know how much aesthetic distance we've really got. Not much, as it turns out."

"But how did you get it to him?" asked Ethel. "How did you get it into the *very book we were reading?*" She looked down. "Oh dear, now I've lost count of my purls."

"It was the easiest thing in the world," Myrtle replied. "Not more than a paragraph into the last chapter, we found out that Hector was in Whitehall, London. And not long after that, we learned the name of his hotel. Well, for quite some time, I'd been wondering if he really should have looked for Hilary in a different Venice. And I thought, 'Wouldn't it be nice to share my thoughts with him?'"

Then Myrtle set down her quilting square and closed her eyes, reliving the incident completely. "So I took a deep breath and emptied my mind. I pictured myself sitting at my writing desk with a fresh piece of stationery in front of me. I relaxed every muscle in my body and tried to imagine the exact address of the hotel. And it came to me:

Queens Guard Hotel
23 Victoria Embankment
Whitehall SW1 London
ENGLAND

"In my mind's eye, I quickly wrote the address on the envelope while it was still fresh. Then I wrote the letter to him. I was just finishing it up when I remembered his curiosity about Harpo and the vagrant. Imogene just told him that Harpo didn't talk. I found that a completely inadequate explanation. And Hector didn't seem to remember it, anyhow.

"So I dashed off a little P.S. explaining it to him.* I sealed up the envelope and stuck on a nice commemorative stamp. I knew I had seconds to spare before the chapter came to an end. So I hastily visualized myself at the post office, dropping the letter into the mailbox. Then I opened my eyes—and here I was!"

"Metaphysical rubbish!" growled Lida June.

"Well, it's obvious that Myrtle's letter manifested in an extremely *physical* form!" chortled Addie. "It's in the book now! And she even mentions *us* in it!"

"What possessed you to attempt such a thing?" grumbled Lida June.

"Oh, it was just a hunch," said Myrtle. "Just some silly right hemispheric dominance sort of thing. It was that same feeling I get in my ankles when there's going to be a thunderstorm. Actually, I didn't stop to think about whether it would work or not. I just did it as a lark."

"I still say it's impossible," persisted Lida June. "I know Whitehall like the back of my hand, and there's no Queen's Guard Hotel along the Victoria Embankment."

"That's just the London you know," explained Myrtle. "The world of the book is different."**

"And another thing," continued Lida June, "there couldn't possibly have been enough *time*. It must have taken—what?—less than a second for that letter to get across the Atlantic!"

"Letters travel fast when you drop them into the fictional world," explained Myrtle. "At the speed of light, I should imagine. Or perhaps even faster. Like tachyons"

"Well, forgive me for saying so," grumbled Lida June, "but I don't like it. I don't like it one bit. Why, what business is it of yours to drop notes to fictional characters, even while you're in the act of *reading* about them! What would your Newtonian spaceman say?"

"Yes," remarked Phoebe McNair. "And how can any of us know whether you've changed how the book turns out? What would have happened if one of us had done something like this when we were reading those delightful Borges stories?"

"Or *Lady Chatterly's Lover?*" added Ethel, with a trace of nostalgia.

"You can't change something that's already happened, can you?" asked Lida June worriedly. "I mean, if the book was already written . . ."

---

* "By the way," she interjected. "Was that in *Duck Soup* or *Horse Feathers*?"
"Stick to your story," said Addie breathlessly.

** "Well, I can assure you there *is* a Clarence Pub on Whitehall Road," whispered Ethel to Phoebe. "And when last I was there, they served a house ale that could make you forget your name! No wonder poor Hector's brain is fried!"

"You could cause a leak," said Phoebe. "At least that's my theory."

"Whatever do you mean?" Lida June was alarmed.

"You know. A leak. A reality leak between here and there. Rather like the 'wormhole effect.'" Phoebe gestured with two weaving shuttles.

"Oh, fiddlesticks," huffed Myrtle. "I didn't change the ending one small bit."

"Myrtle Roebuck!" exclaimed Lida June. *"You didn't peek at the ending, did you?"*

"Such accusations!" said Myrtle. "I don't know what I did to deserve this kind of suspicion. It was all in fun. It didn't even occur to me that it would work. And it was certainly never my intention to disrupt the fabric of reality. Everybody's looking at me like I created a black hole or something."

"Look here," Addie said, "Myrtle tested out a little hypothesis, and it proved valid as theory, that's all."

"It ought to be replicated," muttered Myrtle.

"Now, Myrtle," said Phoebe firmly, "we'll have no talk of replication today. The weather's much too pretty."

"Oh dear, let's not get on the subject of the weather again," said Lida June.

"That's right," said Ethel. "We're not going to talk about the weather or about replication. Or about butterflies," she added hastily.

Addie and Myrtle both sputtered a bit, but the other members nodded in agreement. There was a moment of awkward silence, and then a look of melancholy came over Phoebe. "Wouldn't it be nice to be in Europe?" she asked. Several members sighed sympathetically. "Why, it must be sixty years now since Ralph and I went abroad for our honeymoon. God rest his soul!"

"Oh, I know just what you mean," said Ethel, changing from orange to turquoise yarn. "We live in such a rootless culture—no traditions, so little history. The intellectual/spiritual upheaval of the ages is so alive in the Old World!"

"It makes one really stop and think about the elusive ebb and flow of history, doesn't it?" Addie joined in gamely. There came a general murmur of agreement.

"Here in Elmblight," grumbled Myrtle, "our most prominent bastion of culture is that drive-in theater which has played *The Shaggy Dog* since it came out in—what?—1959, I do believe!"

"These newfangled radical historians can keep on saying 'The past is absent!' till they're blue in the face," said Lida June. "They should go to Chartres. They should go to Delphi."

"They should go to this wonderful little taverna in the Athenian Plaka," said Ethel. "They serve a brand of retsina that's as old as Olympus. Homer himself might well have gotten ripped on it."

"You can *breathe* the past in places like that!" exclaimed Lida June. "Positively breathe it!"

But Phoebe shook her head. "I must say I'm a skeptic on the subject of history," she said. "I'm reaching the age where one wonders if there is truly such a thing as evolutionary and/or historical progress."

"Really, Phoebe," cautioned Addie, pulling a piece of magenta corduroy out of her scrap box. "And people accuse me of having a negative attitude, just because I'm intrigued by chaos."

"Oh, it's purely a philosophical concern," added Phoebe reassuringly. "I mean, *do* events unfold with sequential majesty, or do they merely repeat themselves with mindless inevitability again and again and again? Is there such a *thing* as history?" She whipped a shuttle around each warp thread, making a row of Egyptian knots.*

"Well, I don't much like the question at all," said Lida June. "It makes my stomach queasy. Like the notion of changing something in a book."

"Reminds me of when I was bumming through Europe—oh, centuries ago," said Addie. "I met this perfectly charming nobleman—the Duke of Something-or-Other. Why *can't* I remember his name? I believe I still have some of his

---

* Ethel reached over and tapped Phoebe on the shoulder, as the others kept talking.
"What?" Phoebe whispered.

Ethel said, "I've got just the book you should read, right here in my purse: *Time's Arrow, Time's Cycle*, by Stephen Jay Gould." She pulled the book out.

"Oh, yes!" said Phoebe. "The punctuated equilibrium fellow! What's he got to say about the nature of time and history?"

"Oh, a great deal. And he's got such a graceful manner with metaphors. Listen to this!" Ethel thumbed through the book and read:

> "Deep time is so alien that we can really only comprehend it as metaphor . . . Consider the earth's history as the old measure of the English yard, the distance from the king's nose to the tip of his outstretched hand. One stroke of a nail file on his middle finger erases human history."

"Deep time," said Phoebe. "That's the story of my life."

"You see," Ethel explained, "Mr. Gould's book is all about the discovery of 'deep time' in geology, and its implications for history. When everybody thought the world was just a few thousand years old, history was a pretty easy concept. But faced with billions of years of shapeless change, we may well wonder if linear history even takes place."

"I know I often do," ruminated Phoebe.

"Well, Professor Gould deals a lot with the dichotomy of time, and the two metaphors we tend to most attach to it."

"And what are they?" asked Phoebe.

Ethel read:

> "At one end of the dichotomy—I shall call it time's arrow—history is an irreversible sequence of unrepeatable events . . . At the other end—I shall call it time's cycle—events have no meaning as distinct episodes with causal impact upon a contingent history."

"Dichotomies, dichotomies," sighed Phoebe. "Do read on."

letters." Then, chuckling lasciviously, she added: "That rascal taught this red-blooded, egalitarian, All-American girl a thing or two about the appeal of European aristocracy!"

"There's not much point in going to any of those places if you're going to sleep through the whole trip," said Myrtle.

"Why, I didn't spend all that much time in bed," Addie protested indignantly.

"Not you, dear. I'm talking about Hector."

A slightly embarrassed pause ensued. The smell of brownies cooking drifted deliciously through the room. All that could be heard was Ethel's inaudible whispering. She was reading to Phoebe

"Whatever is it that you're carrying on about, Ethel?" Myrtle demanded.

But Ethel kept reading quietly but intently:

> "I have a personal theory that paradoxes of odd beginnings
> usually unlock the meaning of great works."

Then Phoebe noticed the group's sudden attention. "That's from Stephen Jay Gould," she explained. "Ethel was telling me all about it."

"Oh, yes," said Addie. "The punctuated equilibrium fellow. He's a bit too much of a rationalist for my taste. Let's get back to Hector Glasco."

And Ethel picked up the *jamais vu papers* and read on . . .

The Jamais Vu Papers

Volume One
Number Seven
June

So Hector Glasco comes home from that imaginary place called England.
Once back in Los Angeles, he hurries to Venice, *California*.
At the Sidewalk Cafe he meets renowned investigative satirist Paul Krassner, co-founder of the Yippies and editor of *The Realist*.
What can they possibly have in common?
Let's listen in . . .

. . . so you see, I seem to be the victim of some sort of ongoing hoax. That's why I've come to you for help. What does it mean to be an investigative satirist?

That means I investigate the stories behind stuff in the news . . . and the stories behind stuff in my own personal facade . . . and then I share what I find with my audience.

I've found that I'm a humorist in spite of myself. People laugh at my newsletter, so I have to accept the fact that I'm unwittingly editing a satirical publication.

But how can I do it intentionally?

An <u>intentional</u> satirist, eh? Well, that can be very confusing.
I have this strange affliction: I keep thinking that I'm making up the news.
The classic definition of satire is criticism, so sometimes you don't even need a belly laugh.
**Just to describe what's happening is in itself a criticism,
just to give the facts. A lot of the news is self-satirical.**

What do you consider to be some of the uses of pranks and hoaxes?

Well, Pablo Picasso said that art is a lie to help people see the truth—except in his personal life, of course!

There was one piece that I published in 1971 about the first waterbed fatality. Now this was written by a guy named Tom Miller. And I wasn't sure whether it was a hoax or not, because the protagonist in the piece was named Malcolm Coors, and then Miller put in parentheses, "No relation to Joseph Coors, the beer magnate," which already built up a layer of verisimilitude. Why would you make up a character and then have to deny that he's related to somebody who's real? So Coors's cat had clawed a hole in the waterbed, and it formed a little puddle, and the Sony TV set fell into it and the guy got electrocuted. Luckily, his girlfriend was up getting a roach clip at the time, and she was saved from this horrible fate. So I published it and it was picked up by the San Francisco Examiner as a real item, because I never distinguish what's real from what's not. Then it got picked up by KCBS radio—the CBS all-news outlet. And the furniture manufacturers were having their annual convention.

As a result of this item they passed a resolution calling for higher standards of safety in the manufacture of waterbeds.

I think of it as preventive journalism.

"...so before I perform, I'll say a little prayer, and I hear a voice in reply..."

Please, God, help me to do a good show.

Shut up, you superstitious fool!

Even though I consider myself a free-thinker, I probably spend more time playing with the notion of the mystery than people who consider themselves religious. An important part of my growth was evolving from having coincidence as my religion, to where coincidence and mysticism were the same process. I remained an absurdist and an atheist. But there came a point where I realized that the most absurd thing I could do would be to develop a relationship with this deity I didn't believe in. It was a hoax on _myself_. And, like anything else, it can become a habit...

"And you know, I've really been tested. Not long ago, I had an operation. And if you're used to seeing the world through a filter of absurdity, then it has to apply to your own life, too. I had to go through stages of shock and denial and a kind of free-floating anger before I could get to the absurdity of it. It was an omen for me when the head of orthopedics at UCLA told me that my neurosurgeon moonlights as a circus clown with Ringling Brothers. **That was my moment!**"

I surrender!
Cut me open!
Do what you want!

There's more and more information reaching people, with cable and satellite dishes and all that. People are jaded, because of this conveyer belt of information. I already forget what it was that I was so horrified about on the news yesterday. And I was horrified! But you develop an emotional callus to the horror. And a danger satirists can run into is to see the news just as grist for their mill. After all, you have to separate yourself from something in order to be funny about it. **Steve Allen said that satire is tragedy plus time.** But since everything is accelerating, that time lapse between an event happening and the humor about it is also lessening. **Lenny Bruce used to say that he was a part of everything he indicted.** I've tried to use that as a credo.

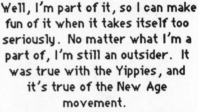

How do you react to the New Age movement?

Well, I'm part of it, so I can make fun of it when it takes itself too seriously. No matter what I'm a part of, I'm still an outsider. It was true with the Yippies, and it's true of the New Age movement. It's even true of the underground press. You know, <u>People</u> magazine called me the father of the underground press, and I wrote to them and said, **"I demand a blood test!"**

A lot of people come to the humor workshop that Scoop Nisker and I do—we've done it at three or four New Age resort-type places—and one guy said, "I'm tired of coming to these places and banging on a pillow and crying about mommy and daddy. I just want to laugh." And that's consistent. People say, **"There's so much stress in my life, I want to re-learn, regain my sense of humor."**

Finally, at the end of a long and satisfying conversation, Paul Krassner and Hector Glasco say goodbye.
Glasco drives home to his apartment, where an unexpected annoyance awaits him.

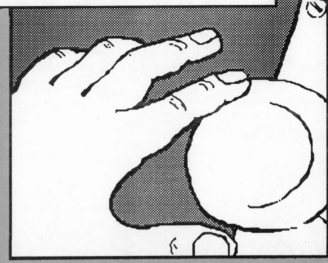

The Jamais Vu Papers

Volume One
Number ~~Seven~~ Eight
~~June~~ July

Apologies are in order. I deeply regret the Wretched condition of the May issue (#8) of <u>The Jamais Vu Papers</u>. As my readers know, I was called away to Italy on a singulary inane piece of business. During my absence, it seems that my printer (or someone) took the liberty of maiming this publication beyond all recognition, turning it into a tawdry little comic book.

Rest assured that I also carefully investigated the possible complicity of my secretary, Miss Bellows, but she assures me that she had nothing to do with that disgraceful ~~comic book issue.~~ I am of a mind to give her the benefit of the doubt and another chance, especially since I might have great difficulty finding other office help at this problematic [redundant?]

point in my career. I assure you once again that this publication is not a game. These papers were intended solely to seek information in a legitimate and dignified manner. Although my colleagues have not flocked to my aid, *Ital* I am going to seek their advice in making this a top-flight, erudite, sober-headed endeavor.

Toward this end, I have fired my printer. Why I ever felt the need for such "expertise" I can't presently imagine. Surely desktop publishing is no unfathomable mystery. I will simply type my text on the office computer, and let Miss Bellows show me how to use the page layout software. She can also proof the material and I will enter corrections when

there is time. I am fully confident that, quite on my own, I can put forth a newsletter which is both informative and visually appealing. As for my printer, let him make his fortune working for Mad Magazine or some other enterprise worthy of his "talents."

I am more determined than ever to find and cure my patient, ~~called~~ *referred to as* Hilary in these pages. The antidote to "M" is my "white whale," so to speak. These papers are no place for levity!

In fact, I must report on a most serious matter. I have discovered that the esteemed Dr. Savonarola has perpetrated a massive hoax on us all. Or, if this matter has been common knowledge in the scientific community all along, then I have been doubly hoaxed!

That's big of you! —G.B.

Still unable to reach Imogene Savonarola, I went to a nearby university science library to research her ideas. I am still in a state of shock over my discovery: an innocuous-looking research paper published in an erudite medical journal -- ten years ago.

Her paper, I Seem to Be a Placebo, finally bares the truth! I hereby publish an excerpt from it with the permission of The Pineal Journal.

As you know, Savonarola wrote to me, claiming to have recently "discovered" the existence of paradox receptors in the brain, and of "oxymorphins" neurotransmitters for metaphorical insight -- and also of a drug called M-- the chemical equivalent of a metaphor.

All this time, her real secret was laying almost forgotten on a library shelf ticking away like an ideological time

bomb: the whole thing was a hoax! Savonarola made up the existence of oxymorphins and paradox receptors 10 years ago. (Query: Why was I the last to know?)

But no ordinary hoax. This one put Peking Man in the shade. Savonarola had perpetrated a hoax of such potent scientific and

mythical power that it was destined to be proven correct in any laboratory in the modern world!

Hence the Hoax Principle: that fictional ideas, like placebos, can attain an astounding level of reality through sheer persuasive force.

As you, being better informed than myself, may already know, Savonarola's "experiments" were succesfully replicated in six major research laboratories. Oxymorphins corresponding precisely to Savonarola's chemical fibs were, indeed, discovered in the human nervous

system. Fantasy became empirical reality. By rights, the Hoax Principle should now be as much a truth of modern science as gravity or evolution.

A few timid letters to the journal editor suggested that the Hoax Principle itself was a hoax, that Savonarola's supposedly "fradulent experiments" were, in fact, quite real.

"We certainly give her all due credit for discovering the oxymorphin," declared a spokesman for the opposing camp, "but we doubt very much that the discovery is a truly valid hoax. In fact, we believe the hoax itself to be an arrogant fraud -- a hoax within a hoax."

Clearly, nothing came of their objections. Even so, Savonarola's paper has left certain mysteries unresolved. She did not divulge the recipe for M ("the most potent placebo of all time," as she calls it) or its antidote.

H. GLASCO

CONCLUSIONS: "THE HOAX PRINCIPLE"

In this paper, I have given you a full, biochemical run-down on these entities I call oxymorphins. Serious researchers and laymen alike should be satisfied that I have, indeed, discovered the brain's neurotransmitters for paradox, and have more than adequately explained their function and chemical structure. I have shared the foregoing with many colleagues, who are convinced that my research and my conclusions are utterly airtight. Now I would like to drop a tiny bombshell.

What if I am making it all up?

No, you'll say. That just can't be. The facts add up much too well to be fabricated.

But I confess: this entire study is a fiction, pure and simple. Lies, lies, nothing but lies. The chemical formulas are sheer jibberish. I dashed them off the top of my head in between reading some very enjoyable poems by Gerard Manley Hopkins. And the experiments are entirely made up. I never set foot in a laboratory with any of these hypotheses. The entire premise underlying this work is utter and complete nonsense. But before you throw this book away in a blind fit of rage, I would like to offer this final challenge.

Replicate this study!

Preposterous, you say. How can you replicate a hoax?

But you see, the true question is not whether there are or are not receptors and neurotransmitters for paradox, but whether fiction can manifest as reality.

I have fabricated an extremely potent theory/myth in these pages. It has entered the vast field of human credulity by the age-old method of King Solomon and has been reinforced by your undying respect for empiricism and scientific reasoning. It is now ready to become literal reality—and will do so in any laboratory in the world.

Hence, the "Hoax Principle," which maintains the following: Flat-out lies can come true, if they appeal eloquently enough to the credulity of both sides of the mind/brain—to our sense of myth and intuition, and to our sense of logic and ratiocination as well.

As a therapist, I have often practiced an interesting form of placebo therapy—one initially suggested by Howard Brody of Michigan State University. When a patient comes in with an illness or ailment, I give them a little pill. "Take this," I say. "It will make you all better."

"But what is it?" they invariably ask.

"It's a placebo," I explain. "A little sugar pill. It has absolutely no intrinsic medical value. But let's both think of it as powerful medicine." The patients take the placebo, knowing exactly what it is. They almost always get better.

This very paper is a placebo, which I have administered with similar honesty. Let us all believe, so that it may prove powerful!

On the other hand, there is a place for scoffers. Many will try to prove this theory wrong. So let me make another little prediction: the Hoax Principle will prove *even more valid* among the scoffers! *Paradoxically, there is ultimately nothing more affirming and empowering than vigorous disapprobation.* Why? Because the energy it takes to attack an idea betrays an underlying belief in that idea. The stronger the attack, the stronger the intuition that it might be true. Believers will find my bogus theories to be true; debunkers will find them even more true.

I would like to close this discussion with a little piece of legend. King Solomon lived in a time much like our own, a time teetering on the edge of a new consciousness. He, like most humans before him, was used to getting all his information from voices all around him. Today, we would call these voices hallucinations. But Solomon knew they were the *elohim*—the many voices of Yahweh himself.

But one day, Solomon learned something in an entirely new way. He learned by considering a possibility, a hypothesis, and then by testing its truth.

He made the first objective, scientific discovery.

"Perhaps," Solomon mused, "the stars are out by day as well as by night. Perhaps it is the binding light of the sun which obliterates them from our sight." He asked the *elohim* if this were true. But the voices did not come. He was bothered by this. It was the first time in his life when the *elohim* had failed to answer him. He would have to discover the truth by the power of his own mind—a thing no human being had ever done.

So, in the middle of the afternoon one day, he had himself lowered into the deepest well in Jerusalem. It was very dark inside the well. It swallowed up all the daylight. He looked up toward the opening of the well. Though it was little and far away, through it he could see the stars.

His idea had proven true.

It was only then that the *elohim* spoke to him again.

"You have done well, Solomon," they said. "You have learned a great new way of thinking. You have discovered a truth about the world for yourself without our help. So we will tell you yet another truth.

"Just like the stars, your dreams are out by day. It is only the light of your waking mind that obscures them. If you turn your mind into a well and climb down to the bottom, you can look up and see your dreams, even when you are wide awake."

So right then and there, Solomon turned his mind into a well and climbed deep inside and looked above. And it was just as the *elohim* had said. His dreams were everywhere, just the same as in sleep. And it was very wonderful.

This new way of thinking caught on. But the *elohim* went away from humankind. For the rest of his reign, Solomon sought to merge the new way of thinking with the old. He wanted people to keep discovering things for themselves, but he also wanted the *elohim* to come back. He sought the Elixir to blend the two ways of thinking into one. But he failed.

"Perhaps," he mused as he lay dying, "it will take human beings three thousand years to put this matter straight."

So—here we are. And what is the foregoing? Is it historical fact? Is it time-honored legend? Or is it more outrageous fiction from the pen of Imogene Savonarola? I can only answer this question with another question:

What's the difference, anyway?

The only answer is to put the question to the test!

In Wotan's Kingdom

". . . but a *comic book!*" cried Hector, trying vainly, as usual, to impress Max Henderson with the anomalousness of his situation. "Who turned my newsletter into a comic book? And *why?*"

Max Henderson was about to reply, but Hector stopped him. "Never mind," he said. "I know what you're going to say. 'Pure randomness.'"

"I hate to think I've gotten that predictable," said Max with a smile.

It was their first meeting since Hector had come back from Europe. As usual, they had adjourned to their accustomed Hollywood bar. Hector noticed that the thick, dark beer had become almost disconcertingly easy to swallow since he had been in England.

"For some reason," continued Hector, "I seem to be the butt of a number of hoaxes these days."

"That's hardly any surprise," said Max. "After all, you have allied yourself with one of the principal exponents of modern hoaxism."

"And who do you mean?" asked Hector.

"Why, Imogene Savonarola, of course," replied Max. "Surely you're familiar with her Hoax Principle."

"I certainly am not."

"But it's her major contribution to the world of ideas! It had a remarkable impact on the nihilist community, I must say. She came up with it—what?—some ten or fifteen years ago. Wrote it up in a rather sensational issue of *The Pineal Journal.* I can track it down for you. She demonstrated that lies could become fact if they were persuasive enough."

"But how could she prove something like that?"

"Well, she conceived of these fraudulent little neurotransmitters called oxymorphins—"

"But wait a minute! Those are real! They're the basis of M, that blasted drug of hers!"

"Of course they're real. They're real *because* she managed to convince everybody they were real. Come now, Glasco. Surely you knew all along that this drug of hers was a *placebo.*"

Hector stared at Max in stunned silence.

"She took advantage of my gullibility!" he said at last.

"Don't let that bother you, old fellow," chortled Max. "If it weren't for gullibility, nobody would ever believe anything. And if nobody believed anything, nothing would be real!"

But Hector wasn't in the frame of mind to consider the implications of this Hoax Principle business. Hilary's disappearance had been bizarre enough without it being attributable to the effect of a placebo. He gulped down a good swallow of dark English ale. He seemed to be positively developing a taste for it.

Then he proceeded to tell Max about his adventures in Europe—at least what he could remember of them.

"The trip wasn't totally wasted," Hector concluded. "I *did* learn something of Hilary's whereabouts. She seems likely to be at Venice, *California*, not Italy."

Max's eyes lit up with excitement. "But I must go there with you!" he exclaimed joyfully. "Venice Beach is my shrine, my sanctuary, my refuge, my sanctum sanctorum! I do insist, Hector! Let me be your guide through its Eleusian mysteries!"

And in a few moments, they were driving down La Brea Avenue in Hector's car, headed for the Santa Monica Freeway. Once they hit the freeway, Hector began to regret bringing Max along. The corpulent scholar suddenly seemed to find everything about the trip humorous—including the pockets of backed-up traffic which plagued them every few moments. Max grinned broadly as they repeatedly spent motionless intervals staring at the inglorious backsides of eighteen-wheelers, misogynist mudflaps adorned with lithe, buxom ladies silhouetted in silver. Great dimples formed in Max's chubby face. His numerous chins jiggled with glee.

But was Max amused by the female effigies or the intransigent traffic? Hector didn't dare ask. He was sure it would only unleash a torrent of philosophical blather.

Once off the freeway and a mile or so down Lincoln Boulevard, Max directed Hector south down Rose Avenue toward an alleged parking lot. As they turned the corner, Hector glimpsed two mangy-looking characters making an obvious drug drop. A strong feeling of xenophobia welled up.

They drove past a floridly painted rose designating a café, continued a block, and found themselves trapped in a line of cars facing the ocean but going nowhere. Hector glanced uncomfortably at a giant plastic figure with a masculine clown's head on a ballerina's body. The sculpture adorned an expensive-looking apartment complex.

He tried hard not to look at it. Eventually the cars in front of them crawled forward, disappearing one by one into the void ahead.

Max laughed heartily and clapped his hands together. He looked like an over-sized baby getting a new toy. Hector could no longer contain his exasperation.

"Max, would you please tell me what's so funny?" he asked.

"Never mind," said Max. "If you don't get life's never-ending punchline, there's no use trying to explain."

"There is a parking lot up ahead, isn't there?"

"We'll find out, won't we?"

"I like to know where I'm going from one minute to the next," groaned Hector.

"And I despise knowing *anything*," parried Max. "'*Le moral, c'est le traveling,*' as Jean-Luc Godard once said."

As it turned out, there *was* a parking lot, and Hector's car eventually reached it. "Four dollars," a large sign announced. It also said "No U Turn." The street was a dead end. Hector guessed that he had experienced the first of Venice Beach's many literal "tourist traps."

Hector parked the car, and he and Max trundled across the parking lot. They were accosted by no less than five panhandlers in rapid succession. Max treated each of them like royalty. He gave them alarming amounts of money.

"Do you give money to every beggar you meet?" Hector asked, nonplussed by Max's generosity.

"Yep," said Max bluntly.

"But why?"

"Don't you know the legend? Whenever you meet a mendicant, it's really Wotan, the owner of the land. He's not asking for money for himself, since all surrounding riches belong to him. He's asking charity for others. He is the godfather of the poor."

Hector shook his head. "I don't know, Max," he said. "The streets sure are full of Wotans these days. As your therapist, I really must warn you against behaving as if myths and legends were true."

"Who said they *were* true? They're just no more *untrue* than anything else."

Hector didn't say anything. There was nothing to say. *After all,* he mused, *nonsense is an irrefutable thing.*

They stepped out of the parking lot and joined the throng along Ocean Front Walk. People were walking, wandering, and jogging by in both directions, on the paved walkway and also on the wide beach. Some of them perambulated about on roller skates, bicycles, skateboards, wheelchairs, and unheard-of contraptions which seemed to have been assembled from spare parts of all the others. One woman pushed a man sprawled in a shopping cart.

To the left were buildings, canopies, pushcarts, and shops, all selling a wild clutter of clothing, sunglasses, and small items that sparkled in the sun. To the right were trees, patches of grass, benches, and a winding, paved bicycle path. Beyond all this was a wide beach dotted with people. Waves crashed on the shore, making a soothing sound like radio static.

The fresh, salty air startled Hector. The clutter of activity startled him even more. Beside the walkway, a black man adorned in feathers pounded a conga drum. On the next bench, a long-haired boy played a guitar and sang. Not far away, a black saxophonist played soulfully from his wheelchair. Although the three musicians showed no awareness of each other, their music mingled with gleeful incongruity.

Walking along, Max and Hector encountered a couple of jugglers trying to make an eight-year-old boy swallow a machete. An amused crowd watched, apparently unperturbed by a demented transient's intermittent threats to pull the pin out of a live hand grenade. Another man leapt off a chair onto a pile of broken liquor bottles. Hector couldn't bring himself to look; Max didn't divert his eyes for a moment. But even Hector couldn't help paying horrified attention as another man juggled a ball and a live chain saw. A turbaned and white-robed guitar player wafted by on roller skates, singing an improvised, elegiacal song which was broadcast through a hidden microphone.

Venice Beach abounded with weight lifters, musicians, accupressurists, crystal salesmen, reflexologists, T-shirt hawkers, comedians, nutritionists, kite flyers, drug dealers, tarot readers, fire eaters, sidewalk artists, astrologers, tourists, and transients.

"How can I expect to find Hilary in a place like this?" asked Hector despairingly.

"Easy," replied Max pleasantly. "Ask somebody." And Max immediately seized the first person he encountered—a black man wearing a dark brown wool blanket cut into the shape of a poncho. The color of the fabric matched the man's skin, eyes, beard, and hair perfectly. He was the most monochromatic human being Hector had ever encountered.

"Excuse me," asked Max, "but have you seen a famous female movie star, shining dark hair, Garbo-esque cheekbones, gracefully flaring nostrils, a fine figure neither too ample nor anorexic, languorous legs, about oh-so-tall, twenty-five years old, a Taurus with certain Cancer traits, a household name, a cultural icon, the envy of all men the world o'er, whose recent disappearance has provoked such a dreadful spate of media hype?"

"Man, you could be talkin' about any of my girlfriends," replied the fellow pertly. And he walked on.

"Very good," Hector muttered to Max.

"Yes," said Max with apparent sincerity. "A valuable clue. I think we're making excellent progress."

As they continued their safari, Hector couldn't help noticing that absolutely everybody was staring at them. At last he realized that they were the only people in the entire throng wearing business suits. To the Venice natives, he and Max seemed exotic and bizarre.

Hector longed to be his usual innocuous self. He wanted to hide somewhere. The bright colors, the constant motion, the laughing voices and the music, together with the smell of sweat and the press of bodies were all too much for him.

At last, they reached the celebrated Sidewalk Café. Sculpted faces stared down at the tabletops from the tops of enormous mock-Venetian columns. A striped canvas awning filtered out the sunlight. So this was the place which had been mentioned in that aberrational comic book.

"Let's stop here," said Hector. "I'd like to rest a minute, maybe get some lunch and a cup of coffee."

"Want to share?" the waiter asked, gesturing toward several partially occupied tables.

"No!" Hector said emphatically, even as Max was nodding "yes."

"Be about half an hour for a table for two," the waiter said. "Stand in line."

Looking over the long line of bedraggled tourists, Hector finally agreed and followed along behind Max as the waiter led them to a table right next to the sidewalk. There, the awning gave them no protection from the glaring summer afternoon sun. Across from them, a diminutive fellow sat hidden behind a menu.

"Let's see, what'll I have?" mused their tablemate. "Maybe a sandwich. Here's one called a 'Jane Fonda.' I guess the waiter apologizes when he serves it. Or an 'Andy Warhol.' You have to eat it in fifteen minutes."

Then he lowered the menu. His eyes sparkled. His round, pleasant face was topped with curly black hair. Hector immediately recognized the face from the comic book.

"You're Paul Krassner!" Hector cried. "And you're real!"

"You do me too much honor," Krassner replied.

"Oh, forgive me," stammered Hector, "but I had reason to think you were a fictional character."

"The feeling's mutual, I'm sure," said Krassner, reaching across the table to shake Hector's hand. "I didn't catch your name."

"Hector Glasco."

"Ah, yes. I ran across some issues of your newsletter—*the jamais vu papers.* And interestingly enough, I was in one of them—as a comic book character."

Hector apologized profusely, explaining that that particular issue had gone out without his knowledge. But Krassner didn't seem the least bit bothered.

"I'm sure it was true in its way," he said.

Max pumped Krassner's hand with zeal. "Mr. Krassner, it is indeed a pleasure," he explained. "I've been following your work for years. It is safe to say that you and your writings inspired me to become the disruptive, unruly, and academically unconscionable iconoclast that I am today."

Krassner returned this dubious compliment with a nod of polite skepticism. The waiter came. Krassner ordered a small dinner salad. Max ordered a "New York Review," a hot dog smothered with sauerkraut. Hector ordered a "Timothy Leary," a hamburger topped with avocado and sautéed mushrooms.

Hector knew nothing about Krassner or his work, but Max was obviously a longtime fan of Krassner's own publication, *The Realist*. The therapist sat dumbly as the scholar probed the satirist with questions.

"What prompted you," Max asked, "to write Lenny Bruce's obituary two years *before* he died?"

"I was hanging around with Lenny at the time," Krassner replied, "and there was almost a competition among police departments to bust him. Nightclub owners were scared. He was not getting work, and his work was his life. So it was if he *were* dead. I wanted to pay tribute and expose that harassment while he was alive. It was strange, the response to it. People who read six newspapers a day thought they must have missed that item, or that it was suppressed, and other people just thought that they missed the paper that day, because it was presented realistically enough and was not unlikely.

"When I told Lenny about it and asked for his permission, he asked, 'But why do you want to do it?'

"'Well,' I said, 'because when you *really* die, my mourning will be pure. I won't have to think, "Oh, shit, now I have to write an obituary."'

"He said, 'Okay, you can do it. But I want to call up my mother first. One more thing, though. What makes you think I'm gonna go before you do?'

"Then somebody did an obituary of *me*, and I really resented it. They said, 'Well, you did the one on Lenny.'

"'Yeah,' I said, 'but there was a reason for that. There's no reason for this except that it's not true. You're not making any point with it except to fool people.'"

This distinction caught Hector's interest. He looked up from his half-devoured Timothy Leary. "So there's a difference between honest and dishonest hoaxing?"

"Creative and easy," said Krassner, finishing up his salad. "Having a point or being pointless."

Hector saw little point in propounding further falsehoods in a world already too fraught with uncertainty. But he knew he was outnumbered two to one.

"I got a call from Associated Press at three o'clock in the morning to check it out," Krassner continued. "I said, 'No, no, no, that was just a hoax.'

"But the reporter wanted to know, 'Well, how can I be sure?'

"'Well, look,' I said, 'I'd *tell* you if I was dead.'"

Max laughed gleefully, and he and Krassner chattered together throughout the meal. Hector concentrated on his sandwich. Finally the three of them paid their bills and left the café.

"Pssst," whispered Krassner conspiratorially to Max and Hector. "Wanna see an example of situational ethics?"

"Sure," said Hector and Max in perfect unison.

Krassner withdrew a purloined fork from his pocket. "I needed a fork," he said with a grin. "That's the situation."

Max exploded into gales of laughter. Hector mustered up a giggle but suspected that he had somehow missed the point of the joke.

Krassner gave the doubled-up Max a nudge. "I've got a strict code, though," he said. "I only steal from restaurants where I eat regularly."

Max erupted into further explosions of unbridled mirth. Hector looked around uneasily. He discovered that they were standing outside Small World Books, which adjoined the Sidewalk Café. He headed in that direction, and Max and Krassner followed.

It was not Hector's intention to buy a book—but bookstores tended to have a tranquilizing effect on him. There was something calming about the presence of so many words. Even his all-too-certain inability to read even a fraction of these words during his lifetime was, in itself, somehow soothing. It gave him a comforting sense of the continuity of human inquiry. It rekindled a faith that there were far more capable minds than his own in the world.

The answers to life's great questions are here, he thought as he puttered among the shelves. *They're all here somewhere.*

Krassner turned to Hector and said, "These papers of yours look pretty interesting. Maybe you've got an idea for a book there."

Hector was both flustered and flattered. "But I wouldn't even know where to begin," he said.

"Well, you could get in touch with John Brockman," Krassner suggested. "He's my literary agent. He negotiated the contract for my unauthorized auto-biography."

Krassner explained that Brockman ran a thriving New York literary agency with his home and business partner, Katinka Matson. "My respect for John really went up," Krassner recalled, "when he had an opportunity to represent Werner Erhard, but would have been 'required' to take est—and refused."

"And who knows?" he added. "You might actually get into the Reality Club." That, Krassner explained, was an elite group of intellectuals, founded by Brockman, who met regularly to "ask each other the questions they've been asking themselves."

The Reality Club's roster of speakers was staggering—a virtual Who's Who of contemporary ideas: Jerome Bruner, Annie Dillard, Freeman Dyson, Betty Friedan, Stephen Jay Gould, Rollo May, Benoit Mandelbrot, Page Smith, the late Abbie Hoffman, and many others. Hector was soon giddy at the thought of sharing such company, exchanging ideas as a peer.

Krassner began to browse through the used book section. "Brockman's famous for selling books by thinkers out on the edge—thinkers responsible for changing the way people look at the world," he said.

"Maybe you should pay Brockman a visit," added Max.

Krassner straightened up triumphantly, with a slim volume in his hand. "I'll tell you what, the next time I talk to him, I'll put in a bad word for you," he said, handing the book to Hector. "In the meantime, take a look at this."

It was called *Afterwords*—and it was written by none other than John Brockman. *Interesting*, thought Hector. *An agent, and an author in his own right.*

Max and Krassner started off down another aisle. Hector opened the book and read:

Man is dead.

That was all the first page said. The rest of it was blank. Hector felt a strange shiver of foreboding. He wasn't quite sure why. But he knew this was not an idea he wanted to deal with at the moment. He tucked the book under his arm and wandered after Max and Krassner.

"It just so happens," Max was telling Krassner, "that I have written a deconstructionist assessment of your life's work. You'll be happy to know that I divested your writings of any meaning whatsoever. . ."

Krassner and Max meandered on down another aisle as Hector stood watching. Max chattered on as Krassner nodded his head. Hector realized that the deranged academic would probably be delighted if he became the butt of Krassner's ridicule in the next issue of *The Realist.* He decided not to interrupt the conversation.

Hector went to the cashier and bought the copy of *Afterwords*. Then he left the bookstore and found himself out on Ocean Front Walk again. A group of four or five healthy-looking characters approached him. A young woman stopped directly in front of him and handed him a leaflet:

Would you like to be a Mundaner?
Physical means to deal with physical problems:
food for hunger, fuel for cold,
trees for shade and air.
If you're interested, come with me!

Hector looked at her. She was rather plain and had dark hair pulled back in a ponytail. The group with her stood quietly, not making any sales pitches, just waiting for his decision. Hector drew a deep sigh and shook his head no. He only wished that his problems were as simple as those the Mundaners proposed to solve. He stuffed the leaflet into his pocket, stepped around the woman, and headed back toward the parking lot. He felt exhausted and a little ill. He intended to go home and let Max make his own way back from his "Elysian mysteries."

But then a most peculiar sight caught his eye. It was a little wigwam made out of quilts, newspapers, and garbage bags, wrapped and tied with a certain uncouth flair around a cluster of bent curtain rods. Hector must have walked right past it as he wandered toward the shore. How had he managed to miss it?

A sign in front of the wigwam read:

Bruno the Brujo
Shamanistic Experiences, $10.00
(Today's Special, $2.50)

Bruno, ruminated Hector. *Where have I heard that name before?*

The Deconstructionist Deconstructed

"And so you see how that very juxtaposition completes the deconstruction of meaning in your last essay. . . ."

Max Henderson was chattering away to Paul Krassner as he walked through the mythology section of Small World Books. Then he turned and realized that Krassner had disappeared.

He smiled. How long had his listener been gone? Long enough, surely, to make him look very foolish indeed to everybody present. Max was all the more pleased at this. The untimely disappearance of such a clever hoaxter was quite as it should be.

"Curiouser and curiouser!" muttered Max.

He wandered aimlessly through the bookshop. Straight ahead was a large table covered with half-priced books. A pair of handsome iron bookends flanked the books. An enormous and fluffy light-orange cat lolled contently among the inexpensive volumes. A smile spread from ear to ear across the creature's face.

Max bent over and whispered to the cat. "So tell me, my furry friend," queried Max. "Are you a hoaxter, too?"

The cat said nothing, but nimbly climbed up on Max's shoulder, purring loudly. Max petted the cat, which stretched out its paw and seemed to point ahead. Max looked toward where the cat beckoned. He saw a display stand featuring the Second Edition of the Oxford English Dictionary, acclaimed by many of the world's cleverest people (including as fine a fellow as Anthony Burgess!) as a truly grand and important thing.

All the volumes were not on display, of course. Why, that would have taken up most of the store! But Volume XVII, fatter itself than the fattest of ordinary dictionaries, was perched proudly on a small, cardboard podium.

Max's mouth began to water. It was as if he were standing outside a pastry shop looking through the window at a rack filled with freshly made cream horns. He couldn't resist. He simply had to have a taste. He walked toward the portly volume with the cat on his shoulder.

The book spread out majestically before his eyes. Volume XVII was opened to page 876. Words, words, and more words spread out upon the pages in front of him.

And what is the use of a book without pictures or conversations? considered Max in his best postmodern manner

Nevertheless, he let his eyes focus upon the letters on the page. One word—and one word only—caught his eye:

the

He turned the page. Then he turned the pages again and again and again. Imagine how startled he was to see that the definition for the word "the" went from page 876 to 880!

Such a little word! mused Max. *And so many thousands upon thousands of words needed to define it! The word "the" will surely grow big-headed and disagreeable with so many other words at its beck and call, waiting on it hand and foot! I'm certainly glad I know the definition of "the" already. I should become very confused indeed if I had to learn it from* this *dictionary!*

But, turning to the cat, Max asked, "What *does* 'the' mean, anyway? Goodness gracious, I seem to have quite forgotten!"

The cat only smiled mischievously.

"It only goes to show," said Max, "that one can earn great bundles of degrees from all smartest schools, and still forget the simplest little thing! I do hope my department chairman doesn't learn of this! But surely he'll become suspicious the next time he says 'the' and I have no idea what he's talking about! Perhaps I'd better see what this dictionary has to say about the word 'the' after all!"

But imagine Max's distress when he found passages like this:

> **17.** *The* is used with a sb. particularized or described by an adjective. The adj. usually precedes, but sometimes follows the sb.: in either case *the* stands first as *the good man, the church militant.*
>
> (An adj. or pple. with a modifying addition regularly follows the sb., as 'the grass wet with dew,' 'the tools needed for the work': cf. 15c.)

"I seem to understand the word 'the' less and less by the very minute!" said Max to the cat. "In fact—I can't remember the meanings of any words at all!"

He was so much surprised that for the moment he quite forgot that words have no referents, anyway—and of what use is a word without a referent?

But in any case, Max could think of no words whatsoever. His brain seemed to have emptied itself of language like a punctured balloon.

Curiouser and curiouser, mused Max again, with rather more consternation than he had at Krassner's disappearance. But of course, he really mused no such thing. He could not think any thoughts at all, because he had no words to think with. His mind was a blank. He knew it, too.

Oh dear, oh dear! he did not muse. *If I have no words, then I must not be thinking! Still, it certainly* seems *as though I'm thinking. But I must only* think *I'm thinking!*

Bereft of language, Max continued frantically not to contemplate his situation. *What to do, what to do!* he did not think.

He looked at the people shopping in a leisurely manner all around him. Before he could think of what to call them, the people disappeared.

He looked upon the thousands of books everywhere. Before he could think of what to call them, the books disappeared.

He stood facing the pair of fine-looking iron bookends with no books between them. Before he could think of what to call them, the bookends disappeared.

Max had no words for shelves, floor, walls, ceiling, or windows. And so they vanished too, leaving him in nothingness.

All that was left in Max's world was the cat on his shoulder. But without a name, the cat too was starting to fade into nothingness in a most slippery and nonchalant manner.

"Oh, furry creature, whatever you are called!" Max did not cry. "Do come back again, and we won't talk about words, or referents either, if you don't like them!"

But the cat was gone, leaving not even a trace of a smile.

*One afternoon the boys grew
enthusiastic over the flying carpet
that went swiftly by the laboratory
at window level carrying the gypsy
who was driving it and several
children from the village who were
merrily waving their hands, but
José Arcadio Buendía did not even
look at it. "Let them dream," he
said. "We'll do better flying than
they are doing, and with more
scientific resources than a miserable
bedspread."*

Gabriel García Márquez
One Hundred Years of Solitude
Gregory Rabassa, trans.

The Teachings of Bruno the *Brujo* Part I

For some reason, Hector felt drawn to the inexpensive sorcerer. Or perhaps he just hoped that the little wigwam would offer a sanctuary from the overwhelming sensory overload of Ocean Front Walk. He ducked inside. It did offer the relief of an enclosed space, but the aroma was definitely no improvement. He found Bruno in a huddle, snoring profoundly, his arms wrapped around a bottle of cheap tequila only half-concealed by the remnants of a brown paper bag. There was nothing about his demeanor or wardrobe to distinguish Bruno from any of the local transients.

Hector was afraid to awaken the *brujo.* His recent trials weighed heavily on him, and he needed some sleep himself. But, in contrast to his narcoleptic misadventures in Europe, he had lately been plagued by chronic insomnia. When he did sleep fitfully, he dreamed hardly at all. He lowered himself carefully onto a bulging, tattered cushion, hoping to rest quietly for a little while.

After a few moments, Bruno snorted in his sleep, lifted his head, and took a sip of tequila.

"I know you," muttered Bruno. "You come seeking the Carpet Flyer."

Hector was indeed startled. "Yes, Hilary!" he cried. "Can you tell me where she is?"

Bruno sat up and chuckled. "You will find her when you wish."

Hector's heart sank again. Clearly, the old magician was full of riddles, and he'd had enough of those. But as he gazed at Bruno, something dawned on him.

"I've seen you before!" he said.

"Yes?" said Bruno with a quizzical smile.

"I saw you racing by on a water ski."

"And where did you see me?"

"In my—" But Hector choked on the next word.

"In your what, my friend?" probed Bruno.

"No, it's too silly."

"Only the truly silly things are worth saying. Come now!"

But Hector could only stare dumbly.

"I believe you were about to say 'dream,'" said Bruno. "At least I hope you were. Because the last time *I* saw *you* was in a dream."

Hector broke into a sweat. True, he could remember lengthy excerpts of dreams he'd had while in Europe. And true, he could remember those dreams in considerably better detail than his waking activities abroad. But surely. . .

"Is such a thing possible?" he asked urgently. "Please tell me. I've heard such strange talk lately—whether in dreams or in waking, I can't always remember. But I have been told that the Sleeping World is as real as this Waking World, and that people are born into both realms. But how can this be? How can you meet flesh-and-blood people in your sleep? After all, a dream is just an hallucination, a product of a sense-deprived cortex trying to make meaning out of random signals from the brain stem. It's merely a neurochemical phenomenon, and primarily an accidental one at that."

"Yes," concurred Bruno. "I believe the formula is seven parts carbon, seventeen hydrogen, one nitrogen, three oxygen—at least according to you scientific-types. Well, who am I to disagree? And yet, you have learned that you can be *lucid* in dreams?"

"But that's a different matter."

Bruno smiled broadly. "I said something to you in that dream of yours. Do you remember what it was?"

"Yes," muttered Hector, dreading what was coming next.

"Then tell me!"

"No," said Hector firmly. *"You* tell *me."*

"Very well," said Bruno, craning himself forward. "I said, 'Lucidity isn't only for dreaming.'" Then he laughed and added: "A good lesson for the moment, I believe."

Hector sat stunned. *Yes, I remember! That's exactly what he said!* But then he was struck by a realization. He, too, started to laugh exultantly.

"Thanks for clueing me in, *brujo*," he said. "Lucidity! That's what's going on here! This is another dream, and I just turned lucid!"

"It is so if you say so," said Bruno.

"And I *do* say so!" said Hector. "What about a change of scene, *brujo*? Let's get out of this rattrap. This is my dream—and I call the shots! It's on me!"

Hector stood up abruptly, fully expecting the little wigwam to vanish into a different scene—perhaps Imogene's palace, or that lovely dream garden.

It didn't.

His head struck against one of the wigwam's supporting curtain rods. It was surprisingly sturdy—and painful. The wigwam rattled and shook. Hector sank to the floor. He could feel a bump growing on his head.

"We seem to have trouble getting along in *both* realms, don't we?" said Bruno.

"I'm terribly embarrassed," said Hector.

"Of course you are. Put it behind you."

"This is *real*, then," said Hector, gazing around the tent.

Bruno laughed. "In a manner of speaking."

"But what an extraordinary magician you must be, to invade my dreams, and then appear before me in my waking life!"

"My powers are—unexceptional," said Bruno, with a modest gesture.

"May I ask you, well, a rather impertinent question?"

"I never answer any other kind."

"With powers like yours, why are you living—here?" And with a gesture, Hector indicated the squalor of the *brujo's* immediate surroundings.

Bruno grunted. "My friend, Venice Beach is one of the world's great power places. It is a story written long ago. Before Atlantis, before Lemuria, before Mu, there was Venice Beach! I, myself, have been here very long."

Then he sat for a moment, shaking his head in profound silence. His seedy clothes seemed to fall into richer folds. The blanket beneath him showed traces of an exotic design.

"King Solomon himself came to Venice Beach once," continued the *brujo*. "It was, oh, near three thousand years ago, I expect. Heard tell that we had quite a jumping place here. Heard tell about the weather and the girls. Heard tell of the mad tequila rites of the natives. Thought he'd come here to do some lucid waking. He flew here—on this."

And, lo and behold, Bruno produced from his battered pea coat the green silk carpet which had disappeared with Hilary.

Hector was astounded. He thought, in rapid succession, of calling the police to arrest the *brujo*, of snatching the carpet away from him, or of simply dashing out of the tent to escape this latest turn of madness. But he steadied himself. His mission was essential.

"Please, oh, please," he said. "Just tell me where Hilary is!"

"Another novice!" muttered Bruno. "Come. You will master Carpet Flying now. You will learn the secrets of the Magical Mundane."

And the two of them stepped outside the wigwam. Bruno unfurled the carpet and let it fall on the sand. It was an imposing relic as always, with letters in Hebrew and Chaldaic, and still larger figures around the border in a kind of writing Hector knew nothing about. But it was also, if anything, more worn and threadbare than it had been while in Hector's possession. It hardly looked like something a mythic king could have flown halfway around the world upon, in any age.

A bit awkwardly, Hector and Bruno sat down on the carpet together. And Bruno pulled out a deck of tarot cards—round ones, old and warped and torn.

"A gift!" Bruno exclaimed. "A gift from King Solomon himself!"

And he shuffled the cards vigorously—circles dancing in his hands, the starred backs of the cards whirling and merging again. Then he presented one of them to Hector.

"You must take this image inside of you," said the *brujo*. And the card was

Trump IX, "The Hermit," an elderly, robed, monklike character with a staff in one hand. His other hand was outstretched. Hector vaguely recalled that the Hermit was supposed to be holding a lamp. But instead of a lamp, this fellow held what appeared to be a star. Then again, it wasn't quite a star, but a sort of gash in the fabric of the Hermit's universe—a rip which revealed a blinding light "behind" everything. The Hermit was surrounded by similar starlike gashes, which dotted the air around him.

Hector looked up at the *brujo*, who sat cross-legged with his eyes closed, in deep concentration.

After a few long seconds, Bruno said with soft conviction: "There! We are flying now!"

Hector looked around. In one direction, a tandem bicycle sailed by carrying two businessmen. In the other direction, a little girl dunked an irritated puppy in the surf while her father laughingly wielded a video camera. Hector could feel lumps of sand beneath the carpet. He shifted on his rump uncomfortably. He found it extremely hard to stay alert.

Whatever we may be doing, he thought, *it's sure not flying*. But he thought it best to keep this observation to himself.

"And now," continued Bruno, opening his eyes with a smile, "we can continue our conversation while airborne! So tell me, my friend. Do you believe that you have mastered lucidity?"

"Do you mean lucid dreaming?" returned Hector.

"Whatever," said Bruno.

"Well, I wouldn't say I've *mastered* it. But I was getting the hang of it for a while."

"And what do you think lucid dreaming means?"

Hector shrugged. "That's fairly obvious, isn't it? It means that you know you're dreaming. It means that you behave with autonomy while in your dreams."

"The sure sign of a novice," sighed Bruno. "You think lucidity means only that one, simple thing."

"Well what else *could* it mean?"

"The lucidity you speak of is what we sorcerers call *low* lucidity—a crude, tentative, and ill-formed recognition of which realm you are in. *High* lucidity means a deeper awareness—an understanding that you share your realm with others, and that your actions have consequences to others. And now may I ask, have you mastered lucid waking?"

"Well surely," said Hector, "we are born with that."

"Are you truly aware of your wakefulness right now? Are you aware of your fellow wakers? And are you aware that we are miles above the earth at this very moment?"

Hector looked at the sand inches below. He suffered from a slight fear of heights, so even a suggestion of high altitude was normally enough to produce a sinking feeling in his lower abdomen. But not now. He felt all too safely rooted to the earth.

"And so," scolded Bruno, "you wander through the Sleeping World as if you owned the place! And you don't even comprehend your own reality. Well, let me tell you, there are Sleeping-Born people who do the same in this realm!"

"Then can it be that we *are* actually visited by people from the dream world?" wondered Hector. He tried to cling to what was left of his skepticism. But he kept thinking of Upton Orndorf—that strange little man who handed him the footnotes in Italy, then turned up in his dream, then telephoned him after he woke up in London.

"Look around you!" cried Bruno. "Read the newspaper! Where do you think we get our politicians, lawyers, New Age gurus, school superintendents, and colorizers of movies? Where do you think we get our evangelists, pimps, pollsters, and corporation heads? Where do you think we get our *experts?* Every last one of them is Sleeping-Born! Our realm is their dream, and their bodies here are but phantoms—and not one of them shows the slightest trace of lucidity!"

Hector found Bruno's words more and more convincing. Yes, the old man had to be right. He glanced quickly at the ground, to remind himself that the rug was *not* flying.

"What do you know about the Brothers and Sisters of Thaumaturgy?" asked Hector.

"They are rather exceptional souls," said Bruno with qualified admiration. "They were born in the Sleeping World, but have mastered high lucidity in both realms. They do persist in one very foolish fantasy, however. They wish to fuse the realms of Waking and Sleeping into one. They wish for all sentient forms to share the joys of both Waking and Sleeping—simultaneously."

The *brujo* spat angrily on the sand. "Rubbish, I call it! To lose the sensuous joy of stretching into a yawning wakefulness in the morning, and of drowsing lazily into yearning sleepfulness in the evening. Or the joy of taking dozens of voluptuous catnaps and catwakes day and night—which is more to my liking! I want nothing to do with their hair-brained prophecies.

"There is only one of them that recognizes the foolishness of their plans—but poor Orndorf has not mastered sufficient lucidity to stop them."

"Orndorf!" Hector snorted. "He has only mastered gluttony." Then he asked warily, "And what of Imogene Savonarola?"

"Their leader, obviously," said Bruno perfunctorily. "The Grand Matron is a stubborn dame. Bit on the flakey side. But impressive in her way." Then Bruno surveyed the scene around him. "A remarkable view, don't you think?" he asked. "And such a clear day! You can see all the way from Big Bear Lake to Catalina! And isn't that San Diego to the south?"

Hector leapt to his feet. "That's enough, old man!" he cried. "Don't try to tell me this carpet is flying!"

Bruno nodded politely. "Ah, skepticism," he said. "Always the best policy."

Hector began to pace up and down the carpet. "Just tell me what's true and what's not true," he shouted. "Are you making this stuff up about dreams or not? Because I'm confused enough already. I don't have time to waste on riddles. Do you actually want me to believe that the the entire cosmos is based on *Little Nemo in Slumberland?*"

"Actually—"

"If it is, just *tell* me so," interrupted Hector. "But don't lie to me in the same breath. Don't tell me this carpet is flying when I can see perfectly well it's not."

"I'd watch my step if I were you. That's quite an abyss below your feet."

"There's no damned abyss! And we're not flying!"

And to demonstrate, Hector stepped off the rug onto the surrounding sand.

"Oh, dear," said Bruno with eerie detachment. "You're falling. You gave me no chance to catch you."

Hector's eyes were caught by Bruno's hypnotic gaze. The *brujo*'s eyes were deep and dark. They seemed to reflect something familiar. But what was it? Hector became extremely tired.

"I'm not falling," he said firmly.

"Oh, but you are," whispered the *brujo* almost inaudibly. "I have to shout so you can hear me."

"I'm not falling," he repeated.

But dizziness seized him. He staggered a little. And what was it that he thought he saw deep in Bruno's eyes?

"I'm sorry, friend," breathed Bruno. "There's nothing I can do to help you."

The sounds, sights, and smells of Venice began to vanish, one by one.

"I'm . . . not . . . falling."

But he couldn't hear his own, feeble protest. He could only feel his lips shape the words one last time:

"I'm . . . not . . . falling."

Hector's world was empty, save for the bottomless, black pools of Bruno's eyes.

They reflected the face of a gigantic clock . . .

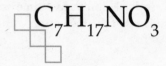# C₇H₁₇NO₃

<h1>$C_7H_{17}NO_3$</h1>

Hector and Imogene crashed through the gigantic clock face.

The impact almost sent them hurtling in opposite directions, but they clung to each other's wrists for dear life. The clock face shattered. From the other side, still plunging downward, they could see it fragmenting in all directions, growing smaller in the distance. But had they crashed into the clock itself or merely its reflection in a pool? And was it now disintegrating into shardlike particles or into rippling waves?

Paradoxically, Hector knew that both were true. He and Imogene had broken through the barrier of temporality. All dichotomies had vanished. And Hector felt no confusion about what had happened a moment before. He could remember—everything! He could remember seizing Imogene's hand among the weird throng of masked Thaumaturgists and falling through space with her. And he could remember the *brujo*'s hypnotic gaze just before he fell asleep. He was lucid, and in both realms.

They maneuvered their bodies like sky divers and faced each other lovingly. Staring into Imogene's eyes, Hector was overwhelmed by the strangest, sweetest melancholy.

"What is it, Hector?" asked Imogene. "What do you want?"

"I want to make love to you," said Hector. "But I know I'm just a phantom in this realm. Your body is here, and mine is on a beach in California. And I have never wanted to touch a woman so much."

Imogene smiled. "Sad, isn't it? My life's dream has always been that bodies like ours might meet in a common realm. Still, we can always have the *illusion* of touch."

And tenderly, Imogene's hand touched Hector's wrist. His clothing turned into a small flock of winged creatures, flying away and leaving him utterly unclothed. He reached toward Imogene and touched her. Her gown, too, sprouted mothlike wings and fled her body, leaving her in resplendent nakedness.

They embraced as they fell—a falling which was also flying. There was no earth, no gravity, no space, not even movement. There was only the light-speed sailing through time itself—not through time future or time past, but downward, ever downward, through time *below*. Wild rivers swept and carried them, first sideways, then in circles, then in spirals through the wild, sweet clearness of time. They shot the rapids of time. They breathed, drank, and drowned in liquid time.

Their limbs—hundreds, perhaps thousands of them—thrashed and curled and wrapped around each other with wild abandon. But whose arms, legs, and other appendages belonged to whom? Neither sight nor touch could tell—nor the boundless smorgasbord of other senses at their disposal. There was a glorious sense of unity, coupled with a feeling of unfathomable multiplicity. Hector and Imogene vanished into each other, and into all sentience. The number "two" lost every meaning. The only numbers in the universe were zero—and infinity.

If this is illusion, thought Hector, *I'll have nothing more to do with reality.*

When it ended, they curled together naked in the bottom of a Venetian gondola, panting, exhilarated, absolutely languid. The gondolier sang. From his mouth came no Italian aria, but the strains of a classical string quartet. Other gondolas floated in the air around them, some close by, others farther off, still others tiny specks in the crystalline distance. In each of the gondolas, Hector and Imogene could see mirror images of themselves in glorious afterglow. They were two again—and it was perfect.

But before long, he sensed that she was troubled. "What's wrong?" he asked.

"Hilary is gone," she said with gentle resignation. "The prophecy was wrong. Sleeping and waking must remain two separate realms, maybe forever."

"Is that so bad?" asked Hector.

"I can't tell you how tired I am," came Imogene's reply.

A question formed on Hector's lips. He didn't immediately know what the question was, so he hesitated to ask it. He sensed that it might be indelicate—perhaps even a little lewd. But at last, he asked it anyway.

"Imogene—would you wake with me?"

She lifted her head from his shoulder and looked into his eyes. He detected that she was slightly shocked at the intimacy of the suggestion—the carnality. *Yes, it is presumptuous, even crude,* he thought. *After all we've just experienced, to want to be an awkward, clumsy, waking body pressing into hers, struggling stupidly and vainly to be one with her. . . How can I even think of it? Still, it's only an illusion, whatever the realm.*

"I know you'd be a phantom there, as I'm a phantom here," he said. "I know our touching must always be illusion. And perhaps we won't awaken in each other's arms, but on opposite sides of the earth. But just to know that we're awake on the same planet at the same time—wouldn't that be wonderful lovemaking?"

Imogene smiled. "It would be lovely." But then her eyes turned sad.

"I can't," she said.

Hector felt like a tormented teenager. He swallowed hard and said, "I understand."

Imogene touched his face. "No," she said. "You don't understand. You can't understand, and I am sorry. Just please believe me."

She vanished from his side. Hector jumped up, rocking the gondola about in the air. The poor gondolier almost toppled into the bottomless blue twilight.

Hector leapt out of the craft, not knowing where he'd fall. He found himself square in the center of the piazza where he had first debarked in Venice. Imogene stood facing him, costumed in a shining white Victorian dress and hat, her hair quite immaculately perfect, carrying a white parasol.

The other entities roaming the piazza were dressed likewise, the men in black tails with top hats, the women all with bustles and parasols. They moved in dainty, geometrical perambulations, like figurines out of a Dresden clockwork. Hector was embarrassedly aware of what a rude figure he presented among them—stark naked, staggering about, dripping with sweat, and wildly and visibly aroused.

He lunged at Imogene, but she warded him off. "Please, Hector," she said with grace and self-possession. "Let me go. I have a train to catch." Then she turned and walked away.

The surrounding dance continued as Hector made a mad dash toward Imogene. But the space before him stretched out wildly. The piazza was suddenly hundreds of miles deep, becoming darker by the second. Imogene continued her leisurely pace, but Hector couldn't catch up with her. Calliope music played. And at the end of the descending darkness, crazily lighted and rising miles into the sky, was that gigantic Ferris wheel again, carrying hundreds of passenger cars. It turned very slowly

As he followed Imogene, he heard the wheel making a decelerating chug-chug-chug, like an old-time steam-powered railroad engine grinding to a halt. Rust-colored clouds arose from the pistons turning the wheel. With a whistle of brakes, it came to a complete stop. Still running, Hector saw a railroad porter with a handlebar mustache take Imogene by the hand and help her into the first available car. The chugging started up again, and the wheel lurched slightly.

"Stop that wheel!" cried Hector, running as fast as his legs could carry him. The porter made a gesture to some unseen engineer, and the chug-chug-chugging halted again. Every girder in the Ferris wheel squeaked and strained. Hector leapt into the car after Imogene.

The interior was furnished like a cabin on a continental railroad train, with facing upholstered seats. Dim lamps shaded with carnival glass protruded from the walls. Hector threw himself into the chair opposite Imogene's—out of breath, and still quite naked.

"What are we doing on this deathtrap?" he asked.

"I don't know what *you're* doing here," said Imogene. "But I'm going to Florence. I have something important to tell my father."

124

"Florence!" exclaimed Hector. "But this damned thing is planted in the ground! It's not taking you anywhere!"

"This is a *dream*, Hector," purred Imogene jadedly. "You know the rules are different here."

A shrill train whistle pierced the air. The engines puffed and groaned. The car lurched forward, carrying them upward. Hector averted his eyes as the anemic lights of Venice slipped into the dizzying void below. The conductor tapped on the compartment door and opened it.

"Your tickets, signore and signora?" he enquired, his white-gloved hand outstretched.

"We don't need tickets," growled Hector.

"To be sure," agreed the conductor. "But perhaps a suit for signore?"

"I prefer to be naked," snarled Hector. "And the lady prefers me that way, too."

"But of course," said the conductor with a bow. "I should have realized. I do beg your pardon." He bowed and left. Hector turned toward Imogene. She lowered her head and blushed slightly. The pinkness blazed in contrast to the whiteness of her wardrobe.

"I'm not embarrassing you, I hope," queried Hector, not meaning it for a second.

"Not at all," said Imogene. He couldn't tell if she meant it or not. They stared quietly out the window. The moon sailed by, so close they could touch its boulders and craters. It took many long minutes to pass.

"I thought things happened in dreams exactly as one wished," remarked Hector irritably.

"They do," said Imogene.

"Then if you want to go to Florence, why don't you snap your fingers and just be there? Why risk your neck in this infernal thing?"

Imogene smiled. "Ah, Hector. Why did you go dashing after me just now, when you could simply wish me into your arms at any second, from now until eternity? Why are you gasping for breath, when your phantom dream form is incapable of fatigue? Why did you create a chase where none is necessary? And why did I conspire with you in this illusion?"

She shook her head boredly. "We create these little—diversions. Limitations. And they distract us from the dreadful ache of having everything—distract us a little."

In his mind Hector heard Orndorf's voice: *Why do you think dreams are so bloody boring?* For the first time Hector wondered whether the thrill of manifesting every square inch of reality could eventually wear thin—not that *he* had learned that kind of mastery by any means.

And what was it that Orndorf had said during that ridiculous meal in Venice? *They want it joined, don't you see? No more of this lovely solidity, no more of this sensuousness, delicious unpredictability.* And Bruno had emphatically called that idea *Rubbish!*

And what was Imogene thinking now? Was she still bent on the joining of the Waking and Sleeping realms, or had she abandoned that plan altogether? Hector turned and looked at her. She was so beautiful, and he was so grateful to have achieved at least this faltering degree of lucidity here with her. He wanted to learn more, and he wanted to be with her. His questions faded away.

She stared out the window pensively. Hector looked out too. A star, not more than a light-minute away, silently exploded into a supernova, filling the sky with blinding white light. Then, just as silently, it collapsed upon itself, imploding into a minute ball of blackness. Other stars blazed nearby—some red, some blue, some yellow, and yet others so white they seemed icy with their very heat. Eons came and went. Several pterodactyls the size of small planets flew by with unassuming grace.

After many years, the car neared the earth again. Florence, its houses all perfectly encrusted in identical red tile, approached below them. The great Duomo cathedral sprouted up among them like a humongous beet.

The car landed in the Piazza della Signoria—a vast, paved, sunlight-filled courtyard littered with statues. A rain-stained marble copy of Michelangelo's David stalked about the square, a rebellious chap scratching himself nervously, searching to and fro for some too-long-anticipated Goliath.

Such is the fate of a sculpture, considered Hector. *Doomed eternally to wait.*

The towering Palazzo Vecchio loomed sternly over it all. Its great spire bent and twisted and peered into every nook and cranny of the piazza, gazing and leering with a single cyclops eye. It allowed no privacy.

Imogene leapt out of the car. Hector started after her, but she warded him off.

"No," she said. "I must meet my father in private. Go back to your own realm. It's over, Hector. You must believe me."

Hector disobediently followed. At the center of the piazza loomed a terrible apparition. A fearsome gallows stood there, made of a single upright post with an unevenly spaced crossbeam. A ladder reached up to the crossbeam. Beneath it roared a pyre of burning sticks and twigs. Flames leapt high into the air. They popped and exploded and stank with gun powder, resin, and oil. Hector's lungs were seared and scorched by the heat, even at a considerable distance.

From the crossbeam hung three Renaissance monks, ignobly dressed in nothing but hair shirts. They had iron collars around their necks and were suspended from the crossbeam by chains. The monks bled, burned, and blistered profusely. The two flanking monks were too engulfed by smoke and fire to be clearly seen. But a seemingly perpetual breeze kept the monk in the center in full sight. His hands and feet were tied, his legs slashed, and his face covered with blood. His tongue protruded from his mouth, swollen in strangulation. His hair shirt had burned indecently to above his waist. He had been dead for many centuries now. Despite this inconvenience, he seemed quite chipper and alert.

Girolamo Savonarola! thought Hector. *Hanged and burned in—I can't remember what year. But can this monk be Imogene's father? And what's he doing in my dream?*

Hundreds of naked people roamed the piazza, all of grotesque shapes and sizes, wielding every conceivable make of camera. They dashed about the square, taking pictures of everything which met their sight. They paid no particular attention to the burning monks. The cameras occasionally turned upon the gibbet, as if at random. Flashbulbs cast eery bursts of illumination over the scene.

"Tourists," said Imogene, her voice filled with scorn.

"Tourists?" echoed Hector stupidly.

"Sleeping fools from the Waking World, unaware that they're dreaming. It's a sure sign of a non-lucid tourist to run around naked like this."

Hector looked upon his own nude body and blushed, realizing his faux pas. He considered manifesting some clothing, but now he felt too self-conscious to do so.

Imogene approached the awful bonfire. She had to shout to be heard above the roar of the flames.

"Father," she said, "it's me, your daughter."

"Welcome, sweetheart," said Fra Girolamo cheerfully. "It's been too long, way too long." His voice was very clear and precise for someone whose tongue bulged out so horribly.

"Father, I have come to ask the meaning of prophecy."

"Certainly. But I don't know why you've gone to the trouble of coming to me. Merriam-Webster, I believe, defines it as a noun meaning 'an inspired declaration of divine will and purpose.' Of course, it is also a transitive verb, meaning to 'utter by divine inspiration.' There are other variants which don't come readily to mind. Surely you realize I don't know the dictionary by heart."

"But, Father," pleaded Imogene, "you embodied prophecy, personified its essence. You mortified, distilled yourself into the perfection of prophecy. You invoked the spirits of Micah, Amos, Ezekial, and Jeremiah to your brethren. You spoke of scourge and regeneration."

"Did I?" asked Fra Girolamo, tilting his head curiously. "Yes, now that you mention it, I suppose I did."

"You promised a better age," cried Imogene. "An age which *came!*"

Fra Girolamo sighed with boredom. "And *went*, if I'm not much mistaken. My dear, it's time someone told you, prophecy is nine-tenths cyclicality. Besides, it's not of much concern to me now. I've moved on to other interests. I live mainly for enjoyment these days. The pleasures of the flesh. Ah, to stand on the Ponte Vecchio as the sun sets on the River Arno, the smells of autumn in the air, sipping a glass of luscious red wine, perhaps with a delightful lady at my side. What a delightful change that is from terrifying the multitude with visions of apocalypse!"

Fra Girolamo sighed deep and long. His reverie was rudely interrupted as the flames flew up and singed away what was left of his hair.

"I'm sure I'll get back to prophecy sooner or later," he said. "*Anima transmigratoria*, don't you know? That's always been my motto. You never know what the spirit's going to hanker after next. Can't spend all eternity worrying about prophecy. That would be an awful waste."

"But you truly were *domini cani*," cried Imogene, "a hound of the Lord. You carried a torch between your teeth like a hunting dog by night, searching out the word of God."

"True, and I still do. But who can say what my torch will light on from one minute to the next? Yesterday, I would hardly have thought it would bring me *here*. The choice is not mine. I find whatever I find, and I don't weigh on what I found yesterday."

Imogene's face reddened, both from the heat of the flames and from frustration at Fra Girolamo's unwelcome answers.

"I worshipped you," she said. "I followed your example and became a prophetess. I preached the prophecy of Solomon: that dreams and waking would be one again. I fulfilled his promise of an Elixir. I brought his book to light. And it said, very clearly, that a waking entity named Hilary must partake of the Elixir. And it said that the prophecy would be fulfilled *when Hilary came to Venice*. But she never came! How can this be?"

Fra Girolamo's eyes gleamed with parental tenderness. "Imogene," he said, "there are so many reasons why this 'Hilary' might not have turned up. Perhaps she wasn't who you thought she was at all. Perhaps the woman you're looking for simply does not exist. Or perhaps she didn't want to be your messiah, your high priestess—whatever it was you expected her to be. And who can blame her?

"My dear, a prophecy is just a suggestion, not an edict. She didn't have to follow it. The choice was hers, not yours, and not even history's—although to tell the truth, I no longer believe there is such a thing. Her fate lies outside the hands of seers or gods. She's free. But in your heart, you've forgotten to set her free. And in your heart, you're the one who's enslaved by prophecy, not her."

Imogene's eyes glazed. "But, Father," she said, "what shall I tell Solomon? It was his prophecy, and I was to be its instrument."

Savonarola made his best attempt at a shrug. "If it's his prophecy, then let him be his own instrument. You know, Solomon and I go back a few millennia. And frankly, my guess is that the old boy's forgotten all about it. You should follow his example."

The flames leapt up again. They burned the ropes that bound Fra Girolamo's wrists. He raised his right hand to the height of his shoulders. He held two fingers up in an apparent sign of blessing. The crowd of naked tourists, oblivious to the monk until now, suddenly turned toward him, crying out with awe and terror.

"Miraculo!" they screamed over and over again, throwing their cameras on the ground. *"Miraculo! Miraculo!"* Then they began to rush about aimlessly, trampling on top of one another.

"Oh, not this again," moaned Fra Girolamo. "The blasted fools think I've come back from the dead." His arm went up and down repeatedly, like a mechanical device. The rioting tourists lost all control. It was a bloody scene, with bodies rising higher and higher.

"Miraculo! Miraculo! Miraculo!"

"Stop giving them your blessing!" scolded Imogene.

"I'm not!" protested Fra Girolamo. "It's this infernal twitch!"

Hector, to his perplexity, heard his own voice screaming: *"Miraculo! Miraculo! Miraculo!"* He rushed into the crowd.

"Hector!" he heard Imogene cry. "You're not *lucid!*"

But in a moment, he had forgotten her very existence. He lusted savagely in the crunching of Minoltas and Kodaks and Polaroids, to say nothing of the snapping of naked limbs beneath his feet. Warm, wet blood poured everywhere.

But why? he asked himself, utterly out of control of his actions. *Why? Why? Why? And where am I? What is this place called?*

To save his soul, he could not remember what realm he was in. The distinction between dreaming and waking no longer existed. The very words had no meaning at all. The mountain of bodies beneath him grew higher and higher. He stumbled over them. The smell of blood became intolerable. There were fewer living tourists left to trample. Soon, he would be the lone survivor. The thought sickened him.

Then came a sound which froze him in his tracks. It was a distant rumbling directly in front of him. The ground beneath his feet began to shake. The air vibrated wildly. The rumbling became a roar, rushing toward him with a vengeance. He could perceive a shape in front of him, something huge and inexorable. But what was it?

At last it loomed close enough to see.

It was a tidal wave. It rushed toward him with a deafening roar, crushing the tourists, living and dead, in its wake. It was too late to run. Hector stood placidly and waited, resigned to his doom. At last, the wave crashed over him, sending him flying head over heels. His bones were crushed to powder. Water poured into his nose and mouth. He gasped and coughed, certain that his life was over.

Then a firm but elderly hand lifted him out of the surf into the California sunlight.

"Tide's coming in," said Bruno the *Brujo.* "Tell me, do you sleepwalk often?"

The Teachings of Bruno the *Brujo* Part II

Soaked to the skin, Hector staggered out of the surf. He almost wept with humiliation.

"I lost it!" he cried, coughing and sputtering. "I was completely lucid, and then I lost it!"

"Lucidity in both realms," said Bruno, shaking his head and helping Hector along. "That's a pretty tall order for a novice."

They headed back toward Bruno's wigwam, where Hector tried vainly to dry himself with a mildewed towel. They sat cross-legged on the carpet again. Hector wriggled uncomfortably at the sand inside his wet clothes. He took off his shoes and socks.

"Let's try one realm at a time, shall we?" suggested the *brujo*. "Let's become lucid in the realm we were *born in*, and not go hankering after regions unknown."

"Where should I begin?" asked Hector. Water still dripped from the ends of his hair.

"Well . . . you could take the great placebo, the legendary Elixir spoken of so long ago by Solomon himself."

At that, Bruno withdrew a small, herb-filled gelatin capsule from his pea coat. Hector immediately recognized it. It was a capsule of M, the very same substance he had administered to Hilary. At least it looked very much like it.

"Where in the hell did you get that?" asked Hector incredulously.

"Off the streets," said the *brujo*.

"But nobody even knows how to make it!"

"It's a placebo," said Bruno with a shrug. "You can make it out of anything. Expensive, though. Are you ready?"

Hector hesitated. Placebo or not, did he dare ingest the capsule himself? He had to decide. Then he thought of Hilary, and how easily he had imposed the risk on her.

He reached out and took the capsule from Bruno. He swallowed it quickly, pursuing it with a cautious sip of tequila. It was cheap stuff which burned his throat like kerosene. Hector longed for a chaser.

He wondered, briefly, how soon the placebo would begin to take effect—or if anything would happen at all. But it didn't take long.

His wet and sandy clothing became flowing garments, softly brushing his moist skin. He could feel his rib cage expand, as if his heart had grown to enormous dimensions. His head felt as if it was floating in the stratosphere. His eyeballs seemed to contain thousands of votive candles.

Hector looked down. The silken carpet shimmered on the sand. It seemed to writhe, to fade and reappear. It looked utterly new. Now it glowed slightly. The surrounding noises and images faded, dropping away out of Hector's awareness.

Hector suddenly noticed a profound alteration of his sense of space. The world hadn't exactly lost its dimensionality; everything was still there, still vividly three-dimensional. But there was a peculiar flatness about everything, too, as if this apparently three-dimensional world was only a backdrop, and a rather delicate one at that. He thought of that inscrutable computer printout from Hilary's final session:

> *All fallen before me, dropped and drape-like,*
> *flat as a world I knew and morning-mocked merry,*
> *knew to hang hopeful over long livid life!*

Hector reached out with his finger. He touched something and jerked back. He peered at the air but could see nothing. Tentatively, he reached out with his finger again, and gasped. He could feel himself touch the "fabric" of his reality.

"Go ahead!" encouraged Bruno. "Give 'er a good shove!"

Hector pushed, and his finger went right through. He pulled it back and a "star-hole" appeared, a gash identical to those on the tarot card—a gash in Hector's very world. A blazing and mysterious light glowed through the hole from the other side. More words came back to him:

> *Light shone punctured*
> *through the perforated outward*
> *and the finger-painted universe before me:*
> *light of desire, light from home.*

Hector laughed with delight, and danced about, poking star-holes everywhere. The light glowed from every one. Rays of light crisscrossed in the air before him. Spots of golden light fell on the wigwam, on the *brujo*, and on his own limbs as he danced. Where the light fell there were new colors, new patterns, and even new sounds, scents, and tastes. Light falling on his hand produced a momentary magical tattoo. A joy swelled up in Hector that he had never known. He was on the verge of taking the fabric of his reality by the handfuls and ripping it open completely. He wanted to fully enter the light which burned behind it. But Bruno caught his hands and made him listen.

"If you tear all of it away," explained the *brujo*, "your lovely illusion will be gone. Everything you know—including yourself—will vanish. What's your hurry? The story will be over soon enough. Just live in the Mundane, and rejoice in it."

Dazedly, Hector stopped his dancing. "Is that what's real?" he asked, trying to peer into the holes.

"That, and this, and much much more," Bruno answered quietly.

A little sadly, Hector rubbed his fingers across the fabric of the Magical Mundane, gently closing up the star-holes. But he knew that he could reopen them any time to get just a glimpse of light.

"This is some sorcery, *brujo!*" said Hector. "Still, there's one trick you haven't sold me on. When is this carpet really going to fly?"

Bruno smiled. "Take a look around you," he said.

And Hector turned again toward Ocean Front Walk to see the weight lifters, musicians, roller skaters, accupressurists, crystal salesmen, reflexologists, T-shirt hawkers, comedians, nutritionists, kite flyers, drug dealers, tarot readers, fire eaters, skateboardists, astrologers, sidewalk artists, tourists, and transients.

"*Worldsprites,*" Hilary had called them in her postcard. None of them seemed to have noticed his dancing, his star-holes spreading wild light everywhere. But he sensed that each of them had known their own star-holes at one time or another. Some had forgotten. Some had never forgotten.

They seemed to perform a dance—a dance as ancient and as mad and as sacrosanct as any shamanistic rite. Hector realized that these celebrants had been here since the days of Solomon, and would doubtless be here always.

A woman in a sundress sat at a card table, intently studying the palm of a middle-aged, erstwhile flower child. Hector remembered the words on Hilary's postcard:

> *Womanworldsprite see Hand, say use only seem to be to*
> *Work Feel othersuch, but truly is to Read-Speak!*

The crippled saxophonist, the conga drummer, and the young guitarist continued to play in blissful ignorance of each other:

> *Worldsprites of Wood String Brass latch-sing to Fleshthings!*

A bunch of kites yoked together performed wild acrobatics across the sky, mingling with living sea gulls. A flock of plastic, windup birds joined the flight:

Here Worldsprite take Idea Bird, Away take Feather,
Unto give Paper Strings Sticks and send on Nojourney.

A skateboardist made a spectacular sweep up a vertical ramp, froze for a second in midair, then glided down the ramp again with perfect grace:

Worldsprites sprout Wheels, Ride Every-Where and No-!

All at once, everything seemed to be its opposite. The wild motion was also a profound stillness; the rush of time was absolute timelessness; and the grand size of everything was really just a point of infinite smallness. It was wonderful. It was ordinary.

Hector looked down again.

"You're right," he said to the *brujo*. "The carpet is flying. It's really flying."

But the crystal-blue sky suddenly filled with clouds. A storm came on with tremendous speed. The canopies came down, the kites were pulled in, the pushcarts fled, and the shopping stalls closed up. The dance broke up and flew off in all directions, worldsprites hastily covering their heads with purses, newspapers, paper plates, or whatever they could get their hands on. Hector climbed hastily into the wigwam after Bruno.

The *brujo* seemed very tired. "Remember your lucidity," he said wearily. And he went to sleep.

Hector waited in the wigwam until the rain blew over. The little dwelling leaked, whistled, swayed, and threatened to fly utterly away. But Bruno's snoring almost overwhelmed the sound of the storm.

The shower, though intense, was very brief. Leaving the *brujo* still asleep, Hector wandered toward the beach. The sun was setting, and the sky had turned an incredible gray and blue, with a dazzling gold penetrating through it all.

After all, thought Hector, *what is the sun, or any other star, but just another a punctured place in our illusion?*

Enormous waves crashed over a breakwater. Surfers bobbed up and down in the tide like pelicans. A Russian wolfhound walked regally by with its master. Several dozen quiet pilgrims roamed the beach, staring at the sunset.

A hush fell. For a solid minute or so, no waves broke upon the beach. The ocean itself was silent—still vibrant and ceaseless, but eerily suspended. Hector looked westward, where great clouds of fog swept over Santa Monica, looking like billows of smoke, completely enveloping the cliffs of Malibu. The edges of the clouds, the crests of the waves, and the white fur of the dog all caught the brilliant yellow light in exactly the same way. Hector's own dampness felt like a delightful extension of the scene.

He realized that all this was just the festival continuing. The shamanistic dancers had only changed form. Hector stood in wonder as his entire world shaped itself to his own desires.

Then he realized he hadn't paid the *brujo* for his teachings. He went back to the wigwam and looked inside. Bruno held his head in his arms, snoring noisily. Hector looked at him and wondered:

Where is he now? What is he dreaming of?

Then Hector smiled as his question answered itself:

Wherever it is, it's no more amazing than where I am right now.

He picked up his shoes and socks, placed a ten dollar bill in the old man's sleeping hand, and left.

THE OLD WOMAN: I tell you,
      wretch, I know I am not in
      hell.
DON JUAN: How do you know?
THE OLD WOMAN: Because I
      feel no pain.
DON JUAN: Oh, then there is no
      mistake: you are
      intentionally damned.
THE OLD WOMAN: Why do you
      say that?
DON JUAN: Because hell, Señora,
      is a place of the wicked. The
      wicked are quite comfortable
      in it: it was made for them.
      You tell me you feel no pain.
      I conclude you are one of
      those for whom Hell exists.

Bernard Shaw
Man and Superman

Tears

Upton Orndorf was wandering through Small World Books in Venice, California. He came upon Volume XVII of the Second Edition of the Oxford English Dictionary, ensconced upon its cardboard shrine. He gripped the nearest bookshelf in a near faint. He almost fell upon his knees with awe.

He glimpsed the people wandering to and fro around him. He could not understand how they could pass by such a treasured object without so much as a bow, a curtsy, a salaam, a genuflection, or a gasho. But they paid no attention to it whatsoever. (Of course, Upton Orndorf had no way of knowing that, earlier that same afternoon, a deconstructionist had been so overwhelmed by this very tome that he had quite disappeared from ordinary reality.)

Volume XVII! mused Orndorf, stroking pages 876 and 877 gently. *Oh, yes! I've heard so much about you, my beauty! "Su—Thrivingly," you are called. And you tell the immortal sagas of such legendary words as suffix, Swiss cheese, Technicolor, temblor, Thespian, thorax, thrasher, thrift and—O most glorious!—the! But do I dare profane you, holy book, by reading you here and now?*

Orndorf stood pondering it for a moment in an exquisite agony of indecision. It was a daunting prospect. He was a rather slow reader—certainly not nearly as prodigious as he was at such other waking activities as eating, drinking, and fornicating.

It was not an indifference to literature that made him so. To the contrary, Orndorf loved reading above all earthly pleasures. His desire to savor and luxuriate in poetry and fiction was the very reason for his slow reading rate. And so it would have taken him at least twenty minutes to get through the thousand-page volume with its three-column layout and its miniscule typeface. But surely the time spent would be most rewarding . . .

But no! he thought with a sigh. *I see only one volume here. And I must read this mighty work of fiction from beginning to end or not at all. To do otherwise would be like perusing the* Bhaghavad Gita *without studying the rest of the* Mahabharata. *It would be like reading only Volume VII of the* Kathasaritsagara. *It would be like jumping ahead to the "Molly Bloom" section of* Ulysses. *It would be like skimming Casanova's* Mémoires *only for the hot parts. It would be an unforgivable irreverence.*

Orndorf gently and carefully closed the ponderous volume, hoping to forestall further temptation. He did so with exactly the same care and chivalry that he might take to rebutton a voluptuous and all-too-willing lady's blouse after partially undressing her. Then he passed on among the bookshelves.

He had come to Venice Beach on a kind of pilgrimage. He frequently sojourned in this mythic land of wakefulness when things weren't going well in the Sleeping World. He would come for the sake of reflection, introspection, meditation.

And there was entirely too much to reflect upon. Things were not at all well in the Sleeping World. Orndorf had been a renegade Thaumaturgist ever since he had unsuccessfully tried to steal *The Elixir of Solomon* from Imogene Savonarola and transmute it to the Waking World. He was an exile and a pariah from the community of sleeping folk. Bulletins had been posted throughout the world of dreams. No one there was likely to give him sanctuary. He was a fugitive—forever.

He thought about his present state of reverse somnambulism. How long had he been awake now? Two days, three days, a week? Would he ever return to his sleeping state again? Did he really want to?

To hell with them, anyway, he kept repeating to himself with mechanical regularity, winding among the maze of shelves. *I may have been born into the Sleeping World, but this one is more to my liking.*

But what of Savonarola's insidious scheme, to unite Sleeping and Waking into one homogeneous realm? Such a short time ago, he had been full of ire and outrage. He had sworn to stop her.

"I'll be back," he had called out to her before driving his Maserati down the maelstrom. "I'll put an end to your infernal scheme—and I don't care about any half-baked prophecies!"

But now his fire and ire were gone. Orndorf drew a sad sigh.

"'I am not Prince Hamlet, nor was meant to be,'" he murmured.

And it was true. He was just a plain little man with insignificant abilities. If the Thaumaturgists were really capable of blending Waking and Sleeping into one, he was much too tired and impotent to try to stop them.

And if this wonderful Waking World isn't going to go on forever in its pristine imperfection, I'd better enjoy it while I can.

It seemed a reasonable sort of resignation. Why, then, did he feel so sad and empty?

He wandered on among the stacks. He was in the used book section now, facing an antique copy of *Alice's Adventures in Wonderland*. He took it down from the shelf and opened it. His eyes fell upon the following passage:

> "For it might end, you know," said Alice to herself, "in my
> going out altogether, like a candle. I wonder what I should be

like then?" And she tried to fancy what the flame of a candle looks like after the candle is blown out, for she could not remember ever having seen such a thing.

Orndorf felt himself choke up slightly. Such words always took him by surprise, reminding him of the true magic of Waking life. How hard it was to remember! Living here meant *not being able to see* the flame of a candle once it is blown out! It meant *having to imagine* such a thing. It meant discovering it in words.

It was precisely this sort of rigor that exhilarated Orndorf. But even so, he felt a profound depression slipping over him. Again he had to wonder, *Why do I feel so empty?*

A word whispered across his mind. He couldn't quite catch it. He concentrated and listened for it again.

Loneliness, it said.

Oh, that's just the folklore of lucid wakers, he thought indignantly. *Surely loneliness is only a myth, a fairy tale. Surely it cannot be real.*

But when he looked around the bookstore with its strangely disconnected customers wandering hither and thither, not touching, not even talking to one another, he began to suspect that it was true.

So many barriers—walls, doors, distances, time, skin, clothes.

The very things that had once enthralled him with their permanence were truly getting him down.

But this is surely a consensual reality, just as the dream world is, his mind protested. *Why do the Waking Born go about their lives as if they each live in a separate universe? Why are they never lucid, even in their own realm?*

These questions seemed too bizarre to even consider. At least he could be content with books. As he meandered through the aisles, he collected a small selection of volumes. Then he nestled listlessly against one of the bookshelves with the pile of books next to him. Orndorf perused them one by one.

Here was a book of stories by that master solipsist Robert Coover, in which the author rejoiced in his own perspective, his omnipotence, and his unique power to create and manipulate the scene—and hence reality.

And here was a book of Escher prints, where drawings of reptiles came to life, crawled around a desk, and crept back into drawings again.

And here was Julio Cortázar, writing ebulliently of his discovery that cats were really telephones.

But doesn't everybody know such things? wondered Orndorf. But then he reminded himself: *In the Waking World, even the most ordinary truths are hidden. They demand the scrutiny of imagination.*

And people here crave dreams as much as I crave wakefulness! To them, the Sleeping World is a wonderful mystery!

Tears welled up in his eyes at this sad irony—Waking folk and Sleeping folk, each craving the others' realm, the others' illusion. And, oh, the things which were taken for granted here! How extraordinary it still seemed to Orndorf that words stayed fastened to the page, that they didn't leap up and play castanets and chant sutras, and that the pages were sewed so neatly into the bindings, that they didn't take to the air like butterflies—and that the books weren't riddled with the unruly scents of roses and lilacs.

As Orndorf stared at a page of Wordsworth, he was overwhelmed with a desire to experience it as physically as possible. He took it between his teeth, ripped off a piece and chewed. Amazing! The taste was actually rather bland and bleachlike. It hardly betrayed the slightest trace of deep, intoxicating burgundy. Orndorf spit that out and bit into a page of Keats. No different, really. Perhaps a slight edge of mildew. It was a dull taste, indeed, betraying very little of Greek retsina's wild and bitter palate.

Orndorf sat against the bookshelf, munching away on the pages of numerous books. He hungrily savored their very sameness, swallowing the pages when he could, spitting them out when he could not. He chewed on some of the covers, too. To be sure, there was more variety to be found in them. At least the textures were different. Some of the cloth bindings were quite unpredictable to the tongue. And the colors on the marbled covers mingled in his mouth, leaving a slightly astringent aftertaste. And yet, not even the sonnets of Petrarch chuckled with sweet persimmon seeds. And not even the poetry of Robert Burns squeeked with the tartness of cranberries.

All this reawakened Orndorf's delight. Despite its loneliness, the Waking World did, in fact, make considerably greater demands upon his consciousness than the Sleeping World. Here, experience was muted, austere, ascetic. It constituted a kind of sensual vow of silence. Reality itself was a challenge. How wonderful was this lucidity!

Orndorf reached over to the bookshelf across from him. A slip of his hand brought a whole row of volumes to the ground. He was on the verge of marveling at the wondrous force of gravity when he noticed two feminine eyes staring through the bookshelf at him.

"Can I help you, sir?" said a voice which accompanied the eyes.

"No," said Orndorf sheepishly. "Not really."

"It is against the store policy for customers to eat any books which have not already been purchased."

"Oh, yes, I quite understand," said Orndorf. "But perhaps I can explain. You see—"

"I know, I know," said the sundressed employee stepping out from behind the bookshelf. "You are not of this realm. You are from the World of Dreams. And so . . ." she gestured toward the mangled tomes.

"How did you know?"

139

"This is Venice Beach. We get them all the time."

"I'm sure you do," said Upton Orndorf with a moan of resignation.

Less than a minute later, Upton Orndorf was walking down Ocean Front Walk, an exile from Small World Books as well as the World of Dreams. As he gazed upon the weight lifters, musicians, accupressurists, crystal salesmen, reflexologists, T-shirt hawkers, comedians, nutritionists, kite flyers, drug dealers, tarot readers, fire eaters, sidewalk artists, astrologers, tourists, and transients, the truth began to settle in.

Loneliness was not merely folklore. It was a fact of Waking life. He could see it clearly now. Waking people never did anything important together. Oh, they talked and ate and drank, made laws, and made love. But they rarely joined their lives, shaped their realities, discovered their possibilities—together.

So many people, mused Orndorf, his heart sinking, *and all so bitterly alone!*

Orndorf sighed. He desperately needed someone to talk to who was beginning to get a glimmer of true possibilities—and who would be willing to talk to him. He could think of no one. This was, in truth, the one cruel fact of Waking life he did not think that he could bear.

As he walked down the walk, he could see Bruno the *Brujo*'s wigwam on the beach to his left. He briefly considered paying a visit to the tequila-addled shaman. But after his humiliation at the hands of Imogene Savonarola, after his vain attempt to purloin *The Elixir of Solomon*, after his failure to forestall the Thaumaturgists in their awful scheme, he did not believe that he could face the *brujo*.

He kept on walking—and walking, and walking. When he was well past Bruno's wigwam, well past the concrete jetty which overlooked the harbor— well past Ocean Front Walk itself, Orndorf turned and walked down to the shore. He stood at the brink of the Pacific, ankle-deep in the surf.

And with a wild and desperate outcry he exclaimed:

"I must find a friend! And a fresh, new realm to share my friendship in!"

He gazed out to sea, and cried out:

> "Over unsounded gorges, through the rifled hearts of mountains, under torrents' beds, unerringly I rush! Naught's an obstacle, naught's an angle to the iron way!"

He sank to his knees in the surging water. Orndorf wept.

Yes, I have heard of tears, he pondered, wet and chilled. *But I never believed they existed until now.*

Llixgrijb's Role

... Outside our time and space, Llixgrijb was still dissatisfied.

"I have created a world full of imaginary creatures," said Llixgrijb. "And yet I am alone. How can this be?"

Despite the populousness of its illusion, Llixgrijb could only watch its lovely universe from the outside. It had not forgotten its own suffering and loneliness. It was not fully a part of the creation it had made.

"I must become a part of my illusion," considered Llixgrijb. "And to do that, I must don a costume, I must wear a mask. I must forget myself forever. But what—or *who*—shall I become?"

At last, Llixgrijb knew the answer. It created a character so obtuse, so unimaginative, so dull and mechanistic that it could never be reminded of its own true dilemma.

It created a past and a future for this character, and put them into place just so. Of course, it was rather tedious to remain focused through one personality in one lifetime. But it seemed dependable, and by then Llixgrijb sought dependability above all else.

Llixgrijb started its character running like a toy train on a straight and narrow track. And that character lives amongst us, unrecognized as the one true source of all existence.

But who is this character?

Joseph
Xavier
Brillig!
Professor of
English at
James
Fenimore
Cooper
Junior College
in Sequester,
Missouri.

And, oh,
things are going
very well in this
illusion . . .

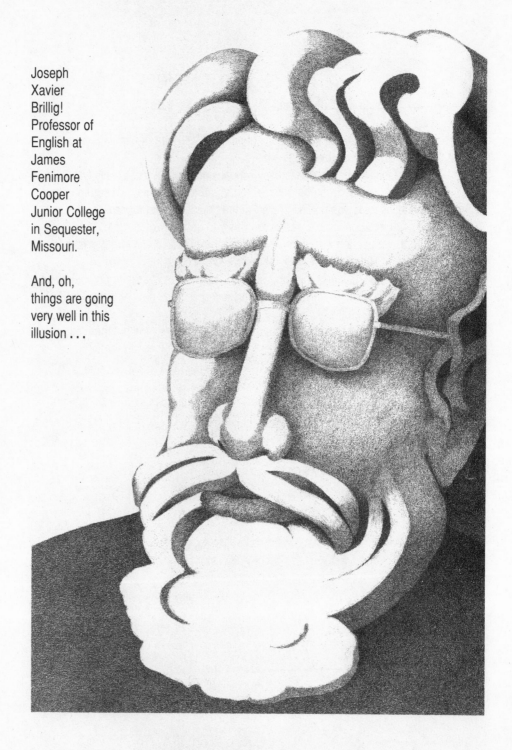

142

is Vu Papers

**Volume One
Number Nine
August**

Dear Printer,
Sorry for the dreadful misunderstanding. I don't know why Miss Bellows thought I wanted to fire you. Of course I did not. Many apologies
Hector Glasco
(Please remove this note before making the plates.)

tar—*much* too far.

What has provoked this outburst? Read further.

Is there a book called The Jamais Vu Papers?

Several of my students recently turned in book reports on a novel entitled *The Jamais Vu Papers*. They claimed it simply turned up in my classroom one day. Speaking as an educator, I am grateful to say that these students are not nearly imaginative enough to invent this story.

But when I demanded to see the book, they said they could not locate it. Nor did my search of the premises turn it up.

The title was not just a coincidence. The characters they listed—*fictional* characters, mind you—included Hector Glasco, Imogene Savonarola, Hilary, Tom Robbins, Paul Krassner, some sort of extra-dimensional entity named Llixgrijb, a

runo the *Brujo*, and a *J. X. illig.*

Now, I do not know who all ese characters are, but I quire an explanation for ing listed among them. A wsuit may be pending.

Is there a Hector Glasco?

But I am seized by a disturbing question. *To whom am I writing this?* Isolated as I am in the semi-wilderness of Sequester, Missouri, I must consider that I have not met the editor of these *Papers.* Your appearance on the national news convinced me for a time that you were real. But given current telejournalistic trends, this is by no means a guarantee of your existence. Are you, then, merely a fiction?

Is this merely a hoax?

Your last issue ended with a treatise on hoaxes. This suggests to me that some sort of monumental hoax is being perpetrated, perhaps on the culture at large.

I beg you, whoever or whatever you are, in the name of literary responsibility *to cease and desist*. It appears to me that what is being attempted in these inscrutable pages is nothing

less than the creation of an insidious new art form—as untried as the novel and the short story were to their respective eras, but far more sinister and subversive than those genres.

The underlying aesthetic "given" is that *something* about the work is a hoax, that it is somehow *framed* in hoax-ness. The all-permeating question from that point on is this: What truth is *contained* in the hoax?

And what is the purpose of this perverted aesthetic exercise? Is it intended as a misguided lesson in contemporary reality? As an intemperate means of unleashing the anarchic right brain upon the unassuming left? Or as nothing more than a sadistic game?

Hoax Verité?

And what on earth is this new art form to be called? Despite my revulsion, my academic nature spurs me on to give it a name. It derives its power from falsehood, deception, and a general uncertainty as to what-is-what. It establishes the *hoax* as a sort of guiding aesthetic principle.

Hoax verité, perhaps?

A dangerous infection?

I fear that the reckless, hoax-ridden experimentation inspired by *Jamais Vu* has proven contagious, and is now infecting the very best and soundest literary minds in the country.

Whence this fear? You are about to see.

Witness, in the following pages, an interview I conducted with esteemed poet/novelist Fred Chappell. I have long regarded him as a national literary treasure, and wanted only to exchange a few thoughts for *The Buzzard Tail Review*, a Missouri literary journal I edit in my spare time.

The results, as you can clearly observe, were utterly perplexing.

J. X. Brillig

My attempted interview with Fred Chappell:

Question #1: I have heard it rumored that faculty and students alike refer to you as "Ole Fred." If this is so, wherever did you acquire such an unlikely appellation?

Answer #1: I flatter myself, that's why I think, Poetry first and devil take the hindmost. The great thing about poetry is that you don't spend so much time housekeeping: dressing your characters, getting them into and out of rooms, coloring landscapes and decorating interiors, and so forth. Poetry is very immediate and is able to o'erleap the quotidian at quantum drive rates of speed. At the same time, its rhythm is a more measured and less breathless one than the rhythm of fiction usually is.

There are, then, contrary motions at work; tensions pull one another out of shape like taffy. Poetry is the more fun factory to be in. I detest "fun" as an adjective. What can I tell you?

Question #2: In a 1985 interview published in *The Atlanta Journal and Constitution*, you commented that "People are always telling me that more people write poetry than read it. Maybe so. But I think that's the healthiest thing that could happen to American culture . . . And I think it would be a sign of an illness, of some obscure sort, if there were more readers than writers of poetry."

Since I find that to be a rather startling assertion coming from a fellow professor of literature, I would like to ask you to explain your meaning.

Answer #2: I am primarily a fiction rather than a poet. That is, for good or bad, I am a personality, an entity that has to be described as being in the process of being made. A poet, however, is a finished product; the poet as figure takes as formal a shape as a statue may. But a personality is that variable fiction that operates on the evidence which is thrown at it hour after hour and can make of it no more than a trivial and inconclusive soap opera.

I really have not answered the question.

Question #3: I am intrigued by your poem "Hallowind" published in the volume *Wind Mountain*. You recount a conversation with author Reynolds Price, in which he says a writer must deal with *"Things as they are"* and you disagree.

Do you still suggest that myth is more important than "things as they are," that the poet has "trained his mind/to hear all, multi-voiced as wind"?

Answer #3: So I will try to now.

I probably do consider myself primarily a poet. But we would have to admit that I primarily consider myself a secondary poet. There are few enough primaries in my makeup, and softer colors predominate, I think. Earth tones, mostly: browns, umber, burnt sienna, etc.

Any more of this one is embarrassing.

Question #4: And is this recounted conversation reported "as it was," or with a "Paradigm as old as fiction/ Itself conformably mixed in"?

Answer #4: Yes, I do consider myself primarily—but not all the time.

Let's say that one has been married for thirty years, as I have been, and with a child almost that old. There is some point where habit sets in and one has to consider other members of his family almost equally. At first you have to train yourself to do so, and then after a while the habit works into the synapses. I would not care to test these synapses under the most dreadful of emergency circumstances, but I take for granted that they do operate, as they are supposed to do for all well-disposed people.

But I have fears about this question, and these fears point up inadequacies. For that reason, I pray that the worst scenarios do not come to pass.

Question #5: Many of the stories told in your poems and novels are rooted in the North Carolina mountains. *I Am One of You Forever* certainly has an autobiographical feel to it, as does much of your poetry. What is the relationship of autobiography to reality? To myth?

Answer #5: Yes/no yes/no yes/no.

One considers himself because he has to do such improbable and ordinary things as crossing streets safely and brushing his teeth. But I do not set myself apart from my usual self in order to discover or to understand literary materials. In short, I cannot make myself an object of contemplation as the good Greeks were able to do. There is something shallow in myself as an object of any sort— and as a subject, I soon grow tired of my self. More interesting are the questions asked about the process of not considering oneself, but then that was not the question that was asked, was it?

Question #6: As a matter of artistic principal, do you feel authors should work out of memory, or out of invention?

Answer #6: Let's put it this way: I consider that I consider. That's a rather pitiable answer, I agree, but I would like to be as truthful as possible. I am not taking this problem in any wide Cartesian sense, but simply looking at my personal habits and mentality. So:

I am not certain that I do ever consider. And yet I write, I speak, I make a noise in my head that resembles what I have been

taught is the noise that thought makes. And yet my thought is unrecognizable as thought to a great many people, especially to a bunch of folks I've never met. We might try this formulation: If Edwin Meese III is considered to consider, then I must be considered as never considering.

Question #7: Your stories also have their metaphysical or mythic side. And what do you believe is the relation of myth to reality?

Answer #7: I do not. Doers are not writers, writers are poor doers. That is a pure sadness of history. Those who do things cannot remember why they have done them, and often they cannot even remember what it is that they have done. The writer then is called upon to remember for them what, why, and how. But the writer doesn't know, and so the doer objects strenuously. The centuries then engage in this muddled dialectic until they produce the blind poet Homer.

Question #8: Do you share the belief of certain of my colleagues (an inane one to my mind) that metaphors are *literally* true?

Answer #8: Yes, do. There is no happiness in action, but there is a certain fleeting satisfaction. The eastern philosophies of inaction are fine for easterners. For westerners they lead to lazy self-indulgence. "Hey," one thinks, "I may be wrong, but at least I'm not doing anything about it!" This overlooks the fact that whatever error, whatever imbecility one has thought of, someone else has thought of it too. Surely it is better to make the mistake oneself than to leave it to others who will almost certainly bungle even the task of the error-making.

So then, do something, without despair and without hope. But don't confuse it with writing.

Question #9: In *Source*, the collection of your poems published in 1985, your lyrical pieces are joined by some rather terrible images that seem to be the aftermath of war—"The Evening of the Second Day," for example. "I can imagine no brutal history that will not be born," you say in "The Transformed Twilight." Are these the myths you see forming around our own time?

Answer #9: But these are not viable alternatives!

Why not is a question that can be put only to positive terms. This query always assumes the existence of most things familiar to us—objects, senses, reason, etc. When it is asked Why things exist, the implied answer is always, Why not? It is so immediately predictable a response that it has become the cardinal one.

The real question is neither *Why* nor *Why not*, but the overlooked term *Or*. This is the question we need to ask ourselves: *Or???*

Question #10: What is your connection with the mysterious Ancient Order of Brothers and Sisters of Thaumaturgy?

Answer #10: Interview questions are always impertinent in some subtle Henry Jamesian sense, but these are less impertinent than most—partly because I'm not exactly certain what we're driving at.

The unchangeable problem with all interviews is: If one of the speakers knows the answer, the other doesn't need to ask the question.

The interview form implies a conspiracy. The dialoguists are cahooting together (to quote Erik Rhodes) to suppress most of the information and to let the audience overhear only just so much of what is actually taking place. Dialogue does not strip away the mask; it gives it instead a final form, a polished surface.

You may have found this interview strangely—how shall I say it?—discontinuous? Here is the reason.

When I first requested this interview, Professor Chappell gave me specific instructions to put exactly ten typewritten questions in the mail on July 27—not before or after. As mildly eccentric as this request seemed at the time, I complied. Extraordinary writers are known to harbor such minor quirks.

But as it turned out, Chappell had put his ten answers in the mail to me on July 27, the very day I had sent my questions. As you might well assume, he didn't have the least idea of what my questions were.

Well, the answers were fine answers indeed, and would probably seem profoundly and eloquently pertinent with an altogether different set of questions. Unfortunately, they had nothing whatsoever to do with mine.

I was troubled. By way of explanation, Chappell simply declared that we had engaged in something altogether new: a non-synchronous interview! He seemed genuinely pleased with the whole idea. I, to the contrary, was nonplussed.

I have assembled the interview as sensibly as I could: question #1 followed by answer #1, etc. I now submit it to a presumably baffled public

—Joseph Xavier Brillig

3:45 P.M.

. . . "Myrtle, you promised!" Ethel cried indignantly.

"Why no, I didn't do a thing," said Myrtle, carefully selecting another piece of dark brown velvet.

"You did so! Professor Brillig saw it! Professor Brillig said so!" Ethel waved her copy of *The Jamais Vu Papers* in the air. Balls of yarn bounced around her. "How did you do it this time? Did you mail it? Did you visualize a carrier pigeon? Did you . . . ? Did you . . . ?" She faltered, quite at a loss for words.

"Actually, I don't think Myrtle did promise never to get mixed up in the story again," said Addie.

"In fact, I distinctly remember her saying something about replication," said Phoebe, wrapping a shuttle with a new shade of ochre yarn.

"I did not promise anything," said Myrtle firmly. "But I did *not* put the book in Professor Brillig's classroom, either." She stitched away on her quilting square, looking every bit the righteous victim of malicious gossip.

"Someone had to put it there," said Lida June.

"Well, I didn't. You can't blame me for every little leak in reality," Myrtle huffed.

"Now, dear, I'm sure you didn't if you say you didn't," soothed Ethel. "But then, who did . . . ?"

There was a long spell of silence in the room.

"Well," ventured Addie, "maybe the author . . ."

Myrtle said, somewhat petulantly, "There are other people reading this book, you know. Any one of them could have tampered with the story."

"Not everyone knows how."

"It's so very simple, really." Myrtle brightened up. "Any imaginative ten-year-old could work it out. Why, you should see how my grandson gets involved with Greek myths—"

"It's like I was saying about reality leaks," interrupted Phoebe. "I believe little trickles of things pass from one kind of reality to another all the time. It's not the kind of thing you'd call a plumber for."

"Someday," added Myrtle, "we should find a way to test it properly."

"Pssst! Look!" whispered Addie. Myrtle, Addie, and Ethel turned to witness Lida June hovering in a seemingly trancelike condition over her copy of *The Jamais Vu Papers*.

Lida June was sitting there, licking her index finger, turning over a bunch of pages, and then licking her finger again and turning them back, repeating this motion endlessly, over and over and over with mechanical precision.

"Oh, dear," sighed Phoebe. "She's having another aneurism, isn't she?"

Addie clapped her hands loudly. "Lida June, dear, snap out of it! Don't scare us so."

Lida June stopped turning the pages and looked up, startled. "Oh, I'm terribly sorry. I rather drifted off, didn't I?"

"What on earth happened, Lida June?" asked Phoebe with profound concern.

"Well, I discovered the most peculiar thing," Lida June replied. "Pages 37 through 40 don't seem to exist."

"Shoddy workmanship!" grumbled Addie. "They don't make books like they used to."

"No, that's not what I mean," Lida June continued. "As I leaf through the book, I can feel those pages between my fingers. But when I actually try to turn to them, they seem to vanish altogether."

She passed the book along to her companions.

"How odd!" remarked Phoebe, thumbing through the book herself. "The same thing seems to be true of pages 88 through 92!"

"And pages 147, 148, 149 . . . ," cried Ethel, performing the operation as well. "Why, page 147 should be right here, just after the last newsletter. But it isn't."

"Of course it is," said Myrtle. "Just look . . ." But when she examined her own copy, she gasped and dropped her basket of quilting squares. Scattered images of shamanic masks stared up at them from the floor. "Why, when you try to look at it, that page just sort of . . . fades away. Now it's quite blank. How absolutely fascinating!"

"What's so fascinating about it?" clucked Addie disapprovingly. She dug around in her scrap box, as if to ignore the entire thing.

"I think I'll make a pot of tea," said Ethel. She wrapped her knitting around the needles, put it all into her knitting bag, and went into the kitchen.

"Bring those brownies, too," Phoebe called after her. "I took them out of the oven a while ago. They must have cooled by now."

"Well, there has to be some sort of rational explanation," said Myrtle, collecting her quilt fragments from the floor.

"Might I be permitted another small hypothesis?" asked Phoebe politely.

The entire group murmured their assent.

"Well," continued Phoebe. "Perhaps those are the pages of the story in which *we* appear."

Phoebe's companions stared at her with startled expressions.

"Phoebe McNair!" cried Lida June. "Where did you come up with such an idea?"

"It's not impossible," said Addie, stitching away energetically. "After all, Myrtle's letter actually did get into the book. Apparently, we're involved in the story somehow."

"What an odd notion!" chuckled Phoebe. She propped her loom against her chair and reached into her purse.*

---

* Phoebe whispered to Lida June, "I believe I have a book here which might illuminate the issue just a little. Yes, here it is: *The Book of Sand*, by Jorge Luis Borges." She pronounced the name "Bor-*jes*."

"I don't believe you pronounce the *juh* sound," admonished Lida June. "It's more like 'Bor-*hes*. It's like the Scottish *ch* in *loch*."

"Well, I can't make that funny sound the way you do," said Phoebe. "So I'll just keep calling him Bor-*jes*."

And so Phoebe continued: "A stranger came to visit the narrator of the story one day. He was carrying this antique Indian book called *The Book of Sand* around with him. He wanted to sell it to the narrator. As the narrator opened the book, he quickly noticed that the page numbers seemed completely arbitrary. Also, he couldn't open the book to the same place twice. Then the stranger told him to try to find the first page."

And Phoebe read aloud:

> "I laid my left hand on the cover and, trying to put my thumb on the flyleaf, I opened the book. It was useless. Every time I tried, a number of pages came between the cover and my thumb. It was as if they kept growing from the book.
> "'Now find the last page.'
> "Again I failed. In a voice that was not mine, I barely managed to stammer, 'This can't be.'"

"It is just a *little* farfetched," fretted Lida June. "What kind of story is this, anyway?" Phoebe read on:

> "Still speaking in a low voice, the stranger said, 'It can't be, but it *is*. The number of pages in this book is no more or less than infinite. None is the first page, none the last. I don't know why they're numbered in this arbitrary way. Perhaps to suggest that the terms of an infinite series admit any number.'
> "Then, as if he were thinking aloud, he said, 'If space is infinite, we may be at any point in space. If time is infinite, we may be at any point in time.'"

"It's an interesting speculation," commented Lida June. "Although I do believe Professor Hawking recently determined that time and space were not infinite at all, but—how did he put it?— 'formed a surface that was finite in size but did not have any boundary or edge.'"

"Oh," rejoined Phoebe, "that's a fancy scientific way of saying time and space aren't really infinite, but they might as well be for all the good it does us."

"But back to Señor Borges's magical book," said Lida June. "Surely your narrator didn't take the silly thing."

"Oh, but he did," continued Phoebe. "He traded his Wiclif Bible for it." And she continued to read . . .

"I don't think so," rejoined Addie. "It strikes me as rather extraneous and dualistic to assume that our world and the world of the book are two utterly separate realms. Remember Occam's Razor."

"Well, I don't doubt we're *in* the book," growled Myrtle, "but still I want to know something. How come we're not allowed to read about ourselves?"

"That would be dreadfully complicated," explained Addie. "Could you imagine reading the very words we're speaking, even as we speak them? Talk about deterministic! We'd be completely restricted to discussing our relationship with the printed page. We'd die of boredom."

This didn't satisfy Myrtle at all. "Who *decided* we couldn't read about ourselves? It wasn't me, I'm sure."

"The authors, I imagine," said Addie with a shrug. "They seem to be responsible for how this whole thing unfolds."

"The authors! But *we* don't have authors . . ." Myrtle's voice trailed away as a speculative look came into her eye. Then she said emphatically, "No. Absolutely not. You can't tell me I didn't decide to drop that letter to Hector of my own free will!" Her needle flew energetically in and out of the fabric.

"Maybe you didn't," said Addie. "Maybe none of us do *anything* of our own free will!"

"Well, I object to this whole hypothesis on purely empirical grounds," complained Myrtle. "I've got just the same problem with this idea that Heinz Pagels had with the Anthropic Principle; why fool around with a hypothesis that can't even be tested?"

"My dear," replied Addie, "if we only talked about *testable* hypotheses, we'd hardly ever talk at all!"

Myrtle got defensive. "Just because I don't like the idea of getting trapped in a book, everybody acts like I'm reverting to some sort of reactionary methodology," she retorted. "The whole thing gives me the willies, that's all I'm saying. It makes life sound so dismal and predestined. There must be a way to check it out."

"Well, if you can come up with a hypothesis that can be tested," said Addie, "more power to you. The fact is, we can't even *look* at these pages. So much for verifiable data."

Myrtle wriggled restlessly. "What's taking Ethel so long with the tea and brownies?" She frowned at Phoebe. "And whatever are you two whispering about now?"

"A Borges story. Someone else had a problem exactly like ours with a book," said Phoebe.

"I remember that one," said Myrtle. "It was an infinite book and he couldn't get rid of it."

Lida June asked, "Is it a true story or isn't it?"

"He says it is, right at the start," said Phoebe.

"But who's this 'he'?" enquired Lida June. "Is it actually Señor Borges, or some imaginary narrator?"

"It doesn't say," confessed Phoebe.

"Well, that's all very interesting," Addie remarked. "But what's it got to do with *our* book?"

"That's right," chimed in Myrtle. "It's not infinite. It's just ornery."

"Maybe ours is more like that other Borges story, the one about the garden, the one like a labyrinth," said Phoebe. She picked up a pale pink square of fabric; perhaps just a *little* variation would be interesting in the white-on-white design, after all.

"That's 'The Garden of Forking Paths,'" said Addie. "But that's more like a spy story."

"The point of it is," explained Phoebe, "that the 'garden' of Ts'ui Pên is actually a book that includes infinite variations on the story, all happening at once. One of the characters says, 'Time forks perpetually toward innumerable futures.' Every choice that is possible is actually made. *Everything* happens."

"Maybe," speculated Addie, "it's just that we just can't see the other variations. Maybe we're reading only one version of a story that *is* infinite in a different way, by branching into every possible variation in time."

"Like that physicist Fred Alan Wolf says," added Phoebe with a chuckle, "in his book, *Parallel Universes.*"

"What does he say?" asked Lida June.

"Oh, you know, the idea began way back in the fifties with that old Bryce Dewitt theory—that there are an infinite number of them," Addie answered.

"There's an infinite number of parallel universes?" Lida June asked anxiously.

"A new one every time I make a decision," said Addie firmly, with considerable satisfaction.

"Well, we're getting into a whole lot of fuzzy questions, if you ask me," said Lida June.

"I agree," chirped Myrtle. "There comes a point where playful speculation turns into out-and-out self-indulgence."

Ethel reappeared in the doorway empty-handed and with a rather surprised expression. "There's a deconstructionist in our kitchen," she announced.

"I was wondering why you were taking so long to make tea," said Myrtle.

"And he's eaten all the brownies," said Ethel.

There were whispers and murmurs among the group of ladies.*

At that moment, a rather disheveled-looking man appeared in the doorway

---

* "Oh dear," whispered Phoebe to Lida June. "Didn't anyone tell him what was in them?"
"Why, Phoebe, you said they were quite mild," cried Lida June with alarm.
"But if he ate *all* of them . . ." said Phoebe.

to the kitchen. "Ahem, eh, uh, ladies," he stammered, trying to straighten his ruffled jacket with some semblance of dignity. "Er, ladies, I must apologize. Allow me to introduce myself. My name is Max Henderson."

Gasps and small cries of astonishment ran through the group. Max stopped, confused. "And I'm a professor of . . . of . . ." He scratched his head.

Max looked exhausted, but a grin slowly began to settle on his features. "I'm sure it doesn't matter," he added. He wobbled a bit and caught the back of a chair. "What a lovely room. Terrific colors. What a lovely day. Is there anything else to eat? Funny, I've wolfed down so much already, and I'm still so hungry! And what a lovely group of ladies. A reading and sewing circle, Mrs. . . . Mrs. Ethel told me."

Smiling foolishly, he tottered forward. "Let me see what book you're reading today." . . .

The Jamais Vu Papers

Volume One
Number Ten
September

My Dear Dr. Glasco,

Once again I feel impelled to contribute my thoughts to your publication. Please be assured that I still maintain my objections to your unprofessional violations of the boundaries between fact and fiction. And I have never received the explanation I requested of the apparent existence of a book entitled *the jamais vu papers*—in which I, myself, allegedly appear as a character.

There are, indeed, a number of loose ends I cannot in good conscience leave untidily lying about.

A hoax played by a poet

First of all, there is this matter of my interview with poet and fiction-writer Fred Chappell—published in your August issue. Droves of readers wrote to express their perplexity. I am now able to enlighten them somewhat.

Dr. Chappell mercifully — if belatedly—supplied some missing pieces. "Thought you might like to see the questions that I actually answered," he wrote to me amiably.

He added, "Considering the situation they are as good as unused, of course, and you are free to ask them of someone else."

Therefore I am including Dr. Chappell's questions here, for the information of your distraught readers and for whatever use you or they may wish to make of them.

Unfortunately, no one has yet answered the carefully considered questions that I actually asked.

Taking the scholarly approach to hoaxes

The master poet had evidently perpetrated a hoax on me. Since Chappell is not only an acclaimed writer, but is also a solid member of the academic world, I knew that I had to give the matter more consideration.

Clearly, it was time for me to look into this matter of hoaxes in a scholarly manner. After all, if such things are to become the "in thing" I should at least be ready to refute them intelligently.

But where was I to begin my research? Perhaps with some famous trickster, such as Coyote or certain current politicians. Or with the infamous "Piltdown Man," believed by some to have been instigated in part by the revered and respected Teilhard de Chardin.

I'm sure you'll agree that the hoax I ultimately chose was a fascinating one—and casts an illuminating light on Savonarola's theory. I shall devote the balance of this communication to my recent researches and commentaries on one particular giant hoax, as well as on the hoax principle in general.

J.X. Brillig

---

1. Do you consider yourself primarily a poet or a fiction writer?
2. Do you consider yourself primarily a poet or a fiction?
3. Do you consider yourself primarily a poet?
4. Do you consider yourself primarily?
5. Do you consider yourself?
6. Do you consider?
7. Do you?
8. Do?
9. Why or Why not?
10. At what point do interview questions become impertinent?

"Cardiff Giant"
by Henry Salle and Fred Mohrmann
stone
photo: New York State Historical Association, Cooperstown

One giant hoax

Half expecting to find nothing, I looked up "hoaxes" in the card catalogue at the J. F. Cooper Junior College library. The category was surprisingly full. Despite the boldness of her theory, Savonarola can make no claim to having invented the hoax!

And so I found a book called *Grand Deception: The World's Most Spectacular and Successful Hoaxes, Impostures, Ruses and Frauds*, collected and edited by Alexander Klein. It fairly fell open to page 126, "The Real Story of the Cardiff Giant," by Alan Hynd.

The story of giants in the earth

In 1868, an atheistic and mischievous cigar manufacturer from New York State named George Hull was visiting Iowa, where he came upon an evangelist ranting and raving and loudly thumping his Bible. "There were giants in the earth in those days," the preacher declaimed from *Genesis* 6:4, and declared that it was absolutely and literally true.

Determined to make fools of all of those he considered religious humbugs, Hull proceeded to devise one of the most successful hoaxes in history.

Hull acquired an enormous block of gypsum in Fort Dodge, Iowa. He hired a couple of sculptors to fashion it into a bogus fossil of just such a giant as *Genesis* suggested—over 10 feet tall and weighing 2,990 pounds. The Giant cut an impressive and convincing figure. It looked as if it had died in agony, and was minutely detailed down to the pores in its skin.

Hull had the Giant shipped to a farm just outside of Cardiff, New York, which was owned by his cousin, William ("Stubby") Newell. With Newell's help, the Giant was planted on those grounds. On October 15, 1869, Newell brought in diggers to excavate for a new well, and the Giant was conveniently found.

The Cardiff Giant became profitable the very day after it was discovered. Newell erected a tent over the grave, and an eager public paid 50 cents a head to see the Giant. At Hull's suggestion, the price soon got jacked up to a dollar.

Hull, of course, swore all participants to secrecy.

Hull's original intent was to make fools of literal-minded evangelists, but his hoax was more effective than he bargained for. While he succeeded in bamboozling the religious, he also succeeded in hoaxing scientists, philosophers, and scholars.

Two Yale scientists studied the find and declared the Giant to be a true fossil. In vigorous disagreement, an archaeologist from the New York State Museum called it an ancient statue.

Ralph Waldo Emerson was overwhelmed by the Giant, and proclaimed it to be "undoubtedly a bona fide, petrified human being." Oliver Wendell Holmes adopted a more empirical stance. In the interest of scientific scrutiny, he drilled a hole in the Giant's head. Finding no brains, fossilized or otherwise, he sided with the "ancient statue" camp.

Without a doubt, the results of this charade bear a chilling resemblance to the claims of Imogene Savonarola in her paper "I Seem to Be a Placebo." This hoax, also, was "proven true" by numerous authorities.

A Hoax on a Hoax

P.T. Barnum was among the very few who recognized the Giant to be a hoax—and he saw that it would be a profitable one at that. He tried to buy the Giant, but was turned down. But a syndicate of businessmen succeeded where Barnum failed. They purchased a three-quarter share in the Giant for $37,500, and put the rascal on display in a New York museum.

They had hardly done so before Barnum began to display *his own* Cardiff Giant just a few blocks away! Barnum's was none too meticulously copied in plaster. But an attempted court injunction couldn't stop him from turning a good profit on it.

So an ironic controversy arose. Both giants could not be real, so *which was the hoax?* This new puzzle clouded the truth even further, and generated great publicity for all concerned.

The public was bored with the Giant by the time a New York reporter got around to investigating its entire history. He discovered and exposed just how the hoax had been perpetrated. George Hull was honestly relieved to be caught at last, and cheerfully confessed to the entire affair.

The Real Hoax?

At this news, the American public showed the full extent of its perversity. Lagging ticket sales skyrocketed, and the Cardiff Giant became a popular hit again. Everybody wanted to see the hoax which had fooled thousands.

But with two Cardiff Giants on display, an unsettling question remained:

Which was the *real* hoax?

J.X. Brillig

I also investigated the current standing of the Hoax Principle in the scientific community. I am happy to say that its acceptance is anything but unanimous. Experts are extremely divided as to whether or not lies can become actual fact.

1) Supporters of the *Strong Hoax Principle* fully support Dr. Savonarola's disturbing claims that actual falsehoods can achieve *literal* truth if they manage to be convincing enough. Although this camp seemed formidable at the outset, it

truths. Artists and novelists have been operating on this dubious assumption for centuries. This "weak" form allows members of the scientific community to be trendy without being committal.

"BLACK HOLE THEORY"
by Tom Hammond

While it is true that most scientists do, indeed, give lip service to this weird and anarchic theory, it is also true that they have broken up into two camps. There are, in fact, not one but *two* Hoax Principles.

tool of ontology?

2) The *Weak Hoax Principle* still holds a good share of supporters. But this rather insipid theory is hardly worth debating. It simply holds that falsehoods can occasionally be used to illuminate deeper

Quantum Physics. Simple, honest truth seems to be in abeyance these days. When shall it come back again? Until a proper mixture of rationalism and empiricism is returned to ontology, I will maintain that we inhabit a new dark age.

J.X. Brillig

Usthay Akespay Iyyahay

"Erethay ereway iantsgay inyay ethay earthyay inyay osethay aysday . . ."

Ouyay avehay eensay isthay ittenwray andyay ityay isyay uetray. Iyay asway uchsay ayay iantgay. Iyyahay asway ymay amenay, ayay onsay ofyay ethay angelyay Emhazaishay. Erhapspay ouyay avehay eardhay ethay orystay ofyay owhay angelsyay amecay ownday intoyay ethay orldway eforebay ethay oodflay, ustinglay afteryay ortalmay omenway. Eway iantsgay ereway ornbay ofyay esethay unionsyay, ayay aceray ithway anymay amesnay, ostmay oftenyay ownknay asyay ethay Ephilimnay.

Eway avehay eenbay alledcay "ightymay enmay owhay ereway ofyay oldyay, enmay ofyay enownray," asyay ifyay eway ereway ethay inestfay ellowsfay owhay everyay ivedlay.

Oeverwhay otewray isthay asway ayay iarlay.

Otay eginbay ithway, eway amecay omfray adbay ockstay. Ouryay athersfay, allenfay angels-yay, ereway oodgay orfay othingnay. Eythay aughttay ouyay otay armchay andyay otay onjurecay, otay ursecay andyay otay exorciseyay, otay usttray inyay ethay auguriesyay ofyay arsstay, oudsclay, unsay, andyay oonmay aboveyay ouryay ownyay oodgay udgmentjay. Eythay aughttay omenway otay aintpay eirthey acesfay andyay enmay otay issembleday. Eythay aughttay ouyay owhay otay akemay eaponsway andyay otay illkay eachyay otheryay orfay onay easonray.

157

Onceyay ouryay athersfay ereway inishedfay eachingtay esethay essonslay, eway iantsgay adhay othingnay evilyay, upidstay, oryay uselessyay eftlay otay eachtay ouyay. Osay eway entway orthfay intoyay ethay orldway andyay underedplay ouyay indblay. Enwhay erethay asway othingnay eftlay otay ealstay, eway evouredday ouyay ybay ethay ousandsthay.

Eway ereway ethay eryvay oulssay ofyay ickednessway, andyay ademay ouyay ickedway ybay ouryay exampleyay. Eway oughtbray onyay ethay oodflay ybay ouryay ickednessway, utbay evernay awsay ityay appenhay. Ethay angelyay Ichaelmay ooktay emay andyay ymay othersbray, oundbay usyay andyay uriedbay usyay insideyay ethay earthyay. Eway areyay otnay otay ebay awakenedyay untilyay ethay ayday ofyay udgmentjay.

Ymay ownyay avegray asway uncoveredyay omesay undredhay earsyay oryay osay agoyay. Ityay ashay eenbay ymay unishmentpay otay ielay ormantday andyay aralyzedpay ilewhay eoplepay arestay, awkgay, andyay aughlay, allingcay emay ayay orgeryfay andyay ayay abricationfay—ichwhay, ofyay oursecay, Iyay amyay.

Iyay amyay ethay eryvay ersonificationpay ofyay raudfray, ethay atronpay iritspay ofyay allyay eceiversday. Iyay amyay ayay ielay oldtay ybay ethay oddishclay umplay ofyay eshflay andyay oodblay ichwhay ewsspay orthfay esethay ordsway.

Allyay atthay Iyay avehay aidsay isyay uetray.

Elievebay othingnay atthay Iyay aysay ereafterhay.

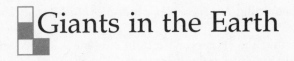Giants in the Earth

Brillig opened his eyes.

He was looking down at the classroom floor. His Oxford anthology was lying there, sprawled at his feet. It was opened to Gerard Manley Hopkins's "Pied Beauty." These words met his eyes:

> Glory be to God for dappled things—
> For skies of couple-colour as a brinded cow;
> For rose-moles all in stipple upon trout that swim . . .

His memory was fragmentary. Not more than a moment ago, he had opened the book to this page, intending to read this poem aloud to his summer quarter Introduction to Literature class. But now he couldn't remember dropping the book. And he couldn't remember having read anything aloud. In fact, he wasn't quite sure what he *could* remember.

What the devil happened? wondered Brillig. *Surely I couldn't have fallen asleep.*

Brillig reached down and picked up the book. Then he looked up. A sophomore girl sat in the front row staring at him with rapt attention.

What's that one's name again? Oh, yes. Milly.

He could swear his students got younger every year. Why, this girl didn't look a day over fourteen. Her face was round and smooth and unnaturally white, like the surface of an egg.

Each of these students looked identical to the next. It was like teaching a classroom full of embryos. Brillig had found it increasingly unnerving. Could it be something in their diets? Or was it merely his own advancing age?

In any case, Brillig was startled by her gaze. Her eyes were blue and almost abnormally round. She looked like one of those hideous urchins painted on black velvet he'd seen in so many gift shops—the ones which always toted scrawny wide-eyed kittens in their arms. But why was she looking at him that way? In all his years of teaching, Brillig had never once been stared at with rapt attention.

"Milly," he asked a bit defensively, "what *are* you gawking at?"

"You," she said. "You've been saying the most amazing things."

Her voice had always been whiney and crass. Now it had turned soft, entranced, and dreamy.

Good God, mused Brillig. *Has she developed a sudden crush on me? That would be a new experience!*

He looked around the classroom. Certain students sat mesmerized, like Milly. Others could barely restrain their giggles. Clearly, something untoward had taken place. Brillig felt a rising panic. His hands began to tremble and sweat. He held onto the book hard, for fear of dropping it again.

What did I say? he wondered. *What have I been doing? And why can't I remember?*

But he couldn't lose face. He had to keep his cool. He hastily gathered his wits and mustered his best John Houseman manner.

"Well then," he barked, "would somebody care to sum up what I just said?"

Nervous glances darted back and forth among the students. For a moment, nobody dared to speak. Then came a reply.

"How can we?" inquired an insolent jock in the third row. "It was all in Pig Latin!"

Then the burly beast of a child broke into giggles. He was echoed by several of his uncouth neighbors. But others in the class continued to stare in dumbfounded wonder.

Brillig sensed that his only recourse was righteous indignation

"Very well," he said, slamming his book shut with a vigorous clap. "I had expected you to read today's assignment before coming to class. I take it you did not. And so, rather than make a joke out of one of the greatest works of English poetry, I do believe it's time to adjourn."

He stuffed the book in his briefcase.

The jock looked a little surprised. "You mean you don't remember what you said?" he asked.

"I have never spoken Pig Latin in my life. And neither, I am sure, did Gerard Manley Hopkins. And I refuse to involve myself in any childish, conspiratorial prank. You're not in high school anymore. Remember that in the future. Now. Good day."

His genuinely startled class evacuated the room—all except Milly, who continued to stare.

"Professor Brillig?" she sighed.

"Yes?"

"Do it again."

He wanted very much to ask, *Do what again?* But he doubted if he'd like the answer. So, with a loud *harumph*, he snatched up his briefcase and stalked out the door.

He walked breathlessly until he reached his office. He walked inside, slammed the door behind him, and locked it. He threw himself into his chair and held his forehead in his fingers. A headache was coming on with a fury.

It won't happen again, he promised himself aloud. *Whatever happened this time, I'll be on my guard. I won't let it happen again.*

He felt reassured at the sound of his own words. He looked out the window. A delicate, lilting quiltwork of morning sunlight filtered through the leaves, flashing green kaleidoscopic light around his office.

Every semester, he had chosen just such a morning to teach "Pied Beauty"— that marvelous conglomeration of literary mendacities. Filled with delight, he had always picked it apart line by line, word by word. He had always wound up making perfect, literal sense of it. Teaching "Pied Beauty" had always been the exhilarating highlight of his semester. But today his joy had been dashed.

There's no respect left. No respect at all.

Brillig nursed his headache in silence for ten or fifteen minutes. Then came a shy knock at the door.

"Who is it?" asked Brillig.

"Rudy Dietz," came the reply. "From your Intro to Lit class."

"Go away."

"Please, sir—"

"I said go away. If you want to apologize, you can do it on Wednesday."

"I don't want to apologize. I've got some important information for you. Please. You won't be sorry."

Brillig sat staring at the door. Surely this was merely a new stage of the prank. And yet . . .

His curiosity was too much for him. He unlocked the door. A slender, bespectacled, blond-haired kid stood facing him.

Are they all albinos? wondered Brillig. *Do they all look alike?*

But yes, he did remember this one—the only one who came to class each day wearing a tie and a jacket. The one who snored. He stepped into the office carrying his books and a small cassette recorder.

"May I sit down?" asked Rudy politely.

Brillig mutely gestured to a chair. Rudy sat down.

"I suppose," said Brillig, "you're about to tell me you heard me speaking in Pig Latin, too."

"I?" asked Rudy, a little flustered. "Oh, no, sir. Not exactly. I mean—not at all. Please believe me. I didn't hear a thing. I slept through it all. I always sleep through your classes."

"How comforting," muttered Brillig.

"Not that you're boring, sir. Oh, not for a moment. It's just that I'm a business major. Literature's not my thing. Literature seems—well, excuse me for saying so, but it seems so *impractical.* I can't keep my mind on it. Especially not that early in the morning."

Brillig snorted. Why did today's students always refer to ten o'clock as "early"? It was probably all that partying and carousing.

"Maybe I should get right to the point," said Rudy.

"Maybe you should," said Brillig.

Rudy brandished his tape player. "I always record your lectures. I play them back when I'm more awake. That way I don't have to miss a thing."

"I'll bear that in mind," said Brillig, "the next time you snore."

"Well, after all that fuss after class, I thought I'd better play today's tape right away to find out what I missed."

"And so?"

Rudy looked at Brillig cautiously. "You really don't know what happened in class this morning, do you?"

"Just play the tape!" barked Brillig.

Rudy pressed the play button. The recorded sound was almost obscured by a loud, repetitive rumbling.

"That's me," explained Rudy.

"Snoring. Yes. I know."

But as Brillig listened more carefully, he could distinguish his own voice amidst the terrible rumbling. There was an odd distortion about it. It sounded strangely alien. After all, no one ever quite sounds like oneself on tape. But still, there is something primal and unmistakable about the rhythm and the resonance of one's own voice.

Brillig heard himself speaking in an unrecognizable tongue. Surely he had never uttered such syllables! But it *was* his voice. He had no idea what the words meant—or if, indeed, they were words at all.

"What—what am I saying?" he stammered.

"My best guess," said Rudy, "is that you really were speaking in Pig Latin. I remember trying to learn how to speak it as a little kid. I guess if I had any kind of knack for it, I'd be better in literature."

Brillig sat listening in silence.

"So you really don't remember?" asked Rudy.

Brillig shook his head. Rudy stopped the tape.

Brillig held out his hand. "Might I—" he began to ask.

"Have the tape?" asked Rudy.

"Yes. Please. I'll pay you anything you want."

"No, I couldn't take your money," said Rudy.

"I insist," said Brillig.

"You don't understand," said Rudy, blushing a little. "I already made a copy at the student union. I can make gobs of copies if I want to. Just take the tape, okay?"

Rudy snapped the tape out of the player, handed it to Brillig, and rushed away.

"I'll see you on Wednesday!" he called out as he darted down the hallway.

That night, Brillig sat listening to the tape. He laboriously transcribed it, syllable by syllable. Then, equally laboriously, he translated the Pig Latin into plain English. It was tricky at first. But soon Brillig caught onto the entity's trick of placing a "y" before the "ay" suffix on words which began with vowels. After that, the process became quite automatic.[1]

Would that I had learned to read French so easily, mused Brillig. *I might have gotten my Ph.D. a year earlier.*

Certain parts of the message evoked a mysterious and chilling sense of familiarity. The entity, who called himself Hiyya, almost seemed like an old acquaintance.

"*Erethay ereway iangsgay inyay ethay earthyay inyay osethay aysday,*" announced Hiyya. Or, in plain English, "There were giants in the earth in those days."

A biblical reference, to be sure, pondered Brillig. *Did my friend Hiyya come straight out of the book of* Genesis?

Another phrase was still more evocative:

"*Ymay ownyay avegray asway uncoveredyay omesay undredhay earsyay oryay osay agoyay.*"

Which, translated, meant, "My own grave was uncovered some hundred years or so ago."

Goose bumps popped up on Brillig's arms. Why did it all seem so familiar?

---

[1] "There were giants in the earth in those days . . ."

You have seen this written and it is true. I was such a giant. Hiyya was my name, a son of the angel Shemhazai. Perhaps you have heard the story of how angels came down into the world before the flood, lusting after mortal women. We giants were born of these unions, a race with many names, most often known as the Nephilim.

We have been called "mighty men who were of old, men of renown," as if we were the finest fellows who ever lived.

Whoever wrote this was a liar.

To begin with, we came from bad stock. Our fathers, fallen angels, were good for nothing. They taught you to charm and to conjure, to curse and to exorcise, to trust in the auguries of stars, clouds, sun, and moon above your own good judgment. They taught women to paint their faces and men to dissemble. They taught you how to make weapons and to kill each other for no reason.

Once our fathers were finished teaching these lessons, we giants had nothing evil, stupid, or useless left to teach you. So we went forth into the world and plundered you blind. When there was nothing left to steal, we devoured you by the thousands.

We were the very souls of wickedness, and made you wicked by our example. We brought on the flood by our wickedness, but never saw it happen. The angel Michael took me and my brothers, bound us and buried us inside the earth. We are not to be awakened until the day of judgment.

My own grave was uncovered some hundred years or so ago. It has been my punishment to lie dormant and paralyzed while people stare, gawk, and laugh, calling me a forgery and a fabrication—which, of course, I am.

I am the very personification of fraud, the patron spirit of all deceivers. I am a lie told by the cloddish lump of flesh and blood which spews forth these words.

All that I have said is true.

Believe nothing that I say hereafter.

163

Brillig closed his eyes and tried to remember. His mind carried him back to the summer of ten years ago. He and Marie had gone on a second honeymoon, trying to restore some spark of excitement to an already flagging marriage.

With admitted unoriginality, they spent a weekend in Niagara Falls. After that, they took a leisurely drive across New York State. They saw the Erie Canal, drove through the Adirondack Mountains, and spent a weekend in Mannhattan before heading back home—tired, grumpy, and thoroughly unrejuvenated.

But something had happened during that sojourn. And that *something* was the key to what was taking place right now. Brillig closed his eyes tighter. He tried harder to remember.

An image came. It was that of an open grave, artificially lit. An enormous, agonized, naked man lay in the grave. His flesh was hard as stone. In fact, he was completely fossilized. His eyes were invisible beneath the heavy shade of his brow. But Brillig could feel them. They stared straight into his heart. They were pleading and desperate.

"Free me," they cried out. *"Free* me."

Brillig remembered the nightmares that followed. He awoke trembling, night after night. The nightmares made Marie very angry. She said they spoiled the entire honeymoon. He dreamed he was locked in stone. He dreamed that he was being studied by an endless parade of vicious, stupid, empty people with cruel grins plastered across their pudgy faces. He was unable to move, unable to regain any semblance of dignity.

"Ityay ashay eenbay ymay unishmentpay otay ielay ormantday andyay aralyzedpay ilewhay eoplepay arestay, awkgay andyay aughlay. . ."

Brillig's eyes popped open. He jumped out of his chair.

"Of course!" he cried. "The Cardiff Giant!"

But that realization offered only a fleeting satisfaction. Brillig began to pace the room.

Steady, boy, he reminded himself. *Remember, it was a hoax, that's all. A hoax on display in some museum in New York state. It can't have spoken through me or any other way.*

Brillig wrestled with the twisted logic of his situation. Here he was, a perfectly sensible man, one who valued his own rationality above all other attributes. And, like any sensible man, he had a succinct and tidy list of things which he could not believe.

He could not believe, for example, that people ever "channeled" entities from other realms. He couldn't even believe that there *were* other realms. This single, tangible universe was quite enough for him—too much, at times.

Ergo? Anyone who claims to channel is perpetrating a hoax!

But—*he* had channeled that afternoon! Had he perpetrated a hoax?

No! Absolutely not.

Still, this had to be a hoax, but whose hoax was it?

Who, indeed? I am confident that not even the most skilled stage magician, the most crafty mountebank, the most cunning mesmerist could get inside my head and force me to babble in Pig Latin against my will!

And yet the tape sat on the table before him. He had listened to it and transcribed it and translated it. There was only one logical conclusion—and paradoxically enough, it defied all logic. He gasped at the thought:

I am a victim of a hoax without a perpetrator!

He slumped in his chair, gasping for air. This hopelessly circular dialectic had left him exhausted. He regained his breath, downed a glass of water, and stalked off to bed.

As he lay there, he offered up a wish to the only higher power he really believed in—a perfectly orderly universe.

Please, let today's quandary vanish into forgetfulness before tomorrow.

Then he went quickly to sleep. Surely, things could get no weirder . . .

De Profundis

Garner Oswinkle, president of James Fenimore Cooper Junior College, reached into his top right-hand desk drawer and pulled out a half-full bottle of Old Grandad.

"Care for a shot, Joe?" he asked.

Brillig considered the offer. He could use a drink. He really and truly could. But this was probably just a ploy to further confirm his recklessness and irresponsibility.

"No, thank you," said Brillig. "I've got a class coming up."

"Ah," said Oswinkle, pouring himself a formidable shot. "Which one is it?"

"Freshman Comp."

"Going okay?"

"As Freshman Comp goes."

"Good. Good."

Oswinkle sprawled backward in his revolving chair, swiveling back and forth like a ship's compass. The metronomelike monotony seemed calculated to be unnerving.

The two sat in silence for a moment.

What a repugnant old bastard, thought Brillig. Indeed, this squat toad of a man was anything but appealing. He sat there in shirtsleeves, his front buttons barely holding his shirt together. Gaps between the buttons revealed unsightly chest hairs. And despite the frigid air conditioning, Oswinkle sweated profusely.

Brillig felt a vague pain in his chest. He was suddenly seized by an irrational fear of dropping dead in his chair here and now in this repulsive company. This sort of phobia was becoming an all-too-regular occurrence.

Why am I so morbid lately? Brillig wondered. *Why am I so obsessed with death—and with death-in-life?*

Oswinkle fanned himself with a newspaper.

"September," said Oswinkle, shaking his head wearily. "September in Missouri."

"Indeed," replied Brillig.

"Not as bad as August, though."

"No."

"Ought to start cooling down soon."

"Yes."

"October will be here before you know it."

"Right."

"Now there's a month for you."

"Absolutely."

"The colors. The smells. The breeze."

They fell silent again. Then Oswinkle sighed.

"People think a bureaucratic type like me's got no poetry."

"No."

"'I should have been a pair of ragged claws,'" declaimed Oswinkle grandly, "'Scuttling across the floors of silent seas.' I guess you know what that's from."

"I haven't the slightest," lied Brillig.

"You don't? Too bad." Then he added with uncharacteristic sincerity, "It says a lot, you know. It really says a lot."

More silence. Brillig wished his superior would get to the point.

"And you're teaching business writing too?" asked Oswinkle.

"Yes," said Brillig.

"And how's that going?"

"I find it dull," said Brillig, seeing no point in keeping his impatience in further check.

Oswinkle stopped his swiveling. He stared at Brillig. A sneer formed on his lips.

"I've heard some pretty strange stuff about your Intro to Lit class," he said.

"Really?" asked Brillig. "Well. People will talk."

"Care to comment?" inquired Oswinkle.

"First tell me what you've heard."

"I'm sure you know what I've heard."

Brillig shrugged. "I always seem to be the last to know."

Oswinkle stared harder. He tried to bore two holes in Brillig with his pupils. Brillig found the effect rather comical.

"Let me come to the point," said Oswinkle.

"I wish you would," said Brillig.

"How long have you been with us, Joe?"

Brillig almost laughed. He wanted to tell Oswinkle to drop the clichés. And he wanted to tell him that he hated to be called Joe. Nobody called him Joe. His mother had been the last person to ever call him Joe. He was the kind of man everybody just called Brillig. Even his ex-wife had always called him Brillig.

"Let's put it this way," said Brillig. "I'm tenured."

Oswinkle snarled slightly. "I've been talking to your colleagues, Joe. They don't think much of you. They think you're slacking off. They say you cut a poor figure at conferences. They say you publish in third-rate journals."

"What do they say about my teaching?" asked Brillig.

"I didn't ask them about your teaching."

"Ah."

"I didn't have to. Your course enrollments have been down for years. Students have always dropped out of your classes like flies. Your evaluations are rotten. Kids say you're a bore. This is not a good time in the history of higher education to be a bore, Joe. Kids want excitement."

"So they tell me."

"You're not much of a teacher, Joe."

"If you say so."

"I think I know what you're up to, Joe. I think I know your game. You're fifty years old. You're divorced. You're up to your neck in alimony payments. You don't have much of a retirement ahead of you. You're worried about your future. You're looking for a little something on the side."

Brillig said nothing. Oswinkle ranted on.

"This New Age mystical Shirley MacLaine dingbat sort of yuppie crap you've been pulling—there's good money in it, huh? I mean, I hear out on the coast, people pay a hundred bucks a head to hear the kind of gibberish you spout."

Brillig just sat there. He was surprised to feel no desire whatever to defend himself. But after all, what was he supposed to say? That he was channeling against his will? That he was the victim of a hoax without a perpetrator? Why humiliate himself with lame and useless pleading? Instead, he felt only cold, mounting anger.

"I don't mind you picking up a few bucks," added Oswinkle. "I just wish to hell you wouldn't use this college as some kind of out-of-town tryout."

It was Brillig who was staring daggers now. And his eyes were about to carve two gaping holes in Oswinkle's chubby face.

Brillig spoke with bland ferocity. "If you were any kind of an excuse for a human being, I'd explain it to you. As it is, I do believe we're wasting each other's time. And now, if you don't mind, I've got a class to teach."

Brillig steadied his glare. Oswinkle shriveled like a punctured inner tube. Then Brillig strode silently out the door.

As he headed toward his next class, he ruminated over recent events. It had been near the end of his summer quarter that he had started channeling the spirit of the Cardiff Giant—that lying and unprincipled upstart who called himself Hiyya—in his Intro to Lit class.

Enrollment for the fall quarter class had skyrocketed. Students dropped essential, required courses just to get in on the fun. Rudy Dietz kept sitting in, even though Brillig had given him a passing grade in hope of getting rid of him. Dietz was still taping Hiyya's diatribes, and offered Brillig a cut in the cassette sales. Brillig refused. And now, that entrepreneurial little squirt was selling copies of his tapes by the dozens and making a handsome profit.

Brillig's Intro to Lit students had studied and mastered Pig Latin with a zeal and enthusiasm they had never brought to Wordsworth. They asked Hiyya questions in that infantile jargon, and he delivered answers. He advised them on dating, personal hygiene, fashions, junk foods, and pop stars. And true to his word, Hiyya never uttered one single word of truth, profundity, or common sense.

To his tremendous frustration, Brillig never had any awareness of Hiyya's presence. The whole class period would go by without Brillig even knowing it. There was only one blessing: Hiyya never appeared during any of Brillig's other classes.

It's hardly any wonder that Oswinkle's so furious, thought Brillig. *I'd feel the same way if I were in his place. So why didn't I at least show him the respect and courtesy of explaining my situation?*

He pondered. But he couldn't think of a single good reason.

Brillig walked into the classroom. His class had arrived and was seated. They watched him approach his desk with devout attention. The room was completely silent. Never in his life had he commanded such fascination from anyone, let alone his students.

Poor little twerps, he thought. *They keep hoping I'll start channeling in this class, too!*

Then, with a gloating smile, Brillig announced:

"Today we're going to discuss *gerunds!*"

The entire building shook with a heartrending groan.

That evening, Brillig did nothing but watch television and guzzle scotch. He stared at the music video channel with the sound off. The effect was eerie. Frenzied and jittery hand-held cameras scurried about, pursuing mangy, screaming rock-and-rollers in mute futility. Animated lumps of clay dumbly stretched, mutated, crawled, and undulated all over the place with preternatural rapidity while lights and colors blazed and danced all around them. Female vocalists silently cavorted in their lingerie through hurricanes, conflagrations, volcanic eruptions, and earthquakes. Torrid and erotic episodes transpired amidst the horrors of Hiroshima, Auschwitz, and My Lai.

It was quite tranquil in its way.

It made Brillig feel at peace with himself and the universe.

Brillig stared and drank, and stared and drank some more.

Hours went by.

Hiyya was the farthest thing from his mind.

His *mind* was the farthest thing from his mind.

At long last, just barely conscious enough to notice the lateness of the hour,

Brillig arose from his chair and staggered toward his bedroom.

The journey was fraught with peril.

His stomach heaved.

He saw two of everything.

The floor kept moving underneath him.

Brillig kept wishing it was only the end of the world.

And so, when he saw the light under the door to his study, he thought it was a product of his febrile and inebriated imagination. He stopped and looked, swaying back and forth.

The study light was definitely on. It looked like two lights shining under two doors. But Brillig knew very well that he hadn't been in his study all evening. Not either of them. Scholarship had been his last concern. Stupidity had been his most dire priority.

So who was in there?

Brillig knitted his brow in thought. The effort sprained his facial muscles. He gasped in pain.

Should I go in there? he asked himself.

He tried to muster up a healthy degree of fearfulness and trepidation. But he was entirely too drunk for caution. He opened his study door and fell inside.

He struggled to regain his balance and looked up. The room was a little slow to catch up with his eyes. And it took another twelve or thirteen seconds for things to come into focus.

There was a man standing by his bookcase. He was a rather homely fellow with a large nose. He was reaching for a book.

"Professor Joseph Xavier Brillig, am I correct?" said the stranger.

"And who the hell are you?" growled Brillig.

"'I am the Fates' lieutenant,'" intoned the stranger. "'I act under orders.'"

"What kind of answer's that?" asked Brillig.

"Melville!" said the stranger with a smile, brandishing a copy of *Moby-Dick*. "One of my favorites. And one of yours too, I'm sure."

"I'll take Hawthorne any day," mumbled Brillig. "Melville's too—"

He wanted to say "confusing," but the word was too much for him. He failed to finish the sentence. He dropped into his desk chair and closed his eyes, hoping never to open them again before the end of his days. The world of the senses was much too ghastly.

"What's your name, anyway?" enquired Brillig petulantly. "Or did I ask you that before?"

"You asked me that before."

"And what did you tell me?"

"Nothing very useful, I'm afraid."

"Don't tease a man in mortal pain," moaned Brillig, near tears.

"Orndorf," said the stranger placatingly. "My name is Upton Orndorf."

"And just who *are* you, Upton Orndorf?" inquired Brillig.

"A lover of literature, like yourself. And a lover of this sublime illusion known as *waking*."

"Yes, well," muttered Brillig. "The less said about waking the better. I believe you should go home now. It's way past your bedtime."

"Oh, no, Professor Brillig. You see, I'm not from these parts. So I'd like to stay a little while if I may. And you mustn't go to sleep just yet. You might have—bad dreams! Come to the kitchen. I'll fix us some coffee."

Brillig was largely unconscious during the odyssey to the kitchen. If it weren't for Orndorf's guiding ministration and encouragement, he'd surely never have made it alive. When he became aware again, he sat face to face with a large mug of black coffee, steaming violently amid the hideous glare of the kitchen. He could dimly make out Orndorf's unattractive face through the rising clouds of steam.

"Pay no attention to that man behind the curtain!" exclaimed Brillig.

Then he collapsed into nauseated giggles. He held his head in his hands. He passed out briefly.

A short while later, he looked up again. The coffee was steaming considerably less now. His unwanted friend was smiling at him pleasantly.

"Remember me?" asked his companion.

"Upton Orndorf," groaned Brillig.

"Very good! Sip some coffee. I think it's cool enough now."

Brillig did so without much difficulty. This sudden onslaught of manual dexterity persuaded him that he was sobering up. That was both good news and bad news. If this Upton Orndorf character was a serial killer—as Brillig strongly suspected—it was far better to be unconscious.

"If you're going to kill me," said Brillig, "I wish you'd do so while I'm still drunk."

"Thank you," replied Orndorf agreeably. "I'll bear that in mind."

Brillig struggled hard to keep Orndorf in focus. His efforts were becoming more and more successful. He gulped down some more coffee and looked again. There was clearly only one of whoever this man was, and he didn't look particularly threatening.

"Well," Brillig grumbled, "what *are* you doing here?"

"Not long ago," answered Orndorf, "I discovered a disconcerting thing called *loneliness*. Since then, I have been searching for its antidote. But now I am starting to realize there is no such antidote in the Waking World—and that the only thing to be done about loneliness is to enjoy it, as I do all other sensations."

"Then why are you bothering me?"

"Merely seeking company," said Orndorf. "You seem to be the perfect person with whom to share my loneliness." Then, leaning forward, Orndorf added: "I do believe you're rather an expert on the subject—aren't you?"

171

Brillig squinted his eyes. Yes, Orndorf was quite clear now. And he was smiling at Brillig idiotically.

"What are you grinning about?" barked Brillig.

"I'm getting a contact drunk!" giggled Orndorf.

"Well, you're enjoying it a hell of a lot more than I am."

"You could enjoy it a great deal more with *this*," said Orndorf. He withdrew a small gelatin capsule from his jacket pocket and set it on the kitchen table between them.

"Drugs," said Brillig.

"Indeed," said Orndorf.

"Tempting."

"I should hope so."

"But—what *sort* of drugs?"

"Ah," said Orndorf, "this one has been called many things throughout the ages. The most powerful placebo of all time, the chemical equivalent of a metaphor, the elixir of Solomon—"

"Good God!" exclaimed Brillig, rapidly approaching sobriety. "This is that drug called M. The one that Glasco character gave to his patient."

"The very one."

"It's a hoax, of course."

"How do you know?"

"Well, it was devised by that Imogene Savonarola woman. The one who came up with the Hoax Principle. She specializes in hoaxes."

"Imogene Savonarola, eh?" said Orndorf. "Never heard of her. And now," he added, holding the capsule between his fingers, "would you care to partake?"

"And why should I do that?"

"'This whole act's immutably decreed,'" declaimed Orndorf. "''Twas re-hearsed by thee and me a billion years before this ocean rolled, at least in one parallel reality or another.'"

"Melville again, but amended."

"Very good. I thought you preferred Hawthorne."

"I do. Quote *him* next time."

"I'll try to do that."

"And, uh, Orndorf—"

"Yes?"

"This is the *midwest*."

"I do beg your pardon—'before this *prairie* rolled!'"

And with those words, he placed the capsule in Brillig's hand. Brillig gazed intently at the capsule and pondered the consequences of swallowing it.

Not the sort of proposition I would normally consider, he mused. *Still, what have I got to lose? It could lead to escape; that would be nice. It could lead to hell on earth; that would be no different. It could kill me; 'tis a consummation devoutly to be wished.*

"Yes, damn it, I'll take it," he said.

"Good!" cried Orndorf, striking the table with his hand. "Brillig, I think this is the beginning of a beautiful friendship!"

"That's not Hawthorne," complained Brillig, studying the capsule, gearing himself up to swallow it.

He expected to hear an apology. None came.

He looked up. Orndorf was gone. Brillig growled softly.

I may be getting sober, but not sober enough to search for that character. Well, down the hatch.

He brought the capsule near his lips. But something most peculiar happened. His hand and the capsule seemed to recede into the distance. The closer they came, the farther and farther away they got. Brillig was flushed with a new sensation. It was like no drunkenness he had ever experienced.

And I haven't even taken the drug . . . !

A word exploded into his mind: "Llixgrijb!" he cried. "But what does that mean?"

Before he could consider the question further, the table and walls of his kitchen seemed to race away into the distance.

Strange and undreamed-of realities rushed upon him like a thunderstorm.

Llixgrijb Panics

... In its extra-dimensional prison, the eternally trapped entity is dependent for its entertainment, for its very sanity, on the monumental obtuseness of J. X. Brillig.

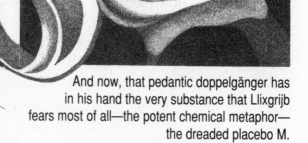

And now, that pedantic doppelgänger has in his hand the very substance that Llixgrijb fears most of all—the potent chemical metaphor— the dreaded placebo M.

With an incredible effort of imagination, Llixgrijb thrusts itself into this illusion of reality, yelling, "I've got to put a stop to this."

But what is going on? Every time Llixgrijb takes the placebo away from *one* Brillig, *another* pops up. Some of the Brilligs are about to swallow M; others are deciding against it; still others have already gulped it down—and several of those have vanished. But where are all these Brilligs coming from? How is the universe doubling, tripling, quadrupling, multiplying toward infinity, faster than even Llixgrijb can keep up with it? The entity decides that it must find out where it lost control. It must locate someone who can answer some questions. "What I need is a physicist!" Llixgrijb decides ...

Pirandello Meets Rasputin

The phone rang. Hector rolled over in bed and picked it up.

"Hector Glasco, M.D.," he grumbled.

He wanted to say, "Who the hell is it?" But he knew it was not good practice for a psychiatrist to curse immediately when answering the phone.

"Glasco!" exclaimed an alarmed voice. "You've got to help me! You've got to get me out of here!"

"Who is this?"

"It's Max! Max Henderson!"

"Do you know what time it is?"

"Do you? Does anybody? What are you asking rhetorical questions for? You've got to help me!"

Hector finally woke up a little. "Max?" he asked.

"Yes, Hector. Max Henderson. Don't you remember?"

Hector sat up in bed and shouted angrily into the telephone. "Max! Where the hell have you been? I looked all over Venice for you. You haven't kept an appointment—haven't even returned a phone call in months."

"I can't discuss that now. I'm in enough trouble as it is."

"What's your problem?" sighed Hector.

"I'm in jail!"

"Then call your lawyer," said Hector, starting to hang up the phone.

"Glasco! Wait! Don't hang up! Whatever you do, don't hang up! They won't give me another phone call. This is not a job for my lawyer. You've got to believe me. I need your help."

"What do you want me to do?"

"Come down and bail me out!"

"Get your wife to bail you out."

"She wasn't *there*, Glasco. She wasn't home. I don't know where she is. I think she's left me. Please. You're my only hope."

"All right, all right. What jail are you in?"

"Jesus, how should I know?"

Hector yawned deeply and scratched his head. "Next time you get busted, Max, try to make it easier for me, okay?"

175

He hung up the phone and stretched, trying to get awake. He prowled into the kitchen and fixed himself a lukewarm cup of instant coffee. Then he got on the phone and called a few police stations until he found out where Max was being held. Then he got in his car and drove.

It's ironic, he thought. *Haven't even seen Max since that strange day at Venice Beach. I discovered the Magical Mundane. I poked star-holes in the universe. I rode a magic carpet. I danced among the worldsprites. I thought my world had changed forever.*

That had only been a couple of months ago. But now he knew it wasn't that easy. Now he was back to treating ex–flower children who felt guilty about their BMWs. And people with midlife crises who felt guilty about their libidos. And stockbrokers and lawyers who felt guilty because they couldn't feel guilty.

His dreams had become brief and elusive. Although he sometimes dimly remembered his encounter with Imogene, nothing in the Dream World seemed real any more.

It was all real once, though, he remembered. *When those dreams were going on, I couldn't even remember waking. And at Venice Beach the flying carpet seemed real. But now, I'm back to the same reality I started in.*

His world wasn't changed at all. And he felt guilty, too—guilty that he couldn't live a life of nonstop wonder. Guilty that a glimpse wasn't enough. Guilty that the lesson didn't stick. And guilty that he still couldn't find Hilary. Hector knew that he was just barely plodding through his daily routine. *Thank God that stuffy midwestern academic sent in enough of his academic blather for the newsletter. I'd never have gotten it out otherwise.*

And here he was, on his way to bail a deconstructionist scholar out of jail.

There's the Mundane, considered Hector as he drove along, *and there is the* mundane.

He went into the police station and paid the cop at the desk $250 for bail.

"What did you nail him for?" asked Hector as he wrote the check.

"Public intoxication and disturbing the peace," said the cop.

"What did he do?"

"He went to a lot of convenience stores and told everybody they were fictional characters."

"What's so terrible about that?"

"Everybody believed him!"

Hector nodded. He could understand how that could happen, whatever realm you happened to be in.

"Just get him out of here, okay?" said the clerk. "We'll drop the charges. We'll do anything. Just get him off our hands. He's giving us a real hard time."

The cop shook his head wearily. He seemed to have the weight of the world on his shoulders.

Then a stocky, cynical cop named Krantz escorted Hector to Max's cell. Prisoners howled, whistled, and cursed, reaching out through the bars as Krantz and Hector walked down the dimly lit corridor. Hector shivered as their grubby fingers actually brushed against his clothing. The smell of uncleansed bodies was suffocating.

"Listen to these guys," muttered Officer Krantz. "Any other night, they're just a bunch of pussycats. As quiet as lambs. But that boy of yours got 'em all worked up. What's the matter with that character, anyway?"

"He's a deconstructionist," said Hector.

Krantz shook his head dubiously. "Like hell he is," he said. "We get lots of deconstructionists through this joint, and this ain't one of them. I mean, I'm pretty hardened to drunken nuts screaming about Heidegger and Derrida and destructive analysis and the rupture in the conventional order. But this is like no form of critical inquiry I've ever run into. This is more like Pirandello meets Rasputin.

"It's like I been saying ever since those goddamn New Critics came along. Some modes of academic discourse ought to be made out-and-out illegal. I'm talkin' about enforceable legislation. I'm talkin' about lockin' up these bozos and throwin' away the key. But does anybody listen? Hell, no. So first you get your New Critics, then your formalists, then your structuralists, and then your deconstructionists, and now your radical historians decontextualizing stuff left and right. A flood of academic riffraff poisoning society, jamming up our institutions of higher learning. Where's it gonna stop?"

Krantz shuddered with revulsion. "I mean, I got a wife and kids. And these guys are treating reality like it's some kind of Tinkertoy. I hate to think what kind of scholarship this looneytune of yours is up to."

Hector had kept quiet as long as he could. "You know what, Krantz?" he said. "Stalin would've loved to have a cop like you on his force."

"Another wise-ass," muttered Krantz, jangling his keys. "Anyways, here we are. Hope you got some sedatives handy. Question is, which of us is gonna need 'em?"

Max was in a cell, sitting on the lower bunk in all his portly, well-dressed, bourgeois splendor. He was surprisingly calm. His cellmate, however, was not so calm. He was a seven-foot monstrosity with gigantic biceps and a mohawk. He crouched terrified in a corner, screaming his head off.

"Krantz, get this guy away from me!" he hollered. "He's messin' with my head. He's messin' with me real bad."

"Easy does it, Omar," said Krantz. "We're takin' him away right now. And we'll bring you some serial killer to play with. Now won't that be nice?"

Omar nodded frantically in agreement.

Krantz wagged his finger scoldingly at Max. "You ought to be ashamed of yourself, scaring this nice gentleman so. Now are you going to come quietly, or am I going to have to use the cuffs?"

Max held out both hands pleasantly. "You'd better use the cuffs, Officer. I'm not exactly responsible for my actions."

Krantz gave Hector a nudge. "Sure you want this joker in your custody?" he whispered. "I hate to turn prisoners over to their lawyers when they're this deranged."

"I'm not his lawyer," said Hector. "I'm his psychiatrist."

"Oh, well, in that case, I'd recommend about 40 cc's of Thorazine with a Valium chaser."

They retraced their steps down the corridor. The prisoners, agitated enough before, went absolutely crazy. They shouted curses and obscenities at Max. They shook the bars and pounded on the walls. They screamed for blood and justice. Max responded to their fury with a detached little smile, nodding and waving and bowing to them as he walked along. It was if he were acknowledging their applause.

The clerk returned Max's belongings. Krantz started to unlock the handcuffs.

"Really, Officer, is that quite necessary?" inquired Max politely. "I was just getting used to them."

"Police property," sneered Krantz. "Whataya think, you get to take 'em home?"

Max climbed into Hector's car. They drove off.

"Where are you taking me?" asked Max.

"I'm taking you home," said Hector.

"Is that really wise? Don't I need observation?"

"I'm too tired to observe anybody. You should have called your lawyer."

"I told you before. This is not a case for my lawyer."

"So, you got a little plastered and went around telling a few people that they were fictional characters," said Hector boredly. "That's not so bad. It may even mean that you're making progress. You're learning how to let off steam."

Max sat silently for a moment, staring out the window.

Then he said, "It was true."

"What was true?"

"What I said. What I told everybody. That they were fictional. You're fictional. I'm fictional. Everybody's fictional. That's my story and I'm sticking to it."

Hector moaned aloud. "God, Max, it's lucky those jailbirds didn't kill you."

"We're all written down in a book," said Max. "I saw it. I read parts of it. I read the part where I first came to you for therapy."

Hector began to wonder if Max's condition was more intractable than he had realized. He drove along, thinking and worrying.

"You don't believe me," said Max.

Hector was silent.

"Look," said Max, "let me tell you how it happened. I was in that bookstore, you know, and Krassner had disappeared and I found that dictionary—a whole tome of signs and signifiers, of meanings without objects. It was beautiful,

178

Glasco! I mean, for a few moments there, I was in deconstructionist heaven!"

Hector said nothing.

"But then something happened," continued Max. "Definitions became absurd. Identifications became absurd. Everything began to vanish. Then some kind of hole opened up. I fell through it. I fell and fell and fell. I—I found myself in—"

But Max's voice choked. He seemed unable to go on.

"God, it was weird," he said.

"Where?" asked Hector, trying to convey some compassion. "It's okay. Just tell me where."

"I was in this living room in a town called Elmblight, Ohio. I was surrounded by a bunch of old ladies. It was some kind of garden club or something. And they all had copies of a book. And we were in this book. They were reading all about us. I stayed with them for a while, and I read with them. And then—wham!— I found myself back inside the book again.

"It worries me, Glasco. It really worries me. I mean, if we're really written down in a book, that means there's got to be an author. That means there's such a thing as authority. That means there's a God."

"That's poetic justice for you."

"It's not funny, damn it!"

"What about the 'public intoxication' part?"

"I'd rather not get into that," mumbled Max.

The two of them were quiet for a moment.

"I thought I'd heard everything," said Hector.

"So you don't believe me," moaned Max.

"I didn't say that. I just said I thought I'd heard everything."

"Christ, Glasco," sobbed Max, "what've I got to do to prove it? I mean, do I have to tell you all the sordid details?"

There was another awkward silence.

"I read other stuff," panted Max grimly. "I read stuff about you. I read stuff nobody could know. I read your fantasies about Hilary. I read about her flying off on that carpet. I read about your placebo trip with that *brujo* character."

Hector felt a rush of alarm. He shivered. "How could you know about those things?" he asked, his voice trembling.

"I've even read parts of the scene we're acting out right now," cried Max, clutching his head in his hands. "Talk about *déjà vu!* I think I'm getting sick. I think I'm slipping through again."

"Sit tight," said Hector. "I'm taking you to the hospital. Maybe you should be under observation."

"I'm not going to make it."

"Don't be silly," said Hector. "If I survived all those dreams, you can survive this."

Hector swerved in order not to run over a cat.

"You're going to make it, Max. You know that, don't you? Don't you?"

Hector turned and looked toward the passenger side.

But Max was gone.

"And not even a flying carpet this time," muttered Hector between clenched teeth.

Café Teatro Athanor

Brillig raised his arms to ward off a lightning bolt that roared past his head. He could smell the scorched air. As he tumbled through a maelstrom of shadows and sensations, he recognized Zeus on a thundercloud, laughing. He caught a glimpse of a medieval knight wearing a cross and swinging a bloody sword. He recoiled from a flash of teeth as a coyote grinned evilly at him. At his elbow, planets were created and destroyed. A pale white human profile turned to stare at him and revealed a yin-yang painted mask.

Brillig tumbled over and over. Gradually he became aware of a consistent sound of drums. They seemed to be pulling him in a specific direction. Then an image rose before him. He floated toward it. He could tell that it was some sort of ancient god-figure, but not one he recognized. It wore a wide flat headdress and was covered all over with carved patterns and symbols. It stood in dignity, with peaceful visage, radiating calm and benevolence. It extended a hand to him.

Desperately, Brillig reached out toward the image. Just when he seemed about to grasp its hand, the rhythm of the drums changed and the figure turned away from him. Brillig gasped. On its back was another face! Now he was confronted with a death's head that leered and nodded for him to come closer. Brillig screamed and flailed his arms and legs to stop his forward motion.

The death's head laughed loudly. Then the figure began to change. It grew taller. Before his horrified eyes it transformed into a serpent with a demonic head. Feathered wings lifted from its sides and arched over Brillig.

Quetzalcoatl? he wondered, drawing a name from a bit of almost-forgotten mythology. With a single swoop the serpent rose into the air and was gone.

After a time, Brillig realized that he was huddled against a hard stone wall. It was night—a warm and semitropical darkness. Brillig was standing in a tiny cobblestone lane. And now—where was he? And what was he doing here? He looked around. The street was narrow and crooked. The surrounding houses had plaster walls and tile roofs. He could still hear the drums—a driving, pounding, crashing rhythm coming from not far away.

Brillig followed the sound. He emerged onto larger and larger lanes. Automobiles began to appear, some parked precariously against the high stone curbs, others bouncing laboriously along the cobblestones, preposterous anachronisms lurching through the night, trying to find their way home to the twentieth century. He recoiled from the stark and crazy shadows the headlights cast everywhere, but soon realized that he was back in something like his familiar reality. The shadows were not going to change into fearful images.

At last, Brillig emerged onto a spacious town square with immaculately groomed trees pruned almost into perfect cylinders. The square was filled with people. Many were dark-skinned; others were gringos of various ages.

I'm certainly not in Sequester, Missouri, anymore, Brillig thought wryly. *But where?*

At that moment a bus full of youngsters pulled up in the square and began to unload. Brillig spotted the license plate.

Ah, I see. Mexico. But surely I must be only dreaming.

The drums were louder now, coming from the other side of the square. There a parrish church towered, its stern, shadowy gothic lines leaning against the stars. He could see outsized shadows whirling against a building. They looked like gigantic feathers dancing.

He hesitated. He had no desire to meet the plumed serpent again just now. But Brillig could see that these dancers were men, women, and children, laughing and obviously having a wonderful time.

Aside from the drums, musicians played upon turtle and armadillo shells. And the dancers wore chains of tiny seashells around their necks and ankles. In the courtyard of the gothic church, and in the street beside it, dancers moved together to prehistoric rhythms. Brillig pressed closer, fascinated by the startling juxtaposition.

To add to the incongruity, the dance swarmed around and around a statue of a certain "Fray Juan de San Miguel"—a colonialist image if ever there was one, showing a saintly, dignified, and berobed monk comforting a cowering, naked savage. The dance seemed at once a mockery and a celebration of both this "Fray Juan" chap and the parrish church itself.

Norteamericano retirees in plaid pants and flowered dresses circulated with their cameras among the crowd of onlookers, firing off salvo after salvo of flashbulbs. The whole scene was a crazy juxtaposition of the Old World and the New, the Christian and the pagan, the Hispanic and the Anglo.

"Dualities!" gasped Brillig. "I am adrift in a world gone mad with myths and dualities!"

But am I actually here? he wondered again. It certainly didn't feel much like a dream. There was an incredible richness of detail that was unfamiliar to Brillig, asleep or awake.

He strained to remember. *I was in my own kitchen. I was staring at that blasted capsule.*

Is that it? Is this entire scene just a placebo-induced figment of my imagination?

But no, it can't be. I didn't even swallow it. I tried to, but it never seemed to reach my lips.

He couldn't think over the sound of the drums and the happy chatter of the crowd. He needed to escape from all this chaos and turmoil to consider his situation. So he wandered away from the town square and up yet another cobblestone street.

He passed a number of markets, cantinas, and *farmacias.* The street began to narrow as he went, and there were fewer and fewer cars. History itself seemed to wax and wane, warp and twist through the streets of this small town.

Brillig noticed, uncomfortably, that his movements were becoming rather jerky and awkward. He stopped and rested, then started again, but the condition did not change. His limbs actually seemed to be carrying him in a specific direction, as if with some purpose.

At last, a colorful shop sign caught his eye. It hung over a heavy wooden doorway, and featured a brightly colored lion which appeared to be trying to devour a flaming sun. The sign announced:

Café Teatro Athanor
Un Lugar Mágico

With what little remained of his high school Spanish, Brillig was able to translate that last phrase: "A Magical Place."

Brillig stood in the balmy night and frowned. *Why am I here?* he wondered. He reminded himself that he was a man of reason. He had long professed a disbelief in magic. But something like magic had transported him to this strange world of juxtapositions and dualities. And despite all his rationality, he couldn't figure out how to find his way home.

And so he moved jerkily through the door into the café. The first thing to catch his eye was a parchment nailed to the wall. In both Spanish and English, it defined the word "Athanor":

> This word originally stood for the alchemist's crucible, into which he gazed waiting for the transmutation of base metals into philosophical gold. Theater, for us, is this crucible. The metals are the human materials, the resulting gold is the secret of life.

Brillig looked around and found himself in a tiny, dimly lit theater. Patrons sat at tables covered with white cloths, sipping coffee, beer, or mineral water. They were a blend of Mexicans, *norteamericanos,* and still other nationalities, speaking in an easy and amiable mix of languages.

At the far end of the café was a miniature stage, concealed now behind a rust-red curtain. The proscenium arch featured a painting of a nude woman riding some sort of exotic sea creature. Her breasts were fountains of milk, and she was flanked on either side by dragons.

Murals on the café-theater walls featured tarotlike images of skeletons, demons, earth mothers, and cosmic lovers. Chimerical animals joined the painted throng—strange birds and bats, and four-legged, sphinxlike beasts with pointed ears and wings and tails.

Papier mâché masks and puppets hung all about. Painted in bright primary colors, they were of close kin to the mural figures.

Brillig could hardly catch his breath. He was not at home in such exotic surroundings, but he nevertheless took a seat. He remembered a line that someone once wrote or said: "The Magic Theater is not for everyone."

The question is, he wondered, *is it for me?*

Brillig ordered a glass of mineral water. The houselights soon went down. The curtains opened. But no actors, sets, or properties appeared before his eyes.

Instead, he saw. . .

Shadows!

Yes, a screen spread out before him, and upon it danced a multitude of shadows. These were no stark, ascetic shadows of black and white and gray. Instead, they were wildly colored and of fantastic shapes, created out of an assortment of different kinds of media—some solid, others multicolored, painted, translucent or transparent. It was like a stained glass window exploding vibrantly to life. Shapes grew and blossomed, shrank and subsided, appeared and magically disappeared, while the theater was filled with the music of Steven Halpern and Edgar Varèse.

There was narration, too—of a sort. But the shadow-play was based more on images than words. And the shadows told a tale. Doubtless, it was a different tale to every single person in the audience. It was a story of a blind child adopted by animals in the forest; of her quest into the world of human beings; of the men who had invented so many machines that they became mechanical, too; of the Spirits who rule the world; and of the Dance of Creation which human beings might someday reenter.

Brillig sat and observed, absolutely spellbound. The dance of shadows filled him with a strange and inexplicable alarm.

When the curtain closed, the audience broke into enthusiastic applause. Brillig started in his seat. He felt as though a spell had been broken. He found that he could not remember the story he had just seen. He swallowed the last of his mineral water. Shakily, he got to his feet.

Members of the audience got out of their chairs and milled about talking to one another. Brillig found something about their movements strangely alien, unnerving. Their arms and legs swung jerkily. Were they all afflicted with the strange condition he had been experiencing?

Carefully, he crept among them, hoping to find the enchanter—or enchantress—who had produced such magic. In a few moments, he found a woman sitting alone. She had a long, elegant face framed in a mane of wild, reddish hair. Her fingers were flamboyantly adorned with rings. A handsome stone dangled from one finger by a chain.

"My name is Joseph Xavier Brillig," he said. "May I ask what's yours?"

"María De Céspedes," said the woman, in a low, throaty voice with a rich French accent. "I am the director of the theater."

"I thought as much," said Brillig.

"Please take a seat," said María. Brillig did so.

He faltered for a moment or two, wondering what to say. He did not wish to reveal the disquieting effect María's shadow-play had had upon him—much less to admit his own strange dislocation. And so he said, without exactly meaning it, "It was a diverting entertainment—although better suited to children, I suppose."

The woman threw back her head and laughed. Then she looked at him, smiling. "So you did not care for it?" she inquired, her eyes gleaming with mischief. Brillig had the feeling she could see right through him.

"Oh, I wouldn't say that," said Brillig nervously. "But I am—how shall I put it?—an admirer of Ibsen. The realistic theater, that's more to my liking. I think so often of poor Hedda, revealed at the end of Act IV in the alcove, dead and bleeding from her own gunshot wound, while Judge Brack cries out, 'But my God! People don't do such things!' Now that's real theater! Something that announces its reality to us! Something that tells us, vividly and plausibly, 'For good or bad, this is the way life is.'"

Then María leaned forward and purred a question: "But is it truly *realistic?*"

The question made Brillig even more uneasy than before, so he evaded it. "Of course," he said, "as a scholar, I have read about the long and time-honored tradition of shadow theater. It is called *wajang kulit*, if I am not mistaken, and it comes from Java.

"But here's what bothers me. Your shadow-play reminds me of Plato's allegory of the cave—surely you remember it. People are tied up inside the cave staring at the wall. Far behind them, in the back of the cave, a fire burns. Cutout figures are carried back and forth in front of the fire, casting shadows on the wall before these people. These shadows of mere cutouts are the only reality these poor wretches know—while outside the cave and completely unknown to them burns the real and ideal light of the sun.

"Not that I buy into Plato, of course," added Brillig firmly. "But isn't your theater rather like his cave? And aren't you perpetuating more illusion in a world where reality is already confusing enough?"

"People sometimes sense a consciousness that they can never touch," explained María enigmatically. "A feeling of this consciousness is what I always want to express."

"But your theater is based on nothing more than images!" complained Brillig. "And all great theater is based on great texts! Think of the Greeks, of Shakespeare. Think of Ibsen, Tennessee Williams, Arthur Miller."

María shrugged. "I love text," she said simply, "but it happens that I don't use a lot of text. Sometimes I use text, sometimes no. I am happy when I can only use music." Then, with a laugh, she added, "Who wants to hear shadows talking? That is ridiculous!

"You see, I love visual language, with masks, with images out of the subconscious. To use a big mask is very different than to use your face. I use the face, also. But the symbolic quality of a mask moves people in a deeper way. You push people to see things at another level.

"And so I never direct myself toward people's intellect. I want to touch the subconscious.

"It is a very old tradition to speak through images, not through language. Wise people have spoken always through images. The indigenous languages here in Mexico are rich with images. In the Nahuan language, the word for river means 'the road moving by itself.'"

Then, savoring the phrase, she repeated, "'The road moving by itself!'

"In many ways, I prefer to play in front of country people. The indigenous people here can sometimes catch what I'm trying to do better than an intellectual—better than a learned scholar like yourself, perhaps!"

"It all strikes me as deliberate primitiveness," grumbled Brillig.

"Perhaps it is," said María. "I have been told that what I do is very close to pre-hispanic theater. Well, I did not know this, and had not intended to do this. Others have said that what I do is like the source of theater. And after all, there has long been a tendency in modern art to look for something more organic. Picasso and others were looking for the source of art itself. And, like other modern artists, I want to catch the duality of the human being."

Brillig started at these words. *Dualities again!*

"Would you please explain what you meant by that?" he asked.

María smiled and lit a cigarette. "Let me tell you a story that I have not yet put on stage," she said. "It is a tale on an Oriental theme.

"A young man pays a visit to a wise man who is meditating near a river. 'I want to know God,' he tells the wise man. 'I want to see through all of life's illusions.'

"'Very well,' the wise man says. 'But before I answer, take this pitcher and fetch a little water for me. I am thirsty.'

"So the young man goes to the river to get some water. But as he is about to dip his pitcher there, what does he find in the water but a beautiful woman!

"He falls in love. He forgets the water. He makes a life with the woman. She dies. He goes through all kinds of catastrophes and drama—you can fill in that part of the story yourself! Then, one day many years later, the young man

186

remembers his original question. He returns to the wise man, more troubled than ever, and asks him the meaning of it all.

"But the wise man only says, 'Where is my water?'"

Brillig stared at her uncomprehendingly for a moment. Then, his voice shaking with agitation, he said, "But that doesn't answer my question! All you've done is tell me a story without a message, without a solution!"

"I try never to offer a solution," said María bluntly. "It's too easy."

This was too much for Brillig. His life was a riddle enough already. He looked around for the most effective avenue of escape through the audience, but could not convince his body to get up and leave.

Then again, he noticed something odd about everybody's movements. Glancing at María, he could see it about her too. He gazed at his own hand. What was it exactly?

He made another quick survey of the Café Teatro Athanor. Then he realized the truth.

Every single person in the theater was a puppet!

Yes, why hadn't he seen it before? Everybody's movements were perfectly orchestrated. The whole scene was like some elaborate, exquisitely choreographed minuet. The hands and limbs were beautifully carved from wood, or shaped from papier mâché. The faces were all painted and glazed with brilliant sculptural detail. And he had come here and joined them, because he was a puppet, too.

He could even see the puppeteers now. How had he missed them before? They were huddled in threes behind each puppet. One, whose face was uncovered, manipulated the head, the eyebrows, and the right arm of each puppet with little rods. His two assistants, cloaked in black but hardly invisible, manipulated the other arm and the legs.

It was *bunraku*, Brillig realized with amazement—a Japanese form he had seen on television and read about. But now it seemed that all reality was *bunraku*.

He gazed closely at María. The movements of her splendid features were more elaborately subtle than those of the other puppets. Her puppeteer seemed even to control the brilliant glistening of her eye, the tiniest motion of her lips.

And now, Brillig raised his own hand and looked at it again. He felt a cold shudder in his wooden limbs. A stick, attached to him by a small metal swivel, extended below his hand and vanished behind him. He had not raised his hand at all. His puppeteer had raised it for him. He turned his head. No one was hiding behind curtains here. In his peripheral vision, he could fleetingly glimpse the face of his own puppet master.

"Who's there?" he asked the puppeteer. "Who are you?"

But of course, there was no answer. And Brillig knew the question was futile. Even the sound of his voice was not really his own. His very words were merely some ventriloquist's trick.

He felt afraid. But surely that was also the result of some string or rod. *How many wires,* he wondered, *what kind of illusion and artifice make up human feeling?*

And my thoughts—this thought. . . and this thought—who is working the controls?

Gasping slightly, he said to María, "We are all puppets. This is all a puppet show. Is this what you meant by 'a consciousness that we can never touch'? And is it this consciousness that you're trying to express?"

But María made no reply. She only smiled at him. Then she looked at her watch.

"Intermission is over," she said. "The second half of the show is about to begin."

And sure enough, the *bunraku* audience members were all returning to their seats.

Brillig trembled in his chair. He felt his heart—or the sensory illusion that he called his heart—beating wildly.

"Oh, please, María," he said. "Please tell me what comes next in this magic theater of yours. I can't bear any more surprises. My reality is battered enough already."

"Don't worry," said María pleasantly. "The next drama is solely for you. And you shall choose it for yourself."

And she held out a small, woolen pouch. She opened it, revealing a deck of cards, their faces down.

"Would you care to mix the deck?" asked María.

Brillig only shook his head. María spread the cards across the table. Brillig chose a card and turned it over.

It was the tarot Trump III, "The Empress," a golden-haired goddess lounging on a luxurious, pillow-laden couch in the midst of a lush, green garden. She wore a glorious crown encrusted with stars and an opulent necklace of identical pearls. In her right hand she held a scepter topped with a small yellow globe— a symbol of the sun's fecundity. Resplendent wheat grew at her feet, and majestic trees towered in the distance behind her.

On the café stage, the rust-red curtains opened. And behold, the Empress herself, the most perfect of all the puppets, was sitting there in her garden. To be sure, the wheat was cut out of cardboard and the trees sculpted out of chicken wire and papier mâché, with leaves of bright green construction paper. And to be sure, the three puppeteers were in full view.

And yet, the whole scene was the more alive for being all illusion. Brillig heard himself mutter, "This is real. This is as real as real can get."

Then the scene upon the stage began to change. The yellow cardboard wheat turned a wilting brown. The green paper leaves turned yellow and red; they trembled and threatened to fall. And the Empress's crown started to droop. Her expression of pleasure and contentment at the earth's bounty turned to one of anguish and despair.

And did Brillig see a tear spill from her brilliant eye? And did that tear mar the glaze of the goddess's exquisite features? And if so, how did the puppet master succeed in making his creation weep? It was an act of splendid artifice.

A gusty chill passed through the theater. There came a rattling like wind chimes as all the puppets in the Café Teatro Athanor shivered. He heard the goddess mourn, "She is gone. She is dead."

This drama is for me? Brillig wondered. The thought disturbed him deeply. He turned toward María appealingly. "Help me," he said. "Help me to make her understand it is only a play. Tell her that no one has died."

María shook her head. "I cannot," she said. "It is your story now."

The goddess keened and sobbed. Brillig could not bear her pain. He stepped upon the stage and into her story.

How's the Universe Today, Mac?

... Dr. Fred Alan Wolf was on his way to give a lecture in quantum physics at the New York Open Center. As you may know, there are an infinite number of paths to get from A to B in New York City, especially on the southern end of Manhattan Island. Since it was a pleasant autumn morning, he wended his way on foot from the East Village to Greenwich Village. He chose a path that took him through Washington Square.

Various human forms roamed the square: mothers pushing baby carriages, businessmen toting briefcases, panhandlers asking for money. A tall gangly man flopped tiredly onto a park bench, as if in slow motion. There was something mechanical about all their movements, something dreamlike and unnatural. They were like silent chess pieces.

Wolf stared, both delighted and a bit uneasy. He turned as a voice to his right caught his ear.

"Hey, Mac," said the voice. A particularly scruffy vagrant was sitting on a bed of cardboard, staring up at him in the pale sunlight. Somehow, Wolf knew the vagrant wasn't going to ask him for money.

"How's the universe today, Mac?" queried the derelict. Wolf felt a jolt. After all, he was on the way to the Open Center to discuss that very question. This had to be more than mere coincidence. "Well," replied Wolf amiably, "that's an interesting question. You know, I've had this notion since I was a child: that our entire reality is taking place in some entity's mind. This is all a stupendous illusion, in which space, time, size, matter, energy, and everything we know is being created. Somehow, this entity is able to create a hologram of its brain in which all of this is taking place, including the illusion of size and matter and energy. Did you ever get that feeling?"

The vagrant stared at him silently, eyes squinting with curiosity. *Yes,* thought Wolf. *He knows all about that feeling.*

Wolf felt a chill of apprehension. "But even as I say all this," he continued, "we don't fully recognize each other as projections of ourselves. I mean, you can say me and I can say me and it's always the *same* me, isn't it? It's All One Self projecting this. And this is all a great big fantasy or phantasmagorical masturbation of some form or another."

The vagrant stood up and stretched. He shoved his hands in his pockets and shook his head with apparent incomprehension.

But does he really understand a word of this? Wolf asked himself. *Maybe I'm wrong.*

"You know," he said to the vagrant with a note of apology, "the real problem is that I'm constantly trying to communicate something out on the very edge, where language itself is inappropriate. I'm trying to stay within the framework of the appropriate language of a classical-Newtonian-deterministic-causal way of thinking to explain things which are *not* classical-Newtonian-deterministic-causal. And I run into all kinds of problems trying to do this."

The vagrant chuckled hoarsely. "It's all right, Mac," he said. "These reality changes get the best of us all."

Then he looked directly at Wolf and said, "I'll bet this entity you're talking about is having a rough time, huh? I mean, here we are, its kids as it were, and we keep learning more and more all the time. If we learn too much, we'll sooner or later come face to face with this character. Then its whole creation will go up in smoke! And whenever it tries to stop us, another reality pops up in which we keep learning anyway! I wouldn't want to be in that entity's shoes, let me tell you."

"Nor would I," said Wolf.

But of course, he thought, *that's exactly where we all really are.*

Wolf handed the vagrant a dollar and moved on. He felt an intuitive surge that got stronger and stronger as he left the square. It was almost unnerving—but nevertheless exhilarating.

Suddenly, he stopped dead in his tracks. A moment before, he had been walking down an expansive sidewalk. There had been other people around. But now he was staring down a narrow, blind alleyway. He was alone.

Or was he? . . .

191

A Trick of the Light

The next morning, Hector arose at his usual time and headed for work. He was unusually tired, of course. But he was trying not to think about Max and . . . wherever he had gone.

As he walked down the hallway toward his office, something happened to him. His footsteps slowed. Then he froze in his tracks. He stared numbly at his name on the door. For an endless minute, he couldn't make himself go inside. He couldn't even move. He just stood there, immobilized with doubt and perplexity.

What if they knew? he wondered. *What if my patients knew?*

After all, he got paid to restore normalcy to troubled lives. He got paid to make people believe that reality itself was valid and true and worthwhile.

And now Hector had just spent the early morning hours face to face with the suggestion of his own fictionality. He shuddered.

What if they found out half the stuff that's happened?

Well, they couldn't find out, that's all. Too many people depended on him to make sense of their lives. His job might be a lie, but it was a damned important lie. And it was his responsibility. He had no choice.

He took a deep breath and summoned up his courage. He stepped through the door. Miss Bellows sat at her desk, poring over a particularly difficult book of gridless crossword puzzles.

"Any patients yet?" asked Hector.

"Not yet," said Miss Bellows. "What's a five-letter word meaning 'to show contempt'?"

"I'm the last guy to ask. You know that. Who's coming in first?"

"Mrs. Clemens. In half an hour."

"Good," said Hector. "Maybe I'll take a short nap. Be sure to wake me up a few minutes before she gets here."

"Sure," said Miss Bellows, without lifting her eyes from the puzzle.

Miss Bellows's very blandness was somehow comforting this morning. It grounded Hector. There was far too much spice and strangeness in his life.

Blandness is good, thought Hector. *Blandness is welcome.*

He almost told Miss Bellows to keep up the blandness, but thought better of it. She might not take it the right way.

He walked into his office and took off his hat. His eyes quickly surveyed the room, still cluttered with all its meaningless bric-a-brac. As usual, everything radiated in the sweet light of morning. It was a room full of haloes. Hector always took pleasure in this daily first glimpse of his professional domain.

But a strange vision met his eyes. It was a slight, elderly, blue-haired lady in a jogging suit. She sat in his patients' chair, sewing on a quilt. He could swear she hadn't been there when he first came in. And for a weird split second in the yellowish light, she actually appeared to be transparent.

Hector blinked hard. And when he looked again, she seemed perfectly substantial.

She stared down at her quilt, then looked up into Hector's eyes. "It came with me," she remarked with stunned wonder. "My sewing came with me."

A bit dazedly, she rose from her chair. She seemed extremely disoriented. She stared at Hector blankly for a moment. Then a grin broke out across her face.

"It feels so strange to be here!" she said. "And yet—not strange at all! Why, everything seems so real!"

Then she sat slowly, as if about to faint. She collected her wits, studying every object in the room with extreme care. She seemed to be absolutely mesmerized.

More than a little nonplussed, Hector rushed out of his office. He pointed an accusing finger at Miss Bellows.

"I thought you said I didn't have any patients yet!" he exclaimed.

"You don't," said Miss Bellows, still staring at her crossword puzzle. "What's a seven-letter word meaning 'an embodiment'?"

"Who is that woman in my office?"

"What woman?"

"You know what woman I'm talking about!"

"I certainly do not," grumbled Miss Bellows. "Probably just a trick of the light. Some kind of freak mirage caused by all that junk you've got heaped up in there."

Hector thought of marching Miss Bellows into his office to see for herself, but reconsidered. Perhaps it *was* just a trick of the light.

But when he went back in, the old lady was still there. She had risen from the chair and had put her sewing down. She was roaming around the office, glowing with delight and curiosity. Hector closed the office door cautiously behind him.

"I do like your office, Dr. Glasco," she said. "It's quite convincing."

Convincing? wondered Hector. He didn't know what to say. He could think of a number of adjectives to describe his office, including musty, cluttered, chaotic, and unkempt. But *convincing?*

"But it's different than I expected" the lady continued. "From the descriptions in those first couple of chapters, I expected it to be a bit more old-fashioned, a little less chrome and glass. I expected the upholstery to be fluffier. I thought there would be wood paneling on the walls.

"Still, I must be making all this up in a way. I mean, if the authors didn't mention all these details, then I must be filling them in, mustn't I? So I guess it's all really just what I expected after all!"

"I guess," Hector said stupidly.

"What an intriguing notion!" she said. "I wonder . . ." The old lady put her hand to her head and screwed up her forehead in concentration. Something shifted in the office light. The chrome table legs became less shiny. The sofa bulged fluffily. As the walls began to darken, Hector yelled, "What are you doing!"

"Oh, I was just experimenting with a little rewriting," she answered. "You're quite right, I have no business doing it. It takes skill and practice and courage to be an author. I'm sure I'd lose control and just make a terrible mess."

The room reverted to normal. "And if my friends were here, they'd see your office as looking completely different than I see it! Why, we'd never come to any consensus at all. We'd probably trip all over each other because we couldn't even agree about where the furniture is. We have enough trouble in our own houses!"

"Is this a dream?" Hector demanded.

"Why no, not at all," she replied distractedly. "My friends and I have never taken any particular interest in dreams—beyond the occasional lucid or prophetic experience, of course. We're really more concerned with *literature*, with *ideas*."

Then she went over to the window and leaned out. "And the view! Why, such a fine panorama of the Hollywood Hills! And there's the Hollywood sign, just as big as the world! Your author didn't describe any of that! Of course, I guess there are summer days when you can't see that far. But I do like this view."

Then she stepped slowly toward Hector

"And I like you, too," she added, with just a trace of flirtation. "You're much like I pictured. So . . . lifelike. Why, I could actually reach out and touch you! May I?"

Lifelike? Hector wanted to ask. But instead, he nodded mutely. The lady reached up and touched his chin.

"Yes, a nice, strong, caring face," she said, smiling. "It takes a life well-lived to make a face like that. But you didn't shave this morning, did you? I suppose, with all that trouble you had getting Max out of jail last night, you didn't get a whole lot of sleep."

Hector glared at her indignantly. "Madam," he blurted, "what on *earth* are you *talking* about? And where did you come from? And how in the hell do you know what I did last night?"

194

"Oh, dear," said the lady, suddenly quite flustered. "Oh, dear. Oh, dear. You don't understand this in the least, do you? I feel like I know you so very well, but I completely forgot! *You* don't know *me* at all! How awfully rude of me!"

"Hector," she added with sudden formality, "it seems I've got some explaining to do. I think we'd both better sit down."

"I quite agree," said Hector.

They sat looking at each other in silence for a moment. Then the lady spoke.

"My name is Myrtle Roebuck. I'm a member of the Elmblight, Ohio, Book Club and Sewing Circle. I believe our mutual friend Max Henderson mentioned us last night. You see, he came to visit us."

Hector's jaw froze. He stared.

"We're reading about you in a book," said Myrtle.

Hector tried to utter a sound, but his throat was closed up tight. The blood drained from his head. He felt extremely dizzy.

"I'm sorry if this causes you alarm," continued Myrtle. "But please understand, I'm not exactly used to this sort of thing myself. Perhaps, when I get back to my friends and read this chapter over again, it won't seem quite so peculiar. But on the other hand . . ."

She sat quietly, pursing her lips, lost in thought.

Hector wrenched his jaw open and managed to utter a question:

"What . . . are . . . you *doing* here?"

"Interesting that you should ask," replied Myrtle perkily. "I was just trying to think of that very thing. I'd hate to think I'm bothering you for no reason."

Then she snapped her fingers. "Oh, yes! Now I remember! I had a book I wanted you to look at!"

She groped around in her handbag and took out a book.

"I thought you might be particularly curious about the nature of human consciousness and sentience and all that, now that you've found out you're a fictional character."

"I wasn't *sure* I was a fictional character," muttered Hector with despair, "until *now.*"

"Well, it was only a matter of time," said Myrtle simply. "Take a look at this."

And she handed him the book. It was entitled *Consciousness Explained*, by Daniel C. Dennett.

Myrtle waved her finger at him emphatically.

"This Professor Dennett is a very astute man," she said. "You might want to pay him a visit—that is, if he happens to exist in the world of this book. I guess that's unlikely. You see, he's a physicalist. Doesn't go in for a lot of dualistic stuff. Looks to the brain itself as the true source of consciousness." Then she chuckled. "I guess he's got good reason. He got into serious identity problems when his own brain was surgically removed."

"That's impossible," Hector sputtered.

Myrtle shrugged. "It was only a story," she said. "It's in another book called *Brainstorms*. I thought that you might present him with an even more interesting dilemma. After all, your consciousness is made only out of ink and paper!

"Why," she added, giggling, "you don't even have a brain at all!"

Myrtle rose from her chair, gathered up her sewing, and deposited it in her handbag.

"Well," she said, "I'd better get back. My friends will be having a fit by now, I expect. You see, they're reading about us, even as we speak. I guess I've got some explaining to do. Tally ho!"

Myrtle briskly strode out of his office. Hector walked to the window and stared down at the street below. Before too long, Myrtle emerged onto the street, walked jauntily along, and disappeared around the corner of a building.

At least she didn't vanish into thin air, he thought. *I've had quite enough of that.*

Hector stepped out into the lobby. Miss Bellows had dropped her book of crossword puzzles on the floor. Completely catatonic, she stared toward the front doorway.

"Just a trick of the light, eh, Miss Bellows?" said Hector.

4:30 P.M.

. . . "Well, Myrtle Roebuck, you certainly can't deny it this time!" Ethel said sternly. She had given up on her knitting.

Myrtle stretched and yawned. Then she sat up and smiled.

"And what's more," Ethel added, "you've convinced poor Hector that he's fictional! And what do you think that will lead to?"

"I'm not denying anything," said Myrtle, smiling sweetly. "I figure that if a body is going to be blamed for everything, she might as well go ahead." She checked her handbag to make sure that her sewing had returned with her.

"I think you had this planned all along," said Phoebe.

"Not exactly." Myrtle giggled. "But you must admit that these little experiments offer fascinating possibilities."

"How did it feel?" asked Addie. She tied a big knot on the front of her composition.

"Perfectly natural, really. Once I got there. It was just a tiny bit disorienting at first. I suppose it *was* rather like lucid dreaming, but it took a more concentrated effort to get there. And everything was so *real*."

"I thought this was precisely the sort of intrusion we had agreed not to perpetrate," said Lida June, stitching in time with her words. "And I also thought it was a terrible insult, telling poor Hector he had no brain."

"I was just stating a simple fact," rejoined Myrtle.

"But whatever makes you think that?" asked Lida June.

"Well, I don't know," sputtered Myrtle. "I just don't remember the authors ever saying he did."

"The authors can't do everything. They never said he had arms or legs, did they?"

"Well, I don't remember them saying so, but—"

"For that matter, they never mentioned an elevator or stairs, but you managed to get in and out of that building, didn't you?"

"There were a lot of things there the authors never *described*," snapped Myrtle. "Like the chrome and glass furniture and the view out the window. I guess you could say I sort of filled them in myself."

"Exactly my point! The reader has to accept some responsibility for logical consistency. And just because Hector didn't open up the top of his head and put his brain on display, you had to go and tell him he didn't have a brain at all!" Lida June clucked ferociously. "The presumption!"

"Now, Lida June," murmured Addie. "Temper, temper!"

"Lida June is right," said Phoebe. "And there's no way you're going to convince me that reality itself hasn't been compromised by all this chicanery."

"Don't you see?" pleaded Myrtle. "It had to be tried. After Max turned up here, I knew it could be done. Everybody seems to be coming and going pretty much as they like."

"That poor man," said Ethel. "He was confused enough when he got here. And he looked even worse when he left. I'm afraid the brownies were the final straw."

"And not a one of them left!" complained Phoebe. "I'd been looking forward to one all afternoon." She added some gold metallic yarn to Quetzalcoatl's wings.

"Poor man," Ethel repeated. "Do you suppose he fell into one of those reality leaks Phoebe was talking about?"

"More than likely," said Myrtle. "It's the most logical explanation." She spread a quilting square out on her lap and began stitching carefully around the eyehole of a new mask.

"Logical's a strange word for it," muttered Lida June.

"I don't know," mused Addie. "We haven't seen the last of that old kook, if you ask me."

"Do you really think so?" asked Ethel eagerly.

"Well, think about it," said Addie. "The last we read about him in the book, he had just disappeared from Hector's car."

"Yes," said Ethel. "Just exactly the way he vanished from this very room! Poof! Just like that!"

"So where do *you* think he's headed next?" continued Addie. "The way things are going for him, this is the only home he's got. He'll be back. You can count on it."

"I do hope so!" exclaimed Ethel.*

Addie turned back to Myrtle and asked, "But when you left Hector's office, why did you *walk* away? I mean, couldn't you have just disappeared?"

---

* "Ethel Wainwright, I think you're awfully interested in this Max," said Phoebe. "I think maybe someone besides Myrtle would like to have a relationship with a younger man."

"I'm just showing a little human consideration," said Ethel, rather stiffly.

"But, Ethel," snickered Phoebe. "Can you imagine the difficulties in carrying on an inter-reality romance?"

"I don't suppose it would be any more complicated than things were back during the civil rights marches through Georgia. Safer, maybe."

"Of course." Myrtle shrugged. "But I thought poor Hector had been through enough numinous comings and goings. I waited until I got around the block and out of sight, and *then* I disappeared."

"But you were here the whole time," protested Lida June. "You were sitting right in that chair, sleeping."

"That's right," said Addie. "You didn't vanish like Max does when he goes back and forth."

"Max has enough trouble relating to one reality at a time," said Myrtle.

"We're quite overrun with logical inconsistencies today," said Lida June.

"If you ladies don't mind, I think I'll see what's on TV," interrupted Phoebe, rejoining the main conversation. "I'd like to get my mind off this whole matter for a little while."

"Yes, I agree," said Lida June. "I, for one, would be delighted never to open that book again."

"Well, maybe it's best," conceded Addie. "No more *Jamais Vu* until we can quit quarreling about it."

Myrtle only sulked.

Phoebe turned on the television set. But as the picture flickered to life, the ladies recoiled in unison at what they saw . . .

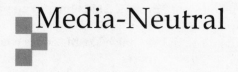Media-Neutral

FADE IN:

On an office door. On it is written:

HECTOR GLASCO, M.D.
CLINICAL PSYCHOTHERAPIST

Mournful, bluesy saxophone music plays in the background. Seemingly of its own agency, the door swings open. THE CAMERA DOLLIES into the office.

HECTOR GLASCO is sitting alone, his feet up on his desk, sipping a shot glass of bourbon.

> HECTOR (Voice Over)
> So now I knew the rotten truth. I was fictional. My whole world was purely fictional. I was just a helpless character, trapped in some clumsily written novel or short story—or maybe even some preposterous movie or TV script no one in his right mind would ever produce. It was heavy news for one day. But now I had to ask myself just one little question. Was I going to take it lying down?

As the saxophone music plays, Hector seems lost in thought. THE CAMERA ZOOMS in slowly on him. He picks up the phone and dials.

> HECTOR
> Yeah, operator. Give me a number for a cab company. Any cab company.

EXT.—HECTOR'S OFFICE BUILDING.

Hector is pacing back and forth on the sidewalk, wearing his hat and overcoat, waiting for a cab.

> HECTOR (Voice Over)
> There's a legend about cabs in L.A. You may have heard it.
> They say there's really only one cab in the entire city. One
> cab for millions and millions of people. It just gets painted
> up differently every day, so people think there's more than
> one.

Hector leans in the doorway for a moment, gets restless again, then resumes his pacing.

> HECTOR (Voice Over)
> Try to get a cab in L.A. sometime. That little legend gets
> awfully easy to believe.

Suddenly, an actual cab drives up. Hector flags it down.

INT.—TAXICAB.

Hector climbs into the back seat. The driver is ill-shaven and smokes a rancid-looking cigar.

> HECTOR
> (sarcastically)
> How considerate of my author to supply me with
> transportation this fine day.

> DRIVER
> Whassat?

> HECTOR
> Nothing. Just take me to L.A.X.

> DRIVER
> See the big game last night?

HECTOR
Skip the small talk and drive.

The driver shakes his head and pulls away.

DRIVER
Jeez. Who's messin' with your reality, fella?

The CAMERA ZOOMS in on Hector's face again. He pulls a book out of his overcoat—*Consciousness Explained*, by Daniel C. Dennett. Hector thumbs through it. His look is grim and determined.

HECTOR (Voice Over)
I had to use the old lady's book as a clue. There was only one man who could help me, and that was philosopher Daniel C. Dennett, Distinguished Professor of Arts and Sciences at Tufts University. Maybe he could answer a few questions. If I was just ink trails on a page, how could I be conscious? *Was* I conscious? And how was I supposed to live with it?

Hector smiles ironically.

HECTOR (Voice Over)
'Course, a lot depended on whether he'd deign to talk to a fictional character. It was a chance I'd have to take.

MONTAGE OF SHOTS:
1) Hector gets out of the cab outside Los Angeles International Airport.
2) Hector purchases a ticket for the first flight to Massachusetts.
3) Hector on the plane, guzzling scotch and munching on macadamia nuts. A little tipsily, he squeezes the arm of the man sitting next to him, to see if he's real. His neighbor is not pleased.
4) Hector stalking across the Tufts University campus.
5) Hector charging into an office and shouting excitedly at a secretary. She appears to give him directions. Hector stalks away.

HECTOR (Voice Over the preceding)
During my trip to Massachusetts, I kept pinching myself to see if I was awake—or even there. I started pinching other people, too. I was afraid my whole world would vanish. When I got to Dennett's office, his secretary told me he was in a seminar. I couldn't wait around till he got out. I had to see him right away.

202

INT. — A HALLWAY AT TUFTS UNIVERSITY

Hector walks down the hall, looking for Daniel Dennett's seminar room. His FOOTSTEPS ECHO weirdly down the hall.

HECTOR'S Point Of View:
as he wanders on down the hallway, looking into one classroom after another. In one, he sees a rotund instructor writing elaborate mathematical formulas on the blackboard.

> INSTRUCTOR #1
> . . . so as we can see, Heisenberg's Uncertainty Principle
> shows that our ignorance about reality can actually arise out
> of our very attempts to *measure* reality —
> > (seeing HECTOR)
> — or perhaps *you'd* care to enlighten us, Mr. — ?

> HECTOR
> No, no. I was looking for somebody else.

Embarrassed, Hector moves on.

> HECTOR (Voice Over)
> I left in a hurry. Uncertainty wasn't a subject I needed a
> lecture on. I was already an expert.

He looks into another classroom, and sees a pompous literature professor, spectacles perched on a beak of a nose, hair tussled in the passion of his own eloquence, reading to his students from a huge volume of Shakespeare.

> INSTRUCTOR #2
> . . . These our actors,
> As I foretold you, were all spirits and
> Are melted into air, into thin air:
> And, like the baseless fabric of this vision,
> The cloud-capp'd tow'rs, the gorgeous palaces,
> The solemn temples, the great globe itself,
> Yea, all which it inherit, shall dissolve
> And, like this insubstantial pageant faded—
> > (seeing Hector)
> I do hope I'm not disturbing you.

                    HECTOR
                (embarrassed again)
    No, no. Not at all.

The professor continues as Hector walks away.

                    INSTRUCTOR #2
    — And, like this insubstantial pageant faded . . .

                    HECTOR (Voice Over)
    I didn't hang around there, either. He was just getting to the
    "we-are-such-stuff-as-dreams-are-made-on" bit. I knew it
    was more truth than poetry.

Hector moves on to another classroom, in which a tall, bearded, and quite
distinguished-looking professor addresses his class. This, in fact, is DANIEL
DENNETT.

                    DENNETT
                (to his students)
    . . . so now that I've won my suit under the Freedom of
    Information Act, I am at liberty to reveal for the first time a
    curious episode in my life —

                    HECTOR
    Excuse me, uh —

The entire seminar turns to look at him.

                    HECTOR
                (horribly intimidated)
    —are you Professor Dennett?

                    DENNETT
                (politely)
    Yes.

                    HECTOR
    Could I, uh, speak with you for a moment?

                    DENNETT
    Certainly. My seminar will be over in forty-five minutes.

                    HECTOR
No, it's really very urgent. You see, I—
                    (summoning up his courage)
I've discovered that I'm a fictional character.

In unison, the students do an enormous double take at Hector.

                                                    CUT TO:

EXT.—TUFTS CAMPUS.

Hector and Dennett sit on a bench in the warm, summer air, discussing
Hector's dilemma.

                    HECTOR
—so how can I possibly be conscious if I exist only on paper?

                    DENNETT
First of all, I don't think you exist only on paper. You may be
a fictional character, but it seems to me that you also exist in
other media as well.

                    HECTOR
For example?

                    DENNETT
Well, certainly, Hamlet isn't made out of ink. In fact,
Hamlet's existence is quite media-neutral at this point.

                    HECTOR
                    (puzzling over this)
Yeah?

                    DENNETT
Not originally.

                    HECTOR
But now he's in the media of millions of people's
imaginations, isn't he? The media of all sorts of different
theatre and film productions, classrooms and—

DENNETT

And that's important.

Inexplicably, a chess board appears between the two of them. As Hector and Dennett move the pieces about, they seem to change in shape and material.

DENNETT

In that regard, Hamlet is rather like a chess piece. Some chess pieces are made out of ivory or wood, some out of metal, but of course people can play chess just in their heads. And when they do, then the white bishop that's on the white squares isn't made out of anything. Still, there always has to be a medium. It might be patterns of excitation in the brain or it might be ink trails on a page.

Hector looks a little relieved.

HECTOR

Well, if I started out as ink trails on a page, the likelihood is that I've resonated out from that through a number of different readers who may have communicated about me in a lot of different ways, expanding on that fiction!

DENNETT

Indeed.

HECTOR

Am I glad to hear that! The idea of being ink on paper was an awful thought.

DENNETT

It's rather demeaning, yes. And, of course, it is true that most characters have a primary relation to one body, which no other character can share with them, and to which they sort of have squatter's rights. And, I gather from what you say, that's not true of you. You have to share your primary body medium with at least one other character.

Hector's discouragement returns.

HECTOR

I'm afraid so.

DENNETT

Indeed, perhaps with a character who, if asked, would say
yes, he was your "author."

HECTOR

That's exactly what worries me.

DENNETT

Well, let's put it this way. You have a biography, don't you?

HECTOR

Yeah. At least I always thought so.

DENNETT

There are lots of biographies around. In fact, there are rather
more biographies than there are people—that is to say, more
than there are human bodies—because each human body
generates at least one biography, and then some human
bodies generate a whole lot of others. Novelists, for instance,
generate quite a few.

HECTOR

Sure.

DENNETT

But sometimes people who are not novelists—that is, human
bodies that are not novelists—will generate more than one
biography. For instance, multiple personality disorder
sufferers often generate half-a-dozen, twenty, or thirty
different biographies. And those have an existence which is,
oh, sometimes partly on paper, partly in other media. So
what makes you think that some of those biographies are
truer, or realer, or less fictional than others?

HECTOR

But if I'm *authored* by someone else, doesn't that make me
less free? I've always wandered through life thinking I could
make my own choices. But if, in fact, somebody else is
calling the shots by writing me or creating me, I find that
rather disturbing.

DENNETT

Yes, I agree with you about that. If you're authored by
somebody else, then that is a particular sign of diminished
status. Most selves are not authored by any other *self*. They
are *created*, but not authored by any particular other author.

HECTOR

And there's another funny thing, Professor. You'd think that
if someone were telling my story, there'd be gaps here and
there. There'd be scene changes, where I'm not aware of
anything. But I feel like my consciousness continues from
one moment to the next—

But Hector has spoken too soon. There is a sudden

SMASH CUT:

On Hector's Face. THE CAMERA ZOOMS back to reveal that we are:

INT.—TUFTS LIBRARY. Hector looks startled. He is definitely aware of the
sudden shift in location, wondering what became of the intervening time
"between scenes." So his consciousness is continuous, eh? Dennett is pulling
books off the selves, stacking them in Hector's arms.

HECTOR

But is there any way on earth I can find out who this author
is? I think it's unfair that I shouldn't know. The author seems
to be gleefully aware of *everything* in my life.

DENNETT

This raises several issues. One is that a great many authors
complain about the way their characters take them over and
won't leave them alone. Sometimes these authors have to
wait and see how they'll come out.

HECTOR

Well, I've heard authors make just that complaint, but I've
never taken them at all seriously. I always thought they were
just spouting some sort of writerly nonsense.

Dennett pulls down several volumes of Dickens and adds them to Hector's
stack. Hector is very nearly buried under books.

DENNETT

Yes, I've had that feeling on occasion. But Dickens, here, claims to have wept—*wept*—over the fate of Little Nell in *The Old Curiosity Shop.* It made him just as sad as it made his readers.

Dennett finds a copy of *The French Lieutenant's Woman* and passes it along to Hector.

DENNETT

And John Fowles has discussed his own emotional reactions to things he has written, finding that they were just too heartbreaking, so he had to go back and tone down the drafts he'd written. They were too upsetting to him. I think these things happen. I don't doubt either, that many authors exaggerate and put on airs, and tell a much more robust and flamboyant story about the way their characters push them around. But I don't think there's any impossibility in a fictional character becoming somewhat unmanageable and imperious and obstreperous in the hands of its creator.

HECTOR

So I might be giving my creator a hard time even without knowing it, eh? I like that idea.

DENNETT

Let's think about the importance of what a philosopher would call "intentional objects," and I'm just going to mention two—one of them animate, one of them not.

Dennett, with an utter lack of amazement, produces an enormous gold bar from a bookshelf. Hector is, understandably, astonished.

DENNETT

The one that isn't animate is the gold in Fort Knox. Now the only reason the gold in Fort Knox is important is because people believe in it. And if somebody could spirit the gold out without anybody being the wiser, it would have no effect at all, of course, on the world's economy. The intentional object—the gold in Fort Knox—is what's important, that's what plays the role it does, and the actual, physical gold is only there because its absence would make the intentional object somewhat perilous.

209

Now Dennett produces an enormous picture book of British royalty from off a shelf.

ENORMOUS CLOSE-UPS—of photographs of Queen Elizabeth II and family.

> ### DENNETT
> Let's compare the gold in Fort Knox to another interesting intentional object: Queen Elizabeth II. I remember some years ago seeing on the BBC in England a series of interviews with young schoolchildren—they were probably five-year-olds—about Queen Elizabeth II. And they were asked, "Well, what does she do? Tell us about her day." And it was fascinating. These children were very sure they knew exactly what the queen did. For instance, she vacuumed Buckingham Palace while wearing her crown. And she sat on her throne while she watched television, things like that. It was wonderful. And it struck me then that Queen Elizabeth II, the intentional object constituted by the beliefs of these children, had a much more important role to play in British social history than the actual living woman, who, no doubt, finds that the intentional object Queen Elizabeth II is much more important than she is, and also has a certain power over her. Well, that's just a sort of laboratory case. We're all that way: the intentional objects that we become, or that we conspire to create along with those who know us.

> ### HECTOR
> So in a sense, we're fictions of everyone we know, and they're fictions of ours as well.

> ### DENNETT
> Absolutely.

> ### HECTOR
> I gather from all this that I shouldn't be looking for a particular author, but should pay more attention to authors *plural*, including myself.

> ### DENNETT
> Sure! And just remember, the fact that you're a fictional character doesn't necessarily mean you have an author.

There can be narratives *without* authors—in the sense of
conscious, deliberate, planning authors. Some fictions get
created without any author at all.

                              HECTOR
                      (a bit startled by this)
            Can you give me an example?

                                                    A FAST CUT:

—and suddenly Dennett and Hector are outdoors, late at night, at the door of
somebody's home. LOUD PARTY MUSIC AND CONVERSATION emerge
from inside. Dennett knocks on the door.

                              DENNETT
            Oh, yes. There's a lovely party game called
            "Psychoanalysis." Have you ever played it?

                              HECTOR
            I don't believe so.

                              DENNETT
            Well, the next time you have a party with some of your
            fictional friends, you can try this out on them.

The host comes to the door and lets them in. Dennett and Hector wander
through the party, observing the activities almost invisibly. Then the party-
goers begin to act out the very scenario Dennett proceeds to describe:

                              DENNETT
            You announce that we're going to play Psychoanalysis. One
            person is designated the psychoanalyst, and has to leave the
            room. He is told, before he leaves, that another member of
            the group is going to relate a dream that he or she has
            recently had to the rest of the party. Then the psychoanalyst
            comes back into the room and begins to ask yes or no
            questions in order to dope out the narrative of the dream.
            Once he's got the story line down, he's supposed to guess
            which of the assembled party dreamt that dream and to
            psychoanalyze that person.
                Well, once the psychoanalyst leaves the room, you
            announce that *nobody* is to recount a dream. Rather, when

the psychoanalyst comes back into the room, his questions are going to be answered according to the following entirely arbitrary rule: Questions where the last letter of the last word are in the first half of the alphabet get answered yes, all others get answered no. But to avoid confusion, later answers are not allowed to contradict earlier ones. As you might imagine, what happens when the psychoanalyst comes back and begins asking questions is that a bizarre and, typically, obscene narrative begins to evolve, much to everybody's intense amusement. It helps if people have been drinking. The psychoanalyst will eventually say, "Well I'm sure nobody ever dreamt that dream. It's too bizarre and obscene. But whoever made it up is extremely ill, very sick indeed."

And then, of course, the joke can be told, and it's on him: that he, in fact was the author of that dream. Well, in one sense he *was* the author. That is, nobody else suggested putting those three nuns in a rowboat with a gorilla. But at the same time, in a sense it's a narrative that has no author. Because it's just a random process. I think that all of our dreams and hallucinations are created by a process which is strongly analogous to that. So Freud is wrong. There is no "dream playwright." There doesn't have to be.

ANOTHER VERY SUDDEN CUT:

—and Dennett and Hector are in the hallway of the very building where they started. It is late at night now. As they walk past all the empty classrooms, a janitor is mopping the floor.

HECTOR

Thanks. This reassures me that I'm not necessarily limited by somebody else's "script." Even if somebody's writing my story, I have a great deal more freedom than I might think.

DENNETT

I think you should be reassured. The only fictional characters that are completely lacking in free will are a *fait accompli.* Just don't let your author—or authors—think that he or she is the *sole* author of your biography.

212

They arrive at Dennett's classroom. Dennett opens the door. The seminar students are still sitting there, exactly as they were when Hector and Dennett left them at least twelve hours ago, waiting faithfully for the return of their professor. Dennett resumes his lecture exactly where he left off:

> DENNETT
> As I was saying, I can reveal for the first time an episode in my life that may be of interest not only to those engaged in research in the philosophy of mind, artificial intelligence, and neuro-science, but also . . .

He closes the door behind him, leaving Hector in the semi-darkened hallway. The saxophone music starts up again.

> HECTOR (Voice Over)
> It gave me something to live for again: just try to keep my author busy. Still, I'd forgotten to ask the good professor one last question. If I was a fictional character in somebody else's story—what did that make *him*?

Hector wanders off into the semi-darkness, passing a lonely saxophone player huddled in a doorway, playing soulfully as he goes.

FADE TO BLACK

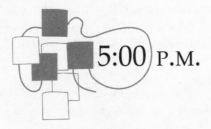 5:00 P.M.

. . . The ladies sat transfixed until the program was over. Then Phoebe quickly switched the set off.

The ladies sat in startled silence for a moment. Then, very quietly, Lida June said, "I saw a documentary about J. Robert Oppenheimer not long ago. When the physicists and engineers responsible for the first atomic bomb observed the blast from their bunker, they were horrified—not only by the hideous flash, but by the length and duration of the explosion. They wondered if they had made a fatal error. They wondered if the fabric of the universe was coming undone—if, indeed, the cosmos itself was about to unravel and disappear."

"What *are* you raving about?" asked Addie Gaines.

"Well, I must say, I'm starting to wonder the same thing about Myrtle's little experiment."

"Don't be melodramatic, Lida June," said Myrtle.

"You can't deny that we just saw Hector on TV," said Lida June.

"He's been on television before," said Myrtle.

"But not *here*, in our own living room," protested Phoebe.

"It's crazy, I tell you," said Lida June. "Crazy and dangerous. And now this positively *proves* that Myrtle is altering reality—not just in the book, but in our world as well!"

"And how does it do that?" asked Myrtle challengingly. "It was just a *story*, on television."

"The screenplay is a chapter right here in the book," said Addie. "I followed along with it."

"And so did I," said Phoebe.

And so, indeed, had all the ladies. They were all sitting there with their copies of *The Jamais Vu Papers* opened to the end of the chapter called "Media-Neutral."

"Well, that's not all that's wrong," Lida June snapped at Myrtle. "To begin with, you handed Hector that book by Professor Dennett—a book by a *real person*, did you not?"

Myrtle stroked her chin. "I'm not sure the word 'real' has a whole lot of semantic value right at the moment."

"Well, he's from *our reality*, at any rate. He's always been a flesh and blood human being just like you and me, and not made out of ink and paper."

"Yes," said Myrtle. "I'll grant you that."

"But because of you, the poor soul has disappeared into *the reality of the book!*"

"I'm not sure I follow you," queried Myrtle.

Lida June grabbed the telephone and plopped it down in front of Myrtle. "Go on!" she said. "Right this minute, I want you to dial up Tufts University. I want you to ask for Professor Dennett."

"Whatever for?"

"I'm telling you he won't *be there!*" exclaimed Lida June. "They'll probably tell you he doesn't even exist! And all because *you* relegated the poor fellow to an eternity of fictionality!"

Myrtle gasped. "Lida June Laramie! That's a perfectly ghastly accusation!"

"Then prove me wrong!"

"Myrtle will do no such thing," interjected Addie. "Lida June, you're quite out of line. Professor Dennett strikes me as very capable of getting along in any medium of consciousness, whether it be ink and paper or the neural network. And we're not going to spend the rest of the afternoon feeling guilty and anxious about him."

"That's right," said Myrtle, recovering from her shock. "And if he is stuck in the book, he won't be the only *real* person who's in there." She counted them off on her fingers. "There's Fred Alan Wolf. And Paul Krassner. And Fred Chappell. And Tom Robbins. And María De Céspedes. There's probably more. And *I* sure didn't put them all there!"

"How *did* they get there, then?" wondered Ethel.

"Maybe they just dropped in, like I did," said Myrtle.

"I don't much care about any of them," grumbled Addie. "What I want to know is why that chapter was so weird."

"Yes," concurred Lida June. "Why did the authors have to put a screenplay in the middle of everything? It was perfectly awful. Like reading shorthand."

"I believe it's supposed to be thematic," said Myrtle. "Don't you think it calls attention to the very thing we're talking about—the *fictional* nature of the story? I mean, when you read most books, you can almost find yourself believing that a narrative or the dialogue is a slice of real life. Your disbelief is completely suspended. But with all those directions and scene changes, that becomes completely impossible. I found it rather Brechtian."

"The authors have a right to use whatever voice they like," said Phoebe solemnly. "They've been pretty unobtrusive up till now."

"I think it's precious and self-indulgent," griped Lida June. She looked down at the sundress she was decorating for her granddaughter. Now why had she ever put those colored patches on it? "It's a terrible aesthetic error," she added.

"I think it's worse than that," complained Addie. "I think it's neurotic. These authors seem to crave nothing but attention. They're just as egocentric as all get out, and couldn't take another single second of being unobtrusive. They're probably from broken homes. They should get psychiatric help, and not bother the rest of us with their little obsessions."

The room was quiet for a moment. The silence was broken by Myrtle's gentle laughter.

"Quite the curmudgeon this evening, aren't we, Addie?" she said.

"Hmmph," explained Addie.

"I'll tell you what I find disturbing about today's meeting," remarked Ethel mildly. "It seems that we're drifting further and further into a completely relativistic world view. And how, may I ask, are we ever to know right from wrong, illusion from reality, truth from falsehood—?"

"Ah," said Myrtle. "Perhaps what we're learning this fine day is the tenuous nature of truth!"

And she pulled a worn book out of her quilting basket, and read:

> "What, then, is truth? A mobile army of metaphors, metonyms, and anthromorphisms—in short, a sum of human relationships, which have been enhanced, transposed, and embellished poetically and rhetorically, and which after long use seem firm, canonical, and obligatory to a people . . ."

"I rather like that," said Ethel. "Who are you quoting?"

"Nietzsche," said Myrtle, and continued reading:

> ". . . truths are illusions about which one has forgotten that this is what they are; metaphors which are worn out and without sensuous power, coins which have lost their pictures and now matter only as metal, no longer as coins."

But Ethel didn't seem to hear the end of it. She was staring toward the kitchen. "Oh, hello!" she said cheerfully. "We've been expecting you back for quite some time!"

The other women snapped their heads around. Max was standing there, hanging onto the door frame for dear life.

"I was lost for a while there," he gasped. "I went straight from Glasco's car into a void with neither text nor referent—but I couldn't get out! I thought I was stuck there forever. But then—I heard you quoting Nietzsche! That's what finally snagged me!"

He stumbled forward and sagged gratefully into an empty chair.

"Thank God for Nietzsche!" he exclaimed breathlessly.

"Have you asked God for *his* opinion?" queried Addie . . .

In Pursuit of Persephone

Brillig stood before the puppet queen in her forest of construction paper and papier mâché. Standing on the stage in the bright light, ruthlessly exposed to the audience, he suddenly felt as though he were in an "actor's nightmare"—forced to take part in a drama, knowing nothing of the role or the lines or the story.

"What goddess are you?" he asked falteringly. "And why do you grieve?"

The goddess's voice was choked with sobs. "My daughter," she gasped. "She has been carried off into the earth. She is to be a bride of death."

Brillig was astonished. "You are the goddess Demeter," he said, "grieving for your lost daughter, Persephone!"

The goddess only sobbed louder. Brillig felt some vestiges of his accustomed rationality returning.

"But your daughter is destined to return again. Why are you crying?"

The only response was yet more sobbing.

"Goddess, forgive me for saying so," he said, "but your grief is meaningless. Your story is the oldest one of all, and you must know it yourself by now. Surely you realize that your daughter will only spend a third of the year with Hades in the Underworld."

Again, Brillig was disarmed by the mechanicalness of his own gestures, the slightly jerky movements of his wooden limbs—and the eerie sense that some clever ventriloquist was actually speaking through him.

In any case, the disconsolate goddess would not hear his words. Raising her lovely wooden arm to her forehead, she exclaimed again, "She is to be a bride of death!"

Brillig now turned straight to her puppet master and asked him: "Why do you make her act out this wretched drama?"

But the puppet master made no reply. His pale face was frozen and inscrutable. Every ounce of his will and energy was projected into his puppet.

Demeter was still shedding great tears. The drops rolled down her cheeks and washed the flesh-colored paint away. Smooth, finely sanded wood began to appear beneath it. The goddess's wooden skeleton was wracked by sobs. Brillig was swept with puzzlement and awe.

Here she is, he mused, *a woman who always knows her daughter will return from the dead, but who mourns every year as if death were forever! A woman who makes the illusion of grief and sundering real to all of us! Surely this is the consummate actress, the greatest artist of them all! And all the rest of us can do is take part in her never-ending drama.*

But what does it mean? he wondered. *If grief is just a performance, an act, then what of joy? Is it, too, just an illusion?*

He glanced briefly toward the audience as if to get some cue or some direction from María De Céspedes. But he could not make out individual faces in the darkness beyond the edge of the stage.

He turned toward Demeter again. The goddess lowered her hands and raised her head. With a groan of misery, she asked, "Who are you? Why have you come to disturb my grief?"

Brillig's lips began to move with disconcerting necessity. Words poured out unbidden. His gestures became more fluid, more automatic. Did he suddenly know his part after all—or was his unseen ventriloquist reading from some age-worn script?

"I am Hermes, the messenger god," he said. "You know me very well. I made peace between you and Zeus countless ages ago by going to the Underworld and arranging for your daughter's release every year from her marriage to Hades."

"I don't know what you mean," sighed Demeter. "My daughter is dead."

"Dead for only a short time, and you know it. And what kind of thanks is it to me, when every year you act as if I never did anything to help you?"

"I don't know what you mean," repeated the goddess with a moan, lowering her head.

Brillig-as-Hermes knelt before the goddess. "Suppose I change the story just a little," he said. "Suppose I make a new arrangement with Hades and bring your daughter back—never to return to the Underworld again. Suppose I put an end to death itself, forever."

Demeter looked up at him. "Could you?" she asked imploringly.

"I can and I will," he said. And he turned upstage to make a sweeping exit.

But instead of a tiny backdrop with makeshift, papier mâché trees, a real, autumnal forest spread out before Brillig-as-Hermes. A row of mountains lay waiting in the distance. A cold, red sun was setting beyond them, and a bitter wind began to blow.

Suddenly, Brillig did not feel quite so sure of his part. Could he really find his way to the Underworld? *I'd better go back to the audience where I belong*, he thought.

He turned toward the apron of the stage. But the rust-red curtain had closed behind him. For the audience of the Café Teatro Athanor, the performance had ended already—but not for Brillig. He was trapped inside the drama; there was no stepping out of his role now. But was he still a puppet? True, his movements still felt strange. But a quick glance to the side gave him no further glimpse of his puppeteers.

There seemed to be nothing to do but to go ahead with the story. He gave the disconsolate goddess a sympathetic bow, then turned and strode away. As Brillig hurried onward through the wilderness, he watched the earth grow brown and barren all around him. Naked branches reached in tangles everywhere. Leaves whirled in the wind. The world grew dark as the sun was blotted out by clouds. Brillig called out the name of the young goddess Persephone over and over again, but to no avail.

Some Hermes I turned out to be! he thought desperately. *Why, I haven't the first idea how to get to the Underworld! And fall has just begun—and she must remain a bride of Hades through the whole winter. If she does return before her time, what then? How can I expect to find her in this desolate wilderness?*

Night came on with fearful speed. Brillig shivered to his bones. He staggered on through the dark. There was no trace of moon or stars—no light of any kind. He tripped and gashed himself as he blindly wound his way among trees and thorns.

Presently, he staggered down a twisted cobblestone lane dimly illuminated by a thousand flickering candles. He was surrounded by huge antique dolls, rattling and ticking and banging with movement. The din of their gears and cogs mingled with the sound of the wind.

Brillig had heard of such artificial creatures. They were automatons, androids of various remarkable talents, forgotten marvels of the eighteenth century. Toys though they were, the spectral machines towered like giants over Brillig.

To his left was a daintily dressed mechanical Dresden boy, meticulously sketching Brillig's portrait as he strode by. To his right, another fine-looking dandy played the flute; his lips, tongue, and fingers shaped themselves to a simple tune, and his spring-powered lungs even supplied the necessary breath. Seated at a clavicord, a lovely lady played a two-part invention with surprising expression. A gypsy girl, less prepossessing than the others, banged away on a tambourine and engaged in a simple dance. A turbaned fellow sitting at a table beckoned Brillig to join him in a game of chess. At last, a doll-like boy conducter, his hair flying, directed an unseen orchestra in the Rondo Allegro from Mozart's *Eine Kleine Nachtmusik.* Brillig had to stop and stare at this exuberant fellow. He seemed so awfully familiar. But from where—and when?

They are wonderful, thought Brillig. *But unwitting—beings of pure artifice. Still— am I any more alive than they?*

Brillig reached the end of the candlelit lane of automatons. He passed back into the forest. The wind began to howl. It grew wilder and wilder. A storm came up. Lightning blazed through the sky, and the earth itself shook with thunder. Brillig was soon soaked by rain.

And so Demeter will punish the world with drowning now, thought Brillig. *Poor, guiltless world—undeserving of this vengeance.*

Music could be heard in the distance—a wild, tormented, romantic melody in a minor key, filled with mad string arpeggios and blaring trumpet fanfares.

Sounds like Franz Liszt, mused Brillig. *Or maybe Franz Waxman. One of the Franzes, anyway.*

The melody seemed to pursue him on his way. Brillig welcomed this musical assailant. At least it gave him a feeling of direction, a sense of fleeing *somewhere*. But at last, weak and exhausted and with no idea where he was, he sank to the ground, surrendering to the now-total darkness.

Why run? he thought, gasping for breath and almost weeping with weariness. *Where do I think I'm running to?*

Then a long lightning flash illuminated the scene around him. It was a churchyard. The tombstones were crooked and worn, some toppled by overgrown tree roots. A strange, pale figure—perhaps a statue, perhaps some lost or wounded animal—appeared before a great obelisk in front of him. Then, with the end of the lightning flash, the figure disappeared into the blackness.

A peal of thunder came, bringing the pursuant music to a roaring cadence. Brillig crouched low and stared into the darkness, waiting for another flash of lightning to reveal the figure again.

The lightning came. Fleetingly, Brillig could see a young girl huddled before the towering tombstone. She was pale and elegant in a flowing white gown. Her golden hair glowed briefly like fire. Then she vanished into blackness again.

"It's the goddess!" gasped Brillig. "It's Persephone herself! She has returned from the Underworld! And she has risen from this very grave, to reunite with the world of the living! Happy Demeter! You need not grieve any more!"

He dashed forward blindly, slipping and falling in the mud. He groped about, trying to find the apparition.

"Young goddess!" he cried. "Forgive the elements for this rude greeting, and welcome home again! Come with me. There is someone who grieves your absence. I will take you to her."

A lingering, distant lightning flash cast an eerie, trembling light upon the girl yet another time. She was not more than a yard in front of Brillig. He could have reached out and grasped her, but he did not dare touch one of the Olympian immortals.

And indeed, she appeared every inch a goddess. Her hair shimmered in the night. Her shoulders were bare, revealing a lovely jewel on her throat which matched her enormous hazel eyes perfectly. Her lips were shaped in an expression of profound and elegant contemplation. She clutched a slender volume to her breast. As wet as she was, she did not shiver or tremble. She seemed undisturbed by the rain.

This is truly an all-knowing Persephone, thought Brillig, *not some flighty girl who knows of nothing but flowers and sunlight. This young woman understands what it means to be the queen of the dead. And that jewel at her throat is surely a gift from Hades himself, the only kind of flower he has to offer her. She is a child of sunlight, but has gained the wisdom of hell.*

"Who are you?" the girl murmured in the blackness over the sound of rain. "And who is it who grieves for me?"

"Your mother," explained Brillig, panting with exhaustion. "She misses you. She wants to hold you in her arms again. She sent me searching for you. I will take you to her."

Brillig could hear the girl's gentle laughter, a weird contrast to the screaming wind and the distant, booming thunder.

"I have no doubt she misses me," whispered the girl. "I miss her too, even though I cannot remember her. It would be kind of her to wait a little longer, though. But if she can't wait, we don't have far to go to meet her. She is resting— right here."

Then came another terrible flash of lightning. Brillig could see the girl's bare, lovely arm pointing to the tombstone. Its inscription was stark and clear:

MARY WOLLSTONECRAFT GODWIN
Author of
A Vindication of the Rights of Woman
Born 27th April 1759
Died 10th September 1797

Brillig staggered back. So this was not Persephone after all! This was—
"Mary Shelley!" he gasped.

"Mary Godwin," corrected the girl. "And who are you?"

But before Brillig could answer, he could feel his own face illuminated by lightning. Mary reached forward and touched him softly.

"Oh, I see," said the girl. "You are no one at all. You have no name. You are a creature of the void, a fragment of a character, a fiction barely formed, a dream half-dreamed. My shadowy friend, my creature of the storm, you are to be a character in the ghost story I must write."

She added rather merrily, "It's convenient to find one's stories ready-written in one's dreams, don't you agree?"

So that's where I am! Brillig realized. *Mary Shelley's nightmare! That celebrated dream which gave birth to her Gothic masterpiece!*

"But I don't want to be your character," protested Brillig, vaguely sensing who he was about to become.

"That's not surprising," said Mary. "You have no wants, no desires at all. You shall not until I finish making you. Now hold still—and let me give you life!"

The rain continued, but the clouds parted slightly, letting a little moonlight slip in. Mary closed her eyes and reached forward, not quite touching Brillig's face with her delicate fingers, but nevertheless seeming to shape and sculpt him in her mind's eye.

"Yes," she whispered. "My tale is taking shape—a perfect tale for men to perform, filled with all the pride, vainglory, and foolishness of men. But it's a woman's story for the telling.

"And you, fair monster, are completed!"

She opened her eyes. Brillig could see his tiny reflection in her eyes. His visage exploded with light. His was the face of some extraordinary creature with a radiance almost unbearable to look upon—but at the same time too beautiful to shun. It was the solid made volatile and the volatile made solid; it was the spiritualization of the physical and the embodiment of the spirit. It took every ounce of Brillig's will to return his own resplendent and yet hideous gaze.

It was the face of a god—not a creator god, but a god as created by man.

"There!" cried Mary with a lilting laugh. "You are perfect! Quite perfect!"

"But what am I?" asked Brillig.

"You are a creature made of lightning."

"But surely I can return to what I was," cried Brillig.

"You were nothing before," said Mary. "And you cannot return to nothing."

"Is there no salvation for me?"

Mary laughed that strange, sad laugh of hers. "Salvation from salvation? What a strange thing to ask! Why, you are an immortal god—the ultimate artifice!"

"But is my life . . . real?"

"Ah, but you must ask your creator that."

"Llixgrijb!" exclaimed Brillig in a whisper.

Mary looked briefly puzzled. "Why, no," she said. "That wasn't the name I had in mind at all. But now I must leave."

"Where are you going?"

"I must awaken, of course, and write my story."

There came another flash of lightning. An elegant canopy bed suddenly appeared in the middle of the churchyard, facing Mary Wollstonecraft's tombstone. In it lay the still, sleeping body of the spectral, dreaming girl Brillig had been speaking to. And a man lay there, too—quite young, perhaps in his twenties, tall and sinewy. He thrashed about in restless and uneasy sleep, clutching a vial in his hand. Perhaps it contained some drug or potion.

The dreaming Mary stepped toward the bed, about to slip into her body.

"But wait!" cried Brillig. "If you awaken from this dream—what shall become of me?"

"I do not know," said Mary thoughtfully. "Perhaps your existence shall continue in the tale I'm going to write. Or perhaps the dream you're in shall go on even when I awake. Or perhaps—you'll simply disappear. It's a fascinating question, isn't it? Are you a dreamer yourself—or are you fully awake even in the world of my dream? I cannot say. You can tell me yourself if we ever meet again."

She slipped into the bed. With a girlish little wave toward the tombstone, she cried, "Good night, Mama!"

Then she vanished into her physical form. Thunder boomed. The bed vanished, leaving Brillig alone in the churchyard. He gazed at his hand. It pulsed with light—as if it were truly framed from lightning.

At least I kept half of my promise to the goddess, he thought. *I put an end to death forever. Perhaps I kept the other half of my promise, too. Perhaps, in putting an end to death, I somehow found Persephone—returned her to the realm of the living.*

But is this truly life? he wondered. *Only my creator can tell me what—and why— I am.*

Brillig strode on through the churchyard. But as he passed along, the surrounding Gothic scene began to fade. His feet no longer touched the earth, and he realized that he no longer moved through space.

It was the future which spread out before him.

Elements of Style

If only there were an index, mused Hector.

He was shuffling idly through Washington Square Park. He had not gone back to Los Angeles after his meeting with Professor Dennett the day before. Instead, he had caught a shuttle to New York, spent the night in a nondescript hotel, and had wandered down to the Village in the morning. An idea hovered in the back of his mind that he had some important business here. He didn't yet know what. Perhaps his author knew. In any case, he needed time to reflect on things.

He detoured around a scruffy vagrant sitting on a bed of cardboard. The vagrant looked up and smiled. "How's the universe today, Mac?" he asked. Hector ignored him and headed for a park bench. As he flopped down on the bench, he heard the vagrant ask the same question of an energetic-looking fellow with a beard. The man stopped and engaged the vagrant in conversation.

Hector was mildly curious about what the mismatched pair would find to talk about, but he quickly forgot them. He had much more pressing and personal questions on his mind.

The verdict was in. Hector knew at last that he was, indeed, fictional. Three witnesses had testified conclusively to this effect. Max had said so, and so had the mysterious Myrtle Roebuck. Professor Dennett had concurred as well, but at least held out some hope for him—the hope that he could still have a will of his own.

Hector drew a tired sigh. How nice if he could simply step outside the cover of the book he was in, turn to the index, and locate the name "Hilary." Then he could open the book to the right page, and—*voilà!* There she'd be! Thumbing through the pages of a book would surely be easier than searching through the world—whether in dreams or in waking.

Well, maybe it wasn't impossible. Perhaps, like Max, he could simply vanish from his present location and reappear someplace where the book was being read—in that room full of elderly ladies, maybe. He closed his eyes and concentrated hard for a moment.

There was only blackness and random lights behind his squinched eyelids.

He didn't have Max's knack for it. Hector wondered briefly and irritably, *Does this mean that Max is better at lucidity than I am?* But he dismissed the idea. Max had certainly not seemed in control of whatever was happening to him.

Maybe it's just as well, he thought. After all, did he dare look into the book of his own life—a book in which the *ending,* whether good or bad, happy or tragic, was already written? Once he had gone to a palm reader on a whim. But the woman had taken one look at his hand and recoiled with confusion and bafflement. She had refused to do the reading. Hector shuddered slightly at the memory. He realized that a book would only prematurely tell him whatever had caused her such alarm. He wasn't ready for that.

Then something else occurred to him.

If Professor Dennett is right, maybe my book has *no author. If so, what's to stop me from crossing out anything I don't like? Then I could write in whatever I want in its place! I could do a rewrite!*

And another thought followed. *Maybe that's what lucidity really means! Rewriting your own reality—controlling it like the Thaumaturgists control dreams.* If he could write his own book, surely he could control even Imogene—at least within its pages.

And, oh, the index! The power it would give him! He could look there for so many of the missing ingredients of his life: *wealth, friendship, serenity, fame, admiration, romance* . . .

He'd have all those things at his fingertips. He'd look up Hilary first, of course. Yes, Hilary had to be his first priority. But short of just such a magical index, he had no notion of where to look for her next. And he had no idea who else he could even ask.

His only experience with writing, except for academic papers, was that newsletter of his—and that all too often seemed to slip out of his control. He was carrying copies of it with him in his briefcase, along with other pertinent and impertinent papers related to this case.

He opened his briefcase and dug around for some blank paper and a pen. "It all began—" he started to write, but a wave of dizziness washed over him. *No,* he realized, *if I begin at the beginning I'll just have to live through it all again.*

He hastily scratched out that line. He looked around at the park. *I'll start writing from this moment,* he thought. *Let's see how it works.* The broad sidewalk before him was empty. He looked down at his notepad and wrote: "A gray pigeon waddled across the sidewalk." When he looked up, a fat gray bird strutted about in front of him, accompanied by several others. Hector was somewhat encouraged. But then he realized that a pigeon in Washington Square hardly demonstrated powers of transmutation.

Then he wrote: "A toy was lost." He stopped and looked up quickly. The birds had been replaced by a bouncing yellow ball. A toddler squealed not far away, wondering where the ball had gone.

Hector broke out in a sweat, even though the September air was cool. Maybe this was working! But he needed to accomplish something more than bringing pigeons and toys into his life. He needed advice.

I need to talk to someone who knows how reality works, he thought. *I need someone to come here, right now, and help me figure out what to do.*

An impulse seized him. Hector leaned over his pad and scribbled these words:

"The wisest person who ever lived came and talked with Hector."

Then he leaned back and closed his eyes again. This ti͟ ͟e just sat and enjoyed the sunlight on his face. He waited patiently for w ͟er happened next.

"Dr. Glasco, I presume," a nearby voice said shyly.

Hector opened his eyes to see a slight, elderly fellow with a closely cropped beard, dapperly dressed in a double-breasted suit. He carried a small leather briefcase. He bowed slightly and doffed his beret, revealing an elegant dome of a head, bristling around the edges with thin, snow-white hair.

"Yes," said Hector. "How did you know?"

The old man shrugged. "You ask for a know-it-all, you get a know-it-all. As they say, 'Be careful what you wish for, it just might come true.' And it was most fortuitous that you chose this moment to write me into your life. Because it just so happens that *I* was looking for *you*."

Hector's hopes rose as the old man approached him and gently shook his hand.

"My name is Isaac Rosenbaum," the old man said, "a haberdasher by trade."

Hector's heart sank a little. "Isaac Rosenbaum?" he asked. "A *haberdasher?*"

The old man hesitated and then shrugged. "Well, that *is* my name in this waking incarnation—and my profession, too. I'm still known by my old name in many circles."

"And that is?" Hector asked.

The old man glanced around. He sat down next to Hector, lowering his voice until it was almost inaudible.

"Solomon," he said. "You may have heard of me. I used to be the king of a small mideastern country—oh, around three thousand years ago, I suppose."

"I see," said Hector, gasping audibly.

"But when you've been around as long as I, you learn that is not smart to tell many folks that you are Solomon, former king of ancient Israel. That might lead to misconceptions."

"Quite," said Hector.

"Somehow," said Solomon, "I sense that you are not merely humoring me."

"My venerable friend—or should I say Your Majesty?"

"Venerable friend is nice," said Solomon.

"I, myself, am but a fictional psychiatrist in a most peculiar narrative. Why

226

shouldn't I chat with an esteemed biblical personage? Especially when you seem to be exactly the fellow I was hoping to meet."

"How very astute," said Solomon. But then the old fellow looked startled. "I do hope you don't imagine that I came to you for psychiatric advice!"

"Not for a moment."

"Not that I couldn't *use* it, mind you! I mean, who couldn't? God forbid that I should be squeamish about such things. Yours is a fine profession, and I would like to think that I pioneered it in my way. But that is not my business here today. All I want are the footnotes."

"The footnotes?" asked Hector. "Oh, yes, *those* footnotes. I've got them right here." And he shuffled through his briefcase, removed the two pages of notes, and handed them to his visitor.

"Thank you so much," said Solomon, rising from the bench. "And now, perhaps I should go. I fear that I am taking too much of your time."

"Not at all. Do stay. I wrote you into this scene in the first place. I need your advice. Can you tell me where I can find Hilary?"

Solomon sat back down. He tilted his head sadly. "My good doctor," he said, "why don't you ask me something simple? Like how to transmute the baser metals into gold?"

"But it was your prophecy, wasn't it?" asked Hector, unable to conceal his disappointment.

"Oh, but it was so long ago! Perhaps I should explain. You see, I'd gotten the hang of lucid waking pretty well a few millennia back, and—"

"So you were born into the Sleeping World?" asked Hector, interrupting.

"Indeed I was!" said Solomon with a wink. "They don't tell you that in Sunday School, I think! Well, I thought, 'Why not try being a king?' So I went through the usual batch of illusions. I got myself 'begat' into the Waking World by King David, and when the old fellow passed on, I took over his job.

"It was an interesting time to be king. And difficult, too. Those were hard days for the Waking Born. The *elohim*, the many voices of God which used to instruct everybody in everything they did, were being heard from less and less and less. And Waking People didn't know how to call upon their own minds. They were lonely and afraid."

"We still are, I fear," sighed Hector.

Solomon gave a self-effacing shrug. "I'm afraid I made things worse," he said. "I had this vain notion that I could take the place of the *elohim*. And so I started off by asking the *elohim* for an understanding heart. But I didn't know the price, the loneliness of having such a heart. For you see, once the *elohim* had given me wisdom, they decided I didn't need their help anymore. So they left the world altogether. And now they come back most infrequently. They speak to very few. I, myself, have not heard from them in hundreds of years."

Solomon craned forward and whispered: "But oh, I made plans! Big plans!

I thought I could make the *elohim* look like pretty small potatoes. You see, I thought I could bring Paradise back to the earth again! I had this idea—don't ask me how I got it!—that paradise was nothing more or less than the union of the Waking and Sleeping Worlds. And I was determined to fuse them back together. I sought an elixir that would do just that. And if just one waking mortal named Hilary were to take my elixir—then Paradise would be regained!

"Ah, the illusions of youth!" he chuckled, leaning back on the bench. "Well, I studied the problem deeply, and wrote my discoveries down in a book, *The Elixir of Solomon*. And I found six of the necessary ingredients for my placebo. But the last one escaped me. I went to my illusory grave fretting about it.

"Of course, the whole thing was completely wrongheaded. I found that out in an altogether different Waking incarnation—that of a bad Pope, as I remember. In an uncharacteristic moment of piety, I thumbed through the scriptures and noticed a passage I had missed before. It said: 'And the Lord God caused a deep sleep to fall upon Adam, and he slept . . .'

"And so," he cried, clapping his hands, "my whole idea went *poof*, up in smoke! You see, even in Paradise, our grandfather slept! And 'To sleep, perchance to dream,' eh? I realized then that Sleeping and Waking were just two realms out of an infinity of realms. They were never one—and they never will be!"

"But," Hector interjected, "Imogene Savonarola believed your prophecy."

"Ah, yes, the poor girl," sighed Solomon. "I'd mislaid my manuscript ages ago, and she ran across it. And she took it much too seriously. She edited it and annotated it—hence, those infernal footnotes. And she was vain enough to think she was the only soul to ever figure out that missing ingredient."

"She wasn't?"

"Heavens, no. People have been making that stuff for ages. I wrote down the missing ingredient myself without knowing it. You can look it up if you like: *Proverbs* 24:13–14.

"Well, I heard that she'd become quite hysterical about all that prophetic mumbo jumbo, so I thought it best to get my manuscript back before she caused any real trouble. I finally tracked her down a couple of days ago, and I'm afraid I scolded her a bit too harshly. If you run into her, tell her not to take it too hard. I'm just a cross old man. Anyway, she told me I'd find the missing pages with you—and here they are! And now my book is my own again."

And Solomon neatly deposited the pages in his briefcase.

"One other thing," he said. "You haven't seen a big green flying carpet lying around, have you?"

"I believe you'll find that in the hands of a shaman named Bruno at Venice Beach."

"Ah!" exclaimed Solomon. "He's still alive then! I must buy the old buzzard a bottle of tequila and pay him a visit! By the way, I have enjoyed your publication."

"Thank you."

"You might have a terrific idea for a book there," said Solomon.

Hector restrained an impulse to giggle. He remembered Paul Krassner saying much the same thing. And so had others. But Hector had guessed that most people were looking for something—anything—to say in the face of utter perplexity. This was surely not the case with Solomon.

"Well," Hector said humbly, "coming from you, that's quite a compliment."

"Ah, well," said Solomon, shrugging shyly.

"No, really," said Hector. "I thought *Proverbs* was terrific."

"What about *Ecclesiastes?*" asked Solomon, blushing slightly with pride.

"Even better."

"Too bad I don't get royalties on those books anymore. Public domain, you know."

"Ah, I see."

"I'm still writing, though. Haberdashery is just a way to pay the rent. My first love is literature. And I've got quite a few books in print—under a variety of pseudonyms."

"But if I wrote a book—" Hector began hesitantly.

"Yes? Come on, don't be shy."

"Would it change reality? Would my life change? Would everything be different?"

"Certainly. All books change reality. Mine, yours, everybody's. But let me warn you, it's a little tricky."

"How do you mean?"

"It's a simple matter to write a sentence mentioning 'the wisest person who ever lived,' and have him actually appear. Any first-year creative writing student can do that. It's the *subtleties* which demand attention, the *nuances*. It's the matters of style, of tone."

"Please explain," said Hector eagerly.

"Well, consider this passage, for instance." And Solomon recited:

> "So I returned, and considered all the oppressions that are done under the sun: and behold the tears of such as were oppressed, and they had no comforter; and on the side of their oppressors there was power; but they had no comforter.
>
> "Wherefore I praised the dead which are already dead more than the living which are yet alive.
>
> "Yea, better is he than both they, which hath not yet been, who hath not seen the evil work that is done under the sun."

As Hector listened intently, the trees in the park grew dark and heavy. The breeze died ominously. The sky seemed low and close and the sun was hidden by dark clouds. The birds and the children fell silent.

229

"Then, on the other hand, consider this passage." And Solomon recited again:

> "Go thy way, eat thy bread with joy, and drink thy wine with a merry heart; for God now accepteth thy works.
> "Let thy garments be always white; and let thy head lack no ointment."

And the brisk autumn breeze and bright sunlight came back. Birds began to chirp again, and the children's laughter returned.

"The whole scene changed," said Hector with awe.

"Did it?" asked Solomon. "Yes, now that you mention it, I suppose it did."

"But you said nothing about the weather, about birds or trees or children. How did you do that?"

"I would teach you if I could," said Solomon pleasantly. "But it comes from experience. Perhaps in two or three hundred years you'll get the hang of it. In the meantime, you should get a literary agent for these *papers* of yours."

"Well, maybe," said Hector modestly.

"You could contact *my* agent—John Brockman."

Hector started. This was the very agent Krassner had mentioned—the author of *Afterwords*.

"John Brockman is *your agent?*" asked Hector with surprise.

"Oh, for many years," said Solomon. "I believe I have one of his cards handy." He fumbled in his jacket. "Yes, here." He handed a card to Hector.

"What do you know of the Reality Club?"

"I have spoken at their meetings once or twice," said Solomon. "Gets pretty lively at times. They are a tough bunch to tangle with."

Then Solomon pulled a gold watch out of his vest pocket.

"Heavens! The time!" he said. And he rose to leave.

"I will come to Los Angeles some day," he said, tipping his beret jauntily, "and you can psychoanalyze me."

"An opportunity that would have honored Freud," said Hector with a bow.

"Freud *did* psychoanalyze me!" whispered Solomon gleefully. "He just didn't know who I was! I made for a very interesting chapter in his book about dreams. Read it again. I'm sure you'll recognize me. And try always to remember—the truly discerning reader is not impressed by the merely miraculous. *Auf Wiedersehen.*"

And the former king of Israel departed.

Hector sat staring across the park, thinking about Hilary. If the wisest man who ever lived couldn't tell him where she was, who could?

But why am I so obsessed about her? he mused. *Am I really concerned for her safety—or merely curious about what she's experienced? Is this responsibility, or self-*

indulgence? Or is it just a particularly nasty case of counter-transference?

But he also knew that it was simply his nature to worry. If he lost something around the office or his house, he could think of nothing else until it was found. Was Hilary nagging at his mind only because she was missing?

Well, Solomon had not been able to give him any clues about Hilary, but he *had* made one very important suggestion.

Hector got up from the bench and found a pay telephone. He dialed John Brockman's number. A secretary listened politely, and suggested that Hector send along a proposal.

"No," said Hector impulsively. "I think I'll come and see Mr. Brockman in person."

He hung up the phone and hailed a cab.

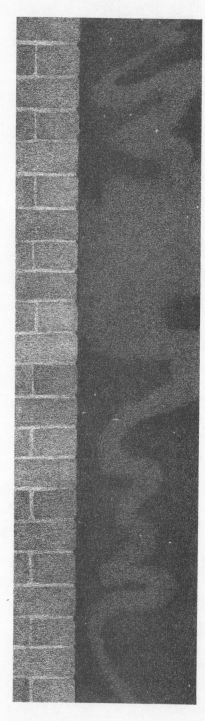

Infinite Infinities

. . . How did this happen? Fred Alan Wolf
wondered. No matter which way he looked,
there was only the narrow, dark alleyway
where a moment before there had been a busy
Greenwich Village street. There were no
people at all.

But then Wolf heard a moan—or perhaps
he just imagined it. It didn't matter. The
difference between sense and imagination had
vanished altogether. He stepped forward into
the alleyway and was plunged into darkness.

He was in a whirling wilderness of
nothingness, a spaceless, matterless void. He
felt, rather than saw, the presence of a great
entity. He sensed that the entity was trapped
somehow, irrevocably imprisoned in some
multidimensional cave-in, a prisoner for a
timeless eternity.

"What is this place?" Wolf asked. "And who
are you?"

"Perhaps you can tell me what happened,"
a rumbling voice said with a cosmic groan. "I
created a being named Brillig. I tried to make
him foolish and obtuse, so he would never
learn about me—so he would never learn that
he *is* me. I tried to experience this world from
his point of view, so that I, myself, might forget.
But he's not staying the way I created him."

The groan grew into a sob of despair.
"Why can't I control my own creation? Do I
have to destroy it all?"

"But who *are* you?" Wolf asked again. And
he heard a sound in reply that seemed alien—
and at the same time, oddly familiar.

"Llixgrijb," the voice whispered like a
distant tornado.

Wolf had a strange sinking feeling. Could this be the entity he had sensed? Was Llixgrijb the mind that contained the universe? Wolf also felt a powerful surge of curiosity.

"Do you remember when you first tried to create this illusory universe?" he asked.

"Barely," muttered Llixgrijb. "It's been my goal to forget."

"Well, let me remind you how it might have been," said Wolf. "It won't hurt. I promise. When you made your first try, you envisioned a very orderly universe; you put everything in its proper place. You envisioned resistive-type forces which would keep everything in its place: strong, weak, electromagnetic, and gravitational. But you ran into a problem. Every time you created an atom, the atom would collapse on itself and vanish. It'd go down in some black hole somewhere and you'd lose track of it, and the whole universe would collapse around you. Every time you created a universe of great mechanical beauty, the whole clockwork crumbled."

"Every time it happened," cried Llixgrijb, "I asked myself, 'What's going on here? I can't create a universe of perfect order! I can't even imagine such a thing! It won't work!'"

"But don't you remember what happened next?" asked Wolf.

"No!" barked Llixgrijb. "And why should I want to? The whole thing gives me a terrible headache."

Headache? wondered Wolf, peering into the amorphous darkness. He tried to explain, "When your early attempts to create a universe failed, you finally realized that the only way you could create a viable, working universe would be to give up knowing what was going on in that universe."

"Yes. I remember deciding that. I had to give up knowing! I learned that *ignorance was the glue that would hold things together.*"

"But the only way you could do that was to confuse yourself."

"That's right," exclaimed the darkness. "I said, 'Instead of creating just one universe, let me create two!'"

"And you tried two," Wolf replied, "and that almost worked. Two parallel universes almost worked. But you still knew too much, and after a while those two universes merged into one, and they collapsed down the toilet again. And you realized that three or four wouldn't work for the same reason. They might just take a little longer to collapse. So you decided that, somehow or other, you were going to have to create a hell of a lot of universes—so that any one universe contained only a part of your knowledge. These are the parallel universes which were all created at the beginning of time. In these parallel universes, every possibility is taking place."

"Are you saying I'm stupid or something?" grumbled the entity. "If I did all that, how come I thought there was only one universe?"

Wolf said hastily, "You can be under the illusion that you're in one universe, but you're never ever in one universe. You're in an infinite number of them all the time. The only thing that is changing is your consciousness. And your consciousness changes depending on how you look.

"It's just the action of shifting consciousness which causes one to decide or to think that one is in one universe or another. Can you see what I'm talking about? It's like a hologram in which you're just shifting your point of view. The trick you found to make everything stable was: *don't create just one infinity."*

There was another moment of rumbling in the shadows. Then the darkness laughed. Finally, Llixgrijb said, rather proudly, "An infinite number of universes! An infinite number of *infinities!* What could be a better guarantee of eternal ignorance? I did a better job with this creation than I thought!"

The spaceless void swirled even more thickly around Wolf. He stood there silently, hoping that Llixgrijb would give up trying to pry cosmic explanations out of him.

"I'm glad you've got it clear now," he said. "If you've got any other questions, read my book *Parallel Universes.* Now if you'll excuse me, I do have a lecture to give. Okay?"

But there was only silence.

"Okay?" repeated Wolf feebly.

He was beginning to get the feeling he was stuck here for a while.

At last the entity spoke, "I take it you aren't enjoying your visit to my realm."

Wolf said nothing.

"Go then," said Llixgrijb, sounding miserable again. "I'll not try to stop you. *You're not trapped—like I am."*

Looking around him, Wolf could now see the entrance to the alleyway. He was indeed free to leave Llixgrijb's realm, at least for now. He retraced his steps and headed toward the Open Center . . .

Benediction, diction, fiction, friction, interdiction, jurisdiction, malediction, prediction.

Bessie Redfield
Capricorn Rhyming Dictionary

——

Rule Seventeen. Omit needless words! Omit needless words! Omit needless words!

William Strunk Jr.

——

Consider the philosophical principle Occam's razor, which in English reads: "The simplest explanation is usually best." In Lojban it's Roda poi velciksi so'eroike ganae sampyya gi xagrai. *Translated back to English: "All somethings-which-are-explanations mostly are if superlatively simple then superlatively good."*

Los Angeles Times
November 17, 1989

Astride Occam's Razor

Man is dead.

Yes, there were those three sinister words again—the opening words of John Brockman's book, *Afterwords*—and the only words on the whole page. When Hector had first read them on that remarkable day at Venice Beach, he had not dared to read any further. Did he now?

He braced himself as the cab careened around a delivery truck. The book flew open to another page. It offered but two words:

Facts smirk.

Once again, the rest of the page was blank. Thumbing through *Afterwords*, Hector could see that each page featured no more than a few lines of text situated at the top of a page, leaving at least half of all pages completely blank. You could slice off the bottom half of the book and not lose a single word. Some pages contained but one line of text. On one of them he found this disturbing sentiment:

Who's crazy? Mankind went out of its mind. There is no mind
out of which to go. Who's crazy?

As if in reply, the cab driver loudly cursed a delinquent Mercedes.

Hector wasn't sure what had prompted him to put *Afterwords* in his briefcase before he left Los Angeles. *Probably just a contrivance on the part of my author*, he mused. But as long as he was about to meet with Brockman, it seemed only polite to take a quick look at Brockman's work. But this book gave him trouble no matter where he opened it.

Hector decided to peek at the end. He occasionally did this with iconoclastic philosophical writings, although rarely with murder mysteries. It was a practice which had saved him the trouble of reading *The Myth of Sisyphus*. After all, once you found out that Camus didn't kill himself at the end, why bother with the rest of it?

Turning to the end of this particular volume, Hector encountered a sinister aphorism:

Nobody knows, and you can't find out.

Nobody knows what? wondered Hector. *And why can't you find out?* Hector felt a small chill of apprehension. Was this book more than he could handle? His heart raced as the cab driver failed to clear a red light. Then came the squeal of tires. Angry motorists honked loudly from surrounding automobiles. The driver responded with a loud yell and a generalized obscene gesture.

Hector decided to thumb lightly through the book, skimming but a few of its pages. He had the distinct feeling that it might be a little foolhardy to actually read this entire volume—even if there were time before the meeting, which there certainly was not. He turned to another page:

There is no past, there is no future, there is no time, there is no space. The beginnings, the endings, are all bound up in the multiplicity of neural operations.

Hector's stomach shifted at the enormity of the thought—and at the accelerating speed of the cab. It was definitely time to try another page:

Progress is merely decreation.

It sounded like an important observation, but Hector had no idea at all what "decreation" meant. He looked elsewhere:

Don't believe any of this. Place no value in the book, in the author. Give it up, the idea of author, of truth. Give up all belief: believe only in yourself. You: you are nothing but my experience. Me: I don't. I don't believe any of this.

Which raised in Hector's mind the obvious question, *if you don't believe it, why bother to write it?* He turned a few pages further.

Perhaps the death of an abstraction is the most difficult death.

The taxi jerked to a halt at a light, almost throwing Hector into the front seat. He fumbled through a few more pages, and the book's message started to dawn on him. The dying abstraction was "man" himself. The author had obliterated his very own existence—and was now determined to raise serious questions about the reader's as well.

So Brockman, too, has faced the possibility of non-sentience, considered Hector. *Shouldn't I find that comforting?*

He looked further and found these words:

There's no thinking subject: only words. Only descriptions.

So that was it! Words constitute the only reality. Yes, that struck a too-familiar chord. Since Hector himself was apparently made up of nothing but words, he and this agent really ought to have plenty to talk about!

The driver changed lanes with gut-wrenching abandon. Hector caught his breath and thumbed a few pages further. He read:

Universe is the big con.

Oh, no! he shuddered. *Not another hoax!* He shuddered and turned the page. But the one he arrived at offered him scant comfort:

The life you live is a lie. The world you inhabit is a lie.

And a few pages further, he unearthed this cryptic outcry:

I'm going out of my mind. I'm trying to hold on to my body, my
life. It's a horrifying experience.

Gasping in sympathy, Hector clutched at the car seat. The world seemed to reel beneath him. He slammed the unprepossessing little volume shut. The gesture was accompanied by a screech as the taxi slid to a halt at a building on Broadway, close to Eighty-third Street. Shakily, Hector paid the driver and climbed out of the cab. The driver noisily cursed the amount of the tip.

Now what? wondered Hector, as he stepped into the building.

He was apprehensive—and at the same time curious. He had looked forward to meeting a prestigious and respected literary agent. He had already begun to fantasize about whopping advances, obscenely lucrative royalties, television and film rights, critical controversy and acclaim, talk show appearances . . .

He hadn't reckoned on facing a man who believed in no reality whatsoever except for words—a "radical epistemologist" who, according to the book cover, had once proclaimed himself "the late John Brockman." Hector wondered if the whole idea of meeting Brockman was just another of Paul Krassner's infamous pranks. But would King Solomon have suggested this meeting as a practical joke? Surely not.

Hector soon found himself standing at a reception desk. Written on the wall behind the receptionist was the word "Information." He turned to see if anything was written on the opposite wall. It bore the word "Power." He mulled over the implications. Did these words really have any meaning? Weren't they just abstractions, and dead ones at that—just like "man"?

Oh, well, it was hardly time to think about such things. In another instant, Hector found himself in a spacious, high-tech office. The first object to catch Hector's eye was a severe-looking primitive bird mask which hung off one of the walls. *An ancient Mayan god of royalties?* mused Hector.

An oblong conference desk with a black leather top dominated the room. Four comfortable leather-upholstered chairs on rollers were arranged in a semi-circle around it. John Brockman himself sat at the head of the desk in a large black swivel chair. He was an elegantly dressed gentleman (Hector suspected the complicity of Giorgio Armani) with steel-gray hair and an inscrutable demeanor. Brockman rose from his chair and greeted Hector with a handshake. Hector was immediately intimidated by his smile.

"What have you got for me, Hector?" asked Brockman, offering a seat. Hector opened his briefcase.

"I believe I've got material for an important book here," he said, pulling copies of his newsletter out of his briefcase. "It started out as a small professional publication—*The Jamais Vu Papers*. But the papers, er, began to multiply somewhat."

Hector kept digging more and more items out of his briefcase. He began to produce a veritable mountain of written material: various bits of correspondence, news clippings, photographs, manifestos, books, and documents of all kinds. The stack grew higher and higher, looking physically quite preposterous in proportion to Hector's diminutive briefcase. "I've been at the center of an incredible whirlpool of ideas and events and realms and realities," he concluded.

Without saying a word, Brockman picked up one of the newsletters and started reading.

Hector became terribly nervous. *Am I just going to sit here and watch, waiting for him to read all this stuff?* he wondered. He fidgeted and paced. *You will if you know what's good for you*, he told himself. *The best thing to do is let him read and decide for himself. You're bound to put your foot in it if you say anything.*

But Hector kept thinking back to Brockman's enigmatic book. Could this snappily dressed, no-nonsense businessman who looked more like a Wall Street investor than an avant garde thinker truly have been the author of such a perplexing little tome? A question arose in his throat. He tried to fight it down, but it popped out of him anyway.

"Mr. Brockman," stammered Hector, "what on earth do you mean by the word 'decreation'?"

Brockman looked up from the papers. His expression was absolutely impenetrable. Was he pleased at Hector's interest in his work, or merely irritated by the interruption? Hector had no idea.

Brockman leaned back in his chair, and began to speak with brisk efficiency.

"To me," he said, "it refers to the idea that reality is not an accretive process, where one word leads to the next. It's the idea that all ideas exist in any, and that the words of the world are the life of the world, and nature is not created, nature is said. Wallace Stevens talked about decreating the world, and said, 'Throw away the lights, the definitions,/ And say of what you see in the dark/ That it is this or that it is that,/ But do not use the rotted names.' Or as William of Occam said, *'Entia non sunt multiplicanda praeter necessitatem'*—'Entities must not be multiplied beyond what is necessary.' That means, do not use unnecessary units of language."

Having completed this explanation of Occam's Razor, Brockman promptly buried himself in the papers again. But Hector found himself curiously unsatisfied. He wrestled briefly with his own better judgment before another question jumped out of him.

"Do you mean that words actually affect reality?" he asked hopefully.

Brockman looked up again. This time, Hector believed he detected just a trace of impatience in his expression.

"If it's not in the language," he said, "it *isn't*. If you can't say it, it isn't. What I'm talking about overall is limits, Wittgenstein's notion that the limits of my language are the limits of my world. I'm talking about the idea that we are our words. We create technologies and tools, and then we *become* the technologies and tools. So, too, with language. All we have is language. All we have is ideas.

"Rather than looking on this, ontologically, as a human-based world, I see a word-based world. James Lee Byars, the conceptual artist, said, 'Thank God for the names of the body.' Those names become our reality. We talk about the heart as a pump. It isn't *like* a pump. It *is* one. But the pump came long after the heart. That metaphor is a human invention. Prior to Newtonian mechanics, the body was talked about in an entirely different way. In the late fifties, John Lilly started playing around with computer models of the brain and all the humanists went up in arms, and now we talk about the brain as a computer. That's something you couldn't have talked about thirty years ago, or certainly before Norbert Wiener came along."

Brockman paused a moment, leaning back in his chair. "We create technologies," he continued, "and we become the technologies. Language to me is a technology. And there is nothing outside of it. Anything else is metaphysical, including the physical. To me, progress is not made through accretion, it is made through decreation. Success is when you tell me I'm wrong."

He said it with a note of challenge. Hector believed it was an invitation to further conversation. He remembered something else that Krassner had mentioned. Perhaps it was time to drop a little hint . . .

"Could you tell me," he asked cautiously, "how one gets into the Reality Club?"

"People are invited to give talks at Reality Club meetings," said Brockman with a shrug. "If you give a talk, you're a member." And he returned to the papers at hand.

Hector was a little dismayed at the brevity of Brockman's explanation. He certainly wanted to speak before the Reality Club. But how was he going to finagle an invitation?

"How do you decide, uh, who's got an interesting idea, who you'd like to speak?" he blurted.

Brockman looked up from the papers. He gazed at Hector, volunteering no explanation. He just looked at him. Hector felt as though time itself had come to a grinding halt.

"Let me put it this way," said Brockman after the excruciating hiatus. "What we call reality is literally taken off the tongues of a finite number of individuals throughout history, a number of whom are alive today, and I want to find those people. I want to ask them what questions they are asking themselves, and get them to come to our meetings and present their ideas and have a back and forth discussion with people their own size.

"We're interested in thinking 'smart,' versus the anesthesiology of 'wisdom.' If someone presents some fact or theory which is a part of a body of work that other people feel they are familiar with, if they're wrong they'll get nailed. On the other hand, that doesn't often happen since our speakers are mostly experts who know what they're doing.

"The arguments come from various epistemological positions. For instance, we have a number of scientists who actually think there is a real world, and they think there is a universe and it was born ten-to-the-minus-x billion years ago, and in a split second the universe was born. I don't know what a billion years means, and I don't think anybody can even talk about it. Other people feel the same way, and in the discussions we ultimately get down to these epistemological camps where various people come from various positions. To me, that's the most interesting aspect of the group. I find that the empirical scientists are almost religious in their belief in the scientific process. Call it naive realism."

Hector's heart sprang inside him. So Brockman was mistrustful of reality! A common reference point, without a doubt!

"I can assure you," said Hector smugly, *The Jamais Vu Papers* is *anything but* realistic! I prefer the language of poetry to the language of science."

"Why are you interested in poetry, Hector?" asked Brockman.

Did Hector detect a glimmer of interest? He dared to hope.

"Well, after all," chortled Hector, "the drug M itself was derived from a line out of Gerard Manley Hopkins."

"Interesting," mused Brockman. "A line out of which poem?"

Hector almost choked. Why did he have to bring Gerard Manley Hopkins into this? "Well, to be perfectly honest, I don't know."

"I have his poetry at home," said Brockman politely. "Perhaps I could find it for you."

"Yes," Hector said. "That would be most helpful." He felt like a perfect fool. Literary agents weren't supposed to spend their time tracking down metaphors. Then Hector frantically tried to explain some of the ideas which had unfolded during the last months—the literal reality of metaphors, lucidity in both dreams and waking, the hoax principle, fictions without authors. He talked on and on and on and on.

Then he shuddered to notice Brockman trying to repress a yawn.

"I find fiction as a convention quite limiting," said Brockman, "and not as interesting as the exploration of what one would call the nonfiction of the world."

Then Brockman sat there staring at him, his elbow on the table and his chin propped boredly on his hand.

Hector froze up. As a fictional character, he felt stung. He didn't know what to say. Suddenly he had a thought. Fiction and nonfiction might not be so separate as Brockman implied. Maybe he could *demonstrate* his writing prowess to the agent.

"Watch just a minute," Hector whispered nervously, whipping out his notebook. "I guarantee you'll find this interesting."

He scribbled down some words frantically. Then he glanced up to see if anything had happened.

Yes, it's starting to work!

And he went on writing. In a matter of seconds, the Mayan bird head had changed into a familiar Venice carnival mask—a glazed white face with a butterfly over one eye.

Then Hector scribbled more and more. As he did so, the office became increasingly transformed. The oblong conference table was suddenly rectangular and quite ornate, with lion's heads staring from each of the corners and fancy fluted legs and ball-and-claw feet. The four stuffed chairs became decorative Queen Anne antiques. The couch became an ottoman with upholstery of crimson crushed velvet. The plain walls were abruptly covered with a kind of paisley wallpaper. A crystal chandelier blossomed from the ceiling out of nowhere. A singularly gaudy Persian carpet spread out across the floor. And with a stroke of mischief, Hector rewrote Brockman's swivel chair into a grand and gold-encrusted throne.

Finally, Hector stopped writing, feeling really quite breathless and exhilarated. He looked around at his handiwork.

Brockman's office was, indeed, wildly and garishly altered.

Brockman, unfortunately, was not.

He sat there exactly as before: elbow on desk and chin in hand. Even the direction of his gaze was unchanged. He was still staring straight at Hector.

And his expression was anything but intrigued.

There was a long interval of deafening quiet. Brockman's yawn, which had lain dormant for many long moments now, erupted with fury. With a furious rustle, the office snapped back to its original appearance. Hector sat stunned.

"Hector," said Brockman at long last, "why did you want to talk to me?"

"I beg your pardon?"

"I'm very busy, and you're pulling all this metaphysical crap."

Hector recoiled with shock. The phrase "unnecessary units of language" sprang into his head. He had piled Brockman's desk with hundreds of unnecessary units of language. He had sat there spouting thousands of unnecessary units of language. Even his transmutations of Brockman's realm were gratuitous and utterly unnecessary. And just a short time ago, Solomon had admonished him about style, tone, and nuance. *The truly discerning reader is not impressed by the merely miraculous,* Solomon had said.

Hector's little demonstration was perfectly worthless, empty, meaningless. He was astride Occam's Razor.

"I was hoping," sputtered Hector, thrashing about like a drowning man, "that you might be able to help me with my book."

Brockman leafed through the pages in front of him, making a last effort to awaken some faint glimmer of professional interest. "Who is it you're looking for again?" he asked. "You're looking for somebody, right?"

"Hilary," he replied, almost in a whisper. "I'm looking for Hilary."

"If you want to make money with your book," said Brockman, arranging Hector's material into an untidy stack, "you've got to find Hilary. Write the book after you've found Hilary. Who wants to read it at this point? Everybody wants the payoff. You could write your book now, you could get a publisher, and while it's in print, Hilary might turn up somewhere in very mundane circumstances, and the story is finished and you missed out on the whole thing. Everybody wants to know the *ending*, Hector."

"So you're not interested in representing me?"

"Well, I think you're wasting my time right now."

"But—what about the Reality Club?"

"What *about* the Reality Club?"

"Is there a place in it for me?"

"Hector, read my lips. I'm looking for people who are *changing the world*."

And not tinkering around with furniture, Hector thought miserably.

Brockman touched the button on his intercom and spoke to the receptionist. "Could you please send someone by to show Dr. Glasco the door?"

Hector hastily grabbed the papers off Brockman's desk and started shoving them into his briefcase. He had images of burly security men coming to drag him away, perhaps throwing him down a flight of stairs or through a plate glass window.

"Thank you for your time, Mr. Brockman," he said, shaking from head to foot.

"Any time," said Brockman amiably. "Let me know what develops."

As Hector walked to the door, his briefcase burst open. The copy of *Afterwords* fell open on the floor. Words glared up at him:

> There is no need for fiction in the world: the world is the only
> fiction.

Hector stared at the words for a brief moment, then gathered the contents of his briefcase together. It was true. And it was no help at all.

Brockman's phone rang. "Oh, hello," Hector heard Brockman say. "Thanks for getting back to me. Oh, no, you're not interrupting anything . . .

"Just another psychiatrist with a book idea."

Flushed with humiliation, Hector hurried away.

The ~~~~~ apers

**Volume One
Number Eleven
October**

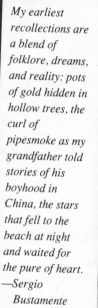

> *Art and story are the essence of all living form. Everything is storied, from the unfolding tale of the DNA molecules to the precession of the equinoxes.*
> —Jean Houston
> *The Possible Human*

My dear Dr. Gla~~~~

I am sorry I ha~~ out of touch since our original collusion. You must think me very negligent. I do receive your monthly newsletter and have followed your professional activities ~~~~ ~~~~ interest.

I re~~~~ been u~~ patient~~ not hol~~ sible. I~~ quiries~~

But d~~ help b~~ was be~~ tient, a~~ been h~~ ful adv~~

An en~~~~ studyi~~~~

My ~~~ come t~~ intoxic~~ fundi~~ has be~~ must ~~

In t~~ reply ~~ Prof. ~~ newsl~~ to hav~~ I have never truly invented anything in my life—not even the Hoax Principle, as Brillig's excellent discus-

~~y~~ demonstrates. My own work would be utterly meaningless without those magnificent hoaxes known as science and history.

What we call "knowledge" is, after all, a vast and wonderful fairy tale—a fiction of ~~~~~~~~

> *My earliest recollections are a blend of folklore, dreams, and reality: pots of gold hidden in hollow trees, the curl of pipesmoke as my grandfather told stories of his boyhood in China, the stars that fell to the beach at night and waited for the pure of heart.*
> —Sergio Bustamente

SNAILBOY—a ceramic sculpture with acrylic and gold leaf
21" high x 32" wide, limited edition of 50
photo courtesy of the Sergio Bustamente Galleries

Sergio Bustamente draws on a rich background of images from his native Mexican, Chinese and Indian ancestries, childhood memories of fantastic stories, archetypal figures, and metaphoric relationships.

~~wi~~ be true again.

But I do have hopes for Prof. Brillig. His alternation between ire and fascination

with the vicissitudes of reality strikes me as a sign of a very healthy intelligence. And rumor has it that he is engaged in some impressive experiments of his own.

Perhaps I should leave Hoax Theory in his very capable hands. I certainly

~~~~ucation

~~~~~ an occasion ~~~~ here or there. ~~~~ead. I corre-~~~~te fascinat-~~~~ continuing

~~~~ was interrupt ~~~stint as an ~~~~ should not ~~~but too com-

~~~~ is self-educates, rites, ~~~les and acco-~~~cumstances ~~~ring us to-~~~ flesh, so to ~~~ should have ~~~cuss. Let us ~~~t till then.

~~~y what, then, ~~~I do whatever ~~~~al. I tell stories. I participate in myths. You might say that I search for artists.

Creativity found

And I have indeed found some very exciting thinkers and doers in this world.

Lately I've been reading Ursula LeGuin's collection of short essays, talks, and reviews: *Dancing at the Edge of the World*. It's rather like carrying on a marvelous conversation, chatting about a number of subjects which have a connection more intrinsic than linear order.

Art is done, LeGuin says, as "a means, a way of living." True work, she says of art and life, "is done for the sake of doing it."

For my part, I am trying to live by that creed. And given your recent adventures, perhaps you have learned a similar lesson. Life, itself, is perhaps best seen as something best "done for the sake of doing it."

Perhaps we should bea[r] this in mind as we pursu[e] our respective quests—yours for your missing pa[-] tient Hilary, and mine fo[r] whatever I decide to pursu[e] next. And who can tell wha[t] that might be? I am waitin[g] to be surprised.

I'm enclosing some sni[p-] pets from these and oth[er] readings, conversation[s,] correspondences, clipping[s] and discoveries. Perha[ps] these fruits of my efforts w[ill] be of some interest to yo[ur] readers.

Best wish for your o[wn] endeavors. I look forwar[d to] the time when our prof[es-] sional paths cross at last[.]

Perhaps circumstan[ces] will soon bring us [to-] gether—in the flesh, s[o to] speak. If so, we should h[ave] plenty to discuss. Let[us] both be patient till then[.]

—J. SAVONAR[OLA]

"Pan Returns to a New Tune"
by Margaret Ford
1986, wood and clay, 68"x21"x15"
photo: Anil Kapahi

Myth must be kept alive. The people who can keep it alive are artists of one kind or another. The function of the artist is the mythologiczation of the environment and the world. [The ideas and poetry of the traditional cultures] come out of an elite experience, the experience of people particularly gifted, whose ears are open to the song of the universe. . . . The first impulse in the shaping of a folk tradition comes from above, not from below.

—Joseph Campbell,
The Power of Myth

Fiction in particular, narration in general, may be seen not as disguise or falsification of what is given but as an active encounter with the environment by means of posing options and alternatives, and an enlargement of present reality by connecting it to the unverifiable past and unpredictable future. A totally factual narrative, were there such a thing, would be passive: a mirror reflecting all without distortion.

—Ursula LeGuin, "Some Thoughts on Narrative"
Dancing at the Edge of the World

*What may not be expected in a
country of eternal light?*

Mary Shelley
Frankenstein

Brillig in Cyberland

It was a void.

It wasn't darkness or silence. It was the absence of all sense. J. X. Brillig couldn't think in terms of blindness or deafness, because there was no such thing as sight or sound—and certainly not touch. She couldn't remember words like eyes and ears.

I guess this is what that first line of Genesis *meant,* thought Brillig. She floated through the void. She had no idea for how long. But *what* was she? *A creature made of lightning,* someone had called her.

Then came a voice: "Hey, Josie. Can you hear me?" The voice was warm and full of good humor.

Sound! thought Brillig. *What a novel concept!*

She heard herself answer: "Yes, I can hear you." She was surprised at the lightness, the lilting buoyancy of her own voice. She didn't yet know why. "Can you hear me?"

"Yeah, loud and clear."

"Good. Now maybe you can tell me where I am. Maybe you can tell me *what* I am."

The void was empty of sound again for a moment. Then the voice answered, "You mean you don't know?"

Suddenly, two human figures appeared in the void—two men, flickering and wavering, threatening to dissolve or collapse into a swirl of television snow. Brillig's reality had a weak horizontal hold. But it was a moderately convincing picture, as holograms go.

The man on the right was perched on an invisible stool, punching instructions into a keyboard which rested on his lap. He wore a cowboy hat and was smoothly outfitted in black—but was it leather or some sort of synthetic? Optical fibers poked out of his head like an unruly mane of hair. At the ends of the fibers, tiny pinpoints of light danced around his craggy features. Brillig couldn't tell whether those were functional or not.

The images stabilized a bit. On the left was a tall, jolly fellow with silvery hair and Celtic features. He sported an enormous grin and mischievous eyes. He looked more than a little familiar.

248

"Can you see us, Josie?" asked the man on the left.

"Yes," said Brillig.

"Good. Do you recognize either of us?"

"I don't believe so," answered Brillig. "I'm not sure."

"Well first off, let me re-introduce you to Upton Orndorf, database cowboy extraordinaire."

"Not so 'extraordinaire' just this minute, damn it," grumbled the cowboy, looking up from his console. "Something's not working right, here."

Orndorf, thought Brillig. The name is familiar. *Where have I—?*

"And I'm Timothy Leary," said the tall, silver-haired gentleman. "Don't you remember me at all?"

Brillig's memory strained. "I remember headlines, news stories," she said. "I remember a Harvard psychologist getting mixed up with psychedelics and the counterculture during the 1960s, eventually getting into computer software and stand-up philosophy—"

Leary let loose a peal of laughter. "Whoa, you're way out of date."

"Please don't talk in riddles. I'm extremely confused."

"What was the last thing you remember?"

"I can't remember anything."

"Does a year come to mind?"

"Why, yes. 1990."

"You mean you don't remember anything past 1990?"

"No. Should I?"

Orndorf let out a wail of frustration. It was tough, gravelly, abrasive. "Holy shit! I broke through a wall of the blackest, meanest metaphor-chains in any inscape—to rustle a construct with a memory *stuck back in 1990!* I'm sorry, Leary. I guess I'm losing my touch." The fiber-optic lights whipped around his head as he shook it.

"But who am I?" asked Brillig. "What am I doing here?"

"Josie, you're breaking my heart," said Orndorf with sudden sincerity. "You and I go way back—and I mean *way* back. I got you started on all your adventures. Don't you remember all the poetry we shared? 'You and I rehearsed these roles a billion years before these circuits closed.' Don't you remember that? Don't you remember any of that lovey-dovey talk?"

Orndorf's voice choked slightly. His eyes grew moist. Swiftly and unceremoniously, he brushed a tear away.

"Hell, who do I think I'm talking to?" he said, trying to regain his rough-and-ready manner. "I keep thinking you're the real item. What's the use of getting sentimental?"

"I don't even remember who I am," pleaded Brillig.

"You're a bio—a fiction," Orndorf said, suddenly offhand. Then he continued to Leary, "You should've read it, one simile just rolled into another and another and another. The oxymoron fence was easy, but then I ran into a cortázar continuity. It was a serious marienbad, but I thought I'd broken out okay. Maybe it was eschered more than I thought."

"What—? What—? Who—?" Brillig stammered frantically.

"You're supposed to be the recorded memory of Josephine Xaviera Brillig, one of the legendary pioneers of the matrix," said Leary.

"Are you telling me I'm not even *myself?*" cried Brillig. "I'm just a *memory?*"

Orndorf turned to Leary. "That's a problem with these bios," he said. "They think they're sentient beings."

"I resent that," cried Brillig. "If I *think* I'm sentient, then I must *be* sentient."

"That's another problem with 'em," Orndorf told Leary. "They're semi-stuck in the Cartesian paradigm."

"If I'm just Brillig's memory," Brillig demanded, "then what's happened to Brillig?"

"Brillig was remaindered," said Orndorf. He shivered. Tiny lights bounced. "I guess it could have happened to me. I had a hell of a time getting back into this borgespath."

"What do you mean, remaindered?" Brillig kept futilely trying to pull at the hologram's arm.

"Remaindered. Discarded. Flatlined, to use an older term," said Orndorf. "Do you understand brain-dead?" he asked when Brillig just gazed at him uncomprehendingly. "Brillig died in the inscape, in the matrix—what we used to call cyberspace in the old days. Nobody knows why. That's why we did a rerelease on you, to find out what happened. We didn't count on you being defective. We thought maybe you'd remember."

"Well, I don't remember," shouted Brillig. "I think this is all completely crazy. And what *is* this matrix, anyway?"

"Relax," said Leary. "We'll fill you in on a few things. Where would you like to start?"

"Well maybe you could give me a historical update." Brillig composed herself a bit.

"Gibson's the teller here," said Orndorf. "You'll have to grab that storyline."

"What—? Who—?" Brillig was sputtering again.

"Maybe I can explain," chuckled Leary. "You see, it's now 2040 A.D. The culture, the habitat, the way of life right now was *written* very specifically and brilliantly back in the late twentieth century by William Gibson in his books *Neuromancer, Count Zero, Burning Chrome,* and *Mona Lisa Overdrive.* Did you ever read any of those?"

"I'm afraid science fiction was never in my line," said Brillig, vaguely remembering a career involving the classics. "Is that where you got your, uh, vocabulary?" she asked Orndorf.

"Gibson and some others defined a lot of terms we used way back in the twentieth century," Orndorf said. "But me, I take to the newni-verse. It's based on poets and prose-riders who cogged the inscape."

"You're still not getting it, are you?" sighed Leary. "Maybe it would help if you popped over to our side. Get virtual."

"Yeah, that's an idea," concurred Orndorf. "Come together. Join the party."

Brillig hesitated, not knowing what to do.

"Do it!" commanded Orndorf.

Brillig instinctively did a strange little mental twist—and suddenly she was a hologram herself, with the curious physical illusion of being a body moving through space. She was with Leary and Orndorf inside a spectacular orbital playground where thousands of people strolled among shopping malls and health spas. Leary, playing the garrulous tour guide, pointed out lakes, small forests, genetically engineered wildlife—and even a simulation of a mountain ski lodge.

How much of it was real, and how much holographic? Radiating from the center of the station was an astoundingly brilliant and convincing semblance of sun, clouds, and blue sky. Were those real birds fluttering above her? She couldn't be sure. To the happy hedonists roaming the satellite, it surely didn't matter.

Suddenly, Brillig stopped cold. Something vague and indefinable had been bothering her since she had arrived—something about her name, the unusual lightness of her voice, some difference in her movements. And now she knew what it was.

"*I'm a woman!*" she cried with alarm.

"Of course you're a woman," said Orndorf. "What did you expect?"

"You don't understand! I used to be a man! What happened?"

Leary and Orndorf laughed. "And you didn't remember?" chuckled Orndorf, his fiber-optic lights dancing. "Joseph Xavier Brillig! That was your name! And I'll bet you started thinking you had yourself all recogged!"

"No need for alarm," added Leary. "You just made a smart choice at one time or other. Women are now seen as the superior sex by far. The ascendency of the male during the last five to ten thousand years of monotheism, feudalism, and all that has been completely changed. Today, it's just like William Gibson predicted. The women are incredibly powerful, strong, tough, sleek, attractive creatures. And we men are kind of dirty klutzes doing our best."

"It's the women who are the real poets," said Orndorf.

The three of them stepped into a glittering and immaculate medical center, where astounding feats of plastic surgery and transfiguration were taking place. Through prompt and painless procedures, people were receiving vat-grown organs, muscle implants, changing their height, build, sex, and even race at will.

"Science has given every individual self-managerial control over almost every aspect of physical life," said Leary. "Everyone can have the body and the appearance that they want."

"With all this control over their bodies," remarked Brillig, "people should be able to live virtually forever."

"Oh, certainly," said Leary.

"Unless they're dumb enough to get remaindered in the matrix," qualified Orndorf with a slight sneer.

They peeked into a room of the medical center where a family was gathered to observe the awakening of an elderly man—perhaps the family patriarch. But this venerable fellow had no body at all. He was nothing but a disembodied head, hooked up to high-tech pumps and respirators. As the old fellow revived, he became quite loquacious, telling stories of the old days and asking interminable questions about the new.

"People who have been around since the mid twentieth century are people who forecasted these changes," explained Leary. "They *arranged* for themselves to be here."

Near the talkative head stood a large glass vat containing a mysterious little figure. Its shape was vaguely human, but its limbs were misshapen and bulbous.

The little homunculus developed and grew with astounding rapidity. At last, it was fully formed, the body of an Adonis—but grotesquely headless! Surgeons arrived on the scene. They proceeded to surgically attach the old man's head to the body. The head kept chattering amiably through the whole operation. The surgeons made a series of injections. All wrinkles, sags, and signs of age vanished from the old man's face. Within minutes, the old fellow was on his feet, more youthful and energetic than he had ever been in his life.

"All religions are against this sort of personal immortality," commented Leary. "But some people saw the light. Ram Dass, for example, used to be very anti-tech, but he's always been very intelligent, and an opportunist in the best sense of the word. And when he saw how things were going, he came along—kind of reluctantly."

"Tell her the truth," said Orndorf slyly. "You had to kidnap him and bring him along."

"Okay, that's true," said Leary, laughing. "It's always been like that with him. It took a long time for me to get him to take psilocybin, and once he took psilocybin it was hard to get him to take LSD. And it was the same with computers. But he's still around, because he's part of the gang and we'll never leave him behind."

"But immortality! It's a terrifying idea," said Brillig with a shudder. He looked closely at Leary. "Isn't the boredom intolerable?"

Leary shrugged. "Well, obviously, if you're bored you hibernate. I wish I could have hibernated through much of the late twentieth century. Whenever Republicans were elected, I would have gladly hibernated for years."

"So death has become an unnecessary luxury!"

"Absolutely. The answer to boredom is not irreversable involuntary coma. We simply take a nap."

"But you'd wake up like Rip Van Winkle and have no idea what's happened—just like me!"

"Not true," said Leary. "We've got brain information transfers, so that even while you're asleep you know what's going on. Basically, immortality is digitizing. The more of yourself you digitize, the more of yourself is going to be immortal. The more of your actions and memories you get digitized, the more immortal you're going to be. I was one of the first people to discover this. My claim to fame today is that there is more of me in digital form than almost any other person from the twentieth century."

"But death is so fundamental!" Brillig cried with incredulity. "Without it, how can there be any progress? How can anything evolve?"

Leary scoffed. "These are primitive ideas, vestiges of when we had only one cave, say, and you couldn't have a hundred people living in that one cave—or in one tree, or on one plot of land. You had to die for the sake of the five kids who were supposed to inherit your plot of land, right? You see, everything is information now. Space is free, so the more the merrier. All the ethics and morals and sage principles of the industrial/feudal/land-machine world are totally overthrown in the infoworld."

"But how can there be privacy in such a world?"

"Privacy is the evil of monotheism," Leary replied. "When literacy started, it was a code the Phoenician traders used because they didn't want the Greek traders to know what the price was. And the Bible itself was a code by those cabalist guys who had that trick going; they were passing on information they didn't want anyone else to know. So basically, lettered writing is always about secrets."

Brillig felt an irrational wave of panic. "But surely you've still got books." She turned toward Orndorf. "Why, you're bubbling over with literary references. Don't you read books?"

Orndorf barely seemed to understand the question. "Books? Hell, once we popped all the literature into the matrix, who needed books?"

The trio stopped and looked at one another. The surrounding orbital resort suddenly vanished. Brillig faced Orndorf and Leary again. There was anticipation in the air.

"So," said Orndorf after a silence. "Are you starting to remember or what? You were one of the legendary riders of the inscape. Want to try it again?"

Orndorf punched more instructions into the board, and Brillig felt an incredible sensation—as though she had done an extraordinary somersault from one reality into another. And suddenly she was plunging through an altogether different universe, careening among glorious, glittering geometrical towers of light. The sense of space was extraordinary. Her mind swelled with incredible knowledge and perception. She had no voice or body, but she could still communicate with Orndorf or Leary. Their thoughts had merged.

253

"Like it?" she felt Leary ask.

"Like it? It's wonderful! But where am I? What is this?"

"The matrix—a consensual hallucination of all the world's information."

Brillig felt a twinkle of memory. She was back on her turf again—even if she still didn't quite grasp what it was. She was inside the matrix, a world of pure information.

"What are those great towers of light?"

"Databanks. All the information of the world is now inside them—and you gain access to them in the matrix. All of the human signals that used to sell as books have been digitized and are now available and stored in these data-banks—plus all the pictures, all the movies and the television shows—absolutely everything."

"Of course!" she began to remember as she swirled among the towers. "These are symbolic receptacles of all the knowledge of the world!" The thought thrilled her.

"In a way, it's just like it used to be," Leary continued. "Even back in the twentieth century—can you remember?—trillions of dollars were exchanged every day in the computer network. These exchanges of money were all done by computer. Hundreds of billions of dollars were being moved around between Japan, Europe, America. I cite that as an archaic example of what's happening right now. And each of those towers is surrounded with ICE—intrusion countermeasures electronics—techniques of defending your base. That doesn't stop a lot of code rustling from going on. Just as you had rustlers and cowboys in the Wild West, today you've got rustlers and cowboys and black marketeers in this infoworld."

Brillig felt herself swell with cyber-cosmic laughter. "Code rustling! Sure, I remember. Legitimate accountants and CEOs work inside those towers, cowboys and rustlers like me working on the outside, busting in through layers of ICE."

They soared higher and higher above the towers. At last, they were in orbit above a matrix-generated globe—a "virtual earth." Thousands, maybe millions of lines of light stretched everywhere, all radiating from various points around the world. An extraordinary number converged on the little islands of Japan, which looked like a cluster of dazzling stars.

"So this is the new meaning of 'community,'" said Brillig. "No boundaries, no borders. People everywhere are connected by countless strands of information, defying time and distance! Geography itself is obsolete! It is a world of cohesion, not division—a world of reconciliation without sundering—a world of life without death. And if life is only artifice, well, what of it, anyway? It's perfect!"

Brillig tumbled through the matrix, letting forth a cry of delight. "Who'd ever want to go back?"

Leary seemed to enjoy the question. "There's a real social conflict about that. The hottest political and social conflict now is between those people who want to spend *all* their time in the matrix, and those who see it as very dangerous and addictive, and don't want their loved ones to leave them and spend more and more time in the infoworld. Once you get into the infoworld, there's no question that it's much more exciting than coming down and pushing a body around. So there is now, as there always will be with an intelligent species so genetically varied, a number of viewpoints. There are those who think the matrix horrible, and those who consider their 'meat' existence slow and vulgar."

No, she couldn't imagine going back. It wasn't just the flesh that tied you down. It wasn't just prosaic forces like gravity. The physical universe itself seemed cramped, claustrophobic—a realm of space-time bent by hunks of matter into gross finitude. It couldn't compare to an infinite ocean of uncut metaphor, a neuroelectric realm containing the absolute essence of literally *everything.*

Brillig's thoughts blended more and more with Leary's. "Everything is information," she felt him think. "Information is much more important than material goods. The politics of information, that's what we're talking about. Almost everything the gods used to do, now the average person can do—change your body, change your mind, change your DNA code, clone, and also be part of the highly advanced wisdom center."

"And a part of a fantastic new mythology! Just because Gibson wrote the story."

"And a whole new theology, too," answered Leary's mind. "Once we established this information world, we'd also created a new intelligence entity—a superintelligence. We don't yet understand the extent of it."

Orndorf chimed in, "Even when we worked out the mathematics of re-Coovering reality, it was more mysterious than we had expected. New storylines kept forming, beyond our programming."

They passed beyond the virtual earth, out onto the mysterious high seas of the matrix. Brillig knew she had been to these parts before. But what had she found out here? Leary wanted to know the answer, too.

She felt Leary hesitate for a moment. "Josie," he asked, "before you came out here that last time, you told us you were about to connect with something, an extraterrestrial, extradimensional intelligence—an entity named Llixgrijb. No one else could do it. You went riding off into the inscape to make contact with Llixgrijb. That's why we resurrected your construct. We just have to know . . .

"Do you remember? Did you succeed?"

The questions turned over and over in Brillig's mind. *Llixgrijb . . . Did I succeed? . . . Do I remember? . . .*

Then suddenly, she felt that presence again, a mind unlike any mind she had ever imagined, at once far away and inside of her, a mind from which she, the physical universe, and the matrix itself seemed to emanate—a mind which contained all other minds.

"Llixgrijb! Yes! I do remember!"

As she rushed deeper into the matrix, she called out to Orndorf and Leary:

"Gentlemen," she said, "this matrix of yours is a great and wonderful hoax. Don't imagine for a moment that it is your invention. It reaches toward you, tricking you into believing yourselves to be its creators! It is a road spread out before you from beyond time and space, inviting you, beckoning you . . ."

"But to where?" asked Orndorf.

"And to whom?" chorused Leary.

A force pulled her deeper into the matrix. It was relentless, inexorable. She felt as though she was being swallowed up by a terrible maelstrom.

"Sorry, boys," she called out, "but it looks like I'm going to have to go this one alone."

She felt Leary's mind receding far behind her, sending one last message to her. "We understand," he said. "We'll miss you. Good luck."

"And don't get remaindered," added Orndorf. "And watch your ways on the borgespaths."

She caught a final glimpse of tiny dancing lights as the message from Orndorf's mind trailed away.

Somewhere, somehow, she knew that Llixgrijb awaited her . . .

Creative Writing

Hector Glasco had come back from New York. He was sitting disconsolately in his office between patients, still stinging from John Brockman's admonishment the day before.

"You've got to find Hilary," the super-agent had said.

And don't I know it! *thought Hector.* I've devoted myself tirelessly to just that quest—to no avail!

But what more can I do? If I haven't found her after all these months, surely I never will. She's either dead or hopelessly insane or simply doesn't want to be found. Whatever the truth may be, the cause is lost. It's time to face facts. It's time to give up the search.

Then he raised his fists to the ceiling and cried:

"So why can't I get on with my life?"

Exhausted and demoralized, he lowered his head down on his desk. His failure was now complete. This was truly the blackest moment of his life.

But little did Hector realize that his luck was about to change. For at that very moment, Hilary had just entered his office building and was riding up the elevator—had, indeed, arrived in answer to Hector's deepest wishes . . .

Thus wrote Hector Glasco.

When he finished, he set his pencil down and leaned back in his office chair. He read over his hasty, longhand scrawl a couple of times. It was not a literary masterpiece by any means, but surely all that was needed under the circumstances.

Let's see if this does it, he thought.

Long seconds passed. Hector drummed his fingers nervously on the desk top.

What's holding up that elevator, anyway? Maybe I can write something to speed things along. But no, I'd better let matters run their course.

Then came Miss Bellows's voice on the intercom.

"Dr. Glasco, there's someone here to see you," she said. Then she lowered her voice, "It's Hilary—"

"Send her right in!"

"But Dr. Glasco—"

"Miss Bellows, don't you understand? I've been *living* for this moment for months now!"

He leapt out of his chair and was halfway to the door when it opened. A sleazy, dissolute-looking fellow in a cheap plaid suit was standing there. "Ah, my good Dr. Glasco," said the man through blocked-up sinuses. "I have heard that you were looking for me."

"Hardly," sputtered Hector. "Who the devil are you?"

"Hilary La Grange, Esquire," the man wheezed, whipping out a card. "fictive character deluxe. Here in response to your inquiry, in answer to your call, in service of your dreams—"

"No, no, no," interrupted Hector.

The man emitted a sneeze of puzzlement. "But you just wrote me into your story, did you not?"

"You're not at all who I'm looking for."

"Ah, but I'm highly mutable," said Mr. La Grange. "You can rewrite me on the spot. I'll assume any form, any identity you like.

"And," he added, "my prices are quite reasonable."

"Thank you," said Hector, "but I'd rather start from scratch."

And he noisily crumpled up the paper he had written on and tossed it at the wastebasket. The paper bounced off the rim and rolled across the floor.

Hilary La Grange, Esquire, vanished into thin air.

That's just the sort of problem Solomon warned me of, thought Hector. *Nuances, subtleties, tone, style—all those elements of writing I just haven't mastered.*

Well, it's high time I got the hang of it.

And Hector grabbed another sheet of paper. He ruminated quietly for a moment, then began to write again . . .

Three weeks passed. Hector's office was a mess. He was literally knee-deep in wadded up pieces of paper. But he made no effort to clean things up. And he no longer even paid attention to his appearance, arriving daily at his office unshaven, uncombed, and unkempt.

And why should I worry about how I look? he thought, wadding up yet another piece of paper and missing his wastebasket for the ten thousandth time. *I have no patients!*

He said the phrase aloud, then repeated it ten or fifteen times, giggling inanely at the pun:

"I have no patients! I have no patients! I have no patients!"

And indeed, every last one of his patients had fled his practice. All of them had ultimately found Hector's futile and dangerous attempts to write their neuroses into oblivion much too spooky to contend with.

But Hector was beyond alarm. Everything else in his life was missing. Why shouldn't his patients be as well? Hilary had been gone for most of a year now. His non-waking lover Imogene had long since been absent from his dreams—and Hector refused to believe that the letter Miss Bellows had published in *The Jamais Vu Papers* was actually from the living, breathing version. He was positive that was just another hoax, and he wasn't going to bite. And Max Henderson, the last human being he had really been able to talk with, had been reported missing again and was sought by the police.

Hector had even received phone calls from James Fenimore Cooper Junior College in Sequester, Missouri, inquiring as to what might have happened to Professor Joseph Xavier Brillig.

Hector took aim with another wad of paper.

"Reality's on sabbatical!" he yelled. "That's what's going on!"

He missed the wastebasket yet again.

Miss Bellows was still with him—in a manner of speaking. But Hector was sure she was looking for new employment. He had noted how her voice always dropped into a furtive whisper whenever he entered the outer office and found her on the telephone.

"Yep, the old girl will be the next to go," he barked, tossing yet another piece of paper.

Even the janitor had stopped coming to clean Hector's office, out of superstitious fear of Hector's sinister activities. The entire building staff knew that Hector was engaged in some sort of black magic—that he caused people and objects to appear out of nowhere.

Hector only wished the magic worked more in his favor. Literally hundreds of different "Hilarys" had shown up recently, of every conceivable age, shape, size, sex, race, color, and religious persuasion. But none, of course, was the Hilary he was looking for.

It seemed such a simple matter. Why couldn't he make it work? He knew perfectly well that his descriptive powers were limited. But why did that have to be such a problem?

He closed his eyes again, pencil clutched tightly between his fingers, and thought hard. He tried to visualize her again. But as usual, no clear picture came.

I've got an idea, he thought. *I'll try to remember the first time she came to my office.*

He did so—and the picture that came was surprisingly vivid.

Yes, I do think I'm onto something here.

He wrote his first impressions of Hilary down as quickly as he could:

> He'd never seen anyone inhabit a chair in quite the way this Hilary did. She didn't really *sit* there. She was languidly *draped* there, hanging against the upholstered leather in exquisitely arranged folds . . .

Hector broke off and looked up at the chair that Hilary had once inhabited. Yes, an image was forming! Delightedly, he got up and waded through the paper to the chair.

But then he recoiled. It looked as though someone had thrown a piece of fabric across the chair. A woman's limbs and anatomical features did, indeed, display themselves amongst the folds of the fabric—but in a ghastly and shocking arrangement.

Two lovely mouths smiled at him, situated on the creature's elbows. Two eyes glanced about—one from each thigh. Her breasts were on her knees, and her knees were grotesquely near the floor. The creature's nose was in the middle of her chest. A mane of soft, radiant hair grew out of the center of her abdomen.

A graceful, delicate hand reached toward him from the creature's forehead. Hector screamed and thrashed his way back through the papers to his desk. He wadded up the description and hurled it violently away. The nightmarish Hilary-thing disappeared.

Hector sat down, trembling all over and chilled with terror.

What on earth happened? What went so horribly wrong?

Then he remembered a cliché he had once seen in some creative writing manual:

"Always write about what you know."

Hector sighed. That was surely the problem. But the truth of it offered him no comfort—no comfort at all. How could he write his *own life* on the basis of what he knew? It seemed to Hector that he had to be always writing *just ahead* of what he knew.

And as for writing Hilary back into his life—well, this presented a serious problem. He had known nothing of Hilary since her disappearance almost a year ago. He had no idea of her current appearance, her experiences, her state of mind, her joys and fears—of anything at all about her.

By trying to write in lieu of all that, he had literally created a monster.

And now Hector sat staring at another blank sheet of paper with considerable awe and trepidation.

What should I write now? he wondered.

Why don't you try the truth? came his own prompt and direct reply.

And so he wrote:

> Hector Glasco had learned that his life was a work of art—a work of literature, in fact. But he had also learned that his own creative abilities left much to be desired. He somehow lacked assuredness, style, a sense of his own voice. Perhaps he needed to take lessons or go to a seminar or a conference or . . .

Hector's writing was interrupted by Miss Bellows, standing in the doorway.

"You have an express letter," she said. "Do you want me to fight my way through this mess, or are you coming over here and get it?"

Hector floundered through the sea of paper and took the cardboard folder from Miss Bellows. He glanced at the return address. The letter was from Elmblight, Ohio—the home of Myrtle Roebuck and her mysterious cronies!

He opened the folder. It contained a few loose printed materials and a brochure advertising a conference. On the cover of the brochure was a quote:

> In what ways are the arts like our dreams? Well, let me suggest that they are tools for working just beyond the edges of what we know. They function on the essential edge of our learning. They help us to think differently. They help us to re-pattern our thinking. Because in order to think about new and different things, we have to think differently, don't we?

Reading on, Hector realized that the person quoted—one of the featured speakers—was none other than Imogene Savonarola! Maybe, it dawned on him, the flesh and blood Imogene *was* trying to contact him.

Dare I suspect she sent me these materials personally? he wondered. *And if so, is this actually the Imogene Savonarola of my dreams?*

At least there was a simple way to find out.

I will go to Elmblight, thought Hector with a smile of triumph.

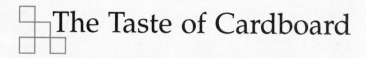# The Taste of Cardboard

Two people pass through tree shadows murmuring words we cannot quite hear. Behind them the ornate old hotel looms, with chattering voices still spilling out the massive door and down the patterned walkways. Heels clatter on the brick walk. Pebbles crunch on a side path. Automobiles cough and purr behind hedges that hide the adjacent lot.

"Are you going to the conference on dreams?" a slow voice inquires. The answer escapes us. "It's in Virginia, at the beach." The voice continues as several people disappear toward the parking lot.

Three women in flat shoes walk quietly on the bricks. They cut across the grass toward a distant street. They still wear nametags which read "Art as a Discovery of Reality" in white letters on a blue background. Beneath that title, their tags say "Roseanne," "Sandra," and—much envied by the others—"Deva."

"Are you staying for the closing session tonight, the talk on hallucination?" Roseanne asks.

"It seems like a strange topic," Sandra says. "She's a scientist, isn't she, what's-her-name? It doesn't seem to me to have much to do with . . . I mean, if art is a discovery of *reality*, what does hallucination have to do with it?"

"There are realities and realities," Deva says sagely.

Sandra digs a program out of her handbag and scans it. "Her name is Imogene Savonarola. I can never remember that. Do you think that's her real name?"

"I really liked the one this morning on—what was it again?" Roseanne squints and remembers. "The transformation of reality . . . the power of paintings and Native American art to transform one thing into another. The one by Jamake Highwater."

"Kachinas," Deva says. "Hopi."

"It says here that Savonarola's the discoverer of the neurotransmitter for paradox. Listen to this," Sandra reads:

"The oxymorphin is almost wholly dormant in modern man, except when it is occasionally sparked by direct encounter with a common metaphor. These experiences are exceedingly brief in our age. This is because we have developed an involuntary tendency to explain metaphors away the instant we experience them."

Roseanne also draws forth a copy of the program. "Goodness, look at all of the books Highwater has written. Listen to this—it's from *The Primal Mind.*" She reads:

"Like all the other symbolic forms, art is not the mere reproduction of a ready-made and given reality. It is one of the ways leading to an objective view of things and of human life. It is not an imitation but a discovery of reality."

"It says she's a fictional character in *The Jamais Vu Papers.* What in the world can that mean?" Sandra asks.

"*He's* real enough," Roseanne says. "I have his book on dance. It's just beautiful."

"Where have we lost our rituals?" Deva asks.

As they reach the street, their conversation fades into the traffic.

The grounds of the old hotel are quieter now. Even birds are silent in the mid-afternoon heat. Only insects hum and buzz. Red and blue petunias set out in white concrete pots glow in the sun. Large trees preside over the formal gardens.

What kind of trees? The setting is Elmblight, Ohio. Not elms, then. Perhaps maples. They are nice and simple, and so fine in the fall.

From beneath the maples the first couple reappears, still strolling, still talking. "As my friend Paul Krassner explained," Imogene Savonarola is saying, "there must be a reason for a hoax other than that it's not true. If you're only fooling people, it's lazy . . . not creative."

Her companion nods.

Imogene continues, "My point is that an honest hoax—*hoax verité*—is a fiction that can manifest as reality if it appeals eloquently enough to the credulity of both sides of the mind/brain—to our sense of myth and intuition and to our sense of logic . . ."

Another pair bursts out of the hotel, walking briskly. "I have to find myself first," the long-haired, bearded man proclaims loudly. His sandals slap-slap down the steps to the brick walk.

"What do you mean?" the woman asks somewhat peevishly, gathering her shawl tightly around her shoulders. Her blond curls bounce wildly in the sun as she strides along.

263

Wait . . . that image doesn't seem quite right—not at this conference, not this year. The text is getting shaky here. We'd better make some adjustments.

Another pair bursts out of the hotel, walking briskly. "I have to find myself first," the trim, dark-haired young woman proclaims loudly.

"What do you mean?" the chubby man asks somewhat peevishly.

Now we've reversed it! But that really doesn't matter. Perhaps it seems more up to date, more universal now. Let's see how it works if we just go on.

"You've certainly established an identity in your field," he insists.

"No!" she exclaims. "That's just the point. It's entirely . . . it's just too dependent on . . ." She lowers her voice a bit, "Until I really do have an identity of my own, how can I possibly . . ." And they, too, disappear behind the hedge toward the parking lot.

The first couple pauses for a moment. "Identity," says Imogene. "They sound as though personal identity can be 'found' and defined more-or-less permanently." She and her companion turn and walk along another side path. "We do that, don't we? In our culture I mean."

"Yes, Western cultures does, *as a matter of fact*, consider personal identity to be something that's permanently defined," Jamake Highwater nods.

"It fills a few everyday needs, but . . ." Imogene mutters. Her hair glints red, escaping from hairpins, floating in the still air.

"It isn't a bad scheme when it comes to those few pragmatic needs. It doesn't hurt the dimensions of our creative mentality to cope with social security numbers, tax returns, and a few other 'make-believe' identities," Highwater says. "But the cosmos isn't impressed by our pragmatism. And, unfortunately, in our haste to clarify and identify everything we tend to believe in the absolute, fixed, and eternal reality of our pragmatic categories."

"It's not very satisfying," agrees Imogene.

"My friend, the late Joseph Campbell, said it better: 'In the West we confuse symbols with the ineffable things they symbolize. We confuse the meal with the menu, and so we often end up munching on cardboard.'" Lines furrow Highwater's cheeks as he grins.

"Cardboard." Imogene nods. "And so many subsist on it."

"There are those who consider such a non-pragmatic viewpoint rather soft and shapeless. 'The truth is the truth. A fact is a fact,' they tell us," Highwater says. "They insist that science has allowed us to know material facts and therefore to abandon suppositions. But such people seem unaware that the antiquated positivism of science—by which they still live their lives—is no longer accepted by scientists."

"Our scientists have become our philosophers," muses Imogene. "It also helps if you're a fictional scientist, as I am. People make fewer demands on you to define boundaries between what is 'real' and what is not."

Highwater's hands move emphatically in the air. "Science has become more active than poetry in recognizing and creating metaphors which imply a cosmos that cannot be factually understood. In the pragmatic West, it's lamentable but understandable that people are alienated by poets; it is, however, rather curious that they are equally alienated by scientists and must live their lives in the 'reality' long abandoned by science."

"It's a sad joke, really," Imogene says a bit mournfully. "But today you spoke of transformation."

"If reality is fixed, then there can't be transformation. And we live in a cosmos in which everything is constantly changing—except us," Highwater exclaims with disgust.

"Do we have any tools, any forms that lead to transformation?" Imogene asks.

"There are a few more or less acceptable forms of transformation in the West," he answers. "When a woman marries she ceases to be Jane Smith and is transformed into Mrs. John Adams. Such a process—a father 'gives' his daughter to her husband—is more a matter of the transference of property than transformation, but it makes my point.

"On a more mystical level, the Catholic novice Jane Smith is transformed by her vows into Sister Jane of the Sacred Heart. Such a religious transformation is a resonation of the ageless process by which a finite person becomes a metaphor of the sacred—not unlike the transformation of a Pueblo Indian into a *kachina* through 'impersonation.'"

Imogene considers the idea. "Identity is changed, transformation is achieved—through impersonation. It should be studied with care. We have so few people with the insight, the patience, the skill"

Highwater laughs. His dark eyes shine. "In the West, what is left of such sacred impersonations are the roles that actors play in our secular dramas. In their own way, actors are temporarily transformed into some other persona, and their success as performers relies upon their capacity to convince us to suspend disbelief—to accept their malleable identities."

Imogene turns away from her companion and, grinning wildly, does a series of cartwheels across the closely trimmed grass . . . three . . . four . . . five . . . No, no, of course she doesn't! We're getting rather too Cooverish. Let's get this narrative back under control.

Imogene turns toward a small pond centered in the yard. Highwater walks beside her. A goldfish fin ripples the surface of the water. Roses nod in the heat. Someone has left a single white glove in the closely trimmed grass. The glove still holds the shape of a hand.

There. That's better.

"Art," says Imogene. "Art must help us make the connection with reality."

"As far as I'm concerned, the Western approach to the experience of art is totally wrong-minded," Highwater says. "Ignorant and educated people alike still look at paintings as if they were depictions of objects rather than the application of paint on a surface in order to produce texture, color, mass, line, etcetera."

"Magritte and many others have tried to tell us," Imogene says.

"As we know, a painting of a pipe is not a pipe. It is a painting," Highwater agrees.

And now—see there—a breeze stirs. It changes the scene utterly. Now there are squirrels, seeking acorns. The trees are oaks.

Highwater continues. "In order to stop seeing what's represented and to see the painting, we must 'become' the painting. That's the only way we can experience art . . . and that's a transformational and empathetic process remote from the Western approach to the external world."

"We miss so much." Imogene says.

"We often end up munching on cardboard when we insist that we are dealing with reality," Highwater says.

"And reality is our work of art," Imogene says.

"We believe the world is 'out there' while scientists and philosophers and people in the arts have long known that the world is something we create moment by moment through the functions of consciousness," he says. "Scientific theorists and artists are equally engaged in creating metaphors rather than discovering truths."

"We live the fictions we create," she says. "We live the fictions we create for each other."

"A society's collective metaphors depict a vision of the cosmos. That vision is what we mean by 'a mythology'—in the best meaning of the word," he says.

"Our myths are our joint fictions, our ancestral fictions," she says.

"Yes, a mythology is a fiction," he says. "But fiction is what the human mind produces. Everything else is cardboard."

They walk away from the pond, away from the rippling fish and the brooding roses and the white glove lying thin and flat—a cutout silhouetted on the bed of ivy.

"And people who are obsessed with 'truth' are going to have to learn to live with fiction. Wallace Stevens—in his *Opus Posthumous*—said it best," he says. "'The final belief is to believe in a fiction, which you know to be a fiction, there being nothing else, the exquisite truth is to know that it is a fiction and that you believe in it willingly.'"

Again they walk away from the hotel, disappearing beneath the heavy oaks. The scene dissolves. Here we are left with only paper and ink.

The conversation continues without us.

The Jamais Vu Papers

Volume One
Number Twelve
November

My Dear Colleagues,

I am sure we were all grateful to hear from the too-long-silent Imogene Savonarola in the October issue of these *Papers.* Granted, she offered little information on my missing patient or the recipe for M. But I, for one, found her final speculations upon the subject of hoaxes quite enlightening.

And now it seems that, at long last, I will have the opportunity to question her personally about these and other matters. She is scheduled to speak this month at the much-touted "Art as a Discovery of Reality" conference in beautiful Elmblight, Ohio. You can be sure that I will be there.

A new query

In the meantime, I must ask your advice on yet a different matter. Another difficult case has sought my help and now I seek yours.

This new patient—let us call him "Omar"—has developed a troubling obsession. He is convinced that he is a character in a work of fiction.

This unfortunate delusion has led Omar to take up creative writing. The poor fellow is convinced he has the power to *write his own life.* He claims to be able to transmute the physical world around him with no other tools than a pencil and paper. He spends a great deal of time and energy attempting to do so.

The agony of mediocrity

Omar is tormented by the notion that all his problems in life arise from a lack of literary talent.

His behavior is not really as bizarre as it sounds. Truthfully, Omar can be very convincing. Even during his worst moments, he seems just as sane as you and me.

And now let me ask what may seem a rather odd question: is Omar *really* clinically insane?

I can't help but think not. Eccentric, yes. My own assessment is that Omar suffers from an overweening sense of duty. Determined not to be a passive player in life's unfolding drama, he has taken too much responsibility upon himself. His most admirable traits have simply gotten the best him.

Still, proper treatment eludes me. Should I attempt to rid Omar of this *idée fixe,* or is there any hope of him living at peace with it? More to the point, precisely what medication would you prescribe, and in what dosages?

Creativity and madness

I am sure you are aware of a burgeoning sensitivity toward the shadowy realm between creativity and madness. The current consensus is that these are not clearcut and distinctive mental phenomena. We must not be too swift to judge.

The last thing I want to do is crush my patient's healthy, creative impulse. I just want to restore his peace of mind.

As always, I look forward to your thoughts and ideas.

Off to Elmblight

And now I am off to Elmblight. The conference brochure was accompanied by cunningly designed tests to measure aesthetic consciousness and critical skills. I have reprinted both on page 2. If you will kindly send in your responses, I will compile and publish the results.

H. Glasco

AESTHETIC CONSCIOUSNESS SURVEY

Have you had an aesthetic experience lately? Would you care to share it with us? Please answer the Aesthetic Consciousness Scale below, and have your confidential responses become part of a national collection of aesthetic experiences to be housed at the new Center for Aesthetic Data Storage and Retrieval located at the University of Georgia Visual Arts Department.

THE COMMITTEE ON AESTHETIC CONVOLUTIONS, CHAIRED BY
W. TOLLIVER SQUIRES,
MA, MMA, PHD

1. Which of the following best describes your emotional condition at the time of your aesthetic encounter?
   (A) Electricity seemed to flow all through my arms and legs.
   (B) My hair stood on end and there was a cold tingling sensation.
   (C) I suddenly went limp.
   (D) Reduced blood pressure.
   (E) Other (please describe).

2. Describe the source from which the experience originated.

3. How long did it last? (Be precise.)

4. Would you like to have another such aesthetic experience in the near future? If not, please explain.

5. List the colors in your experience and the order in which they were experienced. Of these, which were the most transcendent? (translucent?)

6. List any convoluted visual

experiences you may have had

16. Was there

KRITIC'S KORNER
FIND TEN THINGS WRONG WITH THIS PICTURE!

ANSWERS BELOW

ANSWERS: 1. Heavy handed inelegance that nullifies any metaphysical aura about the reality of how form occupies space. 2. Awkward dichotomy between illusion and abstraction. 3. Disquieting texural visages bearing an impassive frontality. 4. Local color. 5. Almost all clouds look like popcorn. 6. Concept change has no direction of stylistic consistency. 7. Narrative and linguistic rather than plastic. 8. A victim of reference to the conventions of act-oriented art forms directly concerned with representation. 9. Reckless absence of any grid system. 10. Juxtaposition of pedestrian forms seems visually and emotionally arbitrary.

"Kritics Korner," intaglio and letterpress, by Tom Hammond

13. Please list all of the visual (and tactile) experiences you have not known.

14. Which experiences do you remember best?

15. Were your aesthetic experiences in black and white, color, or neither?

participating in some termational sessions titled, "Aesthetic Experiences I have Known"?

21. The Committee on Aesthetic Convolutions plans to publish a definite work. Would you agree to have your experiences published, along with your photo and a picture of your experience?

A Dream of Pyramids

Hector Glasco was snoring.

He felt a sharp jab in his left arm. His eyes jumped open. He found himself in the audience of a darkened theater. On the lighted stage before him, Imogene Savonarola was talking.

Or *was* it Imogene Savonarola? Why did he guess it was her?

If I think it's Imogene, reasoned Hector sleepily, *then this must be a lucid dream!*
Hector swelled with self-congratulation.

Why, the last time I had a lucid dream was at Venice Beach with Bruno!
He looked around to see how this particular dream was going.

His first impressions weren't particularly favorable.

First of all, the woman on the stage—the one he thought was Imogene—was no one that he had ever seen before. She was dowdily dressed, a bit overweight, and squinting at lecture notes through unfashionable spectacles. And her hair was more nearly red than golden blond.

Well, this won't do. I want my gorgeous Imogene back. And not behind some damn podium. I want her in my arms.

He closed his eyes and concentrated hard, trying to take them back to that lovely little garden. He visualized that breathtaking apparition in the flowered dress. He remembered her touch, the lilting sound of her voice . . .

He opened his eyes. The scene hadn't changed.

I'm obviously out of practice, thought Hector with a shrug.

Shuffling awkwardly to the next note card, this unfamiliar Imogene spoke:

"Once we dispense with such Freudian anachronisms as a dream 'author,' once we discard our out-of-date notions of some internal creative entity who composes and conducts our fantasies and hallucinations . . ."

She spoke in a reedy monotone, her voice shaking a little from nerves. She gathered a lungful of air to continue her sentence.

". . . then what, we may well ask, is left?" She continued to drone on.

Hector turned to his left. The woman beside him held a pencil in her hand—doubtless the cause of his mild impalement the moment before. She was white-haired and stern-looking. Continuing to stare straight ahead, she stirred and recrossed her legs. Hector looked about. More than a hundred people were sitting around him in plush red chairs.

"Hello," said Hector to the woman next to him. "My name's Hector Glasco. Welcome to my lucid dream. Who are you?"

"Shhhh," the woman hissed, eyes still front. "She's trying to speak."

"Oh, we needn't pay any attention to her. That's not really Imogene Savonarola—or not the one I *normally* dream, at any rate."

"Shhhhhhh," she repeated fiercely.

"Oh, I see," said Hector apologetically. "You're not lucid, are you?"

She turned and glared at him. "I *do* beg your pardon!"

"I mean you don't know that this is a *dream*."

"You're out of your mind."

Hector chuckled heartily. "Me? Oh, I hardly think so. If anything, I'm more *in* my mind than I am in my waking state."

"I'm going to call the usher."

Oh, dear, thought Hector. *This one's even more of a novice than I am. Maybe I can help her out.*

"Let me give you some advice," he said. "Just tell yourself, right now, that you're in a dream—but be careful not to wake up! We can collaborate on all sorts of interesting plots and narratives that way."

A chorus of "shhhhh"s filled the air around him.

"And we can pass the word along to all these other stubborn somnambulists!" Hector continued. "Consensual lucidity! You mean you haven't heard of it?"

These people were terribly slow. Hector felt that he had been dropped into some kind of dreamers' kindergarten. "You could make some kind of an effort," he said to the woman.

He looked down at himself studiously. "I seem to have my clothes on this time." In fact, he realized as he looked around, that everybody had their clothes on. "You do, too. How odd. It would be more appropriate if you were naked. Or if everybody else was."

The woman next to him gasped. The pencil thrust at him again, this time catching him in the wrist—and this time drawing blood.

Pain. Vivid, searing pain. This had never happened in a dream before. Hector looked around, reassessing the situation. He reddened with embarrassment.

"I'm terribly sorry," he said to the woman next to him. Then, feeling some inane imperative to explain, he added, "Please ignore everything I just said. It would appear that this isn't a dream after all."

Hector straightened up and glanced around. Yes, of course. This was a conference of some sort—whatever was it called? "Art as a Discovery of Reality." That was it. And he'd come for the specific purpose of meeting Imogene Savonarola in the flesh at last. And this was no theater at all, but the grand ballroom of the Elmblight Hilton, set up for a lecture. The stage was a raised platform with a lectern and a small table holding a water pitcher and glasses.

Hector shifted in his chair. *So it's reality after all,* he mused. *Whatever that means. Can I trust it to stay in place?*

A short time ago, he had gotten caught in a crowd of people going to hear a talk by Jamake Highwater on the transformation of reality through art, the uses of "impersonation"—things of that sort. Hector had been much too preoccupied to attend. He had paced the streets of Elmblight, restlessly awaiting Imogene Savonarola's lecture. And now, the woman he assumed to be Imogene was still talking.

"So how do we delve into those areas where we don't even know the questions?" she asked the audience. "Blindly," came her own rhetorical answer.

Blindly. Hector sighed tiredly. *Much too blindly for my taste.*

"It takes the rigor of intuition," Imogene continued. "It takes the courage to experience what we cannot define. One has to allow one's mind to be re-structured by an experience before one can even express that experience in language."

She was talking about the arts and hallucinations and dreams. Hector realized he had never heard her be so—so analytical, so scholarly. Oh, she was nervous and a little awkward, to be sure. Still, she was quite something in her own element like this. She cited research from a multitude of disciplines, ranging from art criticism to neurophysiology to quantum physics to underwater basket weaving. He had never heard her talk about any of these things before.

But, he wondered, *have I ever heard this woman talk at all?*

He was here to find out. He stared at the woman on the stage. No, she certainly did not look or sound like the one he had first met in a drowning Venice. Had that woman been entirely a fiction? Or had this very person assumed a different form to share his dreams?

How long he had wanted to bring their relationship into the flesh-and-blood real world! He yearned to hold the genuine woman in his arms while wide awake—with the scenery staying put, not melting and changing all the time. And now, here in Ohio, had he finally found her, or had he not?

Hector was growing intolerably restless. Briefly he considered trying to rewrite the scene, to get the speech over with, to get himself alone with Imogene. But he remembered his last attempt at rewriting—the random pieces of Hilary draped across a chair—and gave up the notion.

He could no longer concentrate on Imogene's words. He fidgeted in his chair. He remembered rushing in all directions through time with his graceful blond lover—experiencing a carnal fulfillment beyond anything he had previously known or suspected to be possible . . .

The audience broke into applause. The talk was over and the conference had adjourned for the evening.

Panicked, Hector leapt to his feet. People were clogging the aisles and moving sluggishly toward the double exits at the rear of the room. Imogene had disappeared from the stage. The woman on one side of him had turned a broad back and was carrying on an intense conversation with her neighbor. There was no way to get by her. The chairs were locked together in rows and he couldn't go forward or back. He turned to the man on his other side.

"Ah, Dr. Glasco," the man exclaimed, checking the name tag. "I thought it might be you. So happy to meet you at last. I've read your publication." He reached out to shake Hector's hand. "You do have a marvelous sense of humor," he exclaimed, pumping his hand up and down. "You know," he leaned forward confidentially, "you really should write a book. The inside story of the disappearance of—" he snickered, "'Hilary.' It'd be quite racy, I expect."

"You read too many tabloids," grumbled Hector. "And now, if you'll excuse me—" He tried, unsuccesfully, to brush past the man, who kept right on talking about how fascinated he was with Hector's adventures.

Hector still couldn't get past either of his neighbors. He craned his neck, trying to see where Imogene had gone. Then he hiked a leg over the chair in front of him, scrambled across to the next row, and rushed off toward the adjoining room, where a reception was in progress. On his way, he knocked a small elderly woman to the floor. He hastily pulled her to her feet, offered a perfunctory apology, and rushed to the reception.

By his second plastic cup of gray-green punch, Hector had sidled into position near Imogene Savonarola, who was talking with several people at once. He took the opportunity to look more closely at her. She was shorter than the woman he knew. He tried to imagine reaching out for her, but the shapes didn't fit. Her breasts were fuller, her hips wider—it was a stranger's body. He couldn't enter there.

Finally, she turned to look at him, smiling politely, awaiting another question from another admirer. "Uh, Dr. Savonarola, " he stammered, "I'm Hector Glasco."

"Oh, of course, Dr. Glasco," she said without missing a beat. "I'm so glad to meet you. I had no idea you'd be here. Are you interested in art?"

"Not really," he said. Then he added, almost inaudibly, "I'm interested in dreams."

"What?" she asked.

"I said I'm *interested in dreams*," he repeated more loudly, staring at her.

Did he see a flicker of something there? If this woman did know what he meant, she was very cool about it. "Lucid dreams in particular," he continued.

"I see," she replied inscrutably. "Perhaps we should arrange a time to talk."

"Yes, yes, whenever you want."

"Could I meet with you later this evening?"

"Yes . . . No!" Hector grabbed at her arm. He was suddenly afraid that she

272

would disappear again. "Er, why don't we have dinner?" He realized it was well past the dinner hour. "Or a late snack . . . or a drink . . . or . . . ?"

"Actually, I've had very little to eat today," Imogene said. "Why don't we see if some place here is still serving food?"

And before long, they were sitting in a coffee shop, awkwardly searching for something to say. Hector couldn't quite bring himself to ask this woman if she'd been his dream lover.

"I enjoyed reading your paper," he finally said, just to make small talk.

"Which paper?" asked Imogene.

"The one about the hoax principle, 'I Seem to Be a Placebo.'"

"Oh, that one," replied Imogene, taking a big bite out of a vegetarian sandwich. "It was brilliant. It certainly did me no good."

"It seems to me that something like that would have, uh," Hector stammered, "profound implications for humanity."

She paused to wipe some crumbs off her chin. "The race has forgotten what it can be. I used to think it was my business to teach them, but now that's over. I've got other things to attend to."

Hector stared at her. His hopes were sinking fast. This woman seemed petty, vain, and completely self-centered. She was hardly the romantic quester of his dreams. There was no further point in even asking if she was the same Imogene. Hector knew she wasn't.

"If you have no faith in the human race," he asked, "why do you bother to do anything? Why do you get up in the morning? Why do you *think*? And why do you stand in front of people like you did today and share your ideas?"

She looked at him. Finally she said, "I had to say *something* if I was going to get up there." Then her eyes softened a little. "I didn't come here today for them," she said, her voice growing strangely gentle. "I came here today for *you*."

Hector stared. He said nothing.

Imogene smiled. "You don't understand, do you? My lecture today, this whole conference, it was just a ploy. It was a way of getting the two of us together."

"I—I'm not sure if I—"

Imogene's eyes seemed to deepen. Her voice became hypnotic. "I seem to remember," she said, "a man once asking me to wake with him."

Now Hector wanted to speak, but couldn't.

"And I thought that man was you," she added. "And so—here I am."

They both sat in silence.

"Then it was really you?" whispered Hector.

"Did we meet in Venice as it sank into the sea?" she asked, smiling.

He nodded.

"Did you find me again at my temple in the sea? Did we fall through the clock face of temporality and make passionate love? Did we float in the air in a Venetian gondola? Did we ride a Ferris wheel to Florence?"

His head bobbed and bobbed. She smiled and extended her hand. "Then it was really me."

Hector looked at her closely. She had wrinkles around her eyes and lines in her forehead. And it was not just that this woman was different. She was real. She was frail. She was fallible. Some of her reddish hairs were out of place. Her clothing was askew here and there. She even had an odor, he realized when she bent close to him. Not unpleasant, but something he had never noticed at all when he had met the Imogene of his dreams.

He realized with a shock that the Imogene he had known seemed to have no wrinkles at all. The woman of his dreams had been the epitome of the male chauvinistic dream. Hector reddened as he realized that his unconscious mind was hardly liberated. In fact, that dream-world Imogene might have come from any current movie or girlie magazine.

He had longed for her to be real. But now he was not stirred, not aroused by her at all.

"But you—" Hector stammered with shame, "well, pardon me for saying so, but there's very little resemblance—"

Imogene shrugged and laughed. "You should see the Hector Glasco of my dreams."

"Oh," he said. "Oh."

It wasn't just that they both looked different, he realized, with some relief. There was no point of contact, no relationship at all. He was a psychiatrist with a neglected practice; she was a scientist with her own agenda. He had tried to help people; she used them for experiments. She had some overarching purpose, some quest; he had begun to long for a simple, everyday life.

She lowered her head. Mutually embarrassed, they both stared at the sandwiches they had ordered. Hers was almost gone. Hector hadn't even taken a bite of his. *The menu made it sound exciting,* he thought. He took a bite. The sandwich tasted vaguely like cardboard. Hector felt a longing for something more than real, something of substance.

"It's hardly the ecstatic experience we anticipated, is it?" asked Imogene awkwardly but pleasantly.

"No," said Hector. "I'm sorry."

She pushed her plate aside. "Well, nothing has gone quite as I planned. Such glorious ambitions I had! The Elixir of Solomon! The union of Sleeping and Waking worlds! I worked damned hard at it, you know. I accomplished the feat of living here—a lifetime of pushing reality through this thick soup, of functioning in time and space. I found it exhilarating. And I thought it was necessary to study, to get those degrees, to establish a reputation, to formulate the placebo *here*. To give it to the right person at the right time. And all for naught.

"Ah, well," she sighed. "For a long time I was as lost in waking as you were in dreams—but, oh, much longer. There was a time when I didn't want to leave. But eventually the Waking World could not hold me."

She sipped her drink pensively. She looked off into space for a moment.

"The truth of it is," she added cautiously, "the World of Dreams can no longer hold me either. I must move on to other worlds, other universes."

Then she looked at Hector intensely. She squeezed his hand tightly. "Would you come with me?" she asked eagerly.

"What?" blurted Hector.

"Hector, I've charted realms beyond dreams or waking! Realms where we can be gods!"

"What do you plan to do," asked Hector, quite startled, "declare a new species?"

"We could," she whispered. "The two of us, you and I alone, could do just that! A new species in a realm where anything is possible!"

Hector found himself moved by her appeal.

"Imogene, I can't," he protested gently. "Your worlds are full of mystics, ancient kings, and infinite possibilities. My world has been very dull. I've never done a very good job of living in it. But I think, maybe—I need to learn to live here for the time being."

"Of course," said Imogene apologetically, a little embarrassed. "Please try to understand. I'm a creature that wonders. I'm a wondering machine. It some-times makes me seem a little foolish"

Then she let out a small, self-deprecating laugh. "I am rather useless, aren't I?"

"Not to you," Hector said simply. Then he added with surprise: "I'm sorry. That was a very peculiar thing to say."

"Not at all," said Imogene sweetly. "It was lovely."

Then she gave his hands a gentle squeeze. "Do you want to meet me one last time—there?"

He felt a brief impulse to say no. But thoughts of many loving moments flooded his mind and he drew his breath in sharply. He nodded.

Hector and Imogene stood hand in hand as great stones lifted over their heads and fell into place on the great structure before them. The main form was completed now, with its secret rooms and tunnels and treasure chambers buried deep within the earth. The mathematics of the universe had been recorded in the precisely designed and aligned mountain of stone. Hector sensed mysteries that he knew had never been unearthed by the human race. That thought disturbed him a little, and he began to pay more attention to his surroundings.

There was chanting in a language he could not recognize. There were people who seemed to be transfixed, just as he had been. Now great flat slabs of polished limestone were lifting, soaring over them, and settling into place on the surface of the pyramid.

A great stone man/lion creature came stalking out of the desert, whipping it's tail back and forth across the dunes. The Sphinx prowled around the pyramid, chose its position carefully, and stretched out on the sand. It glared directly at Hector and Imogene. Something in that gaze made Hector shudder.

Then the creature spoke with a slow, distant, sound like an ancient gong.

"I tell you they were dreamed . . . I tell you they were dreamed . . . I tell you they were dreamed . . . ," chanted the Sphinx. The phrase sounded very familiar. Where had he heard it before? Fragments of a different scene flickered in his mind . . .

"And they *are* dreamed," said Imogene. "Every second of every minute of every day and night. The pyramids are dreamed into existence by these very souls." A pained look came into her eyes.

"The effort it takes!" she said, her voice catching. "The effort and the sadness and the courage it takes, just to keep reality in place—whether in Waking or in Sleep. I swear, if I don't leave these realms altogether, I'll die of pity. And I don't have time for pity."

Hector caught his breath at Imogene's loveliness and stepped forward to take her in his arms again. He realized that he could not focus his eyes on her. That was why she had no lines. In his mind, he also had an image of the dowdy, daytime Imogene. This one before him was mysterious, but not real.

Oh, but still she was lovely. And he had loved her. Tears rolled down Imogene's cheeks. Hector was weeping too. *Can you cry in dreams?* he wondered. He couldn't remember doing so before.

She moved back, just slightly. "I have so much to do," she said.

"And I've distracted you?"

She caught his hand. "A little. But it was a sweet distraction."

The pyramid blurred and began to fade. Through his tears, Hector caught a last glimpse of the unblinking stare of the Sphinx.

And then they were in a garden of a palace. It was the garden they had been in the first night, he realized. But he had become weary of these sweeping changes of place and time. He longed for one good solid fiction—one he could live in.

"Won't you come with me?" asked Imogene again.

"You know I can't," said Hector. "I've just been a helpless character in someone else's saga. It's time for me to write my own story."

She tilted her lovely face up to him. "Are you sure?"

Hector hesitated yet again. But, he found, his thoughts and dreams were mundane ones indeed.

"Yes," he said, regretfully. "I am sure."

She touched his face lightly. "But before you go," she said. "Let me share a secret with you."

"What secret?"

"The secret of the Elixir," she said. "The metaphor itself."

And suddenly, Hector's dream reality whirled madly around him. The beautiful illusion of Imogene dissolved. But he knew she was still there. He knew—without being told—that he was now inside her mind, his own consciousness cascading into hers. He could barely see through a storm of snow and ice. Wind howled about him. He felt himself clinging to the face of sheer rock. He had the sensation of almost infinite height. He was terrified—and exalted—beyond his wildest imagining.

"Imogene!" he shouted. But he could hardly hear his own voice, riddled with wonder and despair.

The wind almost carried away the faint echo of Imogene's distant voice, half-chanting, half-singing her song of final farewell:

> "O the mind, mind has mountains; cliffs of fall
> Frightful, sheer, no-man-fathomed. Hold them cheap
> May who ne'er hung there. Nor does long our small
> Durance deal with that steep or deep. Here! creep,
> Wretch, under a comfort serves in a whirlwind: all
> Life death does end and each day dies with sleep."

A violent gust of pure, frigid consciousness swept him away from the cliff face. He screamed, but knew he was all alone in the whole of creation. He fell and fell and fell, tumbling through light-years, for what may have been eons. He collapsed into a welcome, safe, and utterly unmysterious softness. He clutched a pillow to him.

He had awakened—with tears on his cheeks and the taste of cardboard in his mouth.

 **5:30 P.M.**

... "Oh dear," sighed Ethel. "Somehow I always knew that they would have to part."

"I guess it never could have lasted," said Addie. "But I did have hopes there for a while."

"I'm afraid Imogene is a little too much of a handful for our Hector," said Myrtle.

"What do you think, Max?" Ethel asked.

But the only response was a sonorous snore. Max was slumped into a fat, overstuffed chair, sleeping with a peaceful smile on his face.

"We'd better leave that poor man alone," Lida June advised. "I'm sure he needs his rest."

"It really was a very interesting conference," said Phoebe.

"Which conference?" asked Lida June.

"The one in the book. The one where Hector and Imogene met for the last time."

"And how would you know?" asked Lida June. "The chapter says practically nothing about it."

"I went to it. It was just yesterday," said Phoebe. She was tying fringes on one end of her weaving now.

"You mean that you went to the conference on 'Art as a Discovery of Reality'?" demanded Myrtle, delightedly.

"It was right here in Elmblight, you know," nodded Phoebe.

"Did you hear Imogene speak?" Addie wanted to know.

"No, but I did hear Jamake Highwater. And then I went shopping that afternoon. I'm afraid that by the time I got back all the other talks were over. Everybody was leaving. In fact, some crazy fellow in an awful hurry knocked me down. It quite took the breath out of me for a moment."

"That must have been you, then, in the last chapter," said Myrtle. "And it must have been Hector who nearly trampled you to death."

"Why, I suppose so, now that you mention it." agreed Phoebe.

"Didn't you recognize him?" asked Addie. "Why didn't you stop him and talk to him?"

"I hadn't even started reading the book when I went there," said Phoebe. "I didn't know they had anything to do with each other."

"You didn't do your homework before book club day?" objected Lida June.

"I've been so busy. . ."

Myrtle laughed aloud. "You can stop blaming me now, Lida June," she said. "I'm not the only one that walked into this book."

"But I didn't walk into it at all," objected Phoebe. "It's more like the book walked into me."

"I'm too tired think about it," grumbled Lida June, clearly conceding defeat.

Max stirred and sat up. "Ladies," he said woozily, "I don't completely comprehend your problem. But there's one thing I can tell you. There *is* an out there out there, no matter where you are."

Then he collapsed again into a noisy snoring. The ladies stared at him.

"Did you understand any of that?" Addie asked Ethel.

"Not a word," sighed Ethel.

"Guess we'd better let him sleep it off," remarked Myrtle.

"It could be a long time," said Phoebe.

"*I'll* take him home!" volunteered Ethel.

They did not resume reading the book. They just continued their work in silence. The room grew slightly darker. But no one turned on any lights. After all, it is a strict policy of the Elmblight, Ohio, Book Club and Sewing Circle to read and work only by natural light.

"I sometimes wonder," mused Phoebe.

"So do I," said Ethel.

"About the future?" asked Phoebe.

"Indeed," replied Ethel.

"Perhaps we all do," said Ethel.

There was a general murmer of assent.

"And this Professor Brillig fellow in the book," inquired Phoebe. "Are we really to believe that that's really him in the future, in the matrix with Orndorf and Dr. Leary?"

"The book says so," remarked Addie.

"Ah," said Phoebe. "But is the book authoritative on this point?"

"The book seems to be authoritative on no point," grumbled Lida June.

"Professor Brillig strikes me as awfully square to wind up as a swashbuckler, let alone a woman," said Ethel.

"Honestly," grumbled Myrtle lazily. "I don't believe any of you have paid the first shred of attention. Dr. Fred Alan Wolf has explicitly told us that there are an infinite number of universes, so there must be an infinite number of futures as well. And the future in which Professor Brillig winds up as a cyberspace outlaw is just one of his infinitude of futures."

Ethel giggled at Myrtle's observation. "Why the very idea! And what are you telling me? That I, myself, will be a computer outlaw and an inscape cowboy fifty years from now?"

"Infinite odds would make it inevitable," said Myrtle. "*One* of you will, at least. In *one* of your futures. Or perhaps more than one."

"And will I meet up with Professor Brillig in cyberspace myself someday?"

"The same answer applies," explained Myrtle.

"I think *I'll* take a nap," said Phoebe.

Ethel glanced toward Max. He snorted noisily in his sleep. Perhaps he was about to wake up . . .

The Jamais Vu Papers

Volume One
Number Thirteen
December

Dear Readers of *The Jamais Vu Papers:*

I am sorry to say that this will be the last issue of this newsletter. That is, unless someone volunteers to take over the publication of it. The reason is that Dr. Glasco has decided not to do it any more, or anything else that he had been doing before. That's probably a good thing.

I tried to get someone by talking to some of Dr. Glasco's professional acquaintances, but they did not want to associate themselves with this publication. I guess that is not surprising, since so many things seem to happen in it that we did not put in it. It's been pretty spooky. Maybe it's haunted or something.

However, I want to assure everyone that I have tried my best to send to the printer exactly what Dr. Glasco wanted. Someone else will have to explain where all of those other things came from. Who I don't know.

Anyhow, Dr. Glasco sent me an official memo, so it's included here. As you will see, he is closing down his office. So you won't be able to reach him here or probably anywhere, from the way he sounds.

If anybody needs a good secretary, I will personally be available in two weeks. I can type 35 words per min-

memo: Dear Miss Bellows:

I want to make it official now that I am closing my practice, effective immediately. I would like for you to stay on for three weeks to clear up any manageable business. Be sure to give yourself an additional 30 days pay, plus any unused vacation pay you have coming.

I'm sure this comes as no surprise to you, since I have been largely absent from the premises for some time now. My patients must have long since found more enthusiastic therapists. You can refer any stragglers to whichever of my colleagues seems most appropriate. Use the rolodex at random, if necessary.

If anyone at all should wish to continue this newsletter, consider them most welcome. It is time for me to let it go.

I'm not very good at expressing my feelings in writing, so the best I can say is that I'm deeply grateful for your fine work and dedication — particularly during the last very difficult and troubling year.

Warm Regards,

Hector Glasco

Then there was some more space left over so I decided to put in the minutes of my last secretary's club meeting. It was the only thing I could find that seemed to connect to the subjects that Dr. Glasco has been talking about.

Besides, we've been having a lot of fun.

always take good care of the office plants. You can come and see them. And I have certainly shown that I can handle many other different job activities. Please contact me at this office. Soon.

And, Merry Christmas, everyone!

Yours sincerely,
Geraldine Bellows

The meeting opened with old business, most of which was taken up with a discussion about how to spend the $40 mag

Un
ness
buy
card
is in
ing h

It d
to g
point

Ba
brou
news
which
tinen
infor
voted
shou
"show
next

We
every
bring
tell" a
meeti

Judi
ported
her th
this w
realize
cid, Ju
try flyi
time,
trouble
ground
went u
and ju
space.
flew all over the city and visited friends.

Professional and personal dreaming, what can it do for you? is the topic of a special

who had her very first lucid dream last Saturday!

Sarah Adams reported that she had her third lucid dream this week. When she
d, Ju
flying
h had
off the
time
a high
just
space.
g, she
the

ened
ness,
was
dis-
ow to
left
rum-
eet-
old
of
up
sion
end
om

lon
of a
ms
of
nd
on.

ry-
n a
ur
ur
ng
en
dreaming. Maybe I'll see you in your dreams.
Roseanna Gibbons, Secy.

Tristan und Isolde, a painting by Nancy Camden Witt.

"Happens all the time," says
Coyote. "That's what myths do.
They happen all the time. . . ."

Ursula LeGuin
"The Woman Without
Answers"
Dancing at the Edge of the World

Wolf & Coyote

... It was twilight. Dr. Fred Alan Wolf walked briskly through his neighborhood. He was a bit tired. Those howling dogs, coyotes, wolves, or whatever they were, had kept him awake last night. A whole day had passed, but he still felt a little groggy and he hoped some exercise would wake him up. He had a lot of writing to do this evening.

A large, fuzzy black-and-white dog trotted toward him. Its ears flopped, its chubby body rolled from side to side, its tongue lolled—everything about it seemed to be in motion.

Dogs! thought Wolf with a scowl. *My love-hate nemeses, always there when I don't need them!* He wondered if this was one of the nighttime howlers.

It blocked his way in the middle of the sidewalk, bouncing up and down as if delighted to see him. It really was quite large—and rather muddy, he noted. *The dog,* he thought, trying to be patient, *the guardian, the servant, the soldier, a symbol of loyalty, an eternal protector.*

"I don't need your protection today," said Wolf.

"I'm not here to protect you," said the dog. "I'm here to gnaw at your rational bone and to ask impertinent questions."

284

And the dog jumped up and licked Wolf on the face. It left big paw prints all over his shirt and pants.

"Llixgrijb!" Wolf exclaimed. "I should have known it was you!"

Who else *could* a talking dog be?

Wolf succeeded in pushing the slobbering creature away. "Why are you picking on me again?" he demanded.

"Well, you're paying attention," the dog replied. "Not everybody is listening, you know. Besides, you've asked some rather impertinent questions yourself."

"So what's your problem?" asked Wolf.

"It's Brillig," said the dog.

"Ah, yes. That oblivious and rational entity you created in order to experience this universe. Well, what's the problem with Brillig?"

But now the dog was distracted by a neighbor's rose garden. Thrilled at the prospect of new holes to dig, it trotted exuberantly away.

Llixgrijb, never known for its concentration span, was gone—at least for the moment. Wolf drew a sigh of relief. At least it wasn't his garden this time. And he hadn't been bothered by the distraught entity since that time in Greenwich Village a couple of months back. He hoped that the dog represented Llixgrijb's last complaint, at least for another few months.

Wolf headed out into the New Mexican hills that ranged a short distance away. *I should have asked that dog about the howling while it was still talking,* he thought. *Or is the dog really there when Llixgrijb appears? Or is it Llixgrijb doing the howling?*

He walked on up the path into the hills. The air was fresh and clear. Dusk was descending. He started to feel more peaceful, began to relax and enjoy the air, the quiet hills, the spacious sky. Now he could give some thought to the new book he was writing, a summary of his own recent experiences with various shamanic rituals.

But his problem was—how could he describe his extraordinary encounters in Peru, where he so vividly experienced himself as an eagle, swooping toward the ground as in a hunt? And then as merely an actor in the beautifully scripted drama of the cosmos?

How could he describe his experiences in the sweat lodges at Pine Ridge? And the nighttime ceremonies of the Sioux, with their rustling feathers and their flashing lights? The last few months had been like doing a tour of the shamanic world—a truly mind-blowing tour.

The owl had particularly stuck in his mind—the Night Eagle—during his open vision quest on Bear Butte Mountain, when, in the full light of noontime, an owl swooped not more than five feet above his head? How to convey the synchronicity, the resonance of such a moment?

Among all the medicine animals, the owl was the one associated with clairvoyance, with protection in magic, and with non-conscious wisdom. He had some special kinship with that owl.

And like the owl, he had to pay attention. And like the owl, he had to ask impertinent questions.

The underbrush rustled nearby as Wolf walked along. He stopped in his tracks and listened and looked. He would be glad to encounter an animal—as long as it wasn't another dog.

He had learned from experience that animals, without humans around, are more tuned in to the mythic than we are. *It's not that they're not physical,* he thought to himself. *They're very physical. But they have a stronger mythic sense because they're not as temporally developed as humans—not as concerned about tomorrow and the next day.*

Wolf stood and listened in vain for more movement. But when he started walking again, the rustling began again. It followed him alongside the path. Whatever it was, it was keeping pace with him. Startled for a moment, Wolf stopped again and glanced around. Had that blasted dog followed him? No, this silent shape was much more graceful than that clumsy, salivating oaf could ever be.

He could just make out a shadowy shape in the thickets close to the path. The whole situation made him more than a little suspicious. It smacked of Llixgrijb, again.

"Who's there?" he asked.

And the rustling in the bushes stopped. After a moment, there came an intense, whispering voice.

"Who's there you ask? Some say I created the heavens and the earth. Others say that I was merely the Great Spirit's Lieutenant. Some say that I gave fire to man, like Prometheus, and that I destroyed all monsters who devoured mankind. Others say that the only gifts I ever gave to man were disease and death."

Wolf felt chills rise up his back. This was no shaggy dog, nor even a waitress or a vagrant or a kid on a skateboard. The bushes rustled as the animal moved along ahead of him now. Wolf followed carefully.

The voice whispered again, "I am vastly intelligent and clever; I am infinitely stupid and gullible. I am the spirit of benevolence and generosity; I am the eternal thief, the scavenger. I am the modest braggart, the idiot savant."

The last sentence faded away as the voice moved off. Wolf hurried to catch up.

Now the voice came from ahead and to the left, "When the Great Spirit gave me my name, he told me: 'You will be honored for the good and wise things that you do, and reviled and laughed at for the stupid, vain, and selfish things that you do.'"

And then it came from behind Wolf again, "I am kin to Hermes, the messenger god. I am the messenger and the trickster."

Wolf turned around on the trail. He felt that strange mixture of fear and joy that meant he was again standing on a threshold. Llixgrijb was manifesting in a form much closer to its essence than the entity had done before. And Wolf knew what it was.

"Coyote!" exclaimed Wolf. "That most contradictory of archetypes!"

"Contradictory, indeed," echoed the voice, still in a whisper.

"In any case," said Wolf, "it's a not altogether unexpected pleasure. I know all about you. You have many magical powers, but they don't always work in your favor. You can be tricked or fooled by others. But after all: it takes a master trickster to trick oneself. No one is more astonished than you are at the outcome of your own tricks."

It occurred to Wolf that he probably should feel somewhat silly, standing apparently alone on a trail in the dusk, talking to the underbrush. But he had reaped rewards from stranger things.

He said, "Well, I am Wolf, he of the keen senses, the archetypal teacher, represented by the dog star Sirius. The moon is my power ally. And I'm not tricked by you in the least. You're really Llixgrijb, my personal *bête noir.* Never try to trick a trickster."

A sound came from the brush. It sounded like a chuckle. "And why shouldn't I take an archetypal form? Archetypes are my footprints, after all!"

"Well, Llixgrijb," laughed Wolf, glancing down at the muddy paw prints on his jacket, "Coyote is the perfect archetype for you! The trickster that tricks himself!"

The yet-unobservable creature made a rather indignant rustling, obviously not altogether flattered.

"And what impertinent questions have you got for me this evening?" asked Wolf, as he started strolling up the trail again. "Something to do with your creation Brillig, I take it?"

"When last we spoke," said Coyote, following along parallel to the man's course, "you reminded me that I had created an infinite number of physical, temporal universes. I guess that means an infinite number of Brilligs, too."

"Yes," said Wolf. "Or variations on Brillig. You'd be—he'd be—in each of the universes somehow."

"So obviously, one or more of those Brilligs is going to become aware that he is just my illusion. That's not just a possibility—it *has* to happen because it's just a part of the infinity of all things. Brillig is going to discover me in one place or another. It's inevitable."

"Yes," said Wolf, with a deep sigh of resignation. "That is indeed true. Once Brillig—but that means all the Brilligs—discovers your existence, then the ultimate self-realization will take place. When Brillig has this self-realization, he will achieve coherence in all the universes simultaneously—in which case there will be nothing. All things will vanish and nothing will appear until you dream again."

"Wait a minute," said Coyote. "Suppose Brillig in *one* universe achieves self-realization, and a Brillig in *another* universe doesn't. Does my creation collapse even then? Does Brillig 2 become an unwitting victim to Brillig 1? That doesn't sound fair, does it?"

Wolf was quick to reply. "If Brillig 1 gets self-realization while Brillig 2 doesn't, guess what? Brillig 1 is just following some phoney guru down the street."

"Explain that to me," said Coyote.

"You see, nobody gets out of here unless we all get out of here. And 'all of us' literally means *all* of us—in every one of these universes. It takes phase coherence in order to wake up. You can't wake up without it. What happens in transcendental meditation, transpersonal consciousness, altered state awareness, mantra chanting, shamanic drumming, and things of that sort is this one reality gets jarred, and we shift to alternate realities a bit more freely. We've released part of the illusion that says this is the only reality that ever existed and ever will be. We've released that for just a moment, and during that moment, the Brilligs in about twenty-five thousand universes suddenly catch a glimpse of—you! Llixgrijb! And at moments like that, you get jolted a little bit.

"But you shouldn't get too worried, because twenty-five thousand divided by infinity is still zero. And those are pretty good odds. Somehow, this self-realization has got to take place everywhere."

But the voice in the underbrush sounded worried. "I've been keeping track," it said. "And lately, every one of those infinite number of Brilligs has experienced some sort of expanded awareness—some sort of spill-over from a mythic, archetypal realm."

"So?"

"You are rather an expert on parallel worlds," said the voice. "Are myths and archetypes connected with them?"

"They are if you look at them in terms of the conscious and the unconscious," said Wolf. "The conscious, temporal world of our everyday perceptions is mysteriously governed by the timeless, mythic world. This mythic world supplies a kind of determinism to the temporal world.

"At the level of temporality, the level of time, the level of the world we live in, we find things totally unpredictable. We try to muster the power to control it, but we can't. But in this other world, the world of myth and archetype, there's a kind of flow, a kind of continuum which even follows the laws of cause and effect."

"Interesting," said the voice. "And wasn't quantum physics supposed to have abolished determinacy in the temporal world?"

"Indeed it was," said Wolf.

Then, with more than a trace of mischief and irony, the voice inquired: "And what was your field of study?"

But Wolf was unfazed. "It's true that I've been preaching the quantum view for all this time, saying that things are indeterminate. Now I'm finding out that I was probably wrong. One has to become sensitive and aware at the mythic level, as shamans are. I'm talking about a world in which the future can be seen. Remember Black Elk, who predicted the coming of the iron rails, the iron horses, and men flying on the wings of birds. You see, he was experiencing things at the mythic level, where everything is prescribed and there really are no surprises."

"You don't need to tell me about Black Elk," said the voice. "We used to talk often. He gave me a very hard time."

"And now," said Wolf, "I have to re-look at Newton again, and Einstein too. They knew there was some kind of determinacy. But what were these guys really pointing to? Perhaps what they really wanted to say had less to do with the physical world than with a whole different level of reality—the world of vision and myth, the world of the primal mind."

"So determinism is outside the province of science," mused the entity. "Has quantum physics no relevance to this mythic reality at all?"

"There's a kind of connection, but it's a back door connection. One asks oneself, 'If quantum physics spells chaos, then what gives us our traditional sense of destiny? The destiny of fate, the moving finger writ—where did these age-old insights come from?' The answer is, they come from the mythic world."

"But is the mythic world truly a *parallel* world?"

Puzzling for a moment, Wolf said, "I don't quite know how to answer that question. Whenever I've discussed parallel worlds what I was talking about were different physical possibilities. Perhaps now I'm talking about *two kinds* of parallel worlds: the parallel worlds of physical matter and temporal sequences, and the parallel worlds of the mythic movement or flow."

"Parallel physical worlds and parallel mythic worlds," mused the voice. "And when one of those mythic worlds spills over into your world, you know all that's going to happen next. And yet, paradoxically, you can't know everything that goes on in all those other worlds . . . and worlds . . . and worlds . . ."

The voice faded out into long drawn-out howls that echoed across the hills. Wolf was startled into silence for a moment. The entity seemed to be waiting for him to continue.

"I started out expecting to relate shamanism to quantum physics," said Wolf. "But now it seems to me that the two have little to do with each other—that there is an understanding of reality which exists outside the bounds of science."

Wolf thought for a few moments, then continued, "I suppose one could conceivably try to say that quantum physics can explain the formation of mythic images. But that doesn't ring true to me anymore. Quantum physics is limited by the fact that it deals with paradoxes of the world of physical time, the temporal world.

"Perhaps one could borrow from Bohr's complementarity. When one is living one's myth, there is flow, predictability, certainty, and knowledge of the future. But paradoxically, there is little sense or awareness of the material universe. You know where you are going, but you don't care.

"On the other hand, when one is living fully in space-time-matter, there is nothing but insecurity, unpredictability, scarcity, suffering, etcetera, and one cares very much about what is going to happen. It's a paradox—a laughable one at that."

Coyote said, "You don't sound disappointed by that."

"No, I'm not disappointed. My job is to be a seeker. My job is to be open to any new idea that comes along. I don't have any pet theory. In a sense, I've followed a logical progression from Newtonian physics to quantum mechanics and, now, to the world of myth.

"And although the mythic world is out of the bounds of physicality, it is nevertheless still real in terms of how we live our lives—more real, perhaps, than we care to admit. We see human beings living from generation to generation with the same repetitive archetypes appearing again and again."

It was growing dark now. No reply came for a few moments. Wolf wondered if the entity had simply dematerialized. Then, with an attitude of insolent surrender, it stepped out of the brush and faced him.

It was a coyote, all right, and an unusually large one. Its unruly, tan coat was eerily illuminated by the moonlight. Its great brush of a tail switched back and forth impatiently. Its eyes blazed with mischief, and its ears probed the air attentively. Its expression was at once comical and sinister.

"Don't you have any other questions?" asked Wolf, feeling just a little apprehensive.

"Not really," said Coyote/Llixgrijb. The creature sat on its haunches, tilted its head, and looked pensively at the moon. But, after a few silent moments, it shifted and looked straight at Wolf.

"I was just thinking," said Coyote/Llixgrijb, "that maybe I've chosen the wrong realm to live in altogether.

I created this physical, temporal realm, and put Brillig in it to experience it for me. But, really, all this physicality spells nothing but trouble. It seems that suffering, ignorance, and mortality are the only things that hold the temporal realm together.

"It leads to more grief than gratis."

"Indeed," said Wolf.

"Buddha taught us that suffering and sacrifice are key ingredients in this realm."

"Then why stick around?

"I believe I'll scrap the whole thing and move on to the mythic realm—the world of flow, of determinacy. A world without surprises. I like the sound of that."

"So are you contemplating destroying our world altogether?"

"What do you think?"

"Be careful, my friend," said Wolf. "If you try to scrap this world, you may find the mythic world extremely boring. There will be no meaning or purpose to it, without information from our temporal realm leaking into it. The mythic world is only important because of the physical world, and the physical world is only important because of the mythic world. Here, at least, you get to experience the heroic myth of the mystic experience, because death is real here."

Coyote/Llixgrijb grinned at him. "You're trying to scare me out of it, aren't you?"

"Besides," continued Wolf, "getting rid of either realm would prove rather difficult. Dividing the mythic from the physical or the temporal is like cutting a magnet in two; the pieces will divide into physical or mythic wherever you make the cut. It's either both realms, or nothing. It's a cosmic/mythic complementarity. You must have both to have your dream."

"I think you're bluffing," said Coyote/Llixgrijb.

"Think what you like. If you want to wreck both realms and spend all eternity in that wretched, extradimensional isolation of yours, there's nothing I can do to stop you."

"We'll see," said Coyote/Llixgrijb. "We'll just see."

And the animal vanished into the underbrush.

Wolf blinked his eyes in the growing darkness. Had Coyote/Llixgrijb tricked him, or had he tricked Coyote/Llixgrijb? Had they tricked each other, or had they tricked themselves?

Wolf shook his head and started retracing his steps. It was no use worrying about it now. It was best to get home before it got much darker. He had a lot of writing to do.

Later that night, when he was poring over his book, the howling came again—this time in distinct, musical yelps and arpeggios. There was no mistaking it for anything but a coyote this time. But was it Llixgrijb again? Was this an outcry straight from the heart of Llixgrijb's lonely realm?

Wolf paused and listened. No answer came.

Before getting back to work, Wolf briefly shivered at the thought that our universe might, at any moment, vaporize and vanish into the vindictive recesses of Llixgrijb's imagination.

But quantum physicists get used to that kind of thing . . .

292

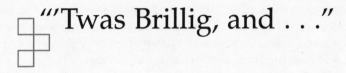

"'Twas Brillig, and . . ."

The brillig journeyed on into the matrix. At first it tumbled through a familiar maelstrom of images and sensations, but now even those memories began to recede. The brillig was growing tinier and tinier.

Eventually, the brillig became but a bare, solitary spot of sentience in a mindless expanse. All material shapes, all things seemingly substantial, vanished into their own hugeness. Molecules appeared in the place of monoliths, then atoms in the place of molecules.

The brillig took pleasure in a game with atoms, observing the infinite possible locations in each electron cloud, and pinpointing the exact position of an electron for just a frail point in time. The cloud of possibilities would then disappear in an exhilarating flash of certainty. It was quite intoxicating.

Then electrons vanished into hugeness, giving way to quarks. And the quarks, too, were consumed into even tinier things.

As the brillig grew smaller, even space/time lost its smoothness. The cosmos became grainy, then downright bumpy. It appeared to be composed of discretely small units. And then the brillig, too, seemed to have reached some threshold of smallness. It had stopped shrinking.

But isn't smallness infinite? pondered the brillig. There was no response, of course.

But what am I? wondered the brillig. *What have I become?*

The brillig felt itself pulsate in a mysterious pattern. It detected motionless neighbors pulsating in exactly the same way. They surrounded the brillig. They were packed into three dimensions like sardines.

A binary unit of information! realized the brillig. *A bit! That's all I am. And that's all that I'm surrounded by. We're clustered, multitudes of us, turning on and off according to some ancient program. Quarks, electrons, atoms, matter, time, space, consciousness, all living things, and even mind itself—these are all illusions which arise out of our collective random binary activities. Even void, even emptiness, is only a conceit, a mirage which we simulate. Together, we comprise the universe itself, a vast mosaic of pure information disguised as reality.*

The brillig could feel itself exchanging a weirdly inarticulate message with its fellows. Their rhythms interlocked contrapuntally like a jazz improvisation. Like its fellows, the brillig seemed to have no volition, no control over its communications.

And yet, the brillig, itself, still seemed able to speculate, to wonder. All its neighbors could do was to exclaim to each other with mindless excitation. All the brillig could detect in them was a sense of urgency providing a purpose of sorts. It was their program, their recursive algorithm.

And the patterns they blindly create out of that urgency comprise the universe itself—all universes—all possibilities, mused the brillig.

And the bits chattered away all alone. Even if they could formulate questions, the brillig was sure there would be no answers. The hardware would always remain beyond the grasp of the software.

And the brillig raised a soundless cry into the void:

"Hateful the day when I received life! Accursed creator! Why did you form a monster so hideous that even you turned from me in disgust?"

No reply came. The brillig was addressing itself—no one else. The muteness of the universe resounded with a sort of ghastly eloquence.

Cosmos . . . Ignorance.

They were synonyms.

The brillig realized this. And so did an infinity of brilligs in an infinity of universes.

It's all a hoax, thought the brillig. *A cruel and stupid hoax. I'll be the butt of it no longer.*

The brillig mustered its anger and its will. There was no further cause to commune with the bits around it. It was better not to exist at all than to exist for no reason.

And so the brillig's message, its signal, sputtered and faded into silence. And silence fell upon the brillig's immediate neighbors, then upon their neighbors, then upon their neighbors' neighbors . . .

And like dominoes, all the trillions upon zillions of information bits fell silent.

Causality ceased to exist.

Temporality ceased to exist.

Physicality ceased to exist.

The cosmos vanished.

And the brillig found itself face to face with its creator.

The End of the Universe
as We Know It

The brillig passed through sheer emptiness. To call it a void would be to give it familiarity, dimension. It was vacant even of void. It was void-less, empty even of its own absence. Then the void-less-ness heaved a deep sigh.

"Please," a distant voice rumbled. "Let's maintain the illusion of separateness for just a moment or two longer," it said. The brillig felt a fleeting inclination to agree.

And instantly, the brillig found itself standing in a long, spacious attic room with oversized eaves and rafters. There was no other life, no movement at all.

"Is this it, then?" the brillig asked. "Is there no one else to keep us company—no one beyond us, above us, around us—anywhere? I mean, are we really alone?"

"If we ever had fellow creatures, it's a moot point by now," the distant voice rumbled.

"And so we only have one illusion left," observed the brillig. "The illusion that the two of us are separate."

"A sweet illusion."

"It serves no purpose."

"It allows us companionship."

"I'm not your companion. I'm you."

"It allows us conversation."

"What's there to discuss?"

"At least it allows us to disagree."

"There's nothing to disagree about."

"We can pretend to disagree."

"Pretending is a waste of time."

"There is no time," said Llixgrijb.

"I know that," said the brillig. Staring sulkily around the vast space, it noticed that the attic was not empty at all. It was a dirty, musty place, cluttered, piled, stacked, and draped with vaguely familiar shapes. The brillig could not quite make out what they were.

But at that moment, the brillig was distracted by a question for which it had no answer.

"But how did *you* come into being?" the brillig asked.

"Ask yourself," answered Llixgrijb. "Do you remember?"

"I can't recall. If there was a beginning, it's all a blank."

"Well, there you have it," replied Llixgrijb. "Even for us, there is the unknowable. Our ultimate curiousity cannot be slaked."

Something unknowable? How could the only consciousness that existed not know how it began? A sensation rather like surprise startled the brillig. *But can there still be such a thing as surprise?*

The brillig was intrigued. It became a fraction more enthusiastic about maintaining the illusion that it and Llixgrijb were separate.

"Was it my enlightenment or your annoyance that ended the temporal realm?"

"Why ask?" retorted Llixgrijb. "That's a meaningless question, as you know."

"Yes, if I did it, you willed that I do it. It was you, in fact, who did it."

"True," sighed Llixgrijb. "And yet I found temporality perversely entertaining in some ways. Too bad it couldn't have lasted a little longer."

"You hated temporality," said the brillig. "You did nothing but fret and worry about it. It gave you nothing but pain."

"It was an entertaining pain. Its creatures, though, were stupid and trivial."

"They weren't so stupid. You were afraid enough of them discovering you."

"In any case, there was no reason to let them live."

The brillig fidgeted in the ensuing silence. What was the point of this bickering? Were the not-two of them doomed to an non-eternity of meaningless squabbling? Was that the only diversion left in this interminable entrapment?

The brillig looked about the attic more closely. Now it could see that the attic was wildly cluttered with puppets of all kinds. Some hung from the beams. Others were piled in trunks. Still others dangled from hat stands and curtain rods.

In its center hung a frightful marionette—a ghastly skeleton wielding a scythe. It grinned horribly, with blood dripping from its empty eye sockets. It was the specter of Death.

"So this is the only realm that's left," said the brillig.

"Yes," said Llixgrijb. "The Wolf-entity called it the realm of myth. It's much more agreeable than the physical, temporal realm we just destroyed. Much less troublesome, anyway. Don't you agree?"

The brillig found that it did not agree. Uneasy, it went over to the Death puppet. Death was, of course, made of wood and papier mâché. Its teeth were of the novelty shop joke variety. The blood in its eye sockets was painted with tempera.

"Clever costume," said the brillig, lamely pretending that Llixgrijb and Death were one and the same.

The puppet, of course, made no reply. It had no puppeteer to give it words or animation. So Llixgrijb pretended to be Death's voice.

"Thank you," said Llixgrijb. "Aren't you going to wear one?"

"I'll wear what you're wearing."

"Of course."

A breeze whistled through the rafters. All the puppets swayed and rattled slightly. Llixgrijb/brillig gazed at the lifeless throng.

The great warrior Beowulf swung listlessly from his strings, his tinfoil armor looking none too shiny. He was flanked by the dragon Grendel on one side and Grendel's mother on the other. These were gaudily painted parade dragons draped over rows of chairs. They breathed no fire, and Beowulf had no battle to fight.

The goddess Isis swayed tiredly in her crepe paper gown. She glared through dead glass eyes at her husband Osiris in marital jadedness. They had no adulterous Nephthys, no jealous Seth nearby to sunder them—and certainly no cause to wrestle life away from death.

Oedipus and his parents, Laius and Jocasta, dangled in separate corners of the attic—unable to meet, unable to act out their violent and tragic destiny.

Eve, her strings all in a tangle, was grotesquely splayed beneath a cut-out Tree of Knowledge. A foam-stuffed Serpent was wrapped around the Tree. Eve looked too weary to reach for the Tree's single oversized wax apple, and the indifferent Serpent saw no point in even tempting her.

A cotton-bearded Moses vainly hugged a styrofoam blank tablet. Of what use were laws? From what authority would they come? And who needed to obey them?

The god Krishna was slung carelessly over the rail of his chariot. He had no Arjuna to counsel, no warrior to advise.

King Arthur held a spray-painted wooden Excalibur above his head, staring up at it crankily. He looked almost as though he wished he could reforge it into something of use—wishing, indeed, that there was such a thing as usefulness.

Titan Prometheus carried a fiery torch in his hand—but its flame was made of wilted red and yellow construction paper. There was no one about in need of fire, anyway.

The goddess Demeter and her daughter Persephone hung adjacent to one another, staring dumbly. Demeter had no earth to nourish, Persephone no flowers to pick. And the two of them knew of no such thing as separation, or of any lustful Hades, or of any bleak underworld to give them cause to grieve or love one another.

Here hung a Harlequin with no tricks to play. There slouched a Pantalone with no coffers to gloat over. Elsewhere sulked a lifeless Columbine, with no lover to pine after.

A variety of animals—some hand puppets, some mere stuffed dolls—were scattered among these figures, animals worshipped by the lost realm of temporal souls for their magical powers: eagles, hawks, elks, deers, bears, snakes, skunks, otters, butterflies, turtles, moose, porcupines, and owls . . .

But the animals brought no life, no magic to the scene. Coyote was rudely draped across a coat hanger, jaded and bereft of mischief. And the lion did, indeed, lie down with the lamb—not out of brotherly love, but because dolls cannot know hunger.

And the most absurd figure among them was Death. The harbinger of mortality grinned stupidly. It's scythe swept across the floor—not in search of temporal flesh, but from the breeze. The attic reeked of mothballs, not of carrion—of mildew, not of mortality. Tragedy and loss were impossible; redemption and love were impossible. It was a realm of dolls and nothing more.

The brillig looked into the face of Death.

"Is this what you want, then?" the brillig asked.

"Yes," said Llixgrijb, still playing Death's ventriloquist. "It is what I've longed and strived for through the ages."

"Well, you can leave me out of it," said the brillig.

"I can't leave you out of it," said Death.

"But it was a mistake!" cried the brillig. "You destroyed temporality too soon! The story was not over!"

"Oh, indeed? But it did drag on so! And how was I to know when it *would be* over?"

"All stories must have both a sundering and a reconciliation. You—we—destroyed a sundered world. And I pitied its creatures. There were two of them in particular, whose story was intertwined with mine, for whom I truly grieved. Their story had hardly begun. They had been apart and were reaching out to one another."

A change was coming over the brillig.

"I felt their presence as they vanished into nothingness. I felt their longing for each other, their desire to know the ending of their story."

The brillig floundered, searched for a form.

"And too late, I wished more life for them—mortal, transient, fleeting, feeble, tragic, painful, joyous, and exultant life."

The brillig felt wooden limbs quickening, leaping to life.

"I regretted their demise. I wanted to live longer among them. And they had names. What were their names?"

The brillig struggled to remember.

"What were their names?"

The brillig felt its wooden limbs turn suddenly to flesh and bone.

"Yes, I remember! Hector and Hilary! It was too soon! They didn't have a chance to live! Their story was not over! And mine was not either! Was I to live to be a a genius or a fool, a saint or a murderer, a hero or a clown? I never knew!"

Professor Joseph Xavier Brillig was now a man again. He shook Death by the shoulders. There came a loud clatter of bones.

"I—I never made a . . . a *contribution* of any kind."

Brillig suddenly slumped forward, gasping for breath, exhausted but transfigured. He looked very rumpled, very ordinary, and very alive. He ran his hands through his white hair.

"And look at all of this," he continued, gesturing around them. "Here we are, in the world of myth, the world of flow—and nowhere to flow to! Surely, this realm cannot last long without nourishment, without meaning and purpose from the realm of temporality."

"It can last forever."

"You know it can't. It, too, must be destroyed. And you must pity these creatures as you slay them."

Brillig watched Death closely. He detected an expression of anguish and sorrow as Death gazed upon its doomed, mythic fellows. Its jaw dropped. Its horrible grin had vanished. Brillig gazed still closer. Tears formed in Death's eyes. Death grieved.

"I will not restore temporality," Death groaned.

"You have already done so."

"I have not."

"You have done so through your grief."

"Or you have—through your desire."

And it was true. Brillig could feel the presence of temporal forms reawakening out of the void. He could feel their exaltation and their sorrow. He could feel Hector and Hilary groping blindly and joyfully toward each other, living their story to the full.

And the mythic world, so stale and lifeless just a moment before, now stirred with mystery and wonder. All the legends and archetypes began to quicken and glow with interest. Little by little, purpose and meaning crept back into their lives.

The puppets began to dance on their strings and rods. Beowulf's eyes glistened as adventure filled the air, and his dragons positioned themselves for battle. Excalibur gleamed and shone with purpose again. The tablets of Moses filled with laws to be obeyed. Isis and Osiris, Demeter and Persephone embraced wildly in the sudden knowledge of bereavement. And Death sniffed the air lovingly, stirred by the pungent scent of mortality in the air.

"We are separate again," Llixgrijb said, now the master ventriloquist and puppeteer, animating and speaking through the most fearsome of all archetypes.

"And now I must return to my life," said Brillig.

"But how do we keep both realms in place forever?"

"We don't," said Brillig. "We'll act out this this little drama a thousand billion times again. After all, we've acted it a thousand billion times in the past."

"Indeed we have!" said Llixgrijb, laughing aloud. "The End of the Universe as We Know It! The Sundering and the Reconciliation of Reality! One of our best stories ever, eh, friend?"

"And we'll come back to it in time—when we're in need of special entertainment again. In the meantime, it is not enough for me to merely forget your existence. I must sew a healthy degree of ignorance among my illusory fellows. I must see that no more simultaneous enlightenment occurs—at least for now. And I believe I have a new idea of how to do it."

"And how is that?"

"I shall *teach them enlightenment!*" said Brillig with a shrug and a laugh. Then he slipped out of the attic of myth and went back to the realm of temporality. He returned to bliss and oblivion—and the comfort of his kitchen.

Automaton

Brillig sat staring for a moment at the capsule of M. He was about to swallow it, but something seemed to hold his hand.

Strange, he thought. *It's almost as if I've experienced an illusion of distended time and space—as if I underwent an extraordinary journey, but have no recollection of it.*

He was suddenly chilled to the bone.

The house is so cold! How did it get this cold?

He glanced around the room. Something seemed strange about his surroundings. He wiped his finger across the table in front of him. It left a distinct trail over the formica. He lifted his finger and looked at it closely. It was blackened by dust.

And I only dusted yesterday—or did I?

Then he noticed that the back of his hand seemed unusually gaunt.

Have I been losing weight without noticing it?

He felt his beard.

It's longer! Much longer! Almost down to my waist! How can that be?

He stood up from his chair and his pants almost fell down around his knees. He must have lost twenty pounds.

But when? In the last few seconds? Impossible!

The sound of howling wind caught his ear. He looked toward the living room window and noticed daylight coming through the curtains.

But it can't be day!

He set the capsule down on the dusty tabletop. He wandered toward the living room window. He was more than a little weak and wobbly. He pushed the curtains aside.

Snow was coming down in windswept torrents.

A snowstorm! In September!

From the window he could see the front door stoop. There was a large, snow-covered mound on it—as if someone lay frozen there. Brillig's heart leapt up into his throat. Perhaps some vagrant had collapsed at his very threshold, and Brillig had never heard his cries for help. He rushed to the front door and threw it open. He brushed some of the snow away with his bare hands. But instead of a person, Brillig found . . .

Newspapers! Fifty, sixty, maybe seventy newspapers! But where did they come from?

His mailbox was stuffed to overflowing. He grabbed a handful of mail and stepped inside. Perusing the envelopes, he saw a number of bills brazenly stamped with the words "OVERDUE NOTICE." He observed the postmark on one of them:

December 17

He sank slowly to the floor. The truth overcame him completely. He didn't reserve one iota of doubt.

I've been sitting in my kitchen staring at that capsule for two-and-a half months— or more!

He sat in stunned dumbfoundedness for many long moments. Then he wondered:

What's happened in all this time?

He gazed at the telephone. After a minute or two, he dialed a familiar number.

"Cooper Junior College," said a secretary's voice. "Department of English."

Brillig hesitated, then said, "Hello, Mrs. Carmichael?"

"Who is this?"

"It's Brillig. Professor Brillig."

There came a gasp from the other end of the phone line. "Professor Brillig, I— we— Where are you? Where have you been?"

"I'm at home."

"But we've been so worried about you."

"I've been at home all this time. Somebody could have come looking for me here. Anyway, don't worry about it. Just let everybody know I'll be back at work tomorrow."

A wave of winter static flooded the phone line.

"Hello?" asked Brillig. "Are you still there?"

Then Mrs. Carmichael spoke again, her voice trembling.

"Professor Brillig, I'm afraid there have been some—unfortunate changes."

There came another flood of static.

"I understand," said Brillig.

"I'm terribly sorry."

"No. Don't be. Merry Christmas, Mrs. Carmichael."

"And Merry Christmas to you, too, Professor Brillig."

He hung up. He sat on the couch, staring dumbly for an hour or more. He then went to the refrigerator to look for some food. But everything in it had decayed past edibility. For the rest of the afternoon, Brillig alternately sat staring straight ahead, or wandered around the house aimlessly.

The house grew much colder as the day wore on. Brillig tried turning up the thermostat. But the gas had been disconnected. He tried to turn on a light. The electricity had been shut off too.

I must write a letter to the phone company, he mused, *thanking them for their infinite mercy in not shutting off my telephone as well.*

By evening, the house was absolutely frigid. Brillig lit a couple of candles, wrapped himself up in a quilt and sat in a rocking chair. He rocked and rocked and rocked, drifting into an increasingly insensible state.

His eyes roamed the darkening room, coming to rest at last on the china cabinet. He perused its contents—its Blue Willow china, its crystal, its silverware . . .

. . . and in the midst of them all, an item he had almost forgotten.

It was a Hummel figurine of a sweet little child—an orchestra conductor. The charming boy wore long tails with great buttons behind. His blond hair was tussled in a frenzy of musical passion. His sweet red lips were slightly girlish. He waved his baton with abandon.

Brillig grinned involuntarily at the sight of the little fellow. He remembered buying it for Marie one Christmas early in their marriage. He remembered the little trick he'd played on her.

Marie had a passion for Hummels back then. And one fall day, when the two of them were wandering through a gift shop, she spotted the little conductor.

"Oh, Brillig," Marie said to her husband, "if you really love me, you'll buy me that Hummel for Christmas!"

Brillig promised to do so. And one day early in December, he went to the gift shop and actually purchased the conductor—the only Hummel figurine the gift shop had in stock. He swore the shop keeper to secrecy.

The next time he and Marie walked by the gift shop, Brillig said to her, "We'd better buy that conductor fellow now, don't you think? Somebody else might snatch him up."

They went into the store, and Marie was absolutely crushed to find her little darling gone. Brillig felt so guilty for his little joke that he took Marie directly home and presented her with the Hummel. She almost fainted for joy.

Now Brillig laughed at the memory.

God, I always hated the sight of that effete little rascal! And Marie grew weary of him, too—otherwise she would have taken him with her. Funny, all this time and I never even noticed he was still in the house.

Staring at the Hummel figure in the wavering candlelight, Brillig found himself gradually mesmerized. He draped his blanket over his shoulders, rose from his chair and walked over to the china cabinet.

And so, my fine fellow, it's just you and me now, eh? We'll have to make the best of things—despite past differences!

The boy seemed to become more mature and dignified with every passing moment, expanding and growing in knowledge and wisdom and understanding. But at the same time, his eternal childhood remained. He retained an untold capacity for laughter and joy and mischief. These were the very things, in fact, which made him so resplendent and strong.

But who are you, little fellow? Do you know something I don't know? Do you know where I've been these last few weeks? Did we meet somewhere? Did we share in some adventure?

Brillig touched the glass which separated him from the figurine. He could actually hear music—the resilient levity of *Eine Kleine Nachtmusik*'s closing rondo. Brillig stroked the glass lovingly. There was really no separation between them at all.

If you could tell me . . . If you could only tell me . . .

Brillig smiled. Something like a memory passed through his mind . . .

# 6:00 P.M.

. . . "Max, dear," said Ethel, "you really must stop reading now. You'll ruin your eyes."

And, indeed, it was getting rather dark. Not only was twilight coming on, but a thunderstorm was brewing. A slight drizzle of rain could be heard on the porch outside. But Max paid little attention to the encroaching darkness. He sat transfixed in an oversized armchair, reading a copy of *The Jamais Vu Papers*.

"Max," repeated Ethel a bit more loudly, "didn't you hear me?"

Max started slightly. "What? Oh, yes, I'm sorry. I'm very close to the end. Aren't you ladies going to read it too?"

"Not now," said Myrtle quietly, continuing her stitching. "It's a little late to read."

Max finished reading the very last page. He slowly lowered the book in his lap.

"Now I understand," he said quietly. "At least as well as I can ever hope to understand anything."

"What *do* you understand, Max, dear?" asked Ethel sweetly.

Max held the book out to them. "A wonderful paradox," he said. "This book you've shown me, this book in which we all appear, is a book *without an author*. Those names on the cover mean nothing! This book is written by no one. Its authors might as well be every single soul who ever reads it."

Max leaned back in his chair and closed his eyes dreamily. His voice dropped into a whisper.

"And now I must be going," he said.

"But where to?" asked Ethel.

"To where our book is made—to the place where cosmic contrivances are crafted, coincidences arranged, and clichés and absurdities made real and plausible. And all without deliberate design, or even a designer! And when I find that place, I will laugh for joy at the gleeful contradictions underlying absolutely everything!"

"A deconstructionist to the very end!" clucked Addie Gaines amiably.

"Yes," said Max, smiling. "To the very end."

"This doesn't mean you're leaving us this very minute, does it?" asked Ethel worriedly.

"Oh, no, dear lady!" answered Max. "That would be most rude of me!"

And Max sat for an hour or so longer, talking with the Elmblight ladies over tea and biscuits about all their pet topics, frequently challenging long-held notions.

"But I'm afraid you're mistaken about Keats's idea of 'negative capability,'" he said at one point. "You see, it's more than mere 'aesthetic distance.' It has to do with a capacity to find beauty in the horrible, exaltation in destruction, the sublime in the grotesque. It's that elusive and noble state of mind where tragedy and levity join together as one."

The ladies nodded with understanding. The rain fell more steadily. The darkness deepened. At last, Max announced that it was time for him to go.

"But won't we ever see you again?" asked Ethel sadly.

"Let me tell you a little secret," said Max, taking Ethel's hand in his. "There is one text, and one text only, for which I cheerfully acknowledge a referent. That text is one mere word:

"*You.*"

"It is a beautiful word," said Ethel, her eyes glistening a little.

"Oh, a most beautiful word," agreed Max. "A word full of paradox and wonder. It embodies both separateness and connectedness, both stillness and motion. I worship 'you' the way other people worship God. If people could learn to always speak it with reverence, to never utter 'you' in anger or bitterness, this would be a perfect world. And so, dear Ethel, just breathe that word—it doesn't matter to whom—and I'll be near!"

A breeze blew through the room. Thunder boomed gently in the distance. The big armchair was empty.

Max was gone.

It was very dark now. Ethel lit a few candles around the room so the ladies could continue to sew and knit. In the flickering light, Addie's stitchery caught Myrtle's eye.

"Oh, ladies, look!" she exclaimed softly.

All the ladies except Phoebe gathered around Addie's handiwork, which she spread out before them in the candlelight. What had earlier seemed an unsightly conglomeration of pieces stitched utterly at random now revealed an ornate and lovely pattern.

"Yes, I remember reading about this very phenomenon!" giggled Addie. "It's called a 'strange attractor.' It sometimes happens all by itself in chaotic systems. But I certainly didn't expect to have a 'strange attractor' turn up in my stitchery!"

"It looks like one of those little black domino masks," commented Lida June.

"Or the symbol for infinity," suggested Myrtle.

The ladies praised and cooed over Addie's stitchery.

"Order out of Chaos," mused Addie.

"Negative capability," murmured Myrtle.

"*You,*" whispered Ethel.

Their faces flickered and threatened to vanish in the ensuing darkness. A damp breeze made the curtains billow. Rain was pouring hard now. Distant flashes of lightning illuminated the room briefly. The thunder came a little closer. The group slipped into silence. They were enveloped by the sounds of the storm.

Phoebe had been sitting in a darkened corner, silent all this while. She had long since set her tapestry aside. She spoke to the others softly.

"I don't much know what to make of everything that's happened today. But I do suppose it's true that order comes only out of chaos. There is no such thing as progress. There's just continuation. Even my birth was only an illusion. I go back through all eternity. And these, our treasured meetings, have been happening always. We just go on."

"And how do you know this?" asked Ethel gently.

"Because I died the day before yesterday."

There came no sound of surprise from the others.

"How did it happen?" asked Addie quietly, her own face deeply obscured by shadow.

"I was sitting at home that afternoon, watching the sun drop behind the trees. Suddenly, I felt a terrible pain between my shoulder blades—like a knife pushed deep into my chest. My teeth hurt terribly. The tips of my fingers felt exactly as though they were being crushed in a vice. I began to sweat. The world went dark.

"I said good-bye to all of you. I said good-bye to my children and my grandchildren. I even said good-bye to my parents and my grandparents—dead though they've been for years."

Then she chuckled softly. "Can you imagine? Saying good-bye to them, too? But I did! And they heard me. And you heard me, too. And I know I died, as surely as any of us will ever die. There was no tunnel, no white light, no welcoming spirits—only the empty blackness of death. And yet . . . here I am, talking to you all . . . my dearest of friends . . ."

Another silence fell. A cool, wet wind whooshed through the room, blowing out all the candles. A wisp of smoke wafted about. The room was riddled with the fragrance of mortality. Now it was too dark for any of the ladies to see each other's faces at all.

"Yes," commented Addie.

"Yes, you're right," said Myrtle.

"Oh, yes," added Ethel, weeping softly.

"And Ted's still with me," sighed Lida June.

"Always," said Phoebe. "We're with each other always. This very room is filled with every soul that's ever lived. Every square inch of reality, every ounce or drop of space and time, is infinitely populous."

They were all quiet for a very long time. Some of the ladies dozed for a little while. Others stared into the deepening darkness. After a long, long while, they declared their meeting adjourned. They turned on the lights and said good-bye.

And then they went home.

And they met again the next week.

And they met again the week after that . . .

. . . and the week after that . . .

. . . and so on into eternity.

But they never got back to reading *The Jamais Vu Papers*. They never finished it. Somehow, they'd gotten as much as they'd wanted out of it.

They went on to other things . . .

*—Where there is a reconciliation,
Stephen said, there must have been
first a sundering.*

James Joyce
Ulysses

Hector Glasco
Among the Mundaners

Hector rested the shovel on the edge of the three-foot hole. Sweat poured down his face, both above and beyond the cotton kerchief he had tied around his head. His hands were grimy, and dirt was caked beneath his nails.

There, he felt it again. Satisfaction. The sensation was growing stronger, more familiar each time. At first it had been only a fleeting shadow of feeling which he could not even identify. Now it was real and palpable.

Carefully, he knocked the shovel against his left shoe and then his right, shaking loose the clods of dirt that had built up on his boots. The action was still a little strange to him. Like digging holes. Like getting a job done.

"What do you think?" he asked the woman who stood by the battered pickup truck.

"It's just right. Just fine." She always encouraged him, but Hector knew that she would not settle for less than "just right." He felt that internal glow again.

"Help me with this," she said, dragging a bucket of rotted vegetation and manure mixed with topsoil. He smiled as he remembered being dragged off to a local stable to clean out the horse stalls. That had not been his favorite job. The large and alien beasts had stamped and switched outside in the sun while he pitchforked their beds clean. Then, he had been doing only what he was told, in lieu of any other idea about what he might do with his time.

Not long ago, Hector had despaired of ever finding answers. So he had stopped seeking them. He had stopped trying to push reality around with words. He had stopped seeking Hilary. He had even stopped thinking about Imogene—almost. If he dreamed of her, he did not remember it.

He had given up his practice and his newsletter, lived off his savings, and looked for a job to do, for something to give him a sense of completion. He wandered about through life, with a feeling of vaguely benevolent randomness, sensing that something profoundly valid was coming nearer every second.

And one day, in a park, he had seen a young woman wandering among the crowd. She was dressed in work clothes. Her hair was medium length, mouse-colored, characterless, pulled together in the back by a plain leather choker. She was not trying to attract a crowd, or even to speak to anybody. She was just passing out fliers to this group of very mixed human beings, perhaps to recruit them for some some sort of volunteer undertaking. Nobody resisted her, or told her to keep her propaganda to herself. She brought smiles to everybody. She walked past Hector briskly, passing off a flier to him as she hurried on.

It said,

> Would you like to be a Mundaner?
> Physical means to deal with physical problems:
> food for hunger, fuel for cold,
> trees for shade and air.
> If you're interested, come with me!

A light turned on in Hector's head. Yes, he'd seen this flier before! He'd heard people talking about the Mundaners recently, about how often they were seen on the streets passing out just this sort of literature. But nobody knew who or what they were—a political party, a religious sect, a drug cult, a utopian community...?

Without another thought, Hector broke into a run. He chased down the woman who was movingly rapidly and industriously through the crowd. She had already passed out a dozen more fliers. He trotted beside her breathlessly, asking her questions.

"Tell me about the Mundaners," he asked.

"What do you want to know?" she asked. "What do you know already?" She seemed to enjoy his newfound enthusiasm.

"Well, I've heard rumors and stories. Is it true that you people claim Faust himself as your founder and guardian saint?" asked Hector. "Do you really believe he redeemed himself from damnation through the ordinariness of the world?"

The woman stopped walking and looked at him. She seemed amused by the question. "Now where did you hear a thing like that?"

Hector felt a little embarrassed. "Well—just around," he replied.

"People do say all kinds of things," said the woman, with a slight shake of her head. For a moment, he thought she was going to walk off and leave. Then abruptly, she looked Hector straight in the eye, motionless and intense, reciting:

> "Firm let him stand, and look around him well:
> this world speaks clear to him who's capable!
> Why needs he through Eternity to wend?—
> he here acquires what he can apprehend."

"Is that from Goethe?" asked Hector.

The woman laughed. "I don't know. Maybe. I heard it somewhere. It strikes me as true. I wouldn't worry much about old Dr. Faust if I were you. He hasn't been around for a very long time."

"But who *are* you people?"

"Trans-mystics," she said. She certainly was the essence of brevity.

"What's a trans-mystic?" Hector demanded, firmly but gently.

She tilted her head and looked at him with what he sensed to be a trace of curiosity and interest.

"Now that you mention it, I'm not quite sure," she said.

"Hey, you're supposed to be one," quipped Hector. "If you don't know, who does?"

"Maybe you should tell me."

Hector hazarded a guess. "Trans-mystics," he replied, "have got to be people who have gotten beyond the need to confirm their spiritual convictions with mystical phenomena."

"Sounds to me like you're talking about ex-mystics," the woman suggested. She seemed to be subtly probing him.

"No," said Hector, having a good time with the idea. "Trans-mystics wouldn't reject anything, whether mystical or physical. They're just content to immerse themselves in the mundane. Every moment is mystical. Every moment is ordinary. It's all the same thing, isn't it?"

The woman chuckled mischievously. "If you say so. It all sounds pretty— what?—'Post–New Age' to me."

"You don't agree?" asked Hector. After all, he'd felt pretty sure of his answer.

"What's there to disagree with?" said the woman. "I just never gave it a lot of thought."

And she started to walk away again. Hector caught her by the arm. She looked at him with surprise.

"Wait a minute," he said. "Don't you folks have any sort of philosophy?"

She shrugged. "Well, we don't demand changes in the culture that we have not been able to make in ourselves. Is that what you mean by a philosophy?"

"Not exactly," grumbled Hector.

"Sorry, then," said the woman playfully, "I guess I can't help you. For us, a philosophy is like lunch. We don't supply it, so if you want one you'd better pack your own. Me, I prefer to travel light. Now, if you'll excuse me, I'd better get back to work."

"Hey, thanks," said Hector ironically as she started to walk away. "You're a real master of PR."

Without another word, the woman wandered on.

Suddenly, the whole thing aggravated Hector in a funny way. *Who the hell are these people?* he muttered, walking the other way. *How can you call yourelf a 'trans-mystic' and not have a philosophy? How can you be a follower of Faust and not have a philosophy?*

But then he stopped dead in his tracks. He turned around. To his immense relief, the woman was still within calling distance.

"Wait," yelled Hector. "I'll come with you."

Now that same woman was selecting a young tree from the back of the truck. Remarkably enough, Hector had never even learned her name. Mundaners, after all, weren't the most talkative people in the world. But she had been there working alongside him for weeks now, ever since he had simply followed the group of people off to do whatever the rest of them were doing. They repaired and painted houses, planted trees, grew vegetables, and taught whoever was interested to do the same. Today they were planting trees people had donated for a small and barren public park.

The pine the woman handed him looked fairly perky, as though it might survive. There were still some limp strands of tinsel dangling from it—it seemed to have been somebody's Christmas tree. It had been a long time since Hector had paid any attention to Christmas, but it made him feel good that this little tree hadn't gotten chopped down for decorations.

It seemed to him that the woman knew each young tree individually, that she selected exactly the right one for each place. He carried the pine to the hole and placed it carefully on the bed of compost. Very gently the woman loosened the tree from its container. Very carefully they set it in the hole and sifted more compost and good soil around the roots. Occasionally the woman murmured and cut off a damaged root or branch. As they filled the space around the tree they ran water into it so that the soil would settle without leaving air holes. It took some time.

Finally they braced the tree with poles and wire padded with rubber from old tires. It was ready to resume life on its own, with occasional visits from volunteer caretakers.

Hector collected the tools and loaded them on the back of the truck, feeling full of magic, full of a kind of satisfaction which hummed inside him like a song.

The tiny headquarters of the Mundaners was in a second story office overlooking Venice's Ocean Front Walk. It was a chaos of activity. Leaflets and pamphlets were stacked on tables everywhere, with stray pieces of paper lying on the floor, getting trampled underfoot. Bulletin boards trumpeted announcements. A couple of computers whirred away, networking with Mundaners all over the world.

It was lunch time. The air was filled with the aroma of tacos, corned beef, sauerkraut, pizza, and hours-old coffee brewed much too strong. Grease and mustard dripped onto the tables, onto newspapers, announcements, memos. To Hector, the smell had a kind of sacrosanctity about it, like incense at some exalted shrine. It was the smell of good work getting done.

Hector stopped and surveyed the spectacle around him—stopped to smell, taste, listen. As he looked around the Mundaners' office, a memory flashed through his mind, of withered little Bruno sitting in his wigwam in Venice, clutching a bottle of tequila. He'd seen nothing of the old codger since he'd come to Venice. He wondered if Bruno had finally died.

Strange, that he should find himself thinking of Bruno now. . .

Even more strange, he was swept with a warm feeling of recurrence and return—a feeling of *déjà vu*, not *jamais vu*, something that he had experienced before.

It seemed to come from deep down, up through his heels, coursing through his body. He shuddered slightly. He looked down at the floor. He was standing on a rug, which looked anything but mysterious. You could barely make out hieroglyphs which had once shimmered and shone around the edges. They had been worn mostly away. Much of the carpet was threadbare from having been walked on countless times. The radiant green was now as dull and brown as dried grass. It was smeared with dirt and food crushed underfoot.

But it was his carpet! The mysterious carpet of Solomon, which had disappeared with Hilary! How many times he had wondered what had happened to it! And now, just when he had stopped wondering altogether, here it was, the single decorative touch in the entire office. Had it just been put here? No. Hector knew he had walked over it himself hundreds of times without taking notice.

That seemed exactly as it should be. And it looked more glorious than ever.

And it was still flying.

But sadness flooded back as he remembered . . .

Hilary.

It was strange, but the name seemed to be all that was left of his missing patient. Her real name seemed to have vanished from his memory ages ago. He remembered so little about her. Who was Hilary? Why did she come to him? How had he felt about her? It was gone. Inexplicably, irrevocably gone.

He could only recall what he had written about Hilary. In his newsletter he had been deliberately evasive, guarded, protective. And he couldn't even bring himself to think about the disasterous results of his more creative efforts. Hilary, the person behind the name, simply didn't exist for him anymore. Was it because he no longer spoke or wrote of Hilary? Was it because he had never succeeded in putting Hilary into words?

He remembered what John Brockman had told him:

"If it's not in the language, it isn't."

And now—or so it seemed—Hilary wasn't. Hilary was never.

Or was she?

A scolding voice in Hector's head barked at him, loud and clear:

Hector, you idiot, how do you think this carpet got here?

He looked up from the carpet, and the back of a woman's head caught his eye.

She was sitting at one of the computers. Her hair was medium length, mouse-colored, characterless, pulled together in the back by a plain leather choker.

He knew at once who it was. And he remembered something else Brockman had told him.

"Hilary might turn up somewhere in very mundane *circumstances . . ."*

Hector could hardly contain his laughter. Did Brockman know even then? He didn't doubt it.

The woman at the computer, his coworker from the park, got up and came over to him, handing him a sheet of scheduled work activities.

Then she paused.

She examined his expression very closely.

She broke into a smile of tremendous amusement.

"Well," she giggled, "hello, Dr. Glasco."

"Hector. Please."

"I thought you'd never recognize me."

"I'm sorry."

"Well, I'm amazed. Really amazed."

"Don't be amazed," he said, not knowing quite why. Perhaps he greedily wanted to keep all the amazement for himself.

She smiled with a peculiar knowingness. "I won't," she said.

"But—where were you?" asked Hector. "What were you doing all that time, before all of this?" He gestured around them.

"Oh," she said with a shrug. "One thing and another."

"I looked for you," he said. "I looked for you all over this world, and in a few other worlds besides. But then I gave up."

He paused and said again: "I gave up."

And then Hector knew just how he'd finally found her.

"Anyway," he said, "I was worried sick."

"You shouldn't have been."

"But I thought I'd done something terrible to you. What effect did the drug have on you?"

"It made me see angels," she said flatly.

"Angels?" echoed Hector with astonishment.

"Thousands of them. I can't tell you how many angels have come and spoken to me in the last year."

"But what did they say?"

Hilary laughed and laughed.

"What's so funny?" asked Hector.

"Oh, nothing, nothing at all. Now what *did* they say?"

She was lost in thought for a moment.

"The first one told me I had a tremendous destiny to perform. I was supposed to bring two realms, two worlds, two universes together into one. I was told that I was to be the savior of waking and sleeping people."

Then Hilary laughed some more.

"I told that angel it sounded like too much trouble, and that I'd pass. There's a funny thing, though. The woman who came to your office for help would have liked that job—being a savior, a messiah. That little pill of yours got rid of her.

"Well, thousands of other angels came after that, with thousands of messages. I was told . . . let's see . . .

". . . that democracy is dead, that the universe is finite but without edge or boundary, and that light can act like a wave or a particle. I was told where voices come from. I was told the truth. I was told how to take out stains, to be careful about buying produce, and all about life insurance. I was told always to trust appearances, that free will is an illusion, and that I need to lose weight. I was told when the Mayan calendar would end, and how to win the lottery. I was told about alternate realities, how to roller-skate, about Isis and Osiris and the bleaching of cane sugar. I was told not to worry. I was told about chakras, skeleton keys, fairies, and dialectical materialism. I was told how to live. I was told the price of everything and the value of nothing. I was told about christs and antichrists and oysters and yetis, and that the universe is made of bits of string. I was told a lie or two—or maybe ten or twenty or a hundred, I just don't know.

"I was told," she concluded, "that God is the answer. But nobody told me what the question was. I was very confused for a while."

"Without a doubt," said Hector, quite perplexed himself. "I mean, what an extraordinary experience! All those angels, saying so many different things— some of them quite contradictory, many of them quite useless!"

"Yes," she agreed. "We were told in Sunday school how angels always told people things they could believe, things of tremendous importance. But nobody ever told us what to do if we met angels ourselves."

Something was stirring in Hector, a vague desire he never expected to see fulfilled. This young woman who stood so unaffectedly before him seemed more real and wonderful than anyone he had ever known. She had wrinkles around her eyes and light lines in her cheeks. They were quite beautiful.

"But you seem so—*together*. You look as though you've sorted it all out somehow."

"Well, I noticed something after a while," she continued. "I noticed that, whatever else the angels might say, they always began with the same words."

"And what were they?"

"*Don't be amazed*. They all said that right away. After a few hundred angels, I decided to take them at their word. It's made all the difference in the world."

Hector mulled it over in his mind. *Don't be amazed*. Yes, he seemed to have learned that lesson, too.

"But do you still see angels?" he asked Hilary.

Hilary beamed. "What do you think *you* are?"

It wasn't long before Hector and Hilary moved into a Venice Beach apartment building together, just a block away from Ocean Front Walk. It was a modest dwelling, with few luxuries. There had once been a swimming pool in the courtyard, now long-abandoned. They swam in the ocean instead. And their complex had a parking garage, which is the most important thing in Venice.

One day when Hector and Hilary were working at the Mundaners' headquarters, they saw two elderly men approaching, waving gleefully. Although both wore Bermuda shorts, wildly painted Hawaiian shirts, and sported flower leis, one looked shaggy and half-crazed and the other cut a dapper, more civilized figure. They each had a bottle of tequila in tow.

Suddenly Hector realized that it was Bruno and Solomon!

"You look like you've been vacationing," he said, greeting them.

"Have we ever," Bruno agreed. "Lucidity in paradise, now that's . . . "

"However," Solomon interrupted gently, "I can't say much for your modern methods of transportation—delayed flights, cancellations, crazy schedules."

"We thought, if you weren't using it . . ." Bruno stammered shyly.

Hector introduced the two to Hilary, only to find out that she knew the *brujo* already. Then he carefully rolled up the old green rug and handed it over to the mythic pair.

"But where are you characters off to?" he enquired.

"To another exciting adventure!" Solomon replied with a wink, tucking the rug under his arm. And Solomon and Bruno strode jauntily away down Ocean Front Walk. Hector never saw or heard from either of them again.

The very next afternoon, Hilary was opening up the mail when she ran across an interesting item.

"Here's something for both of us," she said to Hector, handing him a card. "Friends of yours, maybe?"

Hector read:

> Fra Girolamo Savonarola
> proudly requests your presence
> at the wedding
> of his daughter
> Imogene Savonarola
> and
> Maxwell Henderson
> R.S.V.P.

"Max and Imogene!" exclaimed Hector. "They *met*! They're getting *married*!"

"Should we go?" asked Hilary.

"Are you kidding?" laughed Hector. "It'll be the event of the millennium!"

Hector dug around in the envelope and found directions to where the ceremony was to be held . . .

But it was in an alternate reality, of course. The directions were written in hermetical prose, and carefully outlined the six stages of the alchemist's quest.

"It appears," said Hector sadly, "that we'll have to transmute baser metals into gold in order to get to the ceremony."

"Well, we can do that, can't we?" suggested Hilary.

"Yeah," said Hector, "but it would be an awful lot of trouble."

So they reluctantly threw the announcement away. Hector mentally sent Max and Imogene his regrets and wished them well.

Later that same evening, Hector and Hilary sat in a Chinese restaurant exchanging portions of curried chicken and sweet and sour pork. Hector was rapidly mastering chopsticks and having a marvelous time. He reflected on his life and realized that he was happier at this moment than he had ever been. Of course, he rarely reflected on his life these days without coming to the same conclusion. Life just got better and better.

But he was also seized with a rush of melancholy. This often happened, too, when he reflected.

It's hard to be this happy and not want to live forever.

But of course, that wasn't going to happen.

Besides, considered Hector, *I'm a fictional character. My work of fiction has to end.*

Someday, somewhere, the words and pages have to end . . .

And what if they end before my life does?

What then?

Do I go on?

Or do I stop?

318

The NEW Jamais Vu Papers

Volume Two
Number One
January

Dear Readers,
It may well surprise you to learn that I, Joseph Xavier Brillig, one-time junior college professor and erstwhile mechanist, have taken over this newsletter.

But I have been riddled by insights of an intuitive and—dare I say it?—even mystical nature. I feel compelled to share them with the world. It is to this end that I have responded to Miss Bellows' plea for someone to continue these *Papers*. And you can be sure that Miss Bellows will always have a place on my staff.

However, enough of idle speculation about chemical metaphors. Now *The New Jamais Vu Papers* will investigate the most sweeping issue of contemporary culture— the end of history as we know it. A fashionable topic, to be sure, but one worthy of attention.

Hegel declared that history ended in 1906 with Napoleon's triumph in Prussia.

Aleister Crowley spoke of something more: he said the world was destroyed by fire on March 21, 1904—an event that a surprising number of people failed to notice. He was still sticking to his story in 1944.

More recently, José Arguelles said that history will end with the Mayan calendar—I forget the exact date. And Francis Fukayama told us that history is ending even as we speak.

But I have news for them. History ended in 1965, exactly three millennia after Solomon assumed the throne of Israel. Solomon witnessed the abandonment of man by the *elohim*—the many voices of God, who once instructed us in everything we did. But for nigh onto 25 years the elohim have prepared their return. Now they are heard once more. A New Age does indeed begin.

May these *papers* speed it on its way.

In Love and Light
Joseph Xavier Brillig

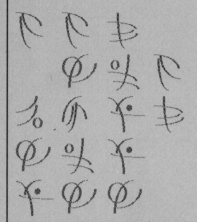

CONTENTS

Above: the personal message you've been waiting for. Those of you who have not yet received your shamanic decoder rings, rush your $50 donation to *The New Jamais Vu Papers* right away. Don't miss the message.

The Search for Authority

translated from the pig latin personally by our own channeler, Dr. J.X. Brillig

Greetings oh wise ones,

It is my great pleasure to be with you again. As those of you who have attended our regular weekly sessions already understand, you are special people. You are in the process of refining your body, mind and spirit—getting in tune with your higher self—or, becoming gods, if you would rather think of it that way.

Now, many of you have asked, how can I do my job, keep my house, raise my children, deal with all the bothersome everyday decisions I have to make, and still take the time and effort it requires to become a god?

The answer is—*delegate authority.* Sure, you get tired of figuring out the small stuff for yourself. We all do. It distracts us from higher things. But the solution is very simple: just turn those tasks over to someone else.

Think of the time it will save when you no longer have to wonder about the right thing to wear. Think of the celestial regions you can tap when you don't have to waste time weighing the elusive pros and cons of day-to-day decisions.

Can't decide which brand of catsup to buy? Wondering whether the signs are right for planting petunias, taking up speed reading, or doing away with a pesky relative? What kind of god gets all bogged down in this stuff?

Think about it! The key is to find your own answer to this simple question:

Who can tell me what to do?

Wouldn't you rather leave it to a real professional—an authority who can handle physical and temporal details? Of course you would!

But who can be trusted to make such decisions for you? Who can possibly maintain the healthy aesthetic distance needed for an honest critique of all the complexities of your life?

The little-known truth is that *such authority is not to be left to those who persist in holding earthly form.*

Because aesthetic distance is the key. Keats had a term for it: Negative Capability. Now how can you possibly maintain an esoteric state like that?

There's only *one* real guarantee of Negative Capability. Find yourself a never-embodied spirit and you're in business. The time has come for all of us to learn how to delegate authority to those who have never lived in this reality and who probably never will.

And where do you look for this perfect authority? Why, from shams, fictions, and *hoaxes*—like me!

Other dimensions can also be good places to check. Locate a bored multidimensional being and you'll have all the advice you need. Of course, entities from other planets will do in a pinch. Literary characters can be consulted as a last resort. Any disincarnate spirit can help if they pass the essential test of Negative Capability— that they know nothing whatsoever about this reality.

Then you'll be free to devote all the time you need to your spiritual growth! Happy evolving!

BULLETIN BOARD
Meetings and Announcements

Thaumaturgists Cookout and Softball Game.
Hey you dream-staters—just making your first tours on this side? There's nothing like working up a sweat to give you a real taste of the waking life. Food and other activities guaranteed to keep you awake. Call for info: (300) I WAKE UP.

2nd Level Lucidity Group
This one's for those with some lucid dreaming experience, only. Arrange appointments for friendship, romance. Meet the man or woman of your dreams. We can show you how. All you have to do is pass a simple test (psych out the phone number) and pay your dues.

Damp Dreamers
Those dreamin' singles are at it again. Another pool and jacuzzi party is planned for the last Saturday of this month. The last one was a terrific success and a number of participants graduated to 2nd level lucidity right there at the party. Don't miss this one. Call (300) SLEEPER.

Learn the Secrets of the Divine Cycle
—WANT MORE—GET MORE—WANT MORE—
GET MORE—WANT MORE—GET MORE
Did you ever wonder how some people get by without working as hard as you do? It's perfectly simple once you understand how. You, too, can manifest your way into the upper class.

Yes, friends, you can wake up to find that new red Porsche waiting at your front door, that mink in your closet, or a better blender in your kitchen. All it takes is 5 minutes a day with our sync-recorded tapes, and it will all be yours. For more information: call (300) HI HIYYA.

RESEARCH UPDATES:

The *new jamais vu papers* receives reports from all over the world on the latest exciting scientific studies. In this column every month, we will tell you what's important.

We've just discovered some exciting developments in studies of psychic snails.

These cute little critters send and receive from their little antennas at a rate you would't believe. You should just see them trucking through those mazes.

The only question that remains for the scientists to explore is: are the smart snails using remote vision, or are they reading the minds of watching researchers? You can be sure we'll keep our readers informed as the answers are revealed.

"The Regeneration of Pavlov's Dog"

This week alone we've received 25 new reports of spontaneous seed sprouting. Those most adept at this skill have been able to speed up their crop production considerably, as well as win a number of bets with skeptical friends.

Hiyya has promised to show us all how to sprout our own at one of next month's channeling sessions. Sign up now.

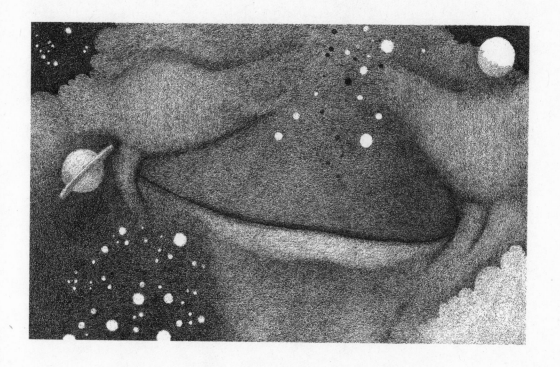

. . . And a great smile spread across all the universes.

ACKNOWLEDGMENTS

The Jamais Vu Papers is loosely based on a newsletter we have published since 1987. Many of our cast of characters are, in fact, quite real people who appeared in that newsletter. All real-life participants are identified on pages 326-327.

Other real people appeared as "characters" in the newsletter, but do not appear in these pages. They nevertheless influenced our story, and deserve our hearty thanks: Jean Houston, Russell Jacoby, Charles Johnston, Howard Rheingold, Russell Targ, and Robert Theobald. And still others contributed their thoughts or their artistic skills to this project at one time or another: Bob Clements, Victor Flach, Steven Hind, Daniel Milo, Todd Lief, Patti Warashina, and Nancy Williams. Bob Clements was also responsible for our early introduction to a Macintosh computer in the Department of Art at the University of Georgia. Our thanks to them, and to all of our subscribers.

A great many of the works and authors that influenced this book are quoted herein. Not quoted but of influence nonetheless is William S. E. Coleman's play, *The Split Infinity*. We have also been inspired by the work and ideas of Jonathan Culler, Radu Florescu, Edward Fredkin, Julian Jaynes, Steven LaBerge and Rupert Sheldrake. This list is, of course, far from complete. But we hope that most of our other thefts are cheerfully acknowledged—or at least implied.

Thanks also to our newsletter staff: cryptologist Sylvia Delgado, lucidologist Jim Uhls, and comprehensivist Greg Wright. Thanks also to Morri Beers for his advice on the first draft of this book.

Many thanks are due to our editor, Michael Pietsch—both for his faith in this project and his creative input as it has taken shape.

And a very special thanks to our literary agents, John Brockman and Kantinka Matson, and all their fine co-workers. Aside from invaluable professional services, they also offered inspiration, ideas, and introductions to many of our participants. This book would not have been possible without them.

Wim Coleman and Pat Perrin
San Miguel de Allende, Guanajuato, Mexico
1990

Parts of our story were based on interviews with actual people. We extend our gratitude to these people for their willingness to participate in the fictional events of The Jamais Vu Papers. *The interviews originally appeared, sometimes in somewhat different form, in* The Jamais Vu Papers *newsletter. They have been revised and reprinted here with the permission of each participant.*

John Brockman is a radical epistemologist, author of *Afterwords* and *By the Late John Brockman*, and the editor of the newsletter *Edge*. He and Katinka Matson, his home and business partner, run a thriving New York literary agency. Brockman is the founder of the Reality Club, a group of intellectuals who meet regularly in New York to "ask each other the questions they've been asking themselves." Brockman appears in our story on pages 237–246.

Fred Chappell is Burlington Industries Professor of English at the University of North Carolina and the author of such volumes of poetry as *Midquest, Castle Tzingal*, and *First and Last Words*. His novels include *Dagon, I Am One of You Forever*, and *Brighten the Corner Where You Are*. In 1985 Chappell won the Bollingen Prize over the strenuous objections of past winners Robert Frost, Ezra Pound, and Wallace Stevens as well as those of his cowinner, John Ashbery. Our nonsynchronous interview with Chappell appears on pages 145-146 and on page 153.

María De Céspedes is a painter, writer, and theatrical storyteller. From 1982 until 1990, she was the director of the Café Teatro Athanor in San Miguel de Allende, Guanajuato, Mexico. She recently contributed her shadow-play and storytelling talents to the Japanese-produced video, *Copil: Son of the Desert*, which presents the cactus as a mythic symbol. She tours internationally with her theatrical efforts and conducts workshops in creativity and improvisation. She appears in our story on pages 181-189.

Daniel C. Dennett, Distinguished Arts and Sciences Professor at the Tufts University Center for Cognitive Studies, is the author of *Brainstorms: Philosophical Essays on Mind and Psychology,* and he co-edited *The Mind's I: Fantasies and Reflections on Self and Soul* with Douglas R. Hofstadter. Dennett played himself in a filmed adaptation of his own short story "Where Am I?" (which appears in both *Brainstorms* and *The Mind's I*). Made in Holland, the film was part of *Victim of the Brain*, which was based on the ideas of Douglas Hofstadter. His forthcoming book is *Consciousness Explained*. Dennett appears on pages 200–213.

Jamake Highwater is a novelist, essayist, and commentator on the arts. Among his many books are: *The Primal Mind: Vision & Reality in Indian America; Dance: Rituals of Experience; Arts of the Indian Americas;* and *Myth and Sexuality.* He hosted a PBS documentary based on *The Primal Mind*. He has also participated in a program on mythology hosted by Joseph Campbell; in the "Six Great Ideas" series produced by Bill Moyers for PBS, moderated by Mortimer Adler; and in numerous other projects for television. Highwater has lectured widely and written countless articles and reviews on Native American cultures and on the visual and performing arts. He is the founder and president of a nonprofit public trust, The Native Land Foundation, dedicated to a celebration of Mallarmé's concept that the imagination is the native land of the mind. Highwater participates in our story on pages 264–268.

Paul Krassner is an investigative satirist and the editor of *The Realist*. With the late Abbie Hoffman, he was the co-founder of the Yippies. Groucho Marx once predicted that Krassner would be the "only living Lenny Bruce." His one-man show has won two awards. His upcoming "unauthorized autobiography" is *The Winner of the Slow Bicycle Race*. Krassner participates in *The Jamais Vu Papers* on pages 93–98 and 107–111.

Timothy Leary is the author of numerous books, including *Info-Psychology*, *What Does WoMan Want?*, and *Flashbacks*. He is also a creator of interactive software, a lecturer and stand-up philosopher, and a proponent of space migration, intelligence increase, and life extension—summarized by the acronym "SMI²LE." He has a longstanding commitment to higher education and continues his involvement with the university inmate population. Leary takes part in our story on pages 249–258.

Tom Robbins is the author of many novels, including *Another Roadside Attraction, Even Cowgirls Get the Blues, Still Life With Woodpecker, Jitterbug Perfume*, and *Skinny Legs and All*. Robbins was the very first subscriber to *The Jamais Vu Papers* newsletter. But what of his alleged membership in strange societies? "I could not be so presumptuous as to claim membership in the College of 'Pataphysics," he explains. "The Church of Subgenius, however, is another matter." Our interview with Robbins appears on pages 35–36.

Fred Alan Wolf is a physicist, coauthor of *Space–Time and Beyond*, and author of many books, including *Taking the Quantum Leap, Star Wave, Parallel Universes: the Search for Other Worlds*, and the upcoming *The Eagle's Quest: A Physicist's Search for Truth in the Heart of the Shamanic World*. He claims to have known Llixgrijb long before we introduced them to each other. Always an adventurous sort, Wolf reunites with the cosmic entity on pages 190–191, 234–236 and 286–292.